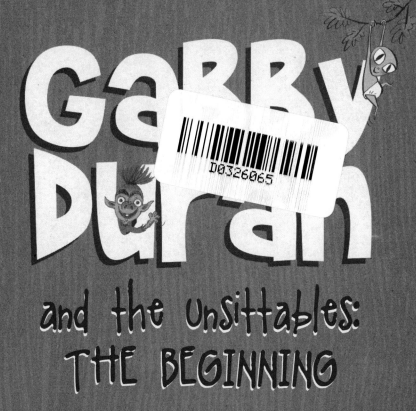

GaBBy Duran

and the Unsittables: THE BEGINNING

BOOK 1
GaBBy Duran and the Unsittables

BOOK 2
GaBBy Duran: Troll Control

ELISE ALLEN & DARYLE CONNERS

Disney • HYPERION
LOS ANGELES   NEW YORK

First Paperback Edition, May 2019
10 9 8 7 6 5 4 3 2 1
FAC-025438-19088
Printed in the United States of America

This book is set in Adobe Caslon Pro, Little Boy Blue, Taberna
Script, The Hand/Fontspring; Officina Serif ITC Pro/Monotype
Designed by Marci Senders

Library of Congress Control Number for
Gabby Duran and the Unsittables Hardcover: 2014029945
Library of Congress Control Number for
Gabby Duran: Troll Control Hardcover: 2015023591

ISBN 978-1-368-04916-0

Visit www.DisneyBooks.com

SUSTAINABLE
FORESTRY
INITIATIVE
Certified Chain of Custody
Promoting Sustainable Forestry
www.sfiprogram.org
SFI-01054

FROM ELISE TO MADDIE, MY
POOH-BEAR, WHO IS MY INSPIRATION
IN ABSOLUTELY EVERYTHING.

FROM DARYLE TO LUNA X. MILLER,
THE MOON CHILD, WHOSE SENSE OF
FUN INSPIRED GABBY FROM
THE BEGINNING.

BOOK 1

GABBy Duran

and the Unsittables

FIRST DOSSIER
When Gabby Met A.L.I.E.N.

WARNING

This book contains revelations so classified that only the most covert layers of the most secretive sects of the Worldwide International Government even know they exist. A single leak could send devastating ripple effects throughout space-time and obliterate the world as we know it.

IF YOU DO NOT BELIEVE YOU CAN
HANDLE THE RESPONSIBILITY,
WE CANNOT STRESS
THIS STRONGLY ENOUGH:

UNDER NO CIRCUMSTANCES
SHOULD YOU TURN THE PAGE

WELCOME, TRUSTED FRIEND,
TO THE FIRST DOSSIER OF
ASSOCIATE 4118-25125A,
A.K.A. GABBY DURAN,
SITTER TO THE UNSITTABLES.

chapter
ONE

t he day that changed Gabby's life started out just like any other ... with a small pitcher of water poured on her head.

"Okay, okay, I'm up!" Gabby spluttered as she bolted upright, though there wasn't anyone to splutter *to*. Gabby was alone. The offending water pitcher had been rigged by her best friend, Zee. It was Zee's solution to Gabby's request for help waking up in the mornings. Zee's first idea was to use her robotics skills to rig Gabby's bed, so at the sound of the alarm it would spring up and catapult Gabby directly onto a beanbag chair across the room. It sounded great . . . until they used a mannequin-Gabby to try Zee's prototype.

The mannequin smashed a giant, Gabby-shaped dent in the back wall.

Zee was sure she could make adjustments and fix the issue, but Gabby opted for Zee's alternate idea instead: the water pitcher. Whenever Gabby pressed the snooze button a third time in a row—*splash!*

It drove Zee apoplectic that after several months of this, Gabby still hit the snooze button that third time. Pavlov's Law demanded that Gabby change her behavior and get out of bed after button-push number two.

Gabby had no answer for this, except to say her love of sleep apparently outweighed the laws of science.

Once she was awake, though, she was unstoppable. She threw off her sopping covers, bundled them up with her equally drenched nightshirt, then stretched her legs over her wild mess of a floor to find the few spots of bare carpet between her bed and her closet. There she dropped her covers long enough to rummage through the tangle of hangers and clothes layering the floor until she found her most comfortable weekend jeans and T-shirt, got dressed, slung her ever-present purple knapsack over her left shoulder, hoisted the giant crumple of bedclothes back into her arms, and picked out a path to her door.

Gabby galloped down her town house's two flights of stairs, deposited her bundle in the dryer and turned it on, then trotted back up to the kitchen, where her mom was juggling a million different pots and pans, all bubbling and steaming and sizzling and giving off such a wild array of smells that Gabby couldn't begin to name a single one.

Okay, her mom wasn't *actually* juggling a million different pots and pans. While the million different pots and pans did their bubbling/steaming/sizzling thing, Alice Duran was *actually* juggling three tomatoes, a feat which she apparently thought would impress Gabby's little sister, Carmen.

"Look, Car! I'm doing it! See? Oh, hi, Gabby!"

The second Alice looked up to say hi to her oldest daughter, all three tomatoes fell unceremoniously to the floor.

Splat! Splat! Splat!

Without looking up from the old-fashioned accounting book on the kitchen table, Carmen said, "Three organic heirloom tomatoes weighing one point five pounds, priced at three dollars and ninety-nine cents per pound, equals 5.985 dollars in the trash."

"Relax, Car," said Gabby. "I think we can eat the six dollars."

"Actually, we can't," Carmen said. "Not anymore. That's the point."

Though only ten, Carmen was as no-nonsense as her

long, flat brown hair with the too-short bangs cut straight across her forehead. "And if you didn't toss your sheets in the dryer every day," she continued to Gabby, "we'd save two hundred sixty-one dollars' worth of electricity."

"Yes, but you'd *lose* two hundred sixty-one dollars' worth of the joy you take in torturing me about it."

"Enough," Alice said as she wrapped her hand in several layers of paper towels ("One quarter Kirkland paper towel roll, at ninety-eight cents a roll, 24.5 cents in the trash," Carmen noted), sopped up the tomato goo, then held it away from her body, so she could pull Gabby into a strong, one-armed embrace.

"Good morning, baby," she said. She gave Gabby a huge kiss right on top of her head, then perked up like a prairie dog. "Do you hear that?" she asked. "It's my baklava calling."

She retreated to her baking corner, which was piled high with a giant stack of phyllo dough. With her Einstein-wild hair and her face and apron smeared with a myriad of splattered colors and textures, Alice looked like a mad scientist as she huddled among her gurgling pots and pans, painting filling onto her pastry. She actually *was* a scientist, or had been before she took up cooking. She'd been a chemist, cooking up concoctions meant to cure the world of all kinds of diseases. But when Gabby and Carmen's dad, an army major, was declared missing in action and presumed dead while Alice was pregnant with Carmen, Alice knew she had to find a way to make money while keeping stay-at-home-mom-ish hours. In no time, cooking cures turned to cooking meals for her catering business, It's All Relativity, a name that played off her look.

Gabby peered into every pot on the stove. She twirled the contents around and inhaled deeply. "Marinara sauce . . . tikka masala . . . and peanut brittle?"

"Pralines," Alice said. "At least they will be. Big Sunday brunch today—a Greek-Italian-Cajun themed Diwali."

Gabby mulled over all the options, then dug into the pantry and grabbed a Pop-Tart, which she slid into the toaster.

"Nutritional content of your choice: zero," Carmen noted.

"You used to worship me, you know," Gabby retorted. "I have video proof."

"It's true," Alice agreed. "When I brought you home from the hospital, only Gabby could make you stop crying."

"It was a psychological experiment," Carmen deadpanned. "I thought you'd be nicer to me if I made you feel important."

"It worked too well," Gabby said. "I feel *so* important that I believe I'm impervious to the evils of Pop-Tartery." She pulled her beautifully browned processed yumminess from the toaster and bounced it between her hands until it cooled enough to hold. "Now what's the scoop?"

"It's what Mom uses to measure out the coffee," Carmen replied as she went back to scribbling in her accounting book.

Gabby never quite knew if Carmen was being exceptionally literal just to mess with her, or because that was how she saw the world. Probably a little of each.

"Got it," Gabby said. "Thanks. And um . . . what's my schedule today?"

Carmen pushed aside the large volume in which she kept track of the family's finances, and replaced it with one of two black binders stacked on the table next to her. The binders looked identical, but Carmen knew one from the other at a glance. One held their mom's schedule, press clippings, and testimonials; the other housed the same information for Gabby.

"Sunday, October eighteenth. Ali, Lia, and Ila. Triplets, age five. Limo to pick you up at—"

A horn sounded from outside the house. Carmen looked at her watch and nodded, pleased by the punctuality.

"—eight A.M. sharp," she finished. "You'll be in the air on the private jet by nine, on set in Florida by eleven, and back home by seven P.M."

"In time to practice my French horn for Friday afternoon's concert!" Gabby said, springing up and heading to the door.

"Where you'll play solo!" Alice cheered.

"Or not," Carmen said. "Maestro Jenkins won't tell her until"—she flipped forward a few pages in the binder dedicated to Gabby—"approximately three fifty-five Friday afternoon."

"Thanks for the vote of confidence, Car," Gabby said.

"It has nothing to do with confidence," Carmen retorted. "Maestro Jenkins never says who will get the solo until five minutes before curtain. Right now it could just as easily be Madison's."

"How do I get you to go back to that wanting-to-make-me-feel-important thing?"

"Can't," Carmen said. "Psychological experiment, re-member?" The tiniest hint of a smirk played at the left corner of her mouth.

"Maestro Jenkins will choose *you*," Alice told Gabby. "I have complete confidence. Got your phone and portable charger?"

"Always."

"Text every hour. If you're in the air and can't, then when you land. Love you!"

"Love you, too!"

Gabby darted out the door and ran down to the curb, where a long black limousine sat waiting. From across the street, she saw Madison Murray framed in her living room's picture window. Madison's perfect blond hair danced gently around her beautiful face as she practiced her flute.

Gabby grimaced. Madison was her archenemy, at least in orchestra. They were both in sixth grade, but they'd played with the Brensville Middle School Orchestra since elementary school. That's how good they were. And while they played very different instruments, they were always up for the same solos. Orchestra leader Maestro Jenkins thought fierce competition was good for his two stars. He tweaked each solo piece just a bit for each instrument, had both Gabby and Madison learn and practice it, then awarded the prize only at the last minute.

Gabby wanted Friday's solo badly, and she'd have a much better shot at it if she were practicing right now, just like Madison. But duty called. Ali, Lia, and Ila needed her, and she couldn't say no to them. Besides, there was still plenty of practice time before the concert.

In her living room, Madison finished a passage and looked up, catching Gabby's eye. Gabby smiled and waved. Madison merely glanced from Gabby to the limousine and back again, then walked pointedly to the window and drew her blinds shut.

It was frustrating. They might be bitter rivals in orchestra, but Gabby always thought that away from the stage, she and Madison should be friends. After all, they had a lot in common. They were both amazing musicians, they'd lived across the street from one another since birth, which was already twelve years now, and . . .

Okay, maybe that was all they had in common. But still, that should be enough! Madison didn't agree, and even though Gabby knew her best friend Zee would say *If someone doesn't have time for you, you shouldn't have time for them,* Gabby still really wanted to win Madison over. She knew she could, too. She just needed the right in.

The limo beeped. Gabby jumped and yanked open the door. She was about to slip inside when something strange caught her eye. A tall, severe-looking older woman stood on the corner. She was dressed all in black and seemed to be staring right at Gabby.

Most of the people in Gabby's neighborhood had lived there for years. Everyone knew everyone else, and the place was a solid car ride from any shopping. This woman was a stranger to Gabby, and strangers didn't generally just find their way here.

Gabby shook off a nervous chill. Most likely the woman was someone's grandmother, here for a visit. Maybe for a funeral, given the outfit.

"Hi!" Gabby called with a smile and wave, but the woman didn't respond. Of course she didn't. She was probably too deep in mourning. Gabby felt awful for disturbing her at a time like this and promised herself she'd ask around the neighborhood when she got back home to find out who had passed away. Then she, Carmen, and Alice could send flowers to the family.

Gabby climbed into the limo and slammed the door shut behind her. "Hi, Albert!" she called.

"Hiya, Gabby," Albert called. "Good to see ya!"

"You, too!"

Gabby settled back to enjoy the ride, but something nagged at her as Albert pulled away from the curb. She turned around in her seat and looked out the back windshield.

The woman in black was still there. And despite the windshield's dark tint, Gabby could swear the woman's eyes were locked directly on to her own.

chapter
TWO

a few hours later, Gabby was sitting in the back of another limo, somewhere in the middle of Florida. The car pulled up to a soundstage, and a tank of a man strode with purpose toward Gabby's door. The man wore tattered army-green pants, with nothing over his ripped-with-muscles chest and abs but two bandoliers of ammunition. A deep scar ran down the left side of his face, the remnant of some long-ago brutality. It twisted his expression into a permanent wicked sneer. With unbelievable force, this man tore open the limousine door, yanked Gabby out by her arm . . .

. . . and pulled her into a huge bear hug.

"Gabby!" he cried. "It's so great to see you!"

Gabby knew that pretty much every other sixth grade girl at Brensville Middle School would die to be in this man's arms right now, but she just didn't think of Adam that way.

"You're doing a *Decimator Four*?" she asked after they pulled out of their hug. She gestured to the telltale scar, but Adam only winked and put a finger to his lips.

"The code title is *Samba Serenade*. Super top secret."

He offered a hand, pinky extended, and Gabby looped her smallest finger through his, swearing to keep mum.

"Is Sierra here, too?" Gabby asked. Sierra Bonita was Adam Dent's wife. The two met when she did the bit part on the first *Decimator* that launched her career, but now she was as big a movie star as him. Maybe even bigger.

"Nah, she's off in Siberia shooting something meaningful," Adam said. "Twenty degrees below zero. Give me action in the heat and humidity any day, am I right?"

"And geckos," Gabby added. She wiggled side to side and climbed her palms through the air, imitating the cute little lizards that always came out at night here, but Adam winced away and shuddered from his chiseled jaw down to his banister-size calves.

"Geckos freak me out," he admitted. "Come on—let's go see the girls. They've missed you like crazy."

"I've missed them, too!" Gabby gushed.

Adam nodded to the security guard at the soundstage door. Like a secret service agent, the guard stood upright and kept his eyes on the field as he held the door open. He didn't even glance at Gabby or Adam. Gabby tried to catch his gaze and give him a friendly hello anyway, but what she saw reflected in his glasses made her voice dry up in her throat.

She wheeled around, her heart racing.

"You okay, Gabby?" Adam asked.

Gabby looked up and down the street. Nothing unusual at all. A couple other soundstages, some golf carts, a few other cars, scattered people walking together to go over business or their lines. . . .

No sign of the tall, severe-looking older woman dressed all in black. The same one she'd seen watching her as she got into the limousine back home. The one she'd seen in the security guard's glasses staring sternly at her from right across the street.

Gabby didn't realize she'd been holding her breath until it came rushing out of her in a long sigh. "I'm fine." She laughed. "Just . . . thought I saw something weird."

"It's a movie lot," Adam said. "There's a lot of something weirds. This morning I had to push past three zombies and an elephant just to get coffee. Come on."

Gabby followed him into the soundstage, glancing back into the guard's glasses on the way in. This time she saw nothing unusual, but why would she? There was no way the old woman could possibly be here.

It must be the humidity. It was messing with her mind. Good thing the stage was air-conditioned. The rush of cold air woke her up inside, and all other thoughts disappeared as she marveled at the incredible giant-size scenery. This *Decimator* apparently took place in New York City, after some near-cataclysmic event for the Earth. Wreckage of buildings lay in massive, crazy-shaped piles. Even the Statue of Liberty was there. Or at least her head. It was sandwiched between a fallen radio tower and half a billboard for a Broadway show.

Two five-year-old girls crawled over it like ants.

"Wheeee!" one of them cried as she slid down a prong of the statue's crown.

"No!" screamed a man in jeans and a T-shirt. The way everyone on set watched him, Gabby assumed he must be the director. "You have to get off!"

The probably director growled to a young man standing next to him holding a clipboard. "This is insane. I swear, if Adam Dent wasn't the biggest movie star in the world right now . . ."

"Look at me!" cried the other little girl. She stood next to Lady Liberty, pushed one finger into the giant plaster left nostril, and twisted it back and forth.

"NO!" wailed the director. "That's the Statue of Liberty!

You can't pick her nose!"

"To be fair," Adam interjected as he and Gabby drew close, "we *did* decapitate her."

The director wheeled around and his entire demeanor changed. "Adam!" He beamed. "Yes! Excellent point. Adorable girls. But, um . . . isn't your assistant supposed to be watching them?"

"She was, yeah," Adam said, then called out, "Romina?"

"She's right here, Daddy! Look! I did it all by myself!"

This was a third little girl, and Adam followed her voice to another corner of the soundstage. The girl stood triumphantly next to a frazzled-looking dark-haired young woman who wore glasses, a gag around her mouth, and handcuffs on her wrists and ankles. Adam smiled.

"Hey, that's great technique! You remembered that from my last film!" Adam knelt down to get face-to-face with his handcuffed assistant. "So you and the girls are having fun?"

Romina responded with a series of gag-bound *mmmph*s.

"Oh right!" Adam realized. He loosened the gag, leaving Romina free to gasp for breath.

"Great fun," she said semi-convincingly. Then she noticed Gabby and her eyes went wide. "Gabby! I'm so glad you're here!"

The second they heard her name, all three little girls wheeled around, their eyes aglow.

"GABBY!" they screamed in unison. They ran and leaped on top of her, tackling her to the ground as each one scrambled for the first hug. Gabby laughed and did her best to wrap her arms around all three of them at once.

"Okay, you have to let me get up," Gabby said. "I need to look at you! Two candy bars each if I can't tell you apart!"

Like cadets falling in line, the five-year-olds sprung off Gabby and stood at attention.

"Um, Gabby," Adam began, "I don't know about the candy bar thing. Sierra keeps them gluten/dairy/sugar-free."

"It's okay," Gabby assured him as she walked up and down the row of triplets. "They won't win."

"But Gabby . . . *I* can't even tell them apart."

Adam had reason to be nervous. The three girls stood exactly the same height, and each wore identical denim shorts with the exact same green-and-white striped shirts and identical black canvas sneakers. While they each wore mismatched socks, they wore the *same* mismatched socks: purple anklets with blue stars on the left foot, red knee-highs with pink polka dots on the right. Their blond hair was fashioned in the same asymmetrical bobs, with bangs the exact same length falling over their right eyes.

They even had matching scabs on their knees.

Gabby knew she was at a disadvantage, but she wasn't worried. She clasped her hands behind her back, plastered on her best knowing-detective look, and paced in front of the girls. As she reached each one she spun toward her, raising one brow and leaning in close to fix the triplet in question with a piercing stare.

The girl in the center giggled. Just the littlest bit, but it was enough.

"Ila!" Gabby shouted, pointing to her.

Ila always broke first.

"How did you know?!" the little girl squealed.

"My freckles give me psychic powers," Gabby intoned. "Now, don't tell me . . ."

Gabby got down on her knees and swayed back and forth, looking from one end-triplet to the other. Ali and Lia were good; they stood identically stone-faced. Luckily, Gabby wasn't looking at their faces. She glanced down and saw the triplet on the far right gently drumming her fingers against her leg, just like Lia always did when she forced her-self to be still.

"My freckles are revealing the answer . . ." Gabby said, dramatically closing her eyes and placing her fingers to her temples. "You're . . . Lia!"

"Yes!" Lia cheered.

Adam shook his head, amazed. "Pretty terrific, Gabby."

"Gabby's the best!" Lia agreed.

"No fair!" Ali sulked. "I wanted the candy bar."

"Oh, I have something way better than candy bars," Gabby assured the girls. "My psychic freckles are telling me the perfect game. Want to hear it?"

The girls did. They leaned into her like daisies reaching for the sun. But before Gabby could speak, Romina cleared her throat.

"I'm sorry," the handcuffed assistant interrupted, "but can you get me out of these?"

"Oh right," Adam said, then turned to his daughters. "Which one of you has the key?"

"I do," Ali said brightly . . . but then her face fell in an impishly exaggerated frown as she rubbed her stomach. "In my belly."

"In your *what*?!" Romina wailed.

"Actually, it *was* in my belly," Ali amended, "until . . ."

She mimed flushing a toilet, making the whooshing and gurgling sounds with her mouth. Romina's jaw dropped.

"Oooh," Adam clucked. "That's a toughie. Maybe we should call special effects? They blow up buildings; I bet they can blow off the handcuffs."

"*Blow* off?!" Romina cried.

Gabby bent down and whispered to the girls. "This is gonna take a while. How 'bout we go play?"

The triplets nodded eagerly and, like little ducklings, followed Gabby to the back of the soundstage. Everyone around stopped and stared. It was the first time since the shoot started that the tiny trio wasn't wreaking havoc on the set.

"It'll never last," the director muttered to his assistant. "Within the hour they'll be back ruining the shoot, or I'll give you my sports car."

Much to the delight of the assistant, who drove away that night in a shiny red convertible, Gabby had a plan. She waited until she and the girls were out of earshot of anyone else, then crouched down low and beckoned them close, all the while glancing around as if to make sure no one was listening in.

The girls were curious—what was Gabby trying to hide? They huddled nearer to her.

"I'm actually here on a mission," Gabby admitted, pushing a lock of brown curls behind her ear, "and I need the three of you to help."

"A spy mission?" Ila asked.

Gabby nodded. "A *secret* spy mission. But it'll only work if we stay *supremely* quiet, and don't let anyone see us for even a second."

The triplets nodded. This was obviously very important.

"Somewhere in these halls"—she gestured behind her, away from the set, to the hallways dotted with dressing rooms, catering stations, working carpenters, prop collections, and wardrobe areas—"is a wooden turtle. Not just any turtle—a secret spy turtle filled with secret spy codes. Our mission is to find it."

The girls were entranced. They hung on Gabby's every word as she pulled from her purple knapsack the tools of their spy trade: little notebooks and pens they'd use to draw pictures and make notes about everything they saw. She gave them the plan: they'd go into each room together, quiet as mice, then spread out and scope the scene without touching a thing or letting anyone know they were there. They'd communicate with hand signals, which Gabby took time to teach them well. After each new room they'd huddle together and whisper about what they found, discuss their upcoming plan of action for turtle hunting in the next room, then continue on with the search.

For thirty minutes the triplets sat rapt. Then they started their mission.

It went flawlessly.

For the rest of the afternoon, the girls and Gabby were as invisible as whispers. Pointedly avoiding any area where they might interfere with the movie shoot, Gabby led the team of super-spies through every room. They made no sounds and disturbed nothing. They took copious notes in their notebooks and exchanged intricate hand signals conveying their many suspicions about everyone they saw. Sure, the crew members looked harmless, but on closer inspection they were clearly secret-spy-turtle-thieves mired in deception and conspiracy. Not even their dad was beyond suspicion.

Gabby waited until the shooting day was almost over, then pulled the girls together to share their clues in hushed whispers.

"What do you think?" she asked, pulling out her own pencil and notebook to compile their thoughts. "Any idea where the turtle is?"

"I know! I know!" Ila jumped up and down and waved her arm in the air. "It was stolen by the woman in black!"

"One of the stagehands," Gabby scribbled, nodding knowingly. "I wonder what plans she has for the turtle's secret codes."

"Not one of the stagehands!" Ila said. "I mean the *old* woman in black!"

Gabby's pencil froze. "The *old* woman in black?"

"Uh-huh," Ali agreed. "I saw her, too. She was *really* old. And she stood super-tall, like she was being stretched up to the sky."

Gabby remembered the old woman who stared at her back in her neighborhood. *She* stood tall like that, too.

And so did a million wicked stepmothers in kids' movies, Gabby reminded herself. Plus, the triplets were little—their idea of "really old" probably wasn't the same as her own.

Gabby forced herself to put silly ideas out of her head

and keep writing. "Okay," she said, "this is good stuff. What else can you tell me about the old woman in black?"

"She was like magic," Lia whispered. "She'd be in a room and I'd see her out of the corner of my eye, but when I looked right at her . . . *poof!*"

"She disappeared? Like in a puff of smoke?" Gabby asked the question hopefully. If the woman poofed in and out of existence, she was definitely a figment of the girls' imaginations.

"No!" Lia retorted. "She wasn't magic, she had *skills*."

"Ninja skills!" Ila added, and demonstrated with a whirling air kick that landed her flat on her bottom. It didn't faze her. She rolled to her knees and pointed a tiny finger in Gabby's face. "And she knew *you* were our leader. Every time I saw her, she was staring right at you."

"Like she was tracking your every move!" Ali added eagerly.

"And wouldn't rest until she'd followed you to the ends of the earth!" Lia finished.

Gabby clutched her pencil so tightly it snapped in her grip. "Ow!" she yelped as a splinter sliced into her finger.

"Gabby!"

"Are you okay?"

"Can we help?"

The three girls huddled around Gabby, concerned. While they examined her shaking hand, Gabby nervously scanned the room, half-expecting the old woman in black to leap out of the shadows and attack her.

No one was there. No one unexpected, at least. Just the regular crowd of people working on the movie; all of them too busy to pay attention to Gabby and the girls.

Gabby took a deep breath. It had to be a coincidence. Even if the girls *had* seen a black-clad old woman around the soundstage, that didn't mean it was the same woman Gabby had seen at home. The woman could still be a stagehand. Or she could be the person Gabby thought she saw reflected in the security guard's glasses. Gabby had jumped to the conclusion that the reflection was the woman from her neighborhood, but it made far more sense that she was actually an extra, or a caterer, or even an Adam Dent fan who snuck her way onto the set. That wouldn't explain her following Gabby around and staring at her, but that part could easily be the girls' imagination.

Gabby concentrated on doctoring her splinter. She let the girls help, and by the time they were done and the stage manager called a wrap, Gabby felt much more relaxed. She made a show of studying the clues the girls had gathered all day and determined that according to their calculations, the turtle with the secret spy codes should be in a prop cannon—the same prop cannon in which Gabby had secretly hidden it earlier in the day. The triplets' screams of delight when they found it brought their dad running.

"Hey!" he exclaimed. "There you are! Is everything okay? You guys were so quiet all day I got worried!"

"We found the turtle!" Ila cried.

"The old ninja woman wanted it, but we thwarted her!" Ali added.

Lia held the turtle high in triumph. "Now we can save the planet from Ninja-Nana Annihilation!"

As the girls jumped and cheered, Adam scrunched his face in thought. "Ninja-Nana Annihilation?" He paused a second, then shouted out to the director, "Reggie! Come here! I think we need to do some rewrites!" Then he wrapped Gabby in a huge hug. "Thanks a million for today, Gabby. You're a lifesaver. You'll do it again?"

"I don't know . . ." Gabby sucked on her teeth like it was a tough call. "Only if the girls *really* want—"

"YES!!!" they chorused, hurling themselves on her for a giant group hug that they only gave up when Gabby threatened to use her psychic freckles to find their ultimate tickle spots. As the girls squealed and ran off, Romina came over to escort Gabby back to the waiting limo.

As the car sped away, Gabby sprawled back in the seat. She giggled, imagining a *Decimator Four* filled with evil old women doing backflips while chasing secret wooden turtles. She'd have to take her friend Satchel to see it in 3-D. The two of them loved cheesy movies, the splatterier the better. They'd been watching them together since birth. Or more precisely, since a week after their same-day births, when their maternity-ward-roomie moms had gotten together to share labor videos. Ugh.

The limo took Gabby to the Bonita-Dents' private jet, where Gabby spent the flight feasting on steak and thick-cut fries. The meal was so giant, Gabby insisted Amelia, the flight attendant, share it with her, and the two chatted happily for most of the flight. When Amelia had to prepare for landing, Gabby leaned back and hummed the solo for Friday afternoon's concert while she pantomimed the finger motions on an imaginary French horn. It wouldn't be as effective as Madison's practice session, but it was something. She got so lost in the notes that she went from the airplane to the limo waiting to take her home in a musical daze. Only when she finished humming the solo did she look up to smile apologetically to the driver.

"Hi, Alber—" she started.

But her voice stuck in her throat when she realized the cold, dark eyes staring at her in the rearview mirror weren't Albert's at all.

Someone else was driving the car.

An old woman, dressed in black.

And the woman did *not* look pleased.

chapter
THREE

g abby lunged for the door and tried to throw it open, but the lock clicked shut.

"I wouldn't do that," the woman's icy voice said. "Unwise to leap from a moving car. And you struck me as so intelligent."

The woman was right. Jumping from the car would be highly hazardous to Gabby's health and her chances of getting Friday's solo, which would be impossible to play from a hospital bed. Still, Gabby couldn't peel her hands off the door handle. She was frozen in place. Only her eyes moved, to stare back at the face in the rearview mirror.

It wasn't a coincidence this time. It couldn't be. That face was the same one she saw reflected in the security guard's glasses in Florida. The same one she saw in her own neighborhood that morning.

But how? And why?

Gabby took a deep breath and tried to slow her thundering heart. She was stuck in this car now, at the mercy of this stalker, and she'd be much better equipped to escape if she stayed calm. She forced a laugh and said, "Sorry about that. I guess you startled me. I thought you'd be someone else."

"Intriguing," the woman said with a nod. "Because so far, Gabby Duran, *you* are *exactly* who I'd hoped you'd be. Aside from the near lemminglike leap to oblivion, of course. That I must admit was disappointing."

Gabby was stunned. "You know my name."

"I know many things."

Outside the window, Gabby watched her exit whiz by. "Um . . . I think we need to turn around," Gabby said. "I live that way."

As she spoke, she eased open her purple knapsack. If she moved slowly and didn't get the woman's attention, she could sneak out her phone and dial 911.

"You can call the authorities if you'd like," the woman said. "But I have no intention of harming you. Quite the opposite. I have a proposition for you. One I believe you'll find intriguing, and one you won't get to hear should you report this event to another human being. Or electronic device, in case you imagined that was a loophole."

Gabby *had* thought that was a loophole. If she texted her mom, she wouldn't *technically* be reporting directly to another human being. So much for that idea.

"You were in front of my house this morning," Gabby said. "And at the studio in Florida."

"And cats bathe by licking themselves, and Henry the Eighth had six wives," the woman sighed. "Would you like to recite more facts I already know?"

Gabby felt chastened, even though she was fairly sure she was the one being wronged in this situation. She sat a little straighter and challenged the woman. "What if I don't want to hear your proposition? What if I tell you to immediately turn this car around and take me home?"

"Well, I certainly hope you'd have the decency to ask rather than tell me, but if you indeed made such a request, I would do just that. After admonishing you for carelessly splitting infinitives, of course. But then you'd never know what you'd missed."

Gabby leaned back in her seat, considering. She wasn't afraid anymore. She supposed she should be. An interstate stalker who spoke in cryptic promises and drove Gabby away from home without asking first was pretty much a textbook call-for-help situation. Yet the more she spoke with the old woman, the less frightened she became. The woman's voice had the clipped tones of a no-nonsense boarding school headmistress. It was the kind of voice that didn't suffer fools and wouldn't waste time on lies. If she said she wouldn't harm Gabby and would take her home if she asked, Gabby believed her.

"Well?" the woman asked. "Would you like to hear my offer?"

Gabby imagined telling the story of this moment to the people she loved most. Carmen would accuse her of idiocy and Alice would worry about her safety. Both would want her to turn around and go home. Satchel would vote for home, too. Much as he could handle anything on a movie screen, in real life he'd freak out if he stepped on a crack or spilled salt. This would have him hyperventilating.

Then she heard Zee's voice in her head. *It's always better to know than not know. Always.*

Gabby smiled. Those were the words Zee said when they'd bonded as lab partners in fourth grade and wondered how much Jell-O powder it would take to turn the school pool into a gelatinous dessert. Gabby had agreed then, and she agreed just as much now. Besides, hearing what the woman had to say didn't commit her to anything.

Still, she felt she had a right to make a demand—a

request—of her own. "First, I'd like to know your name," she said.

"You may call me Edwina," the woman replied.

"Because that's your name?"

"Because it will suffice."

Gabby still didn't say yes. She took a moment to study Edwina. The triplets had thought she was ancient. She wasn't quite that, but the deep lines along her forehead and down her cheeks did peg her as older, maybe even seventy. The white hair piled into a tight bun beneath her chauffeur's cap also aged her. Only her brown eyes seemed young and strong. They were sharp and piercing, filled with keen intelligence. Gabby understood why the triplets had found the woman intimidating, but she highly doubted Edwina had ninja skills. She imagined her leaping into a midair roundhouse kick and laughed out loud.

Edwina raised an eyebrow. "You don't think I could pull off Ninja-Nana Annihilation?"

Gabby clamped her hand over her mouth, then asked, "How did you . . . ?"

"No, I don't read minds," Edwina said, "not even to know you were wondering if I did. I simply surmised it from a combination of your clumsy attempt to subtly size me up, your expression, and what I observed earlier."

Gabby opened her mouth to reply, but she was too

shocked for anything to come out. A hint of a smile played on Edwina's lips.

"Magnificent work, by the way," Edwina said. "With the triplets. You handled them beautifully."

"I didn't *handle* them," Gabby corrected her immediately. "I played with them. It was fun. They're really good kids."

"For *you*," Edwina noted. "As are many children who are impossible for other authority figures."

Gabby screwed up her face. "I'm not an 'authority figure.' I'm just a babysitter."

"*Just* a babysitter?" Edwina arched an eyebrow. "That's not what I've heard. More like a *super*-sitter. Clients all over the world seek you out for the most impossible babysitting cases."

Gabby simply nodded. She was proud of her reputation and happy she could help people who needed her, but she didn't like to brag about it. Starting with her own little sister—despite Carmen's claims otherwise—babysitting was just something Gabby was good at. It came naturally to her.

"Tell me," Edwina said, narrowing her eyes. "What's your secret?"

"I don't have one," Gabby said honestly. "I just love kids."

"*All* kids?" Edwina pressed.

"Never met one I didn't like."

"No matter how . . . unusual?"

Gabby laughed. "The more unusual the better! That's what makes babysitting so fun. Every kid is unique and different, so I never do the same thing twice."

Edwina nodded thoughtfully, then stared at the road and didn't say anything for what felt like ages. Gabby wondered if she'd put her foot in her mouth again, and if Edwina wouldn't offer the proposition after all. She was running their entire conversation back through her head when Edwina's eyes snapped to the rearview mirror and caught Gabby's own.

"I have a job for you," Edwina offered. "One boy, eight years old, ten minutes. I'll pay you four times your hourly rate."

Gabby sat straight up and leaned forward against the seat belt. "What?!"

"I believe you heard me," Edwina said. "Should this job go well, I'll offer you more."

The "Yes!" was about to leap from Gabby's mouth, but Edwina cut her off.

"Before you answer, there's a caveat. You must agree beforehand that you will tell no one about the experience. Not your mother, not your sister, not your friends."

Gabby fell back into her seat. This changed things. "I don't like to lie," she said.

"Nor do I," said Edwina. "It's an admirable quality. However, I'm afraid the circumstance requires it. So what do you say? Are the terms acceptable to you?"

A million conflicting thoughts whirled through Gabby's brain, but only one got bigger and bigger until it stood front and center in her mind.

Gabby's mom, Alice.

She worked so hard to provide for Gabby and Carmen and still be there with the girls all the time, but it was a struggle. Though Alice never complained about it, Gabby knew her mom always felt the pressure to earn more money in less time. And yes, Gabby's income helped, but between school and her French horn and homework and time with her friends, she could only work so many hours. If Edwina really would pay four times her rate, that could make a huge difference in the Durans' lives.

There was something else Gabby wanted, too, but she knew she shouldn't get ahead of herself. Right now Edwina was offering just the one ten-minute job. A nice bonus. A little extra she could put aside and use for something special.

Gabby checked her watch, then picked up her phone.

"Your hourly check-in text to your mother?" Edwina asked.

Gabby wasn't even surprised anymore by how much Edwina knew. She simply nodded, typed, *All good, but running about an hour late b/c of plane stuff. Love u!,* and pressed Send. She felt a twinge of guilt, but it faded. She was doing a little wrong for a greater right. Or at least the opportunity for a greater right. She looked into the rearview mirror and met Edwina's eyes.

"I accept your offer."

Edwina nodded almost imperceptibly and remained silent for the rest of the ride.

Five minutes later, they pulled onto a tree-lined lane with wide sidewalks and houses with lovingly manicured yards. It was early evening, but a dozen different kids still raced around on foot, bikes, or skates. The charming cookie-cutter homes were all spread far enough apart to offer privacy but close enough that neighbors would grow naturally friendly.

The road ended in the swell of a cul-de-sac. Edwina pulled up in front of a green house with white shutters, where a gray Persian fuzzball of a cat rose languidly in the window, stretched, then hopped out of sight.

"Aw!" Gabby cooed. "They have a kitten!"

"Of sorts," Edwina replied.

Gabby understood. The cat had looked small but was probably full-grown. Still, it was really cute. Maybe she and the eight-year-old would find a string and play with it for ten minutes. Easiest assignment ever!

Still playing proper limo driver, Edwina exited the car, then came around to open the door for Gabby. The two walked through the gate in the white picket fence surrounding the front yard, then up a flagstone path to the door.

Edwina made no move to knock or ring the bell. She didn't have to. The second they neared the house, the door swung open to reveal a smiling young couple so beautiful, fresh-faced, and happy they might have stepped off the pages of *Perfect Parent* magazine. They even held hands just to answer the door. Gabby liked them immediately.

"You must be Gabby!" they said in unison.

Exact unison. Even their inflections matched. It was the vocal equivalent of being with Ali, Lia, and Ila all over again. Odd, but sweet.

"I am. Gabby Duran. Nice to meet you."

"No, it's nice to meet *you*," the smiling dad said.

"Please come in!" the smiling mom offered.

"Can we get you anything?" the dad asked. "Water? Coffee?"

The mom's smile strained a bit, and Gabby noticed her squeeze his hand a little harder. "John, honey," she said tightly, "Gabby's still a little girl. Little girls don't drink coffee. All humans know that."

"Of course!" John laughed, but it sounded a little forced. "I was just kidding. So was my wife, Lisa, when she said 'all humans.' I mean, who talks like that?"

Lisa stiffened as if she'd realized she'd made a horrible mistake, but the moment passed so quickly Gabby almost thought she'd imagined it, and a heartbeat later Lisa was laughing right along with her husband.

Loudly. And for a strangely long time.

Edwina sighed and rolled her eyes. "May we see the boy?"

"Of course!" John and Lisa chorused. They turned around but didn't release each other's hands. So instead of simply pivoting, they walked awkwardly around each other in a large circle while Edwina sighed and tapped a foot impatiently.

"This is ridiculous," Edwina finally snapped. "Gabby, come with me."

She walked briskly down the hall and opened a door, revealing stairs leading to a basement. The stairs turned before they made it all the way down, so Gabby couldn't see much of the room from where she stood. Still, she could tell it was finished, with sky-blue painted walls and a thick sandy-brown carpet. Music wafted up, and Gabby heard the jangling of a bell—maybe the cat? Gabby hadn't seen it since she came inside, so maybe John and Lisa had let it downstairs. She also heard boyish laughter.

"Your charge is down there," Edwina said, nodding down the stairs. "I'll fetch you in ten minutes."

"Got it," Gabby said.

She stepped onto the staircase, and the door instantly slammed behind her.

Click.

Had Edwina locked her in?

For the first time, Gabby felt a prickle of unease and

44

wondered if she'd made a big mistake coming here.

"Hey, did you hear that?" she heard the boy ask. "Is that my babysitter?"

Feet pounded across the floor and onto the stairs, and a moment later a towheaded mop top appeared on the landing just below Gabby. He was small for eight, but everything else was exactly what Gabby would expect from a kid with lots of energy. The shins of his jeans looked like they'd lost a brutal battle with a grassy field, his T-shirt had a juice stain down the front, and his hair stuck up wildly on one side. The cat had followed him, and now looked up at him curiously, as if wondering when they'd get back to whatever they were doing. The boy, however, was all about Gabby.

"It *is* you!" he said with a giddy smile. "I'm Philip. Are you here to play with me?"

Gabby laughed at her own misgivings. Philip was a great kid—anyone could see that. Why would Edwina imagine she'd have to pay Gabby four times her hourly rate to spend ten minutes with him?

"I am!" Gabby assured him. "And I'm so excited! What do you want to play?"

"Oh, I know all kinds of games!" Philip enthused. He slipped his little hand in Gabby's and pulled her with him back down the stairs. The basement was all playroom: huge and carpeted, with stacks of toys, scattered beanbag chairs, and lots of empty space to run around.

Gabby shrugged her purple knapsack off her shoulders and knelt down, so she and Philip were eye to eye. "Tell you what," she said. "We don't have a ton of time this playdate, so how about you show me your *favorite* game."

"Okay!" Philip agreed. "I call this one The Brand-New Babysitter and the Giant . . ."

Philip's voice dropped three octaves as he said the word "Giant." His deep rumbling tone filled the room and shook the very walls.

". . . Drippy . . ." the booming voice continued, but now Philip's skin started to bubble and pucker. His clothes seemed to melt *into* his skin, like they weren't fabric at all but part of a body that was now changing . . . and growing by the second.

". . . SLUG-MONSTER!" Philip's deep rumbling voice finished with a shout. He had swelled until he was taller than Gabby herself, and his human body had bubbled and oozed away entirely, leaving a massive curl of gelatinous ooze topped by two googly eyeballs on long stalks. These hung down close in front of Gabby's face, and the creature-formerly-known-as-Philip's mouth opened in a drooling, saber-toothed grin.

"So . . . what do you think of my game?" it asked.

chapter FOUR

*E*dwina sat at the kitchen table, casually thumbing through e-mails on her tablet. None of the sounds wafting up from the basement fazed her. Not the pounding of racing feet, not the wild jiggling of the locked door, not the bloodcurdling screams.

John and Lisa weren't faring quite so well.

"I really wish you wouldn't drink that stuff," Lisa told her husband as she paced the floor. "It's so high-octane."

John lowered the red gasoline container from his mouth and said pointedly, "At least I'm not the one biting my nails."

Lisa removed her hand from the candy dish full of metal fasteners. "They're screws, actually," she said tightly. "And I can't help it. I eat when I'm anxious."

A massive crash from downstairs made both parents jump. Lisa raced to Edwina. "Can't we just open the door and check? Gabby seemed so sweet. I can't live with myself if she ends up like the girl who tried to help the Blitzfarbs."

Edwina didn't answer. She looked up from the tablet and met Lisa's eyes just long enough to communicate that the interruption was most unappreciated. Then she gazed down again. Lisa went back to pacing and chewing on screws. John stopped drinking, but he nervously dangled his eyes in and out of their sockets.

Finally, Edwina's tablet beeped.

"It is time," she said.

"Oh, thank goodness," Lisa gushed. She raced for the basement door and flung it open. The cat was right there. It stood on its back legs and had one of its front paws raised, as if it had been about to knock on the door itself.

"Good, you're here," the cat said in a sweet feminine drawl. "'Cause believe me, y'all don't want to miss this."

Remaining on her back legs, the cat led Lisa, John, and Edwina down the stairs. As they turned the corner, Lisa gasped. The basement was a shambles. The sky-blue walls were riddled with dents, patches of carpet were shredded to

48

bits, and several beanbag chairs had been ferociously gutted, their innards spilled across the floor.

John put a hand on his wife's shoulder. "We're too late," he intoned.

"For the love of Zinqual, will you please keep moving?" Edwina asked sharply. When the parents wouldn't, Edwina sighed and pushed her way past them until she'd fully descended the stairs and could take in the entire room.

"Shhh," Gabby said. "He's napping."

Gabby sat in the one intact beanbag chair. In one hand she held a copy of *Better Homes and Gardens*. With her other she stroked the back of Philip's gelatinous head, which lay in her lap. The rest of his body sprawled across the floor.

"We were playing his favorite game," she whispered to Edwina. "He got really into it—tired him right out, so I read him stories until he fell asleep." She indicated the magazine. "He said he likes this one because it's scary: 'Top Ten Ways to Eradicate Slugs.'" Gabby shuddered. "Gave us the shivers too, right, Vondlejax?"

The cat had made her way to Gabby's side and leaned one elbow on the beanbag chair. "You know it, honeylamb. My tail was so far between my legs I could've tickled my own chin!"

Gabby laughed, then turned to Philip's parents. "I'm so sorry about the furniture. It's my fault. I have to admit I got

49

a little nervous when he first . . . you know."

"A little?" Vondlejax teased. "Sweetcheeks, I thought I'd have to run you to my litter box!"

Gabby let out an embarrassed laugh. "A lot nervous. Pretty completely terrified, to be honest." Then she turned to the cat. "You didn't exactly help."

"I declare, I most certainly did! I shouted right out, 'Don't you panic! Every little thing's gonna be just peaches and cream!'"

Gabby tilted her head and looked at Vondlejax. The cat cleared her throat.

". . . which I suppose might have been a teensy weensy shock," Vondlejax admitted, "seein' as you thought I was an ordinary house cat."

"I *did* panic," Gabby said apologetically to Philip's parents, "and I ran and knocked into some things. . . . I may have even screamed a little. . . ."

"You think?" Vondlejax hooted.

"But then . . ." Lisa stammered, "how did you . . ."

John finished for her. "What changed?"

"Well," Gabby said, "before Philip . . . altered himself, he said he wanted to play a game. So even though I was really scared when he was chasing me, I realized that's what it was to him, a game. But it wasn't a nice game, you know? I mean, he might look like a monster—sorry—but that doesn't mean he is one. He's just a kid. And it's kind of awful that he knows someone like me who's supposed to take care of him is going to run away screaming. It made me really sad."

Lisa sniffled loudly. "That's the nicest thing I've ever heard a human say," she sobbed. John handed her a tissue, and she blotted the tears that trickled from her elbow.

"You ain't heard nothin' yet," Vondlejax said as she leaped onto the back of the couch. "Our girl Gabby spun around all upon a sudden and cried out, 'Now it's my turn to chase you!' Oh, was that boy surprised." The cat fanned herself with a paw and Gabby laughed.

"It's true," she said. "I think that's when we did the most damage down here. But he was having fun. Real fun. I could tell. And then he got sleepy."

Gabby smiled down at Philip. His head was still in her lap. Careful not to wake him, she gave him a gentle hug. Her arm sank a bit into his gooey skin. He sighed happily in his sleep.

John knelt down next to Gabby. "Would you like to move in with us?" he asked. "Forever?"

"Come now, that's hardly appropriate," Edwina clucked. "In fact, it's time for me to get Gabby home. A little assistance, please?"

Lisa gently lifted her son's head so Gabby could slip off the beanbag chair without waking him. Gabby grabbed her purple knapsack, then before she got up she knelt down in front of Vondlejax. The cat used both front paws to scratch behind Gabby's ears. "See?" Vondlejax cooed. "Right there, just like that. Isn't that just pure heaven?"

"You were right," Gabby said. "It feels incredible, thanks."

She gave the cat a hand-to-paw high five, then blew Philip a kiss before she followed Edwina back upstairs and toward the front door. John and Lisa shadowed their every step.

"So when exactly *are* you available?" John asked.

"Do you work during the school week?" Lisa added.

"Do you have room for any more regular clients?"

"How many months ahead can we book?"

Gabby started the same answer she gave all her new clients. "Just call my sister. She—"

"*I* will let you know when and if Gabby's available," Edwina cut her off. "Let us remember, she isn't officially in the program yet."

Before Gabby could say another word, Edwina herded her outside and back into the limousine. Gabby immediately rolled down the window. It was dark outside, but the front porch was well lit, and Gabby could clearly see John, Lisa, and Vondlejax.

"Good-bye!" Gabby called. "It was wonderful meeting you! I hope to see you again soon!"

The threesome all waved back. Then John nudged

Vondlejax, who quickly dropped to all four paws and began an intensive and very feline tongue bath. Gabby kept waving until the house was out of sight, then she rolled up the window. She tried to sit back in her seat, but suddenly she couldn't breathe. She sat straighter, tilting her neck back to gasp for air. Her body trembled all over. Even her stomach felt fluttery.

"There's a thick blanket under the seat," Edwina said. "I recommend wrapping yourself up."

Gabby reached down and felt thick fuzziness. She gratefully pulled the blanket around her and huddled into it. "I don't understand," she chattered. "I'm not scared. Not anymore."

"Delayed shock," Edwina said. "It happens. Much like when you force yourself to be brave for an injection, but faint when you get up to leave. Keep warm. It'll pass."

She turned up the heat in the back of the car.

Gabby felt frighteningly out of control of her own body. She cuddled deeper into the thick blanket and concentrated on the warm air bathing her face. Soon her teeth stopped chattering and her breathing slowed. She was okay. She took a long, deep breath and let it out with a sigh as she relaxed into the seat.

"It was your sister, yes?" Edwina asked.

Gabby's jaw clenched. She was always wary when people

asked about Carmen. "What do you mean?"

"The child who didn't deserve to be treated like a monster," Edwina said. "Seemed like you had a good understanding of what that might be like."

Gabby narrowed her eyes and glared at Edwina through the rearview mirror, but the older woman didn't look critical, just matter-of-fact. Maybe even a little . . . kind? It made Gabby let her guard down.

"Yeah," she admitted. "That was Car. She was tough when she was little. She didn't know how to deal when stuff made her uncomfortable . . . and a lot of stuff made her uncomfortable. So she screamed . . . or yanked at her own hair . . . or threw things. . . . It was no big deal, I knew how to calm her down. But people didn't get it. They stared. Or they didn't stare, but only because they were working really hard *not* to stare, which was worse. Like she was too horrible to even look at. She wasn't. She just needed someone to understand her."

Gabby fiddled with her knapsack. She didn't like to talk about when Carmen was little. It felt disloyal, like she'd just tainted Edwina's vision of her sister.

"All people need someone to understand them," Edwina said. "Just like Philip."

Raising her eyes to look back at Edwina, Gabby said, "But Philip isn't exactly a *person* . . . right?"

"There's something I'd like you to read," Edwina said.

54

She pressed a button on the front console and the television screen in the limo's backseat sprang to life. On it, a glowing green insignia rotated inside a circle—a logo, it seemed—and next to it glowed the words:

Association
Linking
Intergalactics and
Earthlings as
Neighbors

"A.L.I.E.N.," Gabby read the acronym. "Are you saying Philip's an *alien*? Like . . . from-another-planet alien?"

Edwina pulled her tablet out of her bag and handed it back to Gabby. The screen held scans of several newspaper clippings, each cut off mid-article. "Read," she said.

Gabby read.

●————————————●

From the *Philadelphia News Report*, August 30, 1955:

SINKHOLE SWALLOWS SITTER

Emergency workers were thrilled to report the rescue of Abigail Latrelle, 16, after a most harrowing experience. She was babysitting three young children when a giant sinkhole opened and swallowed her whole.

"We built a fort out back," she said. "The kids wanted to give it a basement, but I said we couldn't dig up their yard. They said they'd handle that part themselves, and the next thing I knew, the kids were glowing bright red and the ground was collapsing under me!"

Clearly, there are some strange elements to Ms. Latrelle's story. While doctors have given her a clean bill of health, they do believe the shock of falling into the sinkhole might contribute to her delusions.

●━━━━━●

From the *Miami Gazette*, March 5, 1985:

SCARED SIT-LESS!

How young is too young to babysit? Ronnie Jacobson's parents thought thirteen was the perfect age for their son to sit for their young neighbors. Yet if the story he brought home is any indication, the choice may have been premature.

In the middle of his babysitting job, Ronnie abandoned his charges, raced home, and locked himself in his room. The kids, he claimed, had "turned themselves into mice and crawled all over" him, scaring him so badly he refused to go back.

Thankfully, the story has a happy ending in that Ronnie's parents went to their neighbors' house and found the children safe and sound, albeit covered in shreds of finely nibbled cheese. Still the tale stands as caution to parents of aspiring sitters who might not be ready for the responsibility.

From the *San Francisco Journal*, October 30, 2008:

BABYSITTERS GET VAMPIRE FEVER

We all know the Twilight Saga is an international teen obsession, but nowhere has that been more evident than on Sitipedia. The site touts itself as "the free encyclopedia for all things babysitting." Like Wikipedia, anyone can contribute to articles on the site, and no entry has attracted more traffic than one entitled "Babysitting Vampires."

Apparently, hundreds of thousands of babysitting teens across the world are convinced that the children left in their care are indeed bloodsucking vampires. To share their experiences and offer advice to others, they constantly expand the Sitipedia article with subheads like "Fangs vs. Large Incisors: How to Differentiate," "Bat Training 101," and "Best Garlic Body Lotions."

Bay Area teen Lanie Vendriak says the Sitipedia article has been a literal lifesaver. "I can't tell you how many times I thought I was babysitting regular kids, and it turned out they were vampires!" she said.

• ─────────── •

"I don't get it," Gabby said when she finished the last clipping.

"Inaccurate," Edwina declared. "You're a highly intelligent girl who just had a close encounter with a slug-child and a talking cat. You might be struggling with several layers of denial, but you most certainly *do* 'get it.'"

Edwina was right. Everything Gabby had seen and

read pointed to only one answer. "Philip *is* an alien," Gabby admitted. It felt weird to say it out loud, but it also felt right. "And so are his parents and Vondlejax."

"Very good," Edwina said. "Anything else?"

"Well"—Gabby thought about the articles—"they can't be the only ones, because all those articles were about other aliens from years ago until now, and from different places all over the country. And the Sitipedia one says people are posting from all over the world. And *you* . . ." Gabby looked again at the logo and title, still glowing on the screen on the back of the limo seat. "You must work with A.L.I.E.N., the Association Linking Intergalactics and Earthlings as Neighbors."

"See? You *do* have a talent for deductive reasoning," Edwina noted. "Despite what your math teacher said on your last report card."

"You read my report card?" Gabby asked.

"As you've surmised," Edwina continued, "aliens have been living among us for a very long time. And as you've seen for yourself, while human beings have many points in their favor, accepting things they don't understand is not among them."

Something clicked in Gabby's head. "When you call human beings 'they,'" she asked, "is that because—"

"This is problematic, given that most aliens come in

peace, and they would much prefer *not* to be hunted down and dissected," Edwina said, once again ignoring Gabby's interruption. Gabby noticed that this time, "they" referred to the aliens. So much for clues about Edwina's identity.

"That's where my associates and I come in," Edwina said. "We at A.L.I.E.N. make it our business to maintain peaceful human–intergalactic-being integration. When mishaps occur, we make sure they're perceived as flights of fancy, tricks of the light, or easily dismissible mythologies."

"Like the vampires," Gabby said. "So . . . are *all* monsters actually aliens? Mummies and zombies and werewolves and—"

"And leprechauns and centaurs and fairies and all number of creatures who have disguised themselves so well through the centuries that they haven't inspired any stories about them at all, yes. Overall, we at A.L.I.E.N. are quite proud of our record of success. With one notable exception. Can you guess what it is?"

Gabby looked down at Edwina's laptop and scrolled again through the headlines. She remembered how eager John and Lisa were to hire her.

"Babysitting?" she asked.

Edwina nodded. "It has been a challenge. Time and again mishaps like the ones in those articles threatened to expose the secret we've worked so very hard to contain. The situation has become so dangerous that we had to declare all intergalactic children officially Unsittable."

"Unsittable?" Gabby echoed. "But that's horrible. Every kid is sittable."

"Only given the right sitter," Edwina said. She looked into the rearview mirror and fixed Gabby with a pointed stare.

"Me?"

"You can't be everywhere at once, of course," Edwina said, "and we recognize you have other clients and responsibilities. But if you do this, if you're willing to keep our secrets and join our cause, I assure you that you'll be doing a great service to families very much in need of your talents. And of course, you'll be rewarded most handsomely."

"When you say 'keep your secrets' . . ."

"From everyone," Edwina stated. "That's nonnegotiable."

Gabby flopped back in her seat and thought. *Unsittable* was a terrible thing to call a kid, especially a kid as great as Philip. And she'd made John and Lisa so happy just by spending ten minutes with him. There must be all kinds of families just like them, and Gabby could make them just as happy. Lying to her own family would be awful, but Edwina had already promised four times her hourly rate. With that kind of money coming in on a regular basis, Gabby could do more than just help out at home, she could . . .

She almost couldn't think it out loud. It seemed so selfish, especially when she and Alice and Carmen had to consider car payments and school clothes and college funds. . . .

But with the kind of money Edwina was talking about, Gabby could afford to be a little selfish. No, not selfish. Aspirational. She could give her family everything they needed and still have enough to pursue a dream she'd held close since Maestro Jenkins first heard her play and suggested it.

R.A.M.A. The Royal Academy for the Musical Arts, in London. The finest college for anyone wanting a career in music. Ninety percent of its graduates moved immediately to careers in professional orchestras, and every major philharmonic looked to R.A.M.A. to fill their ranks. Maestro Jenkins said that as a female French horn player Gabby was so unique that if she graduated from R.A.M.A. she could have her choice of the best orchestras in the world. The Berlin Philharmonic, the Royal Concertgebouw Orchestra in Amsterdam, the London Symphony Orchestra, the New York Philharmonic . . . Maestro Jenkins said they'd all fight for the honor of having her on their stage.

It sounded like a dream, and Gabby had immediately looked up the school online and discovered it could *only* be a dream. R.A.M.A.'s tuition was more than Alice made in a year. Even with aid and scholarships, Gabby would have to find money for travel and expenses and textbooks. There was just no way.

But college was six years from now. If she started working for Edwina today and set aside a little each month, she could have enough for R.A.M.A. She could take care of Alice and Carmen and still make her dreams come true. Plus, she'd be there for families like Philip's, who needed her desperately.

All that good had to outweigh the bad of keeping secrets, right?

Gabby put her business face on and leaned forward in her seat. "Here's the deal," she said. "My sister handles my books, so you'll need to set up a payment plan with her. And if you're really paying me four times my rate, we'll have to give her some kind of reason why."

"Unnecessary," Edwina said. "A.L.I.E.N. will deposit your fees in a special account to which you'll have easy access. When it grows to a tidy enough sum, we'll create a very old and very dead long-lost relative who left the family an annuity in his will. Checks will come to your house, at which point your sister can deal with them as she sees fit."

"Okay, good, good." Gabby chewed on her lip as her mind danced through all the other complications. "That leaves scheduling. I do that through Carmen, too, but it's not like you can call and say, 'It's Edwina from A.L.I.E.N.' So here's what I'm thinking—how about we set up a secret code, so when she tells me about the job I know it's actually you? Like you could use the word 'vanilla.' Or 'salamander.'

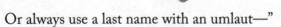

Or always use a last name with an umlaut—"

"We know where to find you," Edwina cut her off, "and we're well aware of your schedule. When we need you, we'll be in touch. That is, if you're saying yes."

Gabby imagined her mom throwing flour in the air and dancing in the flurries when she heard about the long-lost relative's will. She imagined Carmen raising her eyebrow in a grand show of amazement at their new, full bank account. She imagined herself in ten years, standing proudly in a navy blue cap and gown as she accepted her diploma from R.A.M.A. She imagined the families she'd helped cheering her from the audience, stray tentacles accidentally popping loose as they applauded and wiped away grateful tears.

Gabby took a deep breath. There was only one response, but saying it out loud still felt momentous, like everything in her life was about to change.

"Yes," she said. "I'll do it."

Edwina smiled. "Then by the power vested in me by the Association Linking Intergalactics and Earthlings as Neighbors, I hereby declare you, Gabby Duran, Associate 4118-25125A: Sitter to the Unsittables."

chapter
FIVE

*g*abby spent the rest of the ride in silence, her mind too filled with wonder to speak. When the limo pulled up in front of her house, Gabby knew that for appearances' sake, she should fly out like she always did after a job. But the occasion felt too monumental for that.

"Thank you for the ride, Edwina," she said formally. "And of course for the opportunity."

Edwina didn't respond. She simply looked at Gabby in the rearview mirror.

"It was great meeting you," Gabby offered.

She waited for Edwina to tell her it was great meeting her, too. It didn't happen.

"O-kay, then. So I'll just . . ." She reached for the door handle, then thought better of it. "Do you have a cell phone or anything? In case I wake up tomorrow with all kinds of questions I forgot to think of, and—"

Edwina pressed a button on the console. Gabby's door popped open.

"Right," Gabby said. "You'll find me."

She grabbed her purple knapsack and slid out of the limo, which screeched away the second she shut the door. Across the street, Madison was again playing flute in the living room. She wondered if Maestro Jenkins had told her about R.A.M.A., too. Maybe they'd end up there together. Maybe by then, she and Madison would be friends. Maybe they'd be roommates even. And after graduation they'd end up in the same orchestra and they'd tell funny stories to reporters about their early days as bitter rivals at Brensville Middle School.

Madison stopped playing and glanced out her window. Gabby thought she was pretty invisible on the darkened street, but Madison locked eyes with her, then shook her head with a smug smile.

The message was clear. *I practiced, you didn't. I win, you lose.*

Okay, so maybe they wouldn't be R.A.M.A. roommates. Gabby turned and darted inside her house, clomping extra loud so it might seem like she ran in as usual. "Mom? Car?" she called.

"Down here, sweetie!" Alice answered.

Gabby trotted downstairs to the TV room. Alice was sprawled on the overstuffed couch, decompressing to the drone of Food Network. She still wore her stained It's All Relativity apron from the Greek-Italian-Cajun themed Diwali luncheon. Carmen hovered over the Puzzle Place—an old behemoth of a dining room table the Durans had found at a secondhand store, refinished, and turned into a home for Carmen's favorite hobby: impossibly complicated jigsaw puzzles.

"How were the triplets?" Alice asked.

For a second, Gabby had no idea who she meant. John, Lisa, and Philip?

"Oh, you mean Ali, Lia, and Ila!" Gabby remembered, reaching back to what seemed like ages ago. "They were great!"

Carmen looked up from her puzzle. "You sound weird."

"And the flight?" Alice asked. "You said there was trouble, but Carmen checked that Web site that tracks all the planes, and it said the flight left and arrived right on time."

"Really?" Gabby squeaked. Her palms tickled with sweat. "Oh, that's because the trouble was after we landed. Long time on the runway. Is it getting hot in here?" She tugged on her shirt and flapped her arms like chicken wings to get a breeze on her suddenly swampy torso.

"You're acting weird, too," Carmen said.

"Oh yeah?" Gabby countered. "Weirder than choosing a jigsaw puzzle that's a giant math problem?"

"It's a twenty-five thousand piece artistic exploration of pi, taken to two thousand digits," Carmen shot back.

"If the pie was taken to two thousand *flavors*, that would be normal," Gabby said.

"But it wouldn't make sense," Carmen said, scrunching her face. "Pi's a number. It doesn't come in flavors."

"Pie-with-an-e does," Alice said, "and I happen to have a lemon meringue in the fridge. Gabby, why don't you slice some for us?"

That was Alice's favorite way of handling it when the girls bickered: separation, ideally combined with sweets. Gabby tromped back upstairs and sliced three wedges of the pie. She made Carmen's extra-large as an apology. She hadn't really meant to pick on her sister; she just panicked when Car caught her acting strange. If Gabby was going to be a top secret associate for a covert governmental agency, she had to get better at this lying thing. Snapping at Carmen all the time wouldn't work, and if she kept sweating this much every time she stretched the truth, she'd end her first week as a pile of salt and curls.

"You only have two pieces," Alice said when Gabby went downstairs and handed her and Carmen each a plate. "Aren't you having any?"

"Mine's in the kitchen. I thought I'd bring it upstairs and have it while I practice." Translation: *I can't be around you without letting you know I'm keeping a secret.*

"Play loud," Carmen said. "I like hearing you."

Carmen wasn't even looking at Gabby—her full attention was on the puzzle—but Gabby felt like her sister had just given her a huge hug. "Thanks, Car." She kissed her sister on top of her head, and even though Carmen wiped the kiss off like it was bird poop, Gabby swore she saw a hint of a smile.

"My turn," Alice said, holding out her arms.

When Gabby came closer for a hug, Alice held her at arm's length. "You look so much like your father sometimes, it's crazy."

"You think?"

Gabby was only two when her dad died, and he'd been deployed six months before that. She didn't really remember him, and she couldn't see the resemblance in pictures, but Alice swore they had the exact same bright blue eyes and freckles; and pre-army, when her dad's hair had been long, Alice said it had been just as curly as Gabby's.

Alice ruffled Gabby's curls, then pulled her in for a hug. Gabby could smell the tandoori spices still lingering on her mom's clothes. "Don't stay up too late practicing, baby," Alice said. "It's a school night. Carmen and I are going to bed soon, too."

Gabby promised, then bounced up to the kitchen, grabbed her slice of pie, and carried it to her room. After scarfing two huge bites, she opened her French horn case and tried to practice Friday afternoon's solo. She made it through once, playing extra loud for Carmen's benefit, but she wasn't feeling the notes. All she could think about were aliens.

They were real. They lived all around us. She had just personally met four of them. Maybe five; the jury was still out on Edwina. They were everywhere, hidden in plain sight. People Gabby knew could be aliens. People like Ronnie, the bus driver who always shouted, even when she was right in front of you. Or the woman at Alice's favorite bakery who hated kids but loved dogs. Maybe she came from a planet where everyone was fluffy with a tail, so the dogs made her feel at home.

Or maybe *Madison* was an alien. Maybe that's how she could see Gabby in the darkness earlier. Maybe she had creepy mind-tweaking powers, which forced Maestro Jenkins to love her music but messed with her own brain and made it impossible for her to be nice to Gabby, no matter how nice Gabby was to her.

Gabby put away her horn, yanked her phone out of her purple knapsack, and leaped over a pile of dirty laundry to flop on the bed and call Zee. Zee would love this. If Gabby told her there were aliens around, she'd dive in and analyze every detail about every person in their lives until she knew for sure who was earthling and who was intergalactic. It'd be just like the time Gabby found the anonymous "I love you, Gabby Duran" letter in her fifth-grade locker, and Zee went full forensics, dissecting speech patterns, gestures, habits, and daily routines of everyone who had even the remotest contact with Gabby, including some who might have sent the note as a prank. When the culprit turned out to be Wally Ramone, a fourth-grade trumpet player whose lips were always pursed into playing position, Gabby's disappointment was completely overshadowed by her awe of Zee's skills. The clue that closed the case? Turkey jerky. It was Wally's favorite snack. He ate it constantly, and both he and the letter carried its distinctive odor.

Zee would love Gabby's latest mystery even more, but Gabby realized there was no way she could tell her. She'd promised Edwina. If she spilled, she broke the rules, and she wouldn't be allowed to babysit for A.L.I.E.N. No sitting, no money, no helping her family, no R.A.M.A. Plus, kids like Philip would go back to being "Unsittable."

Gabby stopped the call before she even finished dialing. She rolled onto her stomach and screamed into her comforter.

This was impossible. She needed something to distract her.

Could she call Satchel? Even though his mom and Alice had drifted apart a little since their maternity ward roommate days, years of shared playdates, shared birthday parties, and embarrassing-to-look-at-the-videos-now shared baths had sealed their deal. Gabby and Satchel were one hundred percent brother and sister, even if they did have different houses and different parents. Gabby knew him as well as she knew herself, and knew exactly what he'd be doing right now. It was nine at night on a Sunday, so he'd have just finished making bike deliveries for his uncle Gio's restaurant. He'd answer if Gabby called, and there'd be no danger of her talking about A.L.I.E.N. because, unlike Zee, he'd lose it and Gabby would never freak him out that way. But what else could Gabby talk about? A.L.I.E.N. was the only thing on her mind.

She turned off her phone and plugged it in. Better to just go to sleep and deal with everything in the morning. She got ready for bed, crawled under the covers . . .

. . . and didn't wake up until she felt the oozing drool of a strange alien beast dripping onto her face.

"Philip!" she cried as she bolted upright in bed.

It wasn't Philip. It wasn't even an alien. It was that Zee-rigged pitcher of water that doused Gabby every time she pressed the snooze button a third time. As always, she gathered her soaking sheets for the dryer, then got dressed and ready for school and joined Alice and Carmen in the kitchen. Both of them were well into plates of chicken tikka masala, left over from yesterday's brunch. Gabby stared at the heap of chunky yellow-orange goo in front of her own chair and wondered, Could her own mother be an alien? It would explain her penchant for serving decidedly un-breakfasty foods at breakfast.

"Not in the mood for leftovers?" Alice said. "I can make you something else."

"No, it's not that," Gabby said quickly, shaking off the ridiculous idea. "This looks great. I was just thinking about stuff. What's my schedule like this week, Car?"

Between bites, Carmen opened one of her black binders. "Today the Graces, tomorrow the Hayses, Wednesday the Vitaris twins, Thursday the Hayses again," she rattled off. "Friday we left open for the concert."

Interesting. All regulars. Nothing that sounded like code for Edwina.

Then again, Gabby had only been named Sitter to the Unsittables yesterday. It was crazy to think she'd be booked already.

Except John and Lisa seemed like they'd have hired Gabby immediately.

"Do we have anyone unusual coming up in the next few weeks?" Gabby asked. "Anyone . . . I don't know . . . unique?"

Carmen flipped through the book. "Rajit Jethani plays banjo. That's unique. The Cody sisters' grandmother just turned a hundred and two, which is very unique. Adelia Montrose has a dog that won the Westminster Kennel Club's Best in Show. Renee Vel—"

"Got it, thanks." Gabby cut her off before Carmen went through each standout quirk of every single client in the book.

Carmen's watch beeped and she shut the binder. "Time to go," she said. "Bus arrives in three minutes, thirty-nine seconds."

This, Carmen had calculated, was the exact amount of time it took for her and Gabby to put on their coats, gather their bookbags and Gabby's instrument, and get to the stop at the corner. Madison Murray, whose sense of timing was nowhere near as impeccable as Carmen's, was already waiting when they arrived.

"Hi, Madison!"

Gabby said it brightly, but subtly narrowed her eyes, trying to peer through Madison's skin for signs of alien sluginess.

"What are you doing with your face?" Carmen asked. "You look like you smell something bad."

"Carmen! Cut it out. I don't look like that at all." Gabby turned to Madison. "Sorry about that. Don't know what she was talking about."

She offered Madison a chummy laugh. Madison didn't join in. Instead she said, "I noticed the light in your bedroom window was out by ten last night. I was up playing my flute until midnight, then listened to the concerto on headphones, so I'd get extra practice in my sleep. You should probably just go ahead and tell Maestro Jenkins you don't want Friday's solo. It'll save you the suspense of waiting until he gives it to me."

The bus pulled up before Gabby could respond. When Madison turned around to board, Gabby studied her back for any signs of a hidden tail.

"Good morning, girls!" Ronnie the bus driver screamed unnecessarily as they climbed inside. Were her alien ears unable to gauge how loud she was?

Gabby turned down the aisle and stopped in her tracks. The seats were filled with elementary and middle schoolers

75

laughing, shouting, throwing things, zoning out to head-phones, bent over homework, or staring out the window. Were they all human? Had she been riding the bus with aliens all her life? How would she know?

"Butts in seats, or I can't move the bus!" Ronnie cried in her earsplitting bellow.

Gabby quickly slipped into an empty bench a short walk down the aisle, leaving Carmen the only bench she'd accept, the one right behind Ronnie's chair. Gabby took a deep breath and let it out slowly. She had to stop thinking about what happened last night. She couldn't function like this.

Music would help. Gabby pulled out her phone and ear-buds, scrolled to her recording of Friday afternoon's concerto, hunkered down in her seat, closed her eyes, and let the notes fill her head and take her away from everything.

Everything except a sharp pain in her shin. An alien attack?

"Wake up, Gabby," Carmen said. She stood in the aisle next to Gabby's bench. "You fell asleep. We're at your school."

"Oh," Gabby said, rubbing the spot on her leg Carmen had kicked. "Thanks. I think."

Carmen smirked slightly as she went back to her own bench, and Gabby limped herself, her purple knapsack, and her French horn case off the bus.

The minute she hit the curb, a streak of blue and yellow whizzed by, shouting her name.

"Zee!" Gabby happily replied. She raced after her, the knapsack and French horn galumphing against her body with each step.

Stephanie Ziebeck, a.k.a. Zee, rode to school on a motorized skateboard she'd tricked out herself. Hence the super-streak speeds. The super-streak colors came from her blue overalls, every pair of which had a multitude of pockets for gadgets and devices, and her yellow-blond hair, with the almost-equally-multitudinous braids that whipped behind her as she rode.

Gabby caught up with Zee as Zee toe-flipped her skateboard and caught it under her arm.

"Did it finally work?" Zee asked. She was referring, as she did every morning, to the pitcher of water she'd rigged to Gabby's alarm.

"Pavlov totally would have had me put to sleep," Gabby admitted.

"You're killing me," Zee said. She threw her non-skateboard-holding arm around Gabby's shoulders, and they walked into Brensville Middle School. "Come with me, Gabs," she said. "I worked up something new for the L-Man over the weekend."

The L-Man was Ellerbee, the school janitor. His office was right across from the office of the principal. In the first week of school, Zee had rigged some pencils, rubber bands, and a tiny engine into a flying drone that she let loose in the middle of English. She got sent to Tate's, but while she was waiting she saw Ellerbee struggling with a broken vacuum cleaner. Zee fixed it, and the two became friendly. Apparently, Ellerbee's son, who now lived pretty far away and never visited, had been into robotics when he was Zee's age, so Ellerbee understood Zee's dreams of building a bot worthy of a national championship. He also understood why Zee wanted nothing to do with the school's official robotics team, which was manned by Principal Tate. Principal Tate was a man who believed in following rules no matter what, even when those rules sucked the creative life out of something. Ellerbee's son had been more like Zee, and Ellerbee loved sharing his son's old tricks and ideas with her. In return, Zee tried to use her skills to make his job a little easier.

"ZZ Top! Gabby MacGregor!" Ellerbee cried in his thick Scottish accent as he rolled back in his chair. Unlike the principal's palace across the way, Ellerbee's office was little more than a glorified walk-in closet. Shelves crammed with squeeze bottles of cleanser, rags, and buckets lined the walls, while large vacuums, mops, brooms, and buffers crowded the floor. Ellerbee's desk was actually a repurposed lower shelf. His roller chair barely fit beneath it.

"Good to see ya, L-Man!" Zee said.

"Hi, Ellerbee," Gabby added with a smile. She looked at

Ellerbee's framed picture of his hometown—the one he always kept on his desk. He'd told Zee he hadn't been back to Ayr in forty-five years, but he still missed it. Gabby wondered if Philip's family and Vondlejax felt the same way about their home planets.

"Totally hooked you up," Zee said. Her backpack was already on the ground, and she dug inside until she pulled out what looked like foot clips for skis. "Still got the Roombas I juiced for you?"

"Aye, taking up space, I'm afraid," Ellerbee said. He gestured to a pair of round robotic vacuum cleaners Zee had found at a secondhand store. She'd fixed them and rigged them with jet power, so Ellerbee could let them loose and have them finish his work in record time. Unfortunately, the first time he tried one, it slammed into a shelving unit in the science room and spilled sulfuric acid all over the floor. Zee had wanted to pay for the damages herself, but Ellerbee wouldn't let her. He had Tate dock it from his paycheck.

"It's a Newton thing," Zee said as she used the tools in her overalls to tinker with the Roombas and clips. "An object in motion stays in motion unless acted upon by an external force. *You*, L-Man, will be that external force." She stood back and gestured to her creation. "I call it . . . the Shoomba."

Ellerbee cautiously slipped his feet into the shoelike clamps that were now secured onto the robot vacuums.

"You're asking me to ride on these, lassie?"

Zee nodded. "You lean to steer. Try it!"

"Not with you here, ZZ," Ellerbee chuckled. "Don't want you to get in trouble if things fly south. You get ready for class, and I'll let you know how they work."

He and Zee exchanged fist bumps, he waved to Gabby, then the two girls trooped toward their lockers. "Must be hard for Ellerbee," Gabby said as they walked, "living so far away from home."

"I guess," Zee said.

Gabby was talking about the janitor, but she was *thinking* about Philip and his family and Vondlejax. And it was really hard not to talk about them out loud to Zee.

"Did you know they call people who live in this country but aren't from here 'aliens'?" Gabby asked.

Zee scrunched up her face. "Of course I know that. Same thing they call creatures from outer space."

"Right . . . only there's no such thing as *space* aliens," Gabby said quickly.

"'Course there is," Zee said as they hit their lockers and tucked the French horn and skateboard into the deep cubbies beneath.

Gabby's blue eyes widened as she gaped at her best friend. "You know about them?"

"Sure," Zee said. "With all the billions of planets in the

universe, it only makes sense there's alien life somewhere. Maybe even as close as Jupiter's moon Europa. Scientists say the oceans there might support life. Pretty cool, right?" Zee cocked her head, flopping her braids to the side. "Why are we talking about this?"

Gabby's skin prickled. "What do you mean? You're the one who brought up space aliens." She said it a little louder in case any were listening. "I did *not* bring up space aliens."

Zee frowned and studied Gabby, but before she could say anything, another voice called their names.

"Gabby! Zee!"

It was Satchel. He pinballed down the hall, his lanky body ricocheting off every circled-up clique until he reached the girls. "What's up?"

"Gabby's hiding something from me," Zee told him.

"No way! She is?"

"I'm not!" Gabby balked.

"Check it out," Zee said, beckoning Satchel closer. "She's talking too loud, she's blushing, and if you look close, you can see little beads of sweat on her forehead and upper lip."

"Lemme see," Satchel said. His dark hair flopped in his face as he leaned close to investigate. "Oh yeah! Look at that. It's like a little sweat mustache!"

"You guys, cut it out!" Gabby cried, backing away. "I'm not hiding anything."

"See how she's not looking us in the eye?" Zee said. "People do that when they're not telling the truth. And check her arms, flat at her side. When you feel weird about lying, you want to take up as little space as possible."

"I knew that!" Satchel exclaimed. "Gabby and I saw it in *Decimator Two*, when the hijacker was lying to Commando Adam Dent and he totally saw right through it! Oh snap, Gabby, you saw him yesterday, right? Was he on the set? Was it a new *Decimator*? What's it about? I know you're going to say you can't tell me, but you totally have to tell me!"

"I can't say for sure it's a *Decimator*, but I can tell you this," Gabby began, then gave him a few tiny details she knew he'd love. It was more than she'd usually share, but she was anxious to steer the conversation away from aliens and lies. Then the bell rang, and she and Zee split from Satchel to climb the two flights of stairs to Mr. Shamberg's English class. The lecture was about Edgar Allan Poe's "The Tell-Tale Heart," and Gabby realized she was a lot like the protagonist of the story. No, she hadn't killed anyone and hidden them under the floorboards, but she did have a secret she couldn't tell, and she was letting it haunt her. If Gabby wanted a better ending than the guy in the story, she had to get it together.

"Sorry I was acting weird before," she told Zee when class ended. "I think I'm just freaked about the concert

Friday. I worked this weekend, so I didn't practice as much as Madison."

"But you're better than Madison," Zee said, "so you don't have to practice as much."

It wasn't really true, Gabby knew. The French horn was one of the hardest instruments in the orchestra and even the best players needed lots of practice, but it was nice of Zee to say. And thinking about the solo definitely helped take Gabby's mind off her big secret. By lunchtime all she wanted to do was rehearse, so the second she finished eating, she excused herself from Satchel and Zee, grabbed her instrument, and ran down two flights of stairs to the music department practice rooms to play. After school, a job sitting one of her regulars, dinner, and homework, she was at the horn again, and played until *after* Madison's bedroom light went out across the street.

By morning, Gabby was totally herself again. She did ask Carmen if any new and unusual clients had contacted her, but no one had. Days passed, and not a single person asked for Gabby's babysitting services who wasn't a regular or referred by a regular. Gabby didn't see Edwina anymore, she didn't see any pets get up on their hind legs and talk, and no one shed their skin to reveal a body of gelatinous ooze.

Honestly, by the time Gabby sat in Mr. Shamberg's

English class Friday morning, she was sure the entire Edwina/Philip/John/Lisa/Vondlejax experience was only a crazy dream she'd had on the way home from babysitting the triplets. Her mind was far more occupied by the concert. It was today after school, only a few hours away, and of course Maestro Jenkins still hadn't awarded the solo. Gabby had worked so hard all week that, even though she'd be a good sport, she'd be heartbroken if Madison got it instead of her.

That's what she was thinking about when a flutter of movement outside caught her eye, and she nearly screamed out loud.

Edwina's face, half hidden among the leaves of a tree, was framed in the window.

The *third floor* window.

chapter SIX

*g*abby tried to swallow but choked on her own saliva. She wondered if anyone had ever needed the Heimlich for what was basically a spitball.

"May I be excused?" she coughed out.

Mr. Shamberg let her go, so she grabbed her purple knapsack, ignored Zee's curious look, and raced downstairs. She avoided Ellerbee and the scattered students with free periods roaming the halls, zoomed out of the building, ran to the tree outside her English class, and looked up, fully expecting to see Edwina floating in midair.

No. Not floating. She couldn't have been floating. She

85

must have been sitting on a branch. She must have climbed the tree and sat on a branch.

Except the lowest branches were twenty feet off the ground. Edwina couldn't have climbed.

Gabby squinted and peered into the leaves. "Edwina!" she hissed.

No answer. Gabby saw no sign of her either. No black duster. No black wool pants. No chunky black shoes. No shock of white hair around a crimped face.

Nothing.

Was Gabby dreaming again? Did she fall asleep in class?

No. Impossible. She *saw* Edwina. She did.

Heart still pounding from the sprint downstairs, Gabby jumped to get a slightly closer look into the tree's high canopy of branches and leaves. She backpedaled to take in the entire roof of the school. Could Edwina have jumped up there?

She couldn't have. Of course she couldn't have. This was ridiculous. The stress about the solo clearly had Gabby's mind playing tricks on her. As the adrenaline drained from her body she flopped down onto the grass . . .

. . . and noticed a car idling under some trees across the street.

No, not a car. A limousine.

And suddenly she knew without a doubt that it had all been true.

She was a bit surprised, though, that Edwina was back in a limo. She'd assumed the first time it was a matter of camouflage. Gabby had expected a limo to pick her up after sitting the triplets. A limo at Brensville Middle School stood out like a zit on Picture Day.

Apparently, Edwina just liked to travel in style.

Gabby made her way to the limo and peered into the front seat. It was empty. She opened the back door.

Edwina was there, sitting ramrod straight as always, white hair in the severe bun that added two inches to her height. Every bit of her seemed to reach for the sky: the bun, her posture, her dangerously arched brows, the tip of her aristocratic nose. Even her wrinkles seemed angled upward in a pose of superiority.

"My, aren't you dressed like a penguin today," Edwina remarked.

Gabby looked down at herself. "Concert day," she explained. "Black skirt and tights and white blouse. My mom had this black velvet ribbon she wanted me to put in my hair, but I always feel so weird and constricted with my curls pulled back and I—"

"I was making an observation, not looking for a treatise," Edwina said in her clipped voice. "Please, get in and close the door."

Abashed, Gabby did as she was told. She pushed aside

one of several black square throw pillows, so she could slip onto the bench seat across from Edwina's. Then she placed her purple knapsack on the floor at her feet, just like Edwina had done with her own black bag. It was dimmer inside the car than outdoors, and if Gabby squeezed her eyes the littlest bit, Edwina's all-black clothing melded into the upholstery, so she looked like a ghostly head floating in nothingness.

"I'm really glad you came," Gabby said. "I mean, the *way* you came was a little disturbing, but still. I was starting to think I'd imagined everything, you know?" She smiled her most infectious smile.

Edwina didn't return it.

"I *don't* know," Edwina said. "I tend to trust my senses. It's a wiser way to live."

Gabby felt her mouth swell to accommodate her foot. She never had trouble talking to anyone, but chatting with Edwina was like walking a tightrope.

"I have a job for you," Edwina said.

Gabby's heart gave a hopeful little leap. "With Philip and his family?"

"Not this time. Your charge in this case is a little girl named what."

Edwina's coal-dark eyes bore into her. Was Gabby supposed to know the answer?

"Um . . . I'm not sure," she stammered.

"Not sure of what?" Edwina asked.

"Of the little girl's name."

"What."

"The little girl's name!" Gabby said louder. "I'm not sure of it!"

"The little girl's name is what."

"That's just it," Gabby said. "I don't know."

"You don't know *what*?"

"The little girl's name!"

"It is *WHAT*."

"I can't tell you what it is!" Gabby cried. "You haven't told me!"

Edwina closed her eyes and took a deep breath. "The little girl's name . . . is what."

Gabby opened her mouth to object, but Edwina held out a palm. "W-U-T-T," she spelled. "Wutt. *That's* the little girl's name."

"Wutt?" Gabby echoed.

"The little girl's name," Edwina raised her voice. "*Wutt* is what it is!"

"No, no, I get that now," Gabby assured her. "I just meant . . . really?"

"It's quite beautiful in her own language, I assure you."

"I see," Gabby mused. "Then, great! I'm in. When do I sit

for her? I can tell Carmen tonight and she can work it into the sched—"

Edwina picked up one of the throw pillows and thrust it in Gabby's face. "You sit today."

"WHAT?!?!" Gabby cried.

Instantly, the pillow folded out of itself and became a miniature-size girl with long red hair, giant eyes, and an enormous mouth, which opened in a high screeching shriek. Gabby shrieked back at the creature she suddenly held in her hands, then dropped it to the floor, where it scurried behind the bag at Edwina's legs and promptly folded itself back into a throw pillow.

"What *was* that?" Gabby gasped.

"Yes," Edwina snapped, reaching down to pat the pillow gently on its corner.

"Yes, *wha*—" Gabby began, but caught herself as she realized. "Oh . . . what *was* that. I mean, *Wutt* was *that*. That was Wutt."

"Indeed," Edwina scolded. "And I assumed after Philip you'd handle the metamorphosis far more professionally. Now you've frightened the child."

Gabby blushed. "I'm so sorry." She pushed herself off the seat and onto the floor. She wanted to look Wutt in the eye and apologize to her directly, but she wasn't sure which part of the pillow was the girl's face. Or even her head. She opted for an area near the corner Edwina had patted and leaned in close.

"Hi, Wutt. I'm Gabby. I'm so sorry I scared you. I didn't even realize you were here, and then you popped out and screamed like that . . . I guess it kind of took me by surprise."

"Took you by surprise?" Edwina sniffed. "Of course she screamed. You might scream, too, if someone hollered your name into your face."

"Hollered her . . . ?" Gabby replayed the moment in her mind and realized she'd done just that. Her face grew even redder until it matched Wutt's curls. Or what would have been Wutt's curls if the girl weren't currently slipcovered.

"Can we start over?" Gabby asked the pillow. "I'm Gabby Duran, and I'm really happy to meet you. I even have something you might like. Want to see?"

The pillow didn't respond, but Gabby pulled over her purple knapsack anyway and dug around for one of the tiny treasures she always kept on hand, just in case. She found a pink pencil-top eraser decorated to look like a puppy.

"See?" Gabby showed the pillow. "It's an eraser, but I glued on little google eyes and a tiny bead nose and little felt ears. He can still rub away pencil marks, but he's also a pet, and *also* . . ." She slipped the eraser on the tip of her pinkie.

She waggled the finger as she continued in a deep doggy voice, "I'm a happy puppy puppet! I'm lots of things—kinda like you!"

Giggles erupted as the pillow unfolded itself back into a little girl. Wutt still hid behind Edwina's bag, but she was smiling now, and her large eyes danced.

"Hi, Wutt," Gabby said in her regular voice.

"What?"

"I said . . . Oh, wait—you were just repeating your name, weren't you?"

"Wutt," the little girl said happily. She climbed into Gabby's lap, then took the eraser pet off Gabby's pinkie tip and slipped it onto her own. It rode halfway down her finger.

Gabby was entranced watching Wutt play. The little girl was no bigger than a lawn gnome. Her red curls flowed all the way down to her rear end. The eyes Gabby thought earlier had popped wide in surprise really did take up half her face. Their long ovals were filled with endless shiny blackness. Her nose was tiny, barely more than twin paper cuts. Her skin was blue, with thin, darker blue lips that smiled happily as she played with the makeshift finger puppet. Her turquoise gums were unmarred by a single tooth.

She was adorable.

"So, Wutt," Gabby said gently, "you know how I said your name really, really loud before? That was just because I thought Edwina said I was babysitting you *today*. But I must have just misunderstood her. You see, she once told me she knows my schedule, which means she knows I'm way too busy to babysit today."

"Did you know, Wutt, that one of the surest signs of an underdeveloped civilization is when its members pretend to talk to one creature when their message is pointedly designed for another?" Edwina asked.

Gabby blushed yet again, then looked directly at Edwina. "I can't babysit Wutt today," she said. "I'm too bu—"

"Repeating yourself is just a waste of energy," Edwina said. "I *did* hear you." She consulted her tablet and swiped a few screens. "It's nine forty-five now, but we'll start your clock at nine A.M. You'll keep Wutt until midnight."

"*Wha—?!*" Gabby nearly exploded, but caught herself when the girl gave her a furrowed-brow look. Instead she smiled at the child and waved, then scooched along the car floor closer to Edwina and hissed up at her, "My bedtime's eleven on Friday nights."

"We'll pick her up, you won't need to worry about that. . . ."

"I'm in school all day. I have class. I should be in class *right now*."

"Have her eat when you eat, that'll be fine. Anything should do. Just remember, she is gloogen-free."

"And right after school I have my concert with my possible solo and— Did you mean gluten-free?"

"Gloogen," Edwina affirmed. "Nasty little buggers from Sector 358.7. Pulverized for cheap protein by the laziest alien chefs."

Edwina shuddered, but Gabby laughed. "Don't worry," she told Edwina. "Chef Ernie might be lazy, but he's not an alien."

Edwina looked at Gabby meaningfully.

"Is he?" Gabby asked.

"Gloogen-free," Edwina reiterated. "And don't let her anywhere near broccolini. All that vitamin J. You know how it is. Hy-per."

"Vitamin . . . J?" Gabby asked. "Is that real?"

"Now I don't expect you to have any problems," Edwina continued, "but if you do, just keep in mind that Wutt is tenth in line to the throne of Flarknartia, a stunningly peaceful planet that has kept its harmonious place in the galaxy by following the old adage, 'If they knock down our tree, we knock down their forest. If they take over our city, we take over their continent. If they harm a hair on the head of the tenth in line to the throne, we explode their planet into tiny bits.'"

"I'm sorry—what?" Gabby gawped.

"Wutt?" the alien girl looked up in response.

"Exactly," Edwina said. "So that's that, then." She returned her tablet to her bag.

"When you say 'explode their planet into tiny bits,'" Gabby asked, "that's a euphemism, right?"

"Absolutely," Edwina replied. "We'd be blown into something far more like intergalactic dust. Out you go, then. I'll see you at midnight. Ready to go with Gabby, Wutt?"

Wutt looked up at Edwina as if the woman had just offered her a giant ice-cream sundae, perhaps one topped with broccolini. She squealed with delight, then leaped up and threw herself onto Gabby, attaching herself to the front of Gabby's fancy white blouse like a small baby gorilla.

"Wait, Edwina," Gabby said, "I've been trying to tell you. I have school today. I have a concert this afternoon. I'm not free."

"I hardly expect you to work for free, Gabby. I thought we'd established that."

"That's not what I mean. Even if I could keep Wutt with me, how could I keep her a secret?" Gabby put her hands over the little girl's ears. Or at least, she covered the spots on the sides of her head where her ears would be if they were oriented like a human being's. "She's wonderful, but she doesn't exactly blend in."

"You'd be surprised," Edwina said.

The back door of the limousine opened of its own volition.

"Go," Edwina said. "I have complete faith in you. And lovely homes on several outlying galaxies if things go terribly awry."

Gabby sighed heavily, then climbed out of the limousine, Wutt still clinging to her front. Yet the minute Gabby stood, she felt the girl release her grip. Instinctively, Gabby reached out to catch her . . . but what landed in her hands was a brown paper bag–covered textbook. The word MATH was inked on the front in big curlicue letters. Surrounding that, also in multicolored swirls, were a myriad of designs, inside jokes, and craftily hidden initials of particularly adorable middle school boys.

In short, it looked like any other sixth-grade girl's schoolbook.

"Wutt?" Gabby asked the book.

In answer, it lifted its cover several times and riffled its own pages. Gabby almost thought she could hear Wutt's giggle, though it might have just been the *fwit-fwit-fwit* of the paper.

Edwina was right. Gabby *was* surprised. She looked up to tell her so and was far less surprised to discover that the limousine had already disappeared.

chapter SEVEN

Gabby walked back toward the school slowly, staring down at the apparent math book in her hands.

"Normally, I put books in my knapsack," she mused to Wutt, "but with you that kind of feels wrong. Could you even breathe in there? Or maybe when you turn into something you're pretty much just like that thing, so breathing isn't really an issue. Or maybe breathing isn't an issue for you anyway. You know what, Wutt? When we get some time, I'd love to learn all about your planet."

"Are you talking to your math book?"

Disgust dripped from the all-too-familiar voice, and Gabby looked up to see Madison Murray right in front of her. Madison also wore concert dress, but her black skirt and white ruffled blouse looked so impeccable it made Gabby feel small and rumpled. Madison's arms were folded and her mouth curled, and Gabby found it highly annoying that even like that, she still looked really pretty.

"Talking to my math book?" Gabby laughed. "No! That would be ridiculous. More than ridiculous. Ridonculaciallous."

"That's not a word," Madison said. She pulled a small notebook and a pen from the purse slung over her shoulder. "I'm afraid as second period hall monitor it's my duty to write you up. One slip for loitering in the halls during class time, one for disturbing the peace by talking out loud to your textbook, and one for massacring the English language." Madison efficiently ripped off all three sheets, then handed them to Gabby. "I'll escort you to class to make sure you share these with your teacher. I do hope you don't get after-school detention. That would keep you away from the concert, and you can't possibly play a solo at a concert you don't even attend."

Madison's smug look made it very clear that she would *love* it if Gabby got detention.

"You really don't have to walk me to class, Madison. I promise I'll show Ms. Wilkins the notes."

"Citations," Madison clarified. "And of course I'll walk you. It's my duty."

Madison clip-clopped down the hall on low heels that matched her skirt and looked far more formal than Gabby's own black canvas sneakers. For Wutt's protection and her own sanity, Gabby stayed two steps behind Madison and willed Wutt to remain still.

Yet the longer Wutt *did* stay still, the more Gabby worried. *Should* the girl be flipping her pages? Was she all right? Did she need anything?

Gabby fell back a couple more steps and held the book to her mouth. "You okay, Wutt?" she whispered. "If you are, give your pages a little flutter."

Madison wheeled around as they arrived at Gabby's class . . . and saw Gabby with her lips pressed to the math book. Madison's eyes narrowed, and she again pulled out the notebook and pen. She scribbled a note, then ripped it off the pad and handed it to Gabby.

"'Citation for Inappropriate Public Display of Affection with a Textbook,'" Gabby read. "Is that even a thing?"

Madison pulled open the classroom door and cleared her throat loudly. Gabby's entire science class turned in their seats and stared. Satchel waved.

"Yes?" Ms. Wilkins's eyes bugged behind her glasses. "Bugged" was a general theme for Ms. Wilkins. In addition to the thick lenses that magnified her eyes and the endless creatures buzzing around the room's apiaries, ant farms, and terrariums, she always wore bug-themed clothing and jewelry. Today's theme was apparently cockroach.

"Ms. Wilkins," Madison said officiously, "since Gabby Duran is fifteen minutes late, I have delivered her to you personally, along with multiple citations for ill behavior in the halls. Gabby?"

Gabby held out the sheets of paper. Ms. Wilkins took them and crumpled them into a small ball. "Thank you so much, Madison," she chirped, "but I already received written permission for Gabby to arrive late." She tossed the citations in the trash.

Gabby would have enjoyed Madison's drop-jawed horror more if she had any idea how it happened. How did she get written permission to be late?

Ms. Wilkins leaned in close. "That was so kind of you to run to the flower store and have a bouquet sent to the hospital. I do hope your aunt Edwina gets better soon."

Gabby smiled. "Thank you. Yes, I hope so, too."

Now she could enjoy Madison's drop-jawed horror. At least for the two seconds before Madison turned and clip-clopped out of the room. Apparently, there were some side benefits to working for a secret government agency.

As it turned out, Gabby had arrived in science class just in time for a streaming video called *What Bugged the Dinosaurs: Exploring Mesozoic Insects*. Once the lights were out and everyone was either watching or pretending to watch while they snuck in texts, a chapter or two of a novel, or homework for other classes, Gabby cuddled Wutt-the-math-book against her chest, positioned—she hoped—so the little girl could enjoy the show and learn a little something about her adoptive planet.

The video ended at the same time the bell rang. Gabby tossed her knapsack over her shoulder, curled Wutt gently in the crook of her arm, and fell into step next to Satchel. As a percussionist, he was in concert dress too. He walked a little stiffly, constricted by the pressed black pants and button-down white starched shirt.

"How come you're holding the book?" he asked.

"You mean, '*Wutt*'s the book in my arms?'" Gabby teased.

"I know it's a book," Satchel said. "I just wondered why it's not in your bag."

"You mean, '*Wutt* has such a good reason to be outside my bag?'"

"I don't mean that at all," Satchel said. "Are you okay? What's your deal?"

"Yes," Gabby said proudly. "Today she is. Very much. See you at lunch!"

She peeled off into her math classroom, giggling over the perplexed look on Satchel's face. She felt a little bad for playing with him that way . . . but only a little. He'd panic if he knew the truth. Besides, she couldn't help feeling giddy. She had an *alien* in her arms! An alien *princess*: tenth in line to the throne, and *Gabby* got to watch over her. Not only was it an honor, it was the easiest babysitting job she'd ever had. It was also the most fulfilling. Gabby had been dubious about watching Wutt at school, but now she understood why Edwina wanted it this way. At school Gabby was able to both watch and educate Wutt. Already she'd taught her about Earth's early days; now she'd get to introduce her to geometry. The class was usually torture for Gabby, but she was so excited to share it with Wutt she practically skipped inside the classroom.

"Gabby!" Zee waved from the front row. She had her chair turned backward, so she straddled it with her arms crossed over its back.

Gabby almost didn't sit next to her. Keeping Wutt from Satchel was one thing, but for Zee meeting an alien would be a scientific revelation. How could Gabby deny that to her best friend?

Gabby sighed. Doing the right thing wasn't always easy, she told herself, but that didn't mean she should avoid it. She slipped into the seat next to Zee and gently placed the little-girl-in-math-book-form on the desk.

Zee leaned in close. "What happened in English today?

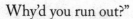

Why'd you run out?"

Gabby felt the words jump onto her tongue and rush her lips to fight their way out. She was dying to tell Zee the truth, so much that it hurt to keep it inside.

"Nothing!" Gabby said fake-cheerily through clenched teeth. "Stomach thing, that's all."

"Stomach thing," Zee said appraisingly, looking her friend up and down. "You do look pale and clammy."

Of course she did. She just told a flat-out lie to her best friend. She clamped her lips into a closed-mouth grimace and nodded.

"You sure you're okay?" Zee asked Gabby. "You seem . . ."

"Alien?" Gabby blurted.

She couldn't *tell* Zee what was going on, but if Zee *guessed* the truth, then it wouldn't be Gabby's fault the information got out. At least, that's how she looked at it.

Zee scrunched her face. "I was going to say 'weird,' but okay, 'alien' I guess."

"Yeah," Gabby said. "Alien. Good word. *Alien.* Very descriptive."

Gabby glanced pointedly at Wutt-the-math-book.

"Okay, something's up," Zee said. "Shoot."

"If I don't tell you, will you feel *alien*ated?"

"Alienated?"

"You won't think I'm violating your in*alien*able right to know?"

"What?"

"Yes, Wutt!" Gabby cried, holding up her math book. "Exactly!"

"Oh hey," Zee noted, "you re-covered your book." She plucked it from Gabby's hands to check it out. "'M.N. plus F.S.'? Who's that?"

"No one," Gabby said, grabbing back the book. "I mean . . . I don't know. I didn't write that. It's not my math book."

"Oh. Should we take it to the lost and found?"

"No!" Gabby shouted, hugging the book close. "She's mine! I mean, *it's* mine. The book is mine. When I said it wasn't, I meant the *cover* isn't mine."

Gabby was floundering now. She could feel the sweat bead on her face. Zee looked confused.

"You put someone else's cover on your math book?"

In response, a voice boomed from the back of the room.

"Did someone say *math book*?"

Gabby and Zee both turned to see a man built like Humpty Dumpty stride into the room. The hair that by all rights should have been on his head had migrated down to a well-manicured soul patch. He wore a purple cape.

"I have a theory about math books," he said as he surged

to the front of the room. "Math books are anathema to arithmetic. Allow me to introduce myself. I am Mr. Lau, and I am not only substituting for your math teacher, I am substituting for your old ways of thought, beginning with your thoughts on math books! Today we say this to math books: farewell!"

Before Gabby knew what was happening, Mr. Lau grabbed her book—grabbed *Wutt*—and hurled her to the ground. She smacked down with a loud *thwack*!

"No!" Gabby cried.

She tried to jump up, but Mister Lau leaned heavily on her desk, blocking her path.

"I know, intrepid student, it's hard to bid adieu to the box in which you've always lived. But today, in this class, we free our minds! Everyone, come to the front of the room and throw your book on the pile!"

"*NO!*" Gabby wailed. She did jump up this time, but Mr. Lau placed a hand on her shoulder and eased her back down in her chair.

"Stay strong, young scholar," he said. "Change can be hard, I know."

Already, the rest of the class was on their feet, books in hand. Gabby could only sit and watch helplessly as student after student—even her own best friend—slammed their books onto the floor, right on top of Wutt.

Gabby cringed. She bit her knuckles. She pounded her

fists on the desk. She yanked on chunks of her hair. She curled into a small ball and whimpered. She suffered through a lecture that had the rest of the class enraptured, while the image of Wutt's huge black eyes and toothless smile danced before her eyes.

The second the bell rang, Gabby raced to the stack of textbooks. She dug through them like a dog, pawing through the pile and hurling the discards behind her as she burrowed down. She vaguely heard the *bangs*, *thwacks*, and *ows* of books hitting desks, chairs, and shins, but none of that mattered. All she wanted was *her* book, and when she found it she snatched it and ran to a corner where she frantically inspected it for scratches or dents.

There were none.

Near tears, Gabby slid down the wall, hugging the book to her chest.

"So, um . . . we need to talk."

It was Zee. She stood in front of Gabby. Behind her, the entire math class spread in a tableau of flabbergasted bewilderment, every jaw on the floor.

chapter
EIGHT

abby looked at the sea of her concerned—or just seriously freaked-out—classmates.

"We totally need to talk," she told Zee. "Later."

Gabby grabbed her purple knapsack, threw it over her shoulder, and raced out of the classroom at a full run, still clutching Wutt to her chest. She knew Zee wouldn't follow. Zee had Art, but Gabby had fourth period free, and unlike Madison Murray, her free periods weren't spent busting other people in the halls.

Gabby tore down the two flights of stairs to the music department. As she ran her phone rang.

Which was strange because she always turned it off before she left for school.

And it wasn't so much ringing as it was honking. This hideous *a-WOO-ga* sound that she would never in a million years assign to anything, and that would bring every faculty member running with detention slips if she didn't shut it up immediately.

Desperate as she was to make sure Wutt was okay, she had to stop the racket. She slowed to a walk and dug in her knapsack for the phone.

It was on and making that horrible sound, but nothing was on the screen except a little swirling wheel. That usually only happened when the phone had to shut itself down and restart. Was her phone broken? Even if it was, why was it making that noise?

Suddenly the sound stopped.

Edwina's face replaced the swirling wheel on the screen. "Well hello, Ms. Duran," she said.

Gabby screamed and dropped the phone.

Edwina tsked. The phone had landed upside-down, so Gabby couldn't see her, but she could imagine the lowered lids, the thin-pressed lips, the head shaking almost imperceptibly in disapproval.

"Really, Gabby?" Edwina said once Gabby picked up the phone again. "Phone dropping? I honestly thought we'd moved beyond that kind of melodrama."

"What are you . . ." Gabby stammered. "How are you . . . How did you get in my phone?"

"The same way the tiny people got into your television set to act out your favorite shows," Edwina said drily.

"I didn't mean that," Gabby blushed. "I meant—"

"I'd love to answer all your questions, but unfortunately I have no desire to do so. I do, however, have news that's rather urgent and can only be delivered to you while you're alone, which is now."

Gabby looked around. It was true. Despite the way the phone had screamed, the stairwell was still empty.

"Can you hurry?" Gabby whispered. "I really need to do something."

"Something as in make sure you didn't bend, fold, spindle, or mutilate the tenth in line to the Flarknartian throne?"

Gabby's stomach sank to her feet. How did Edwina know? "Something like that," she admitted.

"Once a Flarknartian has assumed the shape of another object," Edwina said, "he or she can only be damaged if that object is rent into pieces or punctured clean through. Was Wutt torn apart or impaled?"

"No!" The very idea made Gabby nauseous.

"Then you have bigger things to worry about," Edwina noted. "It seems our anonymity was compromised.

109

Somewhere at your school is a member of the underground Group Eradicating Totally Objectionable Uninvited Trespassers, a.k.a. G.E.T. O.U.T."

"G.E.T. O.U.T?" Gabby scrunched her brows. "They're G.E.T. O.U.T. and you're A.L.I.E.N.? No offense, but for secret organizations you guys come up with really obvious names."

"It's not like we carry business cards," Edwina huffed. "At least, not anymore. But you're missing the point. G.E.T. O.U.T. is a rogue association helmed by an alien-obsessed paranoid named Hubert Houghton."

The image on the phone changed to one of a shadowy silhouette behind a closed window shade. That was replaced by a picture of a man walking outside in a large city. Gabby guessed it was the same man in the silhouette, but she couldn't tell. All she could see were thick-soled shoes, long pants, and a trench coat that covered his entire body. The man's face was hidden by a dark scarf, surgical mask, giant bug-eye sunglasses, and a wide-brimmed fedora. He walked hunched over, hands deep in his pockets. A final picture seemed plucked from a newscast. The name HUBERT HOUGHTON was written under an image so pixelated it was just scrambled color swirls.

"Are these pictures supposed to help me in any way?" Gabby asked.

"They prove a point," Edwina said as her face popped back onto Gabby's screen. "Hubert Houghton is a paranoid germaphobe, agoraphobe, and claustrophobe. To our knowledge, no one has ever seen his adult face. He rarely leaves his house, which is actually a skyscraper covering an entire city block of Manhattan. Houghton is convinced the world's problems stem from pollution. Not ecological pollution, but pollution of the human species by alien invaders. The man has fewer brain cells than a Jilkstarbriak Flusherflom, but billions of dollars in family money to fund what he feels is his moral imperative: the ejection and/or destruction of all extraterrestrials on Earth, as well as those who help them."

"Like you?"

"Like *you*. Our sources tell us G.E.T. O.U.T. suspects you're involved with us, and you're with an alien child. Should they become certain of this information, they will undoubtedly try to capture you, and quite likely kill you both."

"*WHAT*?!" Gabby wailed.

With a ta-da sounding flourish, the math book in Gabby's arms splayed back into a wild-haired little girl. She smiled wide and gave Gabby a huge hug.

"Ah, you see?" Edwina smiled. "I told you she was fine."

Gabby's head was spinning, and she was way too visible holding an alien in the middle of the stairwell. Keeping Wutt clutched close, she scampered down the rest of the stairs and raced through the halls until she got to the practice rooms: eight square rooms, each of which was outfitted with a piano, a music stand, posters illustrating all the instruments in a proper orchestra . . . and nothing else. They were the most private spots in all Brensville Middle School.

Gabby raced into the farthest practice room on the left, slammed herself and Wutt inside, then peered through the tiny door in the window to make sure no one was coming.

"Wutt?" Wutt asked, her giant eyes blinking curiously.

"It's cool," Gabby said. "We're alone. Let me just talk to Edwina a second. You can play with whatever you can find in the bag."

She set down both Wutt and her purple knapsack, then settled onto the piano bench and stared back into the phone.

The screen was blank.

"Edwina!" Gabby cried. She shook the phone. She pressed the button below the screen. She tapped madly at the glass, harder and harder. . . .

"Stop! Stop! You're giving me a headache!" Edwina grimaced as her face crackled back into view.

"You can feel it when I tap the screen?"

"Don't be ridiculous. I can simply see the massive projectile of your finger hurling itself at me multitudinous times, and I assure you it's quite off-putting."

"I'm sorry," Gabby said, "but you were telling me that

no-face guy was going to kill me. I got a little anxious."

"I said he would *likely* kill you," Edwina clarified, "and only if he's certain you're working with alien life. And of course it won't be him directly. He has leagues of rabid followers and plenty of money to hire someone if he doesn't choose to risk one of them."

"Is that supposed to make me feel better?" Gabby asked shakily. "'Cause not so much."

"Protect yourself. Be on the lookout for anyone unusual. Anyone you don't normally see in the school. Anyone odd or out of place."

As Edwina ticked off the traits, Gabby played back her day in her head. Everyone had been the same as always. Same students, same administrators, same teachers . . .

Not the same teachers.

"Mr. Lau!" Gabby burst. "We had a substitute teacher in math. And he was weird. Really weird. And . . . he threw Wutt on the ground and pounded her with textbooks!"

Edwina raised a single brow. "And you allowed him to do this before you knew it wouldn't harm the girl?"

"It's complicated." Gabby's breath came in short gasps, and she paced as she put the pieces together. "It's got to be him, though. He's the one. He figured it out. He knows Wutt's an alien, he knew she was the book, and he was trying to kill her!"

"It's a possibility," Edwina admitted. For the first time, Gabby saw worry on the old woman's face. "If so, he might think the job is done, which is good. Just be careful. Keep away from this Lau. And keep Wutt out of book form, if that's what he suspects she is. As for your own safety, Houghton wouldn't dare have his people harm a human unless he knew beyond a shadow of a doubt that person was actively involved with alien life. As long as anything his other people see is within the realm of normal explanation, you should be fine."

"His . . . other people?" Gabby asked.

"There may well be others. Houghton often likes to tackle a problem from multiple angles. You'll need to be very careful."

"Wuuuuuttt!!!" the girl cried playfully. Gabby looked over to see Wutt had taken several of Gabby's books out of the knapsack and arranged them like stepping-stones. She giggled as she leaped from one to the other, her mass of red curls flying in the breeze with each jump. Gabby laughed out loud. Wutt was adorable, and all Gabby wanted was to spend the day with her and keep her happy and safe, but after what Edwina had just said . . .

"Are you sure I should still sit for her?" Gabby asked, lowering her voice so Wutt couldn't hear. "I mean, if Houghton thinks I work for you, then maybe Wutt shouldn't be around me. Maybe I shouldn't be the Sitter for the Unsittables."

Edwina's entire face seemed to soften. Even the bun in her hair looked looser. "The very fact that you said that makes you the perfect Sitter for the Unsittables, Gabby."

"But—"

"For as long as aliens have lived among us, there have been frightened, misguided people who would stop at nothing to get rid of them. When we give in to those people, we hand them power. Better to continue doing what we know is right. Show vigilance and caution, of course, but remain steadfast. Do you agree?"

Gabby thought about it. It was the kind of statement she thought her father might have made. The kind of thing she saw in the letters he sent home to Alice when he was overseas. Maybe Gabby had a little of her dad's spirit in her. She sat taller on the piano bench. "I do."

"Good," Edwina said. "Then go about your day. I know how to find you if I need you."

"Wait!" Gabby interjected. "What about if I need *you*?"

But the screen was blank. Gabby shook her phone and the picture returned, but it was just her regular home screen. Edwina was gone. Gabby scrolled across the icons—was there one there for A.L.I.E.N.? Had Edwina installed an app that gave her access to Gabby's phone?

If she had, Gabby didn't see it.

She was on her own.

And her math teacher wanted to kill her—literally.

"We won't let anyone scare us, Wutt," Gabby said. "We'll just be super-careful. Right?"

Wutt had moved Gabby's textbooks. Instead of stepping-stones, they were now piled in a tower, and Wutt wobbled on top of them.

Then she fell.

So much for being super-careful.

Gabby lunged and caught Wutt before the girl hit the floor. Then she checked her watch. "Ten minutes till next period. We should probably head upstairs."

"Wutt," the girl grunted. She strained one arm toward a high spot on the wall and her nostril slits pulsed open and shut as she struggled. Whatever she wanted, she wanted it badly. Gabby looked.

"Oh, that?" Gabby asked. "That's a poster. It shows all the instruments in an orchestra. See? This is a piano. Like this one."

She carried Wutt to the piano, set the girl on top of it, and plinked out the only keyboard tune she knew: "Chopsticks."

Wutt loved it. She begged for more: "Wutt! Wutt!"

Gabby laughed and played it again. This time Wutt got to her feet and danced.

"Wutt!" she urged when Gabby finished. "Wutt-wutt-wutt!"

"That's the only piano song I know," Gabby said. "I should have brought my French horn. Then I could play you all kinds of things. And I wouldn't have missed my last chance to rehearse before orchestra period today. That's when Maestro Jenkins will make Madison and me play one last time to try and get the solo."

Wutt tilted her head, confused.

"Don't worry about it," Gabby said. "Rehearsal is good, but it's way more important to be here with you and do stuff that makes you happy."

"Wutt! Wutt! Wutt!" Wutt begged. She leaned down and her red curls cascaded over the piano keys as she tried to plink them out on her own. Then she lifted her head, and Gabby swore her eyes were bigger than ever. "Wuuuuuuutt?" she pleaded.

"I would, I really would, but I only play the French horn," Gabby insisted. "I'll show you." She walked back to the poster and pointed. "That's a French horn. And no matter what any tootley-toot flautist or string-loving violinist says, it's the best instrument in the whole orchestra. I remember when I first started playing—"

A loud *thunk* interrupted Gabby's thoughts and she froze.

Was it Mr. Lau? Had he found them?

"Wutt?" she asked with a trembling voice. "Did you hear that?"

Wutt didn't answer. Gabby silently darted to the door and peered out the window, but no one was there.

Another loud *thunk*.

Gabby wheeled around. Wutt wasn't on top of the piano anymore.

In fact, Wutt wasn't anywhere in the room.

A French horn, however, was on the floor next to the piano. A French horn that hadn't been there before.

Like all French horns, this one was shaped like a wheel ... but a wheel with a giant megaphone of a horn—the "bell"—bursting out one end, and a mouthpiece sticking out the other.

Unlike most French horns, this one was standing vertically, and *thunk-thunk-thunk*ing up and down.

Gabby beamed. "That's perfect, Wutt! That's exactly what a French horn looks like!"

Thunk. The horn jumped again, edging closer to Gabby.

"Yeah, I see you," Gabby said. "You're an amazing French horn."

THUNK! The horn jumped up and slammed against Gabby's legs.

"Ow! Are you trying to tell me something?"

Gabby picked up the horn and looked it square in the bell.

"I'm not sure what you're trying to say, but—"

In an instant, the horn flipped in Gabby's hands and the mouthpiece plooked into her mouth.

Gabby sputtered. "Hey! You don't actually *swallow* the mouthpiece!"

Twid-twid-twid-twid-twid. The horn's valves moved quickly up and down as if someone were pressing them, and the mouthpiece nudged back against Gabby's mouth.

"I'm getting the sense you want me to play for you," Gabby said.

SCRAAAAWNK!!!

Gabby winced away from the hideous squeak Wutt had forced out of the bell. "Okay," she acquiesced. "I'll do it. I just . . . I mean . . . I'll give it a try."

Gabby slid her right hand into the bell of the horn and tried very hard not to think about what orifice this might be on Wutt. She pressed her lips against the mouthpiece and placed her fingers in position on the valves. She hesitated before starting. She'd taken up the French horn in second grade and hadn't played an instrument that wasn't her own in years. This one felt different; a little lighter, with a slightly different balance.

Plus, it was actually a live alien child.

Yet all that faded when she began to play. The notes of the concerto flowed easily, and she instinctively shifted

119

her hand in and out of the bell to muffle or accentuate just the right moments along the way. Gabby had imagined that Wutt would try playing the song *with* her—that she would move her own valves or shift along Gabby's right arm, with a result that was more playful than melodic, a goofy version of her solo co-performed by an eager but untrained partner.

Instead, Wutt *accentuated* the solo. She didn't manipulate the horn in any way, and yet Gabby could feel how much the little girl loved the music. The horn seemed to vibrate with added emotion, and Wutt's own voice seemed to ring in Gabby's ears, humming in perfect unison with the song. Honestly, it seemed to Gabby that on Wutt, she gave the best performance of her life.

Three minutes later, the last note lingered in the practice room. Wutt transformed back to herself and sat in Gabby's cupped hands. Wutt's liquidy black eyes were wider than ever, and Gabby knew the wonder there shone in her own face as well.

"Thank you, Wutt," Gabby said. "That was beautiful."

Wutt opened her mouth to speak, but all that came out was a hooting sound, like a train whistle blowing. Wutt seemed shocked, and clamped her hands over her belly.

Gabby giggled. "Is that how your stomach growls? Are you hungry?"

Wutt nodded dramatically and filled her eyes with in-
finite sadness. Gabby laughed out loud. "You don't have to
give me the pitiful look. I promise I'll feed you. I have lunch
this period. The question is . . . how do I get the food to you?
You can't eat if you're a pillow or a French horn, and I can't
let anyone see you the way you really are. *Especially* when Mr.
Lau's out there."

Wutt wriggled to go down. When Gabby placed her on
the floor, she crawled into Gabby's purple knapsack. She
stuck out a blue hand and waved. "Wutt!"

"That's good for lunch," Gabby mused. "I'll just keep the
knapsack next to me and slip you food. But getting there will
be tough. I don't feel right about zipping you in, but we'll see
so many people on the way . . ." Gabby thought a minute.
"What if you turn into something I can carry? Something
normal and inconspicuous."

Wutt leaped into the air, turned into the math book, and
slammed herself onto the floor.

"Definitely not that." Gabby shuddered. "What else?"

Wutt quickly morphed into the small black throw pillow
she'd been when Gabby met her in the limousine.

"Too weird," Gabby said. "Why would I carry a pillow
around?"

The room seemed to shrink, and Gabby backed all the
way to the wall as Wutt expanded into a baby grand piano.

"Seriously?" Gabby asked.

The piano's highest notes tinkled in what could only be a laugh.

"Come on, we're already late," Gabby said. "I need something easy. Something it makes sense for me to have out." She nibbled the end of one of her curls as she thought. "Oh! You can be a hat! Maybe a beret, so I can look artsy."

Wutt seemed to understand. As the piano shrunk down, Gabby continued to offer suggestions.

"Or a bowler hat! You know those? Like Charlie Chaplin wore. Really cool. To me, at least. Oh! What about a baseball cap? Zee wears those sometimes and they look really good on her. She doesn't have poufy hair like mine, but maybe it would still—"

Gabby realized the piano had stopped shrinking. It was now a two-foot high furry hot-pink monstrosity of a fuzz bomb, with strands that poked out in all directions as if it had just survived a botched electrocution.

It *was* a hat . . . but it was nothing Gabby would put on her head in a zillion years, and it certainly didn't qualify as inconspicuous.

However, it was bouncing up and down, and Gabby got the sense that it was deliriously pleased with itself. Gabby picked it up and held it so she could look it in what she liked to imagine was the eye.

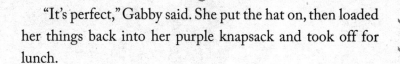

"It's perfect," Gabby said. She put the hat on, then loaded her things back into her purple knapsack and took off for lunch.

chapter
NINE

For the first time ever, the cafeteria looked to Gabby like a den of potential enemies. She stood in the doorway for a moment, overwhelmed by the sheer number of people inside. Any one of them—several, even—could be working for Houghton. Gabby might right now be looking at someone determined to find her and Wutt and destroy them both.

Her best bet was to act natural and attract as little attention as possible.

"Ew!" Madison Murray screamed. "What is that *thing* on your head?"

The entire cafeteria turned to stare. How could they not? Madison had actually jumped out of her chair, sending it plowing into poor Ellerbee who'd been sweeping the aisle behind her, and her voice was almost shrill enough to crack the windows.

If Gabby couldn't have anonymity, at least she could go for quiet dignity.

"Don't you know?" she calmly asked Madison. "This hat is the latest. My mom catered a lunch for *Trend* magazine, and this was in the gift bag. I'm lucky to have it."

Gabby held her head high as she walked to the cafeteria line. Most people stopped staring, though some glanced at her with newly respectful eyes. Even Ellerbee seemed impressed by Gabby's brush with high fashion. He eyed her hat as she passed.

Madison wasn't as impressed. She huffed something to her friends about top styles never looking right on certain people, but Gabby barely noticed. She concentrated on keeping her head steady, so Wutt wouldn't fall off as she grabbed her tray and checked out the entrée of the day. It was turkey tacos, with chocolate pudding for dessert. Normally, the combo was one of Gabby's favorites, but today she wasn't sure. She looked around to make sure Mr. Lau wasn't anywhere within earshot, then gently cleared her throat. "Excuse me," she asked one of the lunch ladies, "is that gloogen-free?"

125

The lunch lady stopped assembling tacos and leaned her girth over the counter. "*Gluten*-free?"

"Um . . . no." Gabby again cast her eyes left and right. "*Gloogen.*"

"I don't know what you're talking about, kid."

From farther back in the cafeteria, the doughy form of Chef Ernie looked up from stirring a large vat of tortilla soup. "Gloogen-free?" he asked. "'Course it's gloogen-free."

But he chuckled under his breath as he turned back to the soup. And did he just whip his tongue out to lick his own eye? Gabby thought he did.

"That's okay," she told the lunch lady. "I'll just have peanut butter and jelly. Two please." That choice was always available for kids who didn't like the hot food, and since Ernie had no hand in the sandwiches, Gabby thought it was a safer bet. Once they were on her tray she grabbed two apples, then left the kitchen area to head toward Satchel and Zee, already at their regular table.

Gabby froze in her tracks as she realized her friends weren't alone. Mr. Lau was kneeling between them. Gabby ducked back into the kitchen and watched. They looked like they were deep in conversation.

"This isn't good," Gabby whispered up to her hat. Then she quickly looked around to make sure no one had noticed her talking to her headwear. It didn't seem like anyone had.

126

Gabby watched as Satchel, Zee, and Mr. Lau laughed like old friends. Then, with a flourish of his cape, Mr. Lau rose and strode away from the table. Gabby waited until he was sitting someplace far away before she joined her friends at their table.

"You just missed Mr. Lau," Zee said. "He's weird, but he's a really nice guy."

Gabby snorted.

"He *is*," Zee said. "He was all concerned after what happened in math class. He asked about you. He wanted to make sure you were okay."

Gabby snorted again.

"Do you need a Kleenex?" Satchel asked. "I have lots. Lots of napkins, at least. Gotta protect the orchestra dress from Aunt Toni's special preconcert meal." Satchel's dress clothes were covered by a mountain of paper napkins. They were tucked into his collar, sleeves, belt, and even between the buttons of his shirt.

"I'm good," Gabby said.

"You might want some napkins anyway," Satchel said. "Aunt Toni said I should share with you. She thinks her food will bring you luck for getting the solo. Dig in."

Satchel indicated the huge spread of food in front of him. His aunt Toni always made lunches for him and his five cousins out of extra food from the family restaurant. Today he had a giant platter of penne with meat sauce, an antipasto salad, and several thick pieces of garlic bread.

"No thanks," Gabby said. She felt a shiver on her head as her hat rocked from side to side. Wutt was hungry. Gabby quickly removed the hat and tucked it into her knapsack, which she left unzipped on the floor next to her seat. Then she slipped one of the sandwiches off her plate and reached it inside. Wutt had clearly already changed back from hat form, because her tiny hands grabbed the sandwich eagerly.

"Ew! Gabby Duran, did you just drop an entire sandwich into your backpack?" Madison Murray screeched from the next row of tables. She was far enough away that she never in a million years should have noticed what Gabby was doing, but of course Madison noticed everything. Her high squeal got someone else's attention, too: Mr. Lau whirled around in his seat, his eyes laser-beaming for Gabby.

"Guess your mom's catering isn't so great if you have to sneak decent food home," Madison snickered. "The *Trend* magazine people probably gave her that hat as a joke."

Madison's friends all giggled appreciatively. Zee whipped around so quickly her braids took a moment to catch up.

"Hey, Madison," she asked, "what's it like to sit at a table so boring you have to spy on other people to make conversation?"

Madison opened her mouth to retort, but Zee shook her head. "Not interested. Over here talking to my friends. Minding our own business. You should try it sometime." She turned back to Gabby and leaned close, so Madison couldn't eavesdrop. "So the math book thing—you gonna tell me what it's all about?"

Gabby wasn't sure she could lie to Zee anymore, especially when Zee just defended her like that. Instead she changed the subject. "Mmmm, Satch, that garlic bread smells really good. Can I have a piece?"

"You'll love it," Satchel said, "but you have to try it with the spread. I know it looks like ectoplasm and smells like bug guts, but I swear it's really good." He opened a small plastic container to reveal a toxic-smelling fluorescent green mush, which he smeared onto the bread. Gabby almost turned it away, but then she knew she'd be back to the conversation about her math book. She held her breath and took a huge bite.

The spread was incredible.

"Wow! This is really great!"

"I know, right? Aunt Toni's new recipe."

From her knapsack, Gabby heard sniffs, then a high-pitched yelping sound, like a puppy begging for a treat.

"What's that noise?" Zee asked.

"What noise?" Gabby asked. She gently nudged her bag

with her foot, but the noise didn't stop.

"Oh snap, I hear it, too," Satchel said.

While her friends looked around for the source of the noise, Gabby quickly slipped the rest of her mush-spread bread into her knapsack. The whines stopped, replaced by a delighted *mmmmm* sound, so low Gabby was sure Zee and Satchel wouldn't hear.

"Whoa, you already finished the bread!" Satchel said when he looked back at Gabby. "Cool, then I can tell you. You know the spread? It sounds totally gross, so I didn't want to say till you ate it, but you know what it is? *Broccolini pesto.*"

"WHAT?!" Gabby exploded. Then she quickly clamped her hand around the top of her knapsack, so Wutt wouldn't jump out to her name.

"I know, right?" Satchel beamed.

Edwina's words from earlier echoed in Gabby's ears. *Don't let her anywhere near broccolini*, she had said. *Hy-per.*

"Do you have any idea how much vitamin J is in broccolini?" Gabby wailed.

"Vitamins run A-B-C-D-E and K," Zee pointed out. "There is no vitamin J."

"I have to go," Gabby said, pushing back from the table. "I have to . . . I have to practice." She pulled up her knapsack from the clenched top, but it was shaking back and forth so hard that she could only lift it an inch before it wrested itself out of her grip and clunked to the floor. Gabby dropped to her knees next to it and fought to grab the zipper.

"Gabby?" Zee asked. "What's going on?"

"Nothing! What makes you think anything's going on?"

She asked this as she knelt on the floor, outright wrestling with her knapsack, which was now shaking even more violently and had started emitting a sirenlike wail.

The zipper thing wasn't going to happen. Gabby grabbed the knapsack around the middle and scooped it up. She ran to scoot it out of the cafeteria as fast as possible, but she only took two steps before the wail reached a high crescendo and the whole cafeteria turned to stare at Gabby holding her struggling bag.

Then the wailing stopped. The bag went still. And in that second of absolute silence, Gabby thought everything would be okay.

Then a two-foot-tall fuzzy hot-pink hat shot out the top of the bag and landed in the middle of one of the lunch tables.

The good news: Wutt had been clever enough to change out of her regular form. Gabby could apologize to the startled diners and come up with a plausible reason for why her hat might have shot out of her bag.

The bad news: in complete disregard for the way a hat was supposed to act, Wutt bounded up to a hanging light fixture, draped herself over it, swung the fixture back and forth until she gained enough momentum, then sailed across the room and landed on the head of Principal Tate.

The impeccably coiffed principal screamed like a soprano. He jumped to his feet and shrieked, "Get it off! Get it off! Get it off!"

Mr. Lau leaped from his own chair to grab the hat. Gabby's heart nearly stopped as he lunged for it, but Wutt was already on the move. She hopped from head to head around the room. Soon the entire cafeteria was on its feet to watch. A bunch of kids cheered like Wutt was part of the coolest prank ever. Others couldn't figure out *what* she was, and screamed and ducked away any time the wild pink fuzziness got near them.

In the midst of all the chaos, Mr. Lau raced through the aisles, his cape flowing behind him. He vaulted onto some tables, then threw himself onto his belly to slide under others. He lunged for the hat again and again, and would have caught it if Gabby hadn't fought to keep him away. Every time he got close to Wutt, Gabby threw a chair, a tray of food, or in one case another student into his path.

Unfortunately, Mr. Lau wasn't the only danger. Ellerbee was chasing the hat with his broom, swatting at it like it was the world's largest fly. Gabby knew that even a direct hit wouldn't hurt Wutt, but it *could* send her careening toward Mr. Lau, or anyone else who wanted to trap her.

"Ellerbee, no!" Gabby cried. "Don't hit her! I mean . . . *it*! Don't hit *it*!"

Ellerbee didn't listen. He smashed Wutt in the side, and the fuzzy pink hat careened toward the one person in the room paying no attention to the chaos. Madison Murray considered herself far above any drama started by Gabby Duran and sat pointedly eating her chocolate pudding as if nothing in the world were amiss. This is why she was particularly shocked when out of nowhere, a hot-pink furry mass landed square on her pudding bowl, slingshotting the contents into her face and all over her white concert-dress blouse.

"GABBY DURAN!" she screamed as she jumped to her feet. Milk chocolate goodness dripped down her bangs.

"I didn't do it!" Gabby shouted.

Seeing Madison coated in dessert inspired someone in the crowd. "Food fight!" he hollered, and immediately the air was filled with soaring tacos, sandwiches, and flying arcs of chocolate pudding.

"Stop this at once!" Principal Tate tried to boom, but "booming" wasn't really his forte even when things were calm. As Gabby ran past, she saw him standing on his chair and screaming as loud as he could, but she doubted anyone else even knew he was there. Gabby's only concern was Wutt, who was zipping down one of the aisles, zigzagging around table legs, sliding along the food-slippery floor, and bouncing off shocked students' and teachers' heads, legs, and torsos. Gabby raced toward the alien girl, sure this time she'd catch her . . .

. . . when Mr. Lau stepped into the other end of the aisle. His bulk seemed to fill the space, and as Wutt bounced ever closer to him, he whipped off his cape and held it out like a matador, ready to snatch the hat inside.

"Here, hatty hatty! Here, hatty!"

The voice was Satchel's, and as he called out he pulled something into Wutt's path that Gabby knew the girl couldn't resist: a tablecloth on which he'd arranged a giant tower of Aunt Toni's garlic bread, each slice spread thick with broccolini topping.

Gabby knew he was trying to help, but he'd made things even worse. Gabby's heart thudded with wild panic as she imagined Wutt turning back into her regular form in front of everyone to eat the food. "NOOOOO!" she cried.

Gabby lunged for the hat.

Mr. Lau lunged for the hat.

The hat lunged for the tablecloth. The second it landed on the pile of bread, the tablecloth folded itself together and snapped shut to make a small, closed sack around the hat.

At the exact same time, the fire bell rang.

If there was one thing everyone at Brensville Middle School instinctively knew, it was what to do when they heard that sound. Within moments the entire room had emptied as the whole student body and faculty moved outside.

Almost the whole student body and faculty.

Satchel lifted the closed, wiggling tablecloth sack and handed it to Gabby. "I got the idea from *Bloodsucker's Revenge*," he said. "Remember the way they trapped the bloodsucker at the end? Zee rigged this out of some stuff in her pockets and a trigger mechanism from a mousetrap I found in the kitchen ... which makes me really glad I bring lunch from home."

Gabby took the bag gratefully. "Thanks, Satch."

"Yes, thank you, Satchel," Principal Tate said, grabbing the bag from Gabby. "*I'll* take this. And I very much look forward to hearing your explanation for what just happened here."

chapter
TEN

*g*abby stared at the principal in stunned silence. She opened her mouth as if to speak, then realized she had no possible words, which meant it was just hanging there, open and probably looking quite ridiculous.

"You're not the only one looking forward to an explanation," Ellerbee blared in his Scottish accent. He was red-faced to the top of his white-fringed head as he stormed over to Gabby, Satchel, and Principal Tate. "Who do you think has to clean up this ghastly mess? Starting with this . . . *thing*?!"

Ellerbee grabbed the makeshift bag out of Principal Tate's hand so roughly Gabby's heart fluttered. She hoped

Wutt had turned back into some kind of object so she wouldn't get too battered.

"You don't have to," Gabby said. "I'll take care of that. And the room, too."

She reached for the bag, but Ellerbee pulled it up and away. "Aye, like fun you will, Gabby MacGregor," he growled. "You'll have to get back to *school* and your precious *classes*." He spat the words like they were medieval tortures. "I'm the one stuck *holding the bag,* so I may as well get started."

"You have enough to do with this disaster zone of a cafeteria, I'm afraid, Mr. Ellerbee," boomed a dramatic voice. Gabby's chest crumbled. She knew that rich baritone. She squeezed her eyes shut, wishing she were wrong, but when she opened them, Mr. Lau was right there, adjusting his cape. "It would be my pleasure to relieve you of this one distasteful duty. It's not much, I know, but it's the least I can do."

Apparently, you didn't have to be a friend of A.L.I.E.N. to dislike Mr. Lau, because Ellerbee flinched away as the round, caped man reached for the bag. It gave Gabby just enough time to jump between them.

"Wait!" she cried. "I have to tell you something!"

All eyes spun to Gabby . . . but she had no idea what to say. She'd only spoken up to buy time and keep Wutt out of Mr. Lau's hands.

"Well, Gabby?" Principal Tate snipped impatiently.

137

"It's okay," Zee said. "You don't have to cover for me."

Gabby whipped her head around. Zee was here?

Ellerbee, Mr. Lau, and Principal Tate looked just as surprised. Only Satchel seemed to know Zee was in the room. She was in a corner, still standing on the chair she'd used to reach the fire alarm. Her braids bounced as she hopped down and made her way to the group.

"The pink thing is mine," she declared. She gave a meaningful look to Ellerbee and added, "It's a robot. For the national robotics championships."

Ellerbee knew all about the national robotics championships. He and Zee talked about them almost every day. So when Zee reached out to him for the sack, Gabby expected him to hand it right over.

He didn't, though. He pursed his lips and held the sack close. He must have been even angrier about the mess than Gabby thought. She was ready to throw herself on the floor, fake some kind of attack, and hope that Zee or Satchel would use the moment to grab the bag, but then Ellerbee sighed and handed the tablecloth sack to Zee.

"Great!" Gabby said brightly. "So now Zee can put the robot back in her locker, and we'll help clean up this mess."

"Not yet," said Principal Tate. He snatched the bag out of Zee's hands and pried open the metal fastener latched around its top. Both Ellerbee and Lau leaned close to peek inside. Gabby nearly swallowed her heart as she chanted over and over again in her head to Wutt, *Be the hat, and be still . . . Be the hat, and be still . . .*

Gabby didn't know if Wutt had actually heard her thoughts, but when Gabby peered into the bag with the others, she saw exactly what she'd hoped to see: a completely normal-looking bright pink fuzzy hat.

"Amazing," Principal Tate mused. "It was so lifelike before."

"That's what I was going for," Zee said. "The bot needs work, though. It wasn't supposed to go crazy like that. So if I could just have it back . . ."

Principal Tate gripped the bag shut. "You know I run a robotics team here at the school," he told Zee for the millionth time. "Why haven't you shared this with us? If you're hoping to win the national robotics championships, why not do it with your school?"

"I prefer to do my own thing, sir."

"And *I* prefer suspending students who irresponsibly release wild machinery into the school population. Should such a student also be responsible for vandalizing school property and triggering a fraudulent fire drill . . . well, that's the kind of student I might have to expel."

Zee paled. "You're going to expel me?"

"Not necessarily," Principal Tate offered.

"I don't understand," Zee said.

But Gabby did. And from the worried murmur of "Oh snap" next to her, she knew Satchel did, too.

"You need a reprieve from your punishment, and I need success for my robotics team. So I'll hold on to this"—Principal Tate held up the tablecloth sack—"and you'll join me and the team after school, when you can disassemble the robot for us and show us how it's made."

"NO!" Gabby screamed so loudly everyone jumped—including the hat in the bag. Luckily, they were all too stunned to notice.

"I mean," she clarified, "Zee's watching my and Satchel's concert after school. She can't go to robotics."

"You'll play many more concerts," Principal Tate clucked. "She can miss today's. Now all three of you, get to class. Mr. Ellerbee can handle this mess on his own."

Gabby could have sworn Ellerbee actually growled at this, but Principal Tate didn't notice. He turned on his heel and strode toward the cafeteria doors, Wutt's sack gripped tightly in his fist. Mr. Lau scurried behind him, his cape flapping in his wake.

"You know, Principal Tate," Mr. Lau said, "I have quite a history with robotics myself, and I've heard marvelous things about your helmsmanship of the team. If it's not too much trouble, I'd very much like to join you this afternoon for the disassembly. It would be a true revelation to see just how that thing ticks. And to watch you in action, of course."

The thought of Wutt being "disassembled" had Gabby in such shock she froze. She could only stare in horror as Principal Tate and Mr. Lau walked out of the cafeteria in lockstep, heads bent close like gossiping middle school girls.

Then she snapped back to life.

"Wait!" she wailed, and scurried after them. She pushed through the cafeteria doors, but Principal Tate and Mr. Lau had already turned the corner and were far away. Worse, lunch period had officially ended, and the hall between Gabby and the two men was filled with students. As Gabby darted her way through the sea of people, Satchel and Zee caught up with her.

"You want to tell us what's really in that bag?" Zee asked as they people-dodged.

"Desperately," Gabby said, "but I—"

"Gabby Duran!" screeched Madison Murray. She stepped in front of Gabby and planted herself like a brick wall. Madison's eyes glowered so ferociously Gabby was afraid hot lava would spew out of them and melt her to ash. Madison's wet, stringy bangs flopped in her face as she screamed, "You did this on purpose!"

"I didn't!" Gabby insisted. She tried to sidestep Madison, but the girl moved with her. Madison tugged at the grotesque blotch of faded brown on her once-white silk-and-lace blouse. It gave off a dizzying mix of soap and chocolate smells that churned Gabby's stomach.

"You thought if you ruined my clothes," Madison sneered, "I couldn't do the concert and the solo. But guess what—my mom's bringing me a new blouse. You failed. I will get that solo, Gabby. I'll play better than you, and even in my second-best top, I'll look better than you, too."

"You always look better than me, Madison," Gabby said. "I'm really sorry, but I have to go." She feinted to the left, then when Madison mirrored her, ducked to the right and ran.

"I'm not going to run in heels, Gabby!" Madison shouted. "But believe me, this is *so* not over!"

Gabby didn't doubt it, but she was far more concerned about Wutt. She thundered down the hall. It had emptied out almost completely now that the next class period had begun. Even Satchel and Zee had disappeared to class.

Mr. Lau and Principal Tate were nowhere to be seen.

Unless . . .

Gabby walked slowly toward Principal Tate's office. She moved carefully, so her shoes wouldn't slap against the floor and alert any teachers to her loitering during class time. She crouched low against the bottom of Principal Tate's door, then slowly slid upward, so she could peer into the window. . . .

"Gabby!"

It was Zee's whisper-hissed voice, but it surprised Gabby so much she screamed.

"What was that?" rang out Principal Tate's voice, and from his office Gabby heard a chair anxiously scraping along the floor.

Principal Tate was getting up. He was going to come out and catch Gabby and send her back to class before she could help Wutt!

But then hands grabbed her from behind and Zee's voice hissed, *"Come on!"*

Zee pulled Gabby across the hall into Ellerbee's office and slammed the door just as they heard Principal Tate fling open his own door and stomp into the hall.

"Why'd you scream?" Zee whispered.

"You scared me!" Gabby whispered back.

"I told you we should have clamped a hand over her mouth before we said anything," Satchel added. He was in the tiny office too. "It's what they do in the movies."

"Shhh!" Zee hushed him. She pulled Gabby down next to her and they huddled on the floor. Ellerbee's door had never fit well—an injustice he didn't feel like he should have to fix himself—so there was a wide space at the bottom between the sill and the door. Gabby crouched there with Zee and peered out at Principal Tate's pinstriped knees, which were joined a moment later by a pair of large black ballooning trousers and the billow of a cape.

"I'm sure it was nothing," Mr. Lau said. "My opinion, you're on edge from all the hullabaloo. Please let me take the robot off your hands. One less thing to trouble you during the day, and I'll bring it back for your robotics meeting."

"No," Gabby whispered. "No-no-no-no-no-no . . ."

"No," Principal Tate echoed. "It's no trouble. The robot's fine where it is. But please, Eumeris, do come check out the disassembly. I'll be interested to get your opinion."

The black-trousered knees seemed to shift back and forth, hesitating, then Mr. Lau said, "I look forward to it. I shall see you then!"

Gabby and Zee watched Mr. Lau's bottom third stride down the hall, then saw Principal Tate's legs return to his office. The door clicked shut.

"Eumeris?" Satchel gawped.

"What did he mean 'the robot is fine where it is'?" Gabby worried. "Where *is* it?"

"Locked in his filing cabinet," Zee said. "Satch and I followed them down and checked it out through the window. Satchel can show you."

"Seriously?" Satchel asked. "We're just going to zoom right over the fact that the guy's name is Eumeris?"

"Satchel!" Gabby urged.

"Fine." He pulled out his cell phone, swiped to video, and handed it to Gabby. "We used my super-spy tactics. We pretended to take a selfie in front of Principal Tate's door but actually shot a video. Check it out."

Gabby pressed Play. She couldn't hear anything over the dull roar of the crowded school hallway, and the foreground of the shot was Zee and Satchel's foreheads as they posed for their staged close-up, but behind them Gabby could see Principal Tate's entire office through his window. Mr. Lau was chatting away saying who-knew-what and reached out to take the bag with Wutt in it, but Principal Tate shook his head. He opened the bottom drawer of his filing cabinet, plopped the still-closed bag inside, then pulled a set of keys from his pocket and locked the drawer again as the video ended.

"I have to get her out of there," Gabby said as she handed the phone back to Satchel.

"I get it," Zee said. "And we've totally got your back. Just maybe you could tell us what 'she' is first."

Gabby looked at Satchel, his brown eyes wide with nervous interest. She looked at Zee, her blond braids cocked to one side as her fixed blue-eyed gaze tried to peer into Gabby's head and dig out the facts for herself. If it weren't for the two of them, Wutt could be in even worse shape than she was now. Plus, they'd sacrificed to help her. Already Zee had risked expulsion and agreed to suffer the tortures of Principal Tate's Robotics class, and they were both in the middle of skipping their sixth period classes. Edwina wouldn't approve, but Gabby owed them the truth.

"I'll tell you," she said, "but you have to swear-swear-swear you won't breathe a word to anyone. Ever. *Ever*. It's that huge."

"Sworn," Zee said.

"I'm out," Satchel said.

Zee wheeled on him. "You're what?"

"I'm in for the helping!" Satchel clarified. "I'm just *really* bad at keeping secrets. I don't want to be the guy who messes up and lets everything out."

"Yeah, but I want to know," Zee insisted, "and we're all in a little room."

Satchel scrunched his face, then lit up with an idea. "Oh snap!" He turned his back to the wall, put his hands over his ears, and hummed. Zee just stared at him.

"I want to make fun of him," she finally told Gabby, "but it'll work. The sound waves he's creating will help counteract ours. Like noise-canceling headphones."

Then Zee folded her arms and raised an eyebrow—Gabby's cue to start talking. Gabby twisted the end of a curl in her mouth, frowned, then blurted out the insanity as fast as she could.

"The-hat-is-a-little-girl-named-Wutt-and-she's-an-alien-from-another-planet-and-I'm-babysitting-her."

"YES!" Zee howled, slapping her palm on Ellerbee's desk. "I knew it!"

Satchel started humming louder and bouncing his head from side to side. Apparently, Zee's outburst overcame his noise-canceling capabilities.

"You knew it?" Gabby asked incredulously. "How could you know it?"

"Hello—the math thing? Even before your freak-out over the book, you must have said the word 'alien' like a zillion times. And on Monday when you were all, 'Space aliens? I didn't bring up space aliens. You were the one who brought up space aliens.' So what's the deal? What planet is she from? What galaxy? Milky Way? No, outside Milky Way. Gotta be an outer galaxy, she probably got here by wormhole. What kind of galaxy? Spiral? Elliptical? Irregular? Are there other people from her planet here, too? Oh wow, human-centric much, Zee? Like she's really a 'person.' Hello, insensitive! Okay, I'm stopping. Give me the scoop."

Zee stared at Gabby, her eyes eager and dancing. Gabby just stood there, slack-jawed.

"Um ... I don't ... really ... know?"

"You *what*? You didn't ask about her planet? About her galaxy? About her *biology*?"

Gabby twirled one of her low-hanging curls around her finger. "I've never been really good at biology. . . ."

"But her biology is incredible!" Zee roared loudly enough that Satchel again had to modulate his humming. "One cell of it could probably change the way we think about *every-thing*! I mean, she can turn into things, right? Like the hat and the math book . . ."

"Uh-huh. And a pillow. And she was a French horn for a little while. And a piano."

"Are you kidding me? And you never asked how she did it?"

"No," Gabby admitted. "I was thinking more about fun things I could show her. You know, keeping her happy. And safe."

Zee's goggle-eyed dismay froze on her face, then melted into an abashed smile. "You're a way better person than I am, Gabs. You're right. Fun and happy and safe. No skin cells."

"Unless Mr. Lau gets a hold of her," Gabby said. "He's from this organization . . . There's a lot to tell, but he knows what she is, and he wants to get rid of her. And me too, if I get in his way."

"Seriously? Mr. *Lau*?"

"He's dangerous. And so is Principal Tate if he brings her to robotics and tries to take her apart. She might look like an object, but if she's ripped apart or impaled"—the words stuck like cotton in Gabby's throat and she had to choke them out—"it'll be for real."

Zee made a gagging face, then brightened. "I promised Tate I'd go to robotics. I'll make sure she's okay."

Gabby shook her head. "Can't risk it. What if he tries to take her out and mess with her before then? I have to get her out of there and someplace safe, but I can't do it while Principal Tate's in his office."

"Done," Zee said. "Satch and I will get his attention, then you can slip in."

"No," Gabby said. "He's already suspicious of you guys. I don't want you to get in trouble."

"I can set off another fire alarm," Zee offered.

It was possible, but Gabby worried that Zee would get caught. She needed another way to distract Principal Tate, and soon.

"Great piles of haggis!" Ellerbee exclaimed as he opened the door and saw Satchel and the girls. "What are you trying to do to me? First the blunderbuss in the cafeteria, now you hide out in my office to ditch your class and nearly scare my heart clean stopped!"

"Sorry," Gabby said.

"Our bad, L-Man," Zee added. "The caf was a total accident, and we're here because Gab's in a major bind."

"And the boy?" Ellerbee asked, jutting a thumb toward

Satchel. "Looks to me like he's dead lost it."

Gabby and Zee looked. Satchel still faced the wall, held his hands over his ears, and hummed; but now he'd given the hum a tune. He danced to it, sliding back and forth across two feet of space and shaking his booty in a way that made Gabby desperately wish she had time to pull out her cell phone and tape it. This was the kind of serious entertainment value that would only skyrocket over time.

Instead she tapped his shoulder.

"Is it over?" he said as he spun to the girls. "Did I miss the big secret?"

"Big secret, did you say?" Ellerbee mused.

Satchel threw his hands in the air. "You see? Even taking all precautions, this is what happens. I am a hazard to myself and others. I cannot be allowed anywhere near the major plot points of my life."

"Does this secret have to do with Gabby McGregor's 'major bind'?" Ellerbee asked.

Gabby locked eyes with Zee, who shrugged—this was Gabby's call.

"Actually," Gabby said, "it does. It's about the hat."

"The robot?" he asked knowingly.

Zee grimaced. "Yeah, okay. It's not really a robot."

"It's not?" Satchel asked. "Wait, don't tell me. Should I start humming again?"

Zee ignored him and kept talking to Ellerbee. "You gotta trust us on this, L-Man. We can't say what the hat is, but it's majorly important to Gabby and she has to get it away from Tate, like, now."

"Except he's locked in his office, and I don't know how long he'll be there," Gabby added. "If someone could distract him, I think I could get the hat out . . ."

"Someone?" Ellerbee asked archly. "Like a certain custodial worker, aye?"

Gabby reddened. She hated to ask Ellerbee for help. It's not like she was Zee and the two of them were friendly. "Well," she started, "only if it's not a big problem. Zee said she and Satchel could do it, but I don't want to get them in trouble."

"And you're not so worried about ol' Ellerbee, is that it?" he asked. The words stung, but he said them kindly, and he smiled afterward. "Wouldn't have it any other way. But even if you get the mysterious hat out of the office, you'll need a place to keep it safe, aye?"

"I think she's got it covered, L-Man," Zee said.

Gabby knew what she meant. Once Gabby had Wutt in hand, the little girl could turn into almost anything and stay hidden in Gabby's knapsack. That trick hadn't thrown off Mr. Lau, though, and it might not throw off any other members of G.E.T. O.U.T. at the school. If there was a better way to make sure Wutt stayed in one piece, Gabby wanted to know about it.

"Do you have something in mind?" she asked.

"Indeed I do, Gabby MacGregor. Tower classroom 3A."

"Wait," Satchel said. "I thought the Tower was closed off because it was haunted. By the spirit of an eighth grader who failed his finals and hurled himself out the window to his death."

Ellerbee laughed. "Very dramatic, that is, but not a bit of it true. They closed the Tower because it's old and expensive to heat and cool. District's been planning to tear it down for decades now, but that costs money, too. Better to make the custodial staff drag his old bones up there to clean it every week. On the plus side . . ." Ellerbee pulled a large, round key chain from a peg on wall and worked off two keys. He handed them both to Gabby. "Gold one works the door to the Tower itself, silver one's 3A. It's the highest one. Best place for a person to hide out, if hiding out was necessary . . . though you didn't hear it from me."

He gave a deep laugh, and for the first time, Gabby really took in Ellerbee's kind, round face and sparkling eyes. Add in long white hair and a beard and he could be a Scottish Santa Claus. It was all Gabby could do to stop from hugging him. "Thank you, Ellerbee," she gushed. "This is perfect."

Just then the bell rang, which was also perfect because

Satchel and Zee could slip out of Ellerbee's office and blend in with the other students heading to seventh period. They still needed an excuse for ditching sixth, and as Gabby watched them disappear down the hall she heard Satchel suggesting they say they were kidnapped by rogue army mech-bots. Zee countered that helping to clean the cafeteria might be a touch more believable.

As for Gabby, she was now about to skip her second school period ever, but it was worth it to save Wutt. Her plan was to hide out with the alien girl through seventh period. Then she could have Wutt turn into something tiny and slip that into her pocket for the eighth period orchestra final solo-showdown with Madison Murray, as well as for the concert itself. After that she could bring Wutt home, and they could play in Gabby's room until Edwina came to pick her up.

"You ready, Gabby MacGregor?" Ellerbee asked. "I promise I'll keep him busy as long as I can."

Gabby nodded, then stayed in Ellerbee's office and peeked through the space in the jamb while he knocked on Principal Tate's door. "Principal Tate, it's Ellerbee, and I could sorely use your opinion in the cafeteria." Gabby couldn't hear Tate's response, but then Ellerbee spoke up again. "Oh, aye, I believe you'll want to be seeing this. Won't take but a minute."

Gabby held her breath as she waited the endless seconds

until Principal Tate decided whether or not he'd leave his office. Finally, he emerged, his entire face scrunched into a frown. "This had better be important, Ellerbee. I have more meaningful things to do than check up on a custodial job."

"No doubt you do, sir," Ellerbee said as he walked two steps behind Tate down the hall. "No doubt you do."

He shot Gabby an okay sign before they turned the corner, and Gabby counted to five before she hoisted her purple knapsack over her shoulder, darted out of Ellerbee's office, and ran into Principal Tate's. It was unlocked; he only locked it when he left school each day. Gabby's heart thumped in her chest as she closed the door behind her. Now she wasn't just skipping class, she was trespassing in the principal's office. If she were caught . . .

She couldn't think about that. She wouldn't be caught. Not if she moved quickly.

Principal Tate's office was three times the size of Ellerbee's closet, complete with a huge wooden desk that gleamed with polish, a plush leather rolling chair, seats and a couch for visitors, and a majestic bookcase that spanned one full wall. The office felt grand but ancient, as evinced by the globe on its tall mahogany pedestal—the globe that showcased a giant red U.S.S.R.

Gabby only scanned all that. Her attention went immediately to the tall vertical filing cabinet. The one piece of cold metal amidst all the warm wood, it looked chillingly to Gabby like the drawers of a morgue. She crouched down and leaned close to the crack around the bottom drawer.

"Wutt, are you there? It's me, Gabby. I'm alone, so you can talk. Can you hear me?"

Nothing. Nothing at all. Panic sizzled across Gabby's skin.

"Wutt? If you're in there, please answer me!"

The voice that came back sounded tiny and far away. "Wutt?"

"Oh good! I'm so glad you're okay!" Gabby gushed. She looked over her shoulder to make sure she was alone, then spoke in a rush. "We don't have time. Turn into something really, really thin, like a piece of paper or string. You know what those are, right? Paper or string? Then you can fit out of the sack and through the crack around the drawer. Do you understand? Wutt? Do you understand what I'm saying?"

When Wutt didn't respond, Gabby pushed her lips against the crack to say, "Wutt?" again . . . and nearly choked when a paper clip flew into her mouth and hit the back of her throat. She coughed it into her palms, where the paper clip morphed into a tiny girl with blue skin, black oval eyes, slit-nostrils, and an impossibly large mane of red curls.

"WUTT!" she cried, throwing her arms around Gabby's neck.

Gabby hugged her close. "Oh, Wutt, I was so worried." She pulled the little girl back to look her in the eye and said, "Don't ever freak me out like that again, okay?"

"Wutt?"

"I know, I know, I'm the one who let you have the broccolini, totally my fault, just . . ." She pulled Wutt close again. "Stay safe, okay?"

"Wutt," the little girl agreed, and hugged Gabby a little tighter until Gabby pulled her back again.

"I'm glad you're out, but we're still in a lot of trouble. I don't know if you were listening when Edwina told me, but there are some bad people after you, and we *cannot* let them see you looking like yourself, got it?"

Wutt's eyes grew enormous, and she trembled in Gabby's arms as she pointed behind Gabby's shoulder. "Wutt?"

Gabby wheeled around. Mr. Lau was standing in the doorway, a wicked grin stretched across his face. "Oh, I think she's got it," he said.

chapter ELEVEN

"We need to converse, Gabby Duran," Mr. Lau said as he stepped closer, his cape swirling around his body, "but first I must insist you turn over that alien child."

Mr. Lau lunged forward, arms outstretched. Gabby knew she wouldn't stand a chance wrestling Wutt away from him. The only move she could think of went against her every instinct, but she had no choice. She cringed, held her breath, then hurled Wutt at the man's feet, shouting, "Something slippery, Wutt!"

Wutt splooshed onto the floor, a puddle of oil on which

Mr. Lau's feet lost purchase and slid out from under him. As he fell, Wutt quickly turned back into herself and darted away as Mr. Lau's bulky body thudded to the ground. He landed flat on his back, his head thumping loudly against the hard wood.

He didn't move. Alarm prickled the skin under Gabby's arms into a cold sweat. Was he alive? Terrified, she tiptoed slowly to his side and leaned close to look for a pulse in his neck.

"Uuuuuugggghhh," he groaned, breathing a gust of moldy-fish breath straight up Gabby's nose. She recoiled and grabbed Wutt, then tossed the girl into her purple knapsack.

"Something small, Wutt," she said. "I'm going to zip you in and get out of here."

Gabby didn't know what the girl became, but the knapsack had just enough heft when she tossed it over her shoulder that she imagined it was some kind of book or binder. She checked the clock. Seventh period was more than halfway over. She was lucky Ellerbee had kept Principal Tate away as long as he had, but he could be back any second. She leaned out the door to make sure the coast was clear, then barreled down the halls as fast as she could. She turned corners, racing past the stairwell that led down to the music rooms, past the stairs that led to the upper-floor classrooms, all the way down to the far end of the school, and the never-used door that led to the Tower.

Gabby glanced over her shoulder, pulled the gold key from her pocket, unlocked the door, then shut it behind her. The air smelled of must lightly covered by pine cleaner, and though Gabby would have loved to peek in at the post-apocalyptically abandoned classrooms, she instead stormed up the stairs to the top floor, scanned the doors for 3A, then used the silver key to open it. It didn't have a twist or push-button lock on the inside; the key locked it here as well. Gabby eagerly twisted the key in the lock to seal herself safely inside.

The room was large, its carpet streaked with ancient skids and splotches, and divoted by long-gone chairs and desks. It also held fresh vacuum tracks. Clearly, Ellerbee had tried his best, but the damage here was permanent. The walls were faded orange, with a giant rectangle of brighter orange along one, where the blackboard once hung. A row of cracked-paned windows ran along another wall, each one so wide that Gabby understood how the suicide rumor had started. If someone did want to jump, the windows could easily accommodate them. When she peered out, the sidewalk below looked like a child's toy.

This was the kind of room that would have given Satchel nightmare visions of zombie teachers and vampire students, but it was tucked away and locked, and that made it perfect for Gabby. She plopped down in the middle of the floor, shrugged off her knapsack, and opened it.

"Wutt?" the girl asked, popping her red-curled head out of the bag.

"Yeah, we're good," Gabby said.

She winced as an idea crossed her mind, and Wutt noticed. The little girl crawled the rest of the way out of Gabby's knapsack and clambered into her lap. She looked up at Gabby with deep concern in her eyes. "Wutt?"

Gabby smoothed her hand over the girl's curls. "I don't know . . . I just wonder if maybe we should stay here all day. Skip orchestra, skip the concert . . . sneak you out afterward and keep you in my room until Edwina comes to get you."

Wutt cocked her head to one side as if confused, then leaped off Gabby's lap and twirled like a ballerina. Her long nostril-slits vibrated as she hummed the notes to Gabby's solo.

"I know," Gabby agreed. "I don't *want* to miss it, but if it'll keep you safe . . ."

She pulled her phone from her knapsack. She planned to text Satchel and have him tell Maestro Jenkins she was sick and would have to miss the concert, but before she could do it, she heard a key turning in a lock. Gooseflesh chilled Gabby's skin. She shoved her phone in her back pocket, tossed her knapsack on her back, grabbed Wutt into her arms, and backed into a corner. "Change, Wutt," she whispered. "Quickly."

When the door swung open, Gabby was holding her breath . . . and a giant beach ball in her hands.

"Gabby MacGregor?"

"Ellerbee!" Gabby cried with relief. She stepped out of the shadows to see the old man standing in the door. He held a large sack, heavy enough to pull him down on his left side, and breathed heavily from the climb upstairs.

"I should've known it was you," Gabby said. The beach ball in her arms was so wide that Gabby had to struggle to see the janitor around it. "I can't thank you enough for this place. You're the best."

Ellerbee smiled and his shoulders drooped humbly. "Not at the moment I'm not, lassie. But I will be. When you give me the alien child and I get my million-dollar reward."

Gabby felt her stomach curdle. She clutched the beach ball closer. When she spoke, her voice sounded like a frightened squeak. "Wait . . . what?"

"Aye, you know what I'm talking about. Let's not play games. It looks like a pink fuzzy hat, but we both know it's more than that."

Gabby's breath flowed a little easier. At least Ellerbee thought Wutt was still a hat. He didn't know she could change. That could buy her some time to figure a way out of this.

"I don't understand," Gabby said. "I thought Mr. Lau was the one after her."

Ellerbee's furry white brows shot up. "A girl child, is she? Eh, all the same." He bent over to re-lock the door from the inside and seal in Gabby and Wutt. "As for *Mr.* Lau, I saw what he was trying to do. The rich man with the scrambled face on the phone chat told me there'd be others. But I had the inside track, didn't I now? We're friends, you and I. So let's make this easy. Hand me the child, and we can forget this ever happened. Where is she, in your backpack?"

Gabby's mind whizzed with options. She could give him her knapsack and try to run out with the beach ball, but he'd look inside and know she'd tricked him before she could unlock the door. She could throw Wutt at him like she did with Mr. Lau, but Ellerbee was too old to handle a smack on the head. If anything happened to him . . . No matter how crazy he was acting now, Gabby couldn't live with herself if he got hurt because of her.

Gabby placed the beach ball on the floor behind her and moved closer to Ellerbee, trying to reason with him. "Ellerbee, you're a really good man. If you understood what Houghton—the scrambled face guy—if you knew what he'd do to her, I don't think you'd want to hand her over. He'll hurt her. Or worse. And she's an innocent kid."

Ellerbee laughed so hard he started to cough. He doubled over, and Gabby wondered if she should help him or try to sneak past while he struggled for breath. The choice was

162

made for her when he stood tall again and pointed something at her that he'd pulled off his belt.

"Is that a gun?" Gabby gasped.

"Easy there, lassie. Just a stun gun. I don't want to use it,
but I will if I have to. As for the girl, I've spent forty years
cleaning up after innocent kids and got not a lick of respect,
nor a lining of my pockets. If one little alien girl has to have
a tough time for me to get my due, I can live with that."

Gabby considered her options. The stun gun could knock
her out, but only if Ellerbee touched her with it. Gabby could
easily outrun him. If she had to let him chase her around the
room until he got tired enough that she had a second to unlock the door and escape, that was fine with her. She crossed
her arms and made her face stony. "I'm sorry, Ellerbee. I can't
let that happen."

Ellerbee sighed, then pulled two large items from the bag
at his side. Gabby recognized them immediately. They were
the Shoombas—the two robot vacuum cleaners Zee had
rigged with foot clamps and jet power for him. As he slipped
his feet into the clips on top of each machine, he said, "I'm
sorry, too, Gabby MacGregor, but I'm done cleaning up after
other people."

"But . . . aren't those vacuum cleaners?"

"They are, lassie," Ellerbee agreed. "And they're also how
I'm going to shut you down and get what I need." He kicked

his vacuum-clad heels together, and the twin engines roared to life. Holding the stun gun in front of him, he zoomed toward Gabby. Panic froze her for just a second, which was all it took for Ellerbee to lunge at her with the sizzling mouth of the gun.

"Here!" Gabby shouted. She shrugged off her purple knapsack and hurled it across the room. It landed near the door, and Ellerbee quickly swerved to get it. With his attention on the bag, Gabby ran to the nearest window. Her breath rasped in her throat as she pushed up on the ancient edging to try to open it, and she cried out when it stuck. Grunting with effort, she leaned in and pushed once more. The window flew upward, and Gabby drank in the cold fall breeze.

"It's not in here!" roared Ellerbee, tossing aside the knapsack. His jet engines zoomed to life again, and Gabby knew she had no time. She grabbed the beach ball and shoved it out the window, but it was too big around. It stuck halfway through.

"I've got you now, lassie!" Ellerbee growled right behind her, and as Gabby pushed on the ball with all her might she cried, "Change, Wutt! Change to something smaller!"

Wutt did as she was told. She turned from a giant beach ball to a tennis ball . . . just as Gabby thrust all her weight into a final shove. With nothing to push against, Gabby's momentum spilled her out of the window.

Gabby's stomach climbed into her throat, and she had no idea if she was pointed up or down. She scrambled and clawed for something to hold, but there was nothing. She was falling. If she were lucky, she'd break every bone in her body. If she weren't lucky . . .

Gabby shut her eyes tight. She remembered the tennis ball falling out of the window first. At least Wutt would be okay. If the girl was smart, she'd roll into some tall grass and stay there until Edwina found her.

The wind flapping against her hurt Gabby's ears. She clapped her hands over them and waited for it all to be over. She tried not to imagine the final thump. How much it would hurt. How long she'd lie there until someone called an ambulance. Or what Ellerbee would do if he found her first.

THUMP!

The shock of landing knocked out Gabby's breath . . . but she didn't feel any pain. She lay still, waiting for it to kick in, an agonizing torture so overwhelming she'd beg to lose consciousness.

It didn't happen.

In fact, she felt comfortable. Cozy, even. She rolled onto her stomach and opened her eyes.

She was lying on a five-foot-thick air mattress that had cushioned her fall.

"Wutt?" Gabby cried delightedly.

The little girl gently deflated, easing Gabby to the ground before turning back into her own shape and raising her arms with a ta-da shout, "Wutt-WUTT!"

"You are *amazing*!"

Gabby hugged the alien girl, then a faraway gasp of "Hollerin' haggis!" made her look up.

Ellerbee leaned out of the top Tower classroom window. Even from this distance, Gabby could see his mouth gaped open and his eyes wide. Ellerbee knew Wutt could change now, and he'd seen her in her true form. That was bad. At least he was all the way up in the Tower. By the time he got down here, Gabby would have Wutt far away from the school.

Then twin jets roared, and Gabby watched in horrified awe as Ellerbee lifted first one Shoomba-clad foot and then the other out the Tower window. He stepped out into sheer nothingness, the jet-powered vacuum cleaner robots supporting him as he lowered slowly to the ground. He still wielded the stun gun, and Gabby knew once he landed he could use the jets to outpace them almost instantly.

"We have to get out of here, Wutt," Gabby murmured. "Fast."

She was answered by another engine roar, this one much closer than Ellerbee's. She wheeled around. Where Wutt had been a second ago sat a large motorcycle, the same blue as the girl's skin, with painted flames the color of her fiery curls.

"I don't know how to drive a motorcycle, Wutt!" Gabby yelled.

The motorcycle revved.

"I don't have a helmet!"

The motorcycle scooted forward a few feet.

"I'm only twelve! I don't have a license!"

The next roar was from Ellerbee's Shoombas, and when Gabby spun she could see the sizzle of the stun gun, ready to bite into her skin.

Gabby screamed and climbed onto the motorcycle, which shot away so quickly Gabby was nearly thrown off. She forced herself to lean forward over the handlebars and grip until her knuckles went white. Her curls smacked across her face and blindfolded her eyes. She peeked over her shoulder. Ellerbee was following them on the Shoombas. He wasn't as fast as Wutt, but his teeth gripped in determination as he leaned into the chase and tried to put on speed.

a-*WOO-ga!*

It was the same hideous noise she'd heard earlier in the day, when she was on her way down to the music room. She pulled her phone out of her pocket and pressed the button on the bottom. Edwina's face filled the screen, calm and efficient as always.

"Gabby?" she began.

"Edwina!" Gabby shouted. The wind blew curls into her mouth as she spoke and she spit them away. "I really need your help!"

"Excuse me?" Edwina asked, raising an eyebrow. "I can't hear you. We seem to have a bad connection."

"Can you *see* me?" Gabby wailed as Wutt zoomed them beneath some low-hanging branches that slapped leaves into her face. They were racing through the woods that separated the school from a residential area, and the walking paths weren't made to accommodate motorbikes. "I'm having a little trouble here!"

"Things are going well, you say?" Edwina said. "So glad to hear it. I just wanted to check in with you because there's been a change of plans. I'll be picking up Wutt at your school right after your concert. I'll meet you both in the auditorium."

"No, Edwina, I won't be at the concert!" Gabby said as several bugs smacked against her cheeks. "We're being chased by G.E.T. O.U.T.! I need backup! Come get us now—I need you!"

"Hmm . . . Still crackling in and out, but I assume you understand and we're all settled. I'll see you in a bit, then." The screen clicked to black.

"NO!" Gabby screamed to the now-blank phone. A ball of disappointment swelled in her throat and she thought she might cry. "What are we going to do, Wutt?"

Then Gabby looked up and screamed. They had left the woods and were on a street . . . in the wrong lane . . . with a car zooming right toward them. "Wutt!" Gabby wailed as the car's horn honked. "Look out!"

Wutt swerved to miss the car, but her wheels skidded out from under her, and the motorcycle careened to a steep grassy embankment at the side of the road. Gabby could picture her legs being crushed by the motorbike as it fell on top of her. She winced, but Wutt changed just as they lost balance and toppled. She became a rag doll version of herself and tumbled into Gabby's arms as they rolled down the hill. The ground and the sky kept changing places as Gabby tumbled. When she stopped, she jumped to her feet.

The world was still spinning, but she wasn't hurt. She even knew where they were. She and Wutt had landed not far from a huge sprawling playground—the same one she came to all the time while babysitting. It was full of kids right now, all of them squealing with glee as they scrambled around jumping, swinging, and playing. Gabby recognized a lot of them, and was so happy to see *them* happy she almost forgot the terrible danger she was in . . .

. . . until she heard a twin-jet roar and wheeled around to see Ellerbee, his stun gun poised as his Shoombas zoomed him swiftly down the hill and right toward Wutt and Gabby.

chapter TWELVE

there was no time to think. Gabby scooped up rag doll Wutt and ran toward the playground.

"Hey!" she called out. "April! Sienna! Jordan! Madeline! Look what I've got!"

Gabby's voice must have sounded as panicky as she felt, because several parents and nannies who sat on benches around the playground turned around, alarmed. Their faces relaxed when they saw Gabby though, and they waved and smiled.

The kids were more exuberant. Most of them had known Gabby since they were infants. "GABBY!" they screamed, and stampeded toward her in a swarm. Gabby knelt down as the squealing kids cascaded over her, hugging every part of her they could reach. Gabby tucked Wutt under one arm and used the other to hug back every kid she could. As she did, she glanced over her shoulder. Ellerbee stood glowering from a group of trees several yards away. He'd removed the Shoombas to look less conspicuous, but he didn't dare come closer. Much as he might want to grab Wutt, a lone man causing a commotion at a kids' playground would only send every mom, dad, and nanny reaching for their phones to dial 911. The longer Gabby could keep Wutt with the throng of kids, the better off she'd be.

"Is that your doll?" a little girl named April asked.

"Yes, she is!" Gabby replied. She pulled Wutt from under her arm and held the rag doll out so she was standing on the ground. As always, Wutt had done an impeccable job of transforming herself. She stood about three feet tall, which was about the same size as most of the kids. Like the real alien, her doll-skin was blue, and she had giant black button eyes, thick red curls of yarn, and a painted-on smile. She wore a red gingham dress, knee socks, and black strappy shoes. Her face was dotted with freckles just like Gabby's.

She was enchantingly adorable. The kids backed away a bit to admire her.

"She looks so soft," a doe-eyed four-year-old named

Bianca cooed. "Can I hug her?"

"You sure can," Gabby said.

Bianca wrapped her arms around Wutt and squeezed her tight. Wutt tried to hug her back, and Gabby had to move fast to make it look like she was the one moving the doll's arms around Bianca's body.

"I love her!" Bianca said. "What's her name?"

"It's Wu—"

Gabby stopped herself. *Wutt* would not do for the doll's name. She scrambled to think of something else.

"Wendy," she said. "It's Wendy."

"Can I hold her next?" a girl named Zara asked.

"And then me?" asked a preschooler named Ella.

That opened the floodgates. Many of the boys had already made their way back to the playground equipment, but most of the girls were entranced. They all clamored for a turn hugging the doll and reached for her hungrily, but before they accidentally caused damage with their overeager hands, Gabby hoisted Wutt safely onto her shoulders.

"Here's the deal," Gabby told the group. "Wendy is very special to me. You can *all* play with her, but it's very, very, *very* important that you don't poke any holes in her, or rip her apart in any way. You can hug her, you can throw her, you can love her up like crazy, but no holes and no rips. Understand?"

Gabby said it with her serious face, which all the kids

only saw in the most vital of times. They nodded solemnly, and Gabby gently lowered "Wendy" back to the ground. Immediately, Ella took one of the doll's hands, Bianca took the other, and they ran to the seesaw. Gabby thought she might have noticed Wendy's feet running along the ground with them, but she hoped if anyone else saw they'd chalk it up to a trick of the sunlight. Soon Wendy was sandwiched between Ella and Bianca on one side of the seesaw, while Zara and a boy named Scott took the other. For a second Gabby wondered if she'd done the right thing handing Wutt over to this group of strangers, but then she noticed "Wendy's" painted-on smile. It was twice as wide as it had been when the girl first changed form, and Gabby wondered if Wutt had ever had the chance to play freely with a group of kids her own age.

Scott's mom, Mrs. Lewis, frowned and checked her watch. "Gabby, it's the beginning of eighth period. Shouldn't you be with Maestro Jenkins in orchestra getting ready for the concert?"

In addition to Scott, Mrs. Lewis had an older son named Andrew, who was in orchestra with Gabby and Satchel. Gabby hated to lie to her, but there was no good way around it.

"Maestro Jenkins didn't want me over-rehearsed. He gave me the class time off so I could perform with more energy."

It was a semi-plausible lie, since Maestro Jenkins had

made offers like that in the past, but Mrs. Lewis still pursed her lips. "I love that you're here playing with the kids, but I'm assuming this isn't the kind of rest he had in mind. And I'm positive he wouldn't want your concert dress to look like that."

Gabby looked down at herself. Her white blouse was streaked with bright green grass stains and splotches of brown dirt, her knee-length black skirt was wrinkled and twisted the wrong way around her body, and her black tights were ripped at the knees. She lifted a hand to her face and could feel the layer of grime. She gave Mrs. Lewis an embarrassed smile. "I have a change of clothes at school. And I can clean up there, too."

"I hope so," Mrs. Lewis said. "After all, I'm sure you'll be playing solo. You need to make a good impression."

Gabby didn't have the heart to tell her that she wouldn't be at school until *after* the concert, when she'd deliver Wutt back to Edwina. She was thrilled when a moment later, Mrs. Lewis took Scott home to grab a snack before the concert. Now she wouldn't have to keep up appearances. She could concentrate on Wutt and on Ellerbee, who was still lurking in the trees. At some point she'd have to find a way past him, but so far she had no idea how.

In the meantime, the kids played with Wutt. From the seesaw, they all scrambled to the slide, and took turns going down with "Wendy" cuddled in their laps. Then they brought the doll with them for secret clubhouse meetings at the very top of the play structure and afterward gave her a turn getting her legs buried in the sandbox. They even strapped her into the baby swing and took turns pushing her as high as she could go.

Despite everything, Gabby felt warm and happy inside. Earlier in the day she'd thought the best thing she could do for Wutt was teach her about Earth through her school classes. Now Gabby understood she was giving the little girl something far more important—the experience of not just understanding Earth, but *belonging* on it.

The kids moved away from the playground equipment to play catch on the lawn. "Wendy" was the ball. Gabby imagined how free and fun it would be to soar through the air and not have to worry about hitting the ground. She could imagine Wutt's happy giggle with each toss and the comfort of landing in a pair of little hands. Or getting scooped up again after a tumble into the grass.

Gabby wasn't the only one charmed by the kids' games with Wutt. Several parents and nannies stopped their sideline conversations to watch the fun, and when the kids asked for a couple of grown-ups to throw Wutt, so the children could all stand between them for Monkey in the Middle, April's mom and Zara's dad eagerly volunteered. Zara's dad tossed

Wutt to April's mom, and all the kids leaped and squealed as they reached for the flying doll. The same thing when April's mom threw it back to Zara's dad.

"Throw her *far*, Daddy!" Zara shouted, and then all the kids joined in. "Yeah, throw her far!" "Make Wendy fly!" "Make her fly through air!"

"You really want to see her fly?" Zara's dad asked. He grinned at April's mom and waved for her to move back. She did, and the kids beamed eagerly as Zara's dad wound up to throw Wutt. Even Gabby was excited to see her friend soar across the field. Zara's dad cocked his arm back and threw . . .

. . . but he didn't know his own strength. Wutt soared not only high over the heads of the kids, but also over the head of April's mom. Wutt flew well beyond the woman's leaping reach, all the way toward a group of trees.

The group of trees. The one where Ellerbee was hiding in wait.

"NO!" Gabby wailed. She raced toward the still-soaring doll, but Wutt was on a beeline for Ellerbee. Long before Gabby was even close, the janitor stepped forward and held out his hands, eager to make the catch. He looked so hungry for success that Gabby could practically see him drool.

Suddenly, the roar of a motorcycle made everyone look up, but only Gabby died a little inside at what she saw.

Mr. Lau, his cape flying out behind him, rode the bike.

He zoomed toward Ellerbee, and without slowing for even a second, he stood on the foot pegs, reached one hand off the handlebars, and plucked Wutt from the air. In a single motion, he stuffed her into a large metal box on the side of the bike, then flicked a lock to seal her in.

"Ha-*ha*, old man!" he cried to Ellerbee as he zoomed away. "You lose—*I win!*"

"NO!" Ellerbee roared. He struggled to put on his Shoombas again so he could chase Mr. Lau, but Gabby didn't stick around to watch. She tore after Mr. Lau's motorcycle, pumping her arms and legs as hard as she could. When her dress shoes got in her way she kicked them off. She felt the bottoms of her tights give way until she was barefooted, sprinting over grass, dirt, and through clumps of brush. She ignored the pebbles and sticks that poked her feet, ignored the low branches that tore her tights and scratched her legs and arms. She ran long after the motorcycle was out of sight, ran toward the sound of its engine until even that was gone. She ran until every breath clawed its way into her throat, and when she finally stopped she bent double, her hands on her knees, gasping for air. Her lank curls hung in her face, damp with sweat.

Wutt was gone. Mr. Lau had taken her to Houghton. To a man who wanted to "eradicate" her. Gabby had thought she was a big hero, giving Wutt a real playdate with humans her own age, but all she'd done was give Wutt's enemies the chance to capture her . . . which they had.

Wutt had trusted Gabby. Wutt's parents and Edwina had trusted Gabby—trusted her with Wutt's *life*—and now the girl was gone. Gabby could see Wutt's face in front of her: the blue skin; big black eyes; red curls; toothless, trusting smile. She could feel Wutt's arms around her neck and the weight of her small body in her arms.

Gabby couldn't hold herself up anymore. She toppled onto the ground, curled her knees into her chest, and cried.

"Wutt?" a small voice asked.

A tiny hand touched Gabby's arm.

Wutt was back! She got away from Mr. Lau! An atomic blast of joy exploded inside Gabby, and she sat straight up, already beaming and ready to hug the girl close.

Except it wasn't Wutt. It was Evan, a two-year-old boy who had been at the playground. His nanny, Davida, crouched down behind him. Both Davida and Evan's faces scrunched with concern.

"What?" Evan asked again. "What wrong?"

"Are you okay, Gabby?" Davida asked. "Maybe I should call your mother."

Gabby couldn't explain this to her mother. Not yet. She needed time. "No, it's okay," she said. "It's just the doll. It was really important to me."

Davida nodded. "Yeah, that was strange what happened over there. We asked the Scottish guy about it, but he didn't say much. The other one . . . I'm afraid he's long gone."

The words clanged in Gabby's stomach. She nodded dully.

"Are you sure you don't want me to call your mom?" Davida offered again. "You're kind of . . . well, you're kind of a mess."

"I know," Gabby admitted. She tried to scrape the last of her mental energy for some kind of excuse, but came up empty. "I overreacted, I guess."

Davida smiled. "You're twelve, right? I remember twelve. It's the hormones coming in."

Gabby didn't have the strength to be mortified. She just nodded and let Davida help her up.

"You need a ride anywhere?" Davida asked. "I'm taking Evan home; I could drop you on the way."

Gabby knew Davida. Accepting a ride from her would be fine, but the only place Gabby wanted to go was some small, windowless room, far away in another country, with nothing in it but a giant bed with layers of comforters and a blanket with a silky edge. Then she could crawl in, rub the blankie edge on her cheek, and sleep for years and years and years until maybe she could forget everything that just happened.

She had a responsibility, though. She had to let Edwina know what happened. She had to admit her failure and face

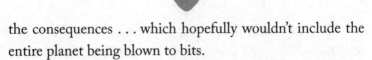

the consequences . . . which hopefully wouldn't include the entire planet being blown to bits.

"I need to go to school," Gabby said. "Can you take me there, please?"

chapter
THIRTEEN

he Brensville Middle School Orchestra performed in the Melchamp Auditorium, a large, stand-alone theater that sat right next to the school and rivaled the downtown home of the city's orchestra. Melchamp Auditorium was Gabby's favorite place in the world. Normally, just the sight of it made her happy, and on performance days she swelled with pride knowing she'd earned the privilege of playing in such a beautiful venue.

Yet today, when Gabby waved good-bye to Evan and Davida and looked at the auditorium, she felt hollowed out and miserable. She didn't deserve to play here. She didn't deserve anything.

She looked at her watch. Eighth period had ended ten minutes ago. The school day was over, and kids roamed the pavement in front of the school, talking in happy clumps. Some looked at Gabby, raising their eyebrows or laughing at her disheveled messiness, but Gabby barely noticed. She heard everyone as if through water, and they all felt far away from her.

"Gabby! Hey, Gabby!"

Andrew Lewis, Scott's older brother, was racing out of the middle school along with five other boys from orchestra. The whole group followed Andrew toward Gabby. They looked her up and down. "What happened to you?" Andrew asked.

He sounded interested, not judgey, but Gabby was too numb to give him an answer. She just shrugged, and Andrew left it at that. "Come in with us," he said. "Maestro Jenkins won't get mad at us for being late if we're with you."

Gabby hadn't planned on facing Maestro Jenkins. Edwina had said she'd meet Gabby in the auditorium after the concert, so Gabby had hoped to wait outside and catch her before she went in, or just slip in afterward once the crowd had left and find her then. Actually going backstage and explaining to Maestro Jenkins why she'd skipped orchestra and why she couldn't play in the concert . . . that wasn't on her agenda.

Still, when the boys surrounded her, she didn't have the energy to object. She let them herd her along through the backstage door and into the high-ceilinged chamber filled with all the ropes, pulleys, and lights that would make the stage come alive once the thick blue curtain was lifted.

"*O . . . M . . . G!*" Madison Murray whined in a voice so loud that anyone already in the audience must have heard it. "What is *wrong* with you?" She clip-clopped over in her shiny heels, and the small part of Gabby that was still paying attention noticed that Madison had indeed changed her clothes since lunchtime. This might have been her second-best skirt and blouse, but it was even frillier than her best one.

Once she reached Gabby's side, Madison took an exaggerated deep breath, then proclaimed, "Gabby Duran, you *reek!*"

Everyone turned, stared, and sniffed the air. Satchel, who had been drinking from a water bottle, actually did a spit take, spewing like a hose all over the backstage floor.

"Not the entrance I expected, Gabby." Maestro Jenkins's long, towering form strode backstage center. "Nor the look I expected, though as a rule I do support the creative eccentric."

As little as it mattered now, Gabby supposed she owed Maestro Jenkins some kind of explanation. "Maestro Jenkins, about orchestra period . . ."

"Patience, Gabby! I was about to get to that." Maestro Jenkins spread his arms and urged all the orchestra members into a close huddle. Satchel maneuvered his way next to Gabby and tried to catch her eye, but she felt too wretched to let herself connect with him.

"You are correct, though," Maestro Jenkins continued. "Everyone here noticed that you were not in our eighth period session today. However, I did not tell them why. I left that honor for you. Would you like to divulge the contents of the note I put in your locker at lunchtime?"

Gabby didn't understand. She hadn't been back to her locker since well before lunch. If Maestro Jenkins had left a note there, Gabby hadn't seen it.

"Actually," she said, "if you don't mind . . . would *you* please do the divulging?"

Maestro Jenkins smiled approvingly. "Losing your humble veneer, I see. Very well then, I'll share the accolades myself." He lifted his voice to address the whole group. "I told Gabby," he said, "that I happened to be walking to my office during fourth period when my ears were rewarded by an absolutely stunning version of tonight's solo emerging from a practice room. I peered through the window, and there was Ms. Gabby Duran, making utter magic. I slipped a note in her locker to tell her that as far as I was concerned she could do no better. I would take that as her final audition and leave it to Ms. Madison Murray to try to top it during eighth period. As for Ms. Duran, she could have the period free"—he sniffed down his nose at Gabby, a mix of disgusted and amused—"to do as she saw fit."

This information was clearly as new to Madison as it was to Gabby. Her eyes grew fierce and she opened her mouth as if to object, but then she cleared her throat and pulled herself tall. "Maestro Jenkins, may *I* divulge what happened in eighth period? When I performed the solo and received a standing ovation from the entire woodwind section and most of percussion except one extremely biased drummer?"

Satchel bumped his arm against Gabby's to let her know he was the extremely biased drummer in question. Gabby still couldn't meet his eye, but she gave him a wan half-smile.

"I believe you just did divulge, Madison," Maestro Jenkins said. "And indeed you gave a fine audition. Just not fine enough. Gabby Duran, I reward you this afternoon's solo! Now everyone get ready. House lights off in two minutes, then get to your places!"

Gabby dully registered calls of congratulations, as well as some arm squeezes, pats on the back, and one stomp on her toe from Madison that couldn't possibly have been accidental, but none of it sank in. She beelined for Maestro Jenkins.

"Maestro Jenkins," Gabby said, "thank you, but I can't do the solo this afternoon."

"Don't be ridiculous," Maestro Jenkins clipped. "You can and you will."

How could Gabby make him understand? She couldn't possibly play right now. She was empty inside. She had nothing to give the music.

Then she realized she had an excuse. "I don't have my instrument," she said.

It wasn't exactly a lie. Yes, her French horn was right next door in the cubby under her locker, but Gabby didn't have it *here*.

Maestro Jenkins looked at her like she was crazy. Then he pointed past her. "Gabby, your horn is on your chair, right where it's supposed to be."

Gabby turned. From here she could see out the wings to the stage. It was already set up for the orchestra, with the musicians' instruments sitting on their chairs or at their places. Maestro Jenkins was right. Gabby's horn was on her chair, exactly where it belonged. Satchel must have brought it over for her. Normally, she'd be thankful, but now her heart sank. Now she needed a new excuse.

"But Maestro Jenkins . . ." She tried to object, but the maestro shushed her and whisper-hissed to the entire orchestra, "House lights down now! Everyone to your places!"

He eyed Gabby and nodded for her to move. What could she do? It was dark with the house lights down, but glow-in-the-dark tape on the floor helped Gabby and the others shuffle successfully to their seats. By the time the house lights came up and the audience applauded, all the musicians and Maestro Jenkins were in place, the musicians standing next to their chairs.

Gabby saw her mom and Carmen in the front row, just like always. She forced a smile. If they noticed how disheveled she was, they didn't show it. Carmen clapped with great gravity, while Alice beamed and practically bounced in her seat.

Gabby shriveled inside. Her mom and sister seemed so proud of her. They had no idea how horrible she really was.

The applause died down as the orchestra sat. At a wave of Maestro Jenkins' baton, they moved their instruments to ready position and prepared to play.

For the first time ever, Gabby dreaded placing her French horn to her lips. She wasn't sure she could do it.

As if sensing her fear, the horn did the job itself. It leaned forward of its own volition and plooked its entire mouthpiece into Gabby's mouth.

She spluttered a little and pulled the horn away. The other horn players looked at her curiously. Gabby's horn silently tootled its valve levers, as if it was laughing, and Gabby quickly placed her hand over them, so it looked like she was making them move herself.

But she wasn't.

Hope tingled through her body and she leaned close to

the instrument. "Wutt?" she whispered.

The horn leaped up and down in Gabby's lap, and Gabby hugged it tight to stop the motion. She leaned over the instrument and whispered into its side. "But I don't understand. How did you—"

Gabby didn't finish her thought. Even though she hadn't been paying attention to Maestro Jenkins, Wutt apparently had. She pushed her mouthpiece against Gabby's lips just as the orchestra started to play, and Gabby instinctively dove in and played along. All Gabby's questions dissolved into the music, and everything but her overwhelming joy faded away as she and Wutt happily played song after song.

Then a spotlight shone on Gabby. The rest of the orchestra grew silent.

It was time for the final moment of the concert: Gabby's solo.

"Here we go, Wutt," Gabby whispered.

She rose, and a low murmur ran through the crowd. At first Gabby thought the audience was impressed with the way the spotlight glinted off Wutt's French horn body. The instrument almost seemed to glow.

Then Gabby remembered her ripped and stained clothes, matted hair, and dirt-smeared face. They'd been somewhat hidden by the rest of the orchestra at the beginning of the concert, but now they were in full view.

Gabby almost laughed. How she looked was the last thing she cared about right now. She gently placed her lips to the horn's mouthpiece and began to play.

The first time she and Wutt played this song, Gabby had been transported. She'd thought nothing could be as beautiful.

That performance was a pale ghost of this one.

From the first notes, Gabby and Wutt played a true duet. Wutt moved the valves not *for* Gabby, but *with* her, and each tone shift that came from Gabby moving her hand in and out of the bell held stronger and richer emotion. Though Gabby peeked at Maestro Jenkins and her sheet music, what she saw was every moment of her day with Wutt and how deeply she had connected with the little girl. Halfway through the solo, Gabby closed her eyes. She didn't need any more guidance. She and Wutt were in a musical world of their own, using the notes to tell their story in perfect unison.

When they finished, there was silence.

Then the whole audience burst into applause. Gabby heard the creaks and rustles as they rose to their feet. Even some of the other musicians stood and clapped, and Gabby laughed when she heard a hoot and turned to see Satchel doing a full-on celebration dance behind his drum kit. Maestro Jenkins himself gave her a small bow and a smile before waving his arms to guide the entire orchestra to their feet. The house lights came on, illuminating the audience, and Gabby beamed with glee at her mom and Carmen. Carmen nodded as she clapped, which for her was wild exuberance, and Alice screamed Gabby's name out loud. The orchestra bowed twice as a group, then Maestro Jenkins had Gabby step forward for a final solo bow. Instead, Gabby gestured to her French horn and leaned it forward—Wutt's own personal curtain call.

As everyone applauded, Gabby noticed someone else in the audience. A woman about halfway back, dressed all in black, with white hair pulled back in a severe bun. The seat to her left held two giant bouquets of roses. The bouquets seemed normal, though Gabby noticed the blooms seemed extra red. Almost unearthly so. And each bouquet trembled with what seemed like overwhelming emotion. Pride, maybe?

Gabby's heart jumped. The roses were Wutt's parents! They had to be! Wutt must have noticed them too, because the French horn let out an involuntary *BLATT* that should have been physically impossible without anyone blowing into it, but no one seemed to notice over the continued roar of the crowd. No one except Madison Murray, who opened her mouth in shock, then gave Gabby the stink eye.

Only as the curtain lowered, Gabby noticed the seat to Edwina's *right*. The man seated there was large and round . . . and wore a cape . . . and had a soul patch.

Mr. Lau.

Mr. Lau was with Edwina? And Wutt's parents?

Gabby wanted to see more, but the curtain came down all too quickly. Immediately, Gabby was swallowed by a maelstrom of congratulations. She hugged Wutt close and heard herself thank everyone, but her brain buzzed with such a wild mix of elation, relief, and confusion, she didn't even know what she said.

"That was *amazing*, Gabby!" Satchel said as he caught up to her and walked by her side. "Seriously amazing! I mean, I know you're always amazing, but this was like *amazo-amazing*! Like, *amazingly* amazo-amazing! Like—"

Gabby glanced around to make sure no one else was listening, then whispered, "Want to know *why* it was so amazing?"

She looked meaningfully at her French horn then smiled knowingly at Satchel. He plopped his hands over his ears, started humming, and strode away as fast as he could.

"Nice solo, Gabby," came another voice.

The compliment sliced across Gabby like a sword, and Madison leaned so close that Gabby could smell the peppermint from her breath spray. It smelled like evil.

"Thanks, Madison," Gabby said brightly. "No hard feelings?"

She stuck out her hand. Madison sneered down like she was more apt to spit in it than shake it.

"Feelings have nothing to do with it," she minty-hissed.

191

"I *know* something's up, and I'm going to figure out what it is." She reached for Gabby's French horn, but Gabby turned and blocked the grasp.

"I have no idea what you mean," Gabby said innocently. "Great show, though!"

Gabby didn't wait for Madison's rebuttal. She hugged Wutt even closer and pushed her way out the backstage door into another throng of well-wishers. She smiled and nodded to all of them, but craned her neck and pushed through. She was looking for Edwina, but stopped when she found Carmen and Alice.

"Why isn't your horn in its case?" Carmen asked.

"*That's* the first thing you say to her?" Alice chided. "Gabby, you were incredible!"

"You were incredible in the concert," Carmen agreed. "You're also incredibly stinky. And why do you look like you were ground up in a food processor with our lawn?"

"Thank you," Gabby said. "And why do *you* look like you cut your own bangs with kids' scissors and a ruler?"

"Because I *did* cut my own bangs with kids' scissors and a ruler."

"*Exactly,*" Gabby said, then turned to her mom. "You really think it was good?"

"It was incredible, Gabby," Alice gushed. She wrapped her arms around both Gabby and her horn and rocked them back and forth. "Truly, truly incredible."

"*I* heard your solo was so hot, it boiled tungsten!" Zee cried. She had been at Principal Tate's robotics club as she'd promised, but now ran over to throw her arm around Gabby in a congratulatory half hug. "That's really hot," she added. "Tungsten has a boiling point of 5,660 degrees Celsius. That's, like, around *ten thousand* degrees Fahrenheit."

"Melt-a-human-body-to-ash hot, is how I put it," Satchel noted as he joined them from the auditorium. "Which if you ask me, way easier to understand."

"I couldn't have done it without my fabulous French horn," Gabby pointed out with a knowing smile to Zee.

"It's a French horn solo," Carmen noted. "By definition you couldn't have played it without a French horn. You also can't have a pastrami sandwich without pastrami."

"Oh snap, I would love a pastrami sandwich right now," Satchel said.

"I was making an analogy," Carmen said. "I wasn't actually talking about—"

"I think I might have some pastrami in the fridge," Alice interrupted. "How about we all go back to our house and celebrate?"

"Think you might have some cake with that pastrami?" Zee wondered.

"Cake with pastrami?" Carmen gawped. "That would taste terrible."

"Pretty sure she meant one after the other, Car," Gabby said, but even as she spoke, she saw something out of the corner of her eye.

A limousine. It was parked halfway around the corner, almost out of sight among the trees, but it blinked its headlights as if sending a coded signal through the dusk.

"I'll be right back," Gabby said. "I, um . . . have to grab my horn case from the main building. It feels really *alien* to carry my horn without it."

Zee understood. She quickly engaged everyone in a conversation about the full snack lineup they should enjoy back at Gabby's house. Once they were all distracted, Gabby slipped away. She rounded the corner behind Brensville Middle School and saw Edwina. The old woman stood alone near the back end of the limousine.

"Edwina!" Gabby gushed. She placed her horn on the ground and threw her arms around Edwina, but the woman stood stiffly and didn't move a muscle to respond. It was like hugging a steel pole. Gabby quickly felt ridiculous and embarrassed. She let go and stepped back a few steps. "It's . . . um . . . good to see you."

"I'm sure," Edwina said, not-so-subtly brushing any traces of Gabby's touch from her shoulders and black suit jacket. "I have something for you."

She opened the back seat of the limousine and pulled out an item Gabby recognized instantly.

"My purple knapsack!" she cried, slipping it onto her shoulders. "But I thought it was—"

"Far aloft in the highest room of the Tower?" a voice boomed as Mr. Lau emerged from the limo. "Indeed it was, but once I had Wutt safely back to Miss Winnie here . . ."

He slung an arm around Edwina's shoulders. Edwina glared.

"I have access to Blichtencritch cringling acid that would dissolve you in two-point-one seconds," she said.

Mr. Lau removed his arm from her shoulders.

"As I was saying," he continued, "once Wutt was safe with *Edwina*, I retired to the place from whence I'd seen you and Ellerbee soar out the window and retrieved your misplaced item."

"I don't understand," Gabby said. She turned to Edwina. "I told you I thought Mr. Lau was from G.E.T. O.U.T. Why didn't you tell me he's with A.L.I.E.N.?"

"Because I'm not *with* A.L.I.E.N., my young friend," Lau answered. "I *am* an alien. From the planet Zeeliwhiz Five, in the Stradflarn System."

He took a deep bow, and Edwina tamped down an impatient sigh.

"He wasn't in our database," Edwina admitted. "Many still aren't."

"By choice!" Mr. Lau crowed. "Large registry systems rarely bode well in my experience. I fly under the radar as I ply my trade as a humble substitute teacher, but I pride myself on sussing out and befriending those secretly like me. You might say I have excellent *A*-dar."

"I might not," Edwina sniffed, then turned back to Gabby. "Though I will say that unbeknownst to myself, your Mr. Lau substituted last year for a second grade class that included a certain sluglike friend of ours."

Gabby thought about it, then lit up as she realized, "Philip? You know Philip?"

"Quite well, yes," Mr. Lau said. "And John and Lisa, who had been monumentally troubled over their inability to find a sitter. So when they met a young whelp named Gabby Duran, they told me. And when I saw that selfsame Gabby Duran would be in my math class at Brensville Middle School, I kept an eye on her. Then lo! You came into my class, and what to my wondering eyes did appear—"

"It's not *War and Peace*," Edwina snapped, then returned her focus to Gabby. "The man figured out Wutt's true nature, he'd heard the rumors about Houghton—"

"It's all the buzz on Spacebook," Lau interjected before Edwina silenced him with another glare.

"—and being on the inside at the school, he was able to peg Mr. Ellerbee as Houghton's man on the take."

"Indeed! But I played it up around Mr. Ellerbee like I was working for Houghton as well," Mr. Lau admitted. "That way he couldn't reveal my true identity to G.E.T. O.U.T."

The pieces were all falling into place now as Gabby played back her and Wutt's day in her mind. All except one.

"Okay," Gabby said. "So, Edwina, when you called me and said we had a bad connection, were you already in touch with Mr. Lau? And was that just your way of getting him some kind of GPS location on me?"

"Oh no, we truly did have a satellite out at the time and you were in terribly grave danger," Edwina said. "But you handled it beautifully, so thank you for that."

The French horn Gabby had placed next to her started bouncing up and down and tootling its valves.

"No, of course I didn't forget about you, Wutt," Edwina said. "And neither did they."

As she spoke, she peeled a pair of white silk gloves from her hands, then set them on the ground. Just as Gabby remembered that Edwina was bare-handed during the ovation, the gloves changed form. They sprouted into two small creatures, each one no higher than Edwina's knee. Both had giant liquidy-black eyes, paper cut nose slits, blue skin, and blue toothless mouths. The one on Edwina's right had long, flowing purple curls. The one on her left had short hair that was bright red.

"Wutt's mom and dad," Gabby breathed.

Wutt immediately popped back to her true form with a shriek so high and shrill it hurt Gabby's ears. The little girl raced to her parents, who sandwiched her in a huge hug. When she pulled away, the three of them spoke in rapid currents that sounded to Gabby like a buzzing hive of bees.

"Indeed," Edwina agreed, gesturing to one and then the other. "Her mother, Hoo, and her father, Ayedunno."

The two parents turned their massive eyes on Gabby, and she suddenly felt a chill. Would they be angry with her that Wutt had come so close to getting hurt on her watch? In unison the two moved closer, flanking her, their eyes unreadable. Together they nodded solemnly, and Gabby understood what they wanted. Nervously, she crouched low to the ground.

Both Hoo and Ayedunno threw their arms around Gabby for a tight hug, on which Wutt pounced, so she could join in. Gabby laughed and hugged them back.

"Wutt told them she had the most wonderful day of her life," Edwina said. "This is their way of thanking you."

"I got that." Gabby giggled. When they pulled back from the hug she added, "And I want to thank you, too. Wutt's very special. I'm really happy I got to know her and be her friend."

The three started buzz-talking again, but Edwina quickly cut them off. "Time for that on the way home. Let's go now." She unhooked a straight pin brooch stacked with simple beads from her lapel and held it out. "All right, Hoo's on first, Wutt's on second, Ayedunno on third."

The three aliens transformed into beads and strung themselves onto the brooch, which Edwina then hooked back onto her lapel.

"That'll do then," she said to Gabby. "Mr. Lau?"

Mr. Lau climbed into the limousine and Edwina was poised to do the same, but Gabby wasn't ready to let her go. Her mind was still reeling with questions. "Wait!" she said. "What about Mr. Lau? What happens to him? And what about Ellerbee? He's really not a bad man, he just—"

"Mr. Ellerbee has agreed to tell us everything he learned about Houghton," Edwina said, "and in return we'll settle him in a job he'll find much more satisfactory. Mr. Lau will go back to his regular life as a substitute."

"And Wutt? Will I get to babysit her again? Because I'd really like to. And G.E.T. O.U.T.—are they watching me now? Should I be looking over my shoulder? Like . . . I mean . . . should I be worried? Or could I be doing spy work for you between jobs? Because I would! I mean . . . assuming there will be another job . . . Will there be another job?"

"We'll be in touch," Edwina said.

She slipped inside the limousine, pulling the door shut behind her. The engine started, and Gabby was sure it was about to drive away, but then the window lowered.

"It was a fine beginning, Associate 4118-25125A," Edwina said as the hint of a smile curled her thin lips. "You should be very proud. I am."

The window closed and the limousine rode away.

Gabby smiled.

A good beginning. That meant there'd be more. More aliens, more secrets, more danger.

Gabby couldn't wait.

BOOK 2

GABBY DURAN

Troll Control

FROM ELISE TO MADDIE,
ALWAYS—AND TO RAHM
AND EVERETT FOR LOVING
GABBY RIGHT AWAY.

FROM DARYLE TO LIZ
LEHMANS, WHO IS OFTEN
THE ONLY GROWN-UP IN
THE ROOM.

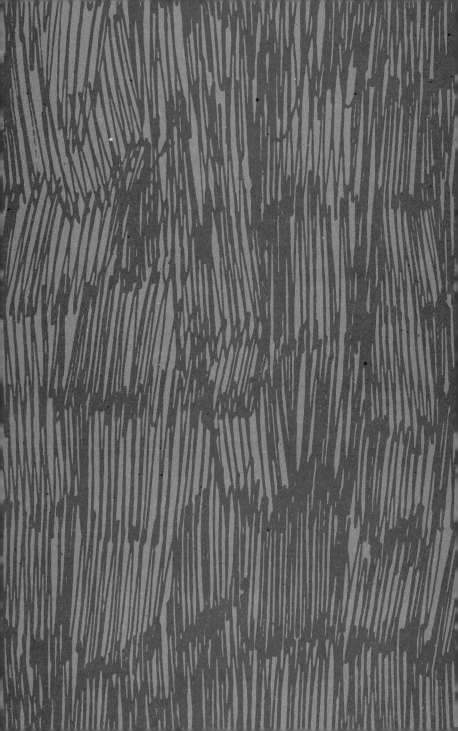

SECOND DOSSIER
Troll Control

WARNING

This book contains revelations so classified that
only the most covert layers of the most secretive
sects of the Worldwide International Government
even know they exist. A single leak could send
devastating ripple effects throughout space-time
and obliterate the world as we know it.

EVEN IF YOU READ THE FIRST DOSSIER, YOU MIGHT
NOT BE PREPARED FOR THE DISCLOSURES IN THIS
SECOND DOSSIER. IF YOU HAVE ANY UNCERTAINTY
AS TO WHETHER OR NOT YOU'RE PREPARED TO DELVE
DEEPER INTO THE ONGOING FILE OF GABBY DURAN,
WE MUST BEG YOU IN THE NAME OF ALL YOU
HOLD DEAR . . .

UNDER NO CIRCUMSTANCES SHOULD
YOU TURN THE PAGE

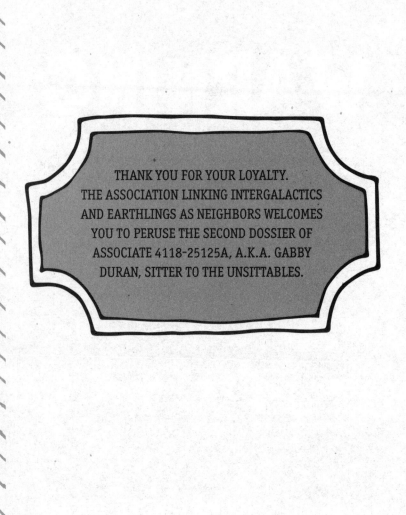

THANK YOU FOR YOUR LOYALTY.
THE ASSOCIATION LINKING INTERGALACTICS
AND EARTHLINGS AS NEIGHBORS WELCOMES
YOU TO PERUSE THE SECOND DOSSIER OF
ASSOCIATE 4118-25125A, A.K.A. GABBY
DURAN, SITTER TO THE UNSITTABLES.

chapter
ONE

"Alien . . . Alien! . . . ALIEN!!!!"

Satchel Rigoletti's eyes bugged out and his long body curled into itself as his voice rose to a high crescendo of terror.

Next to him, Gabby Duran bobbed her brown curls in a nod.

"It's an alien," she agreed.

Satchel turned to her. His face was pale and his normally floppy hair stood out in all directions. "How are you not freaking out about this?" he demanded. "That guinea pig just turned into a giant, slavering, razor-toothed alien!"

Gabby shrugged. "The movie *is* called *My Guinea Pig Is an Alien.*"

Satchel relaxed back into Gabby's overstuffed couch, and his ill-fitting 3-D glasses bounced on his face. "Yeah, but you're supposed to freak out like you don't expect it. That's what we always do."

"I know," Gabby said, adjusting her own 3-D glasses a bit. "But I'm just not buying that guinea pig as an alien."

"Interesting," said Gabby's other best friend, Stephanie Ziebeck, a.k.a. Zee. She was sitting cross-legged in front of Gabby and Satchel, but unlike them, she wasn't wearing 3-D glasses. Zee wasn't interested in cheesy action-horror flicks the way her friends were. Instead, she bent over a wild hodgepodge of metal chunks and tangled wires that she had named Wilbur. Now that Zee was on the Brensville Middle School robotics team, Wilbur came with her everywhere, and she was all about turning him into a champion.

"So what *would* you buy as an alien, Gabby?" Zee asked in an affectedly casual voice as she screwed one twisted hunk of metal into another. "Maybe . . . a *math book*?"

Satchel snorted out loud. "A math book? That is the lamest alien idea ever."

"It's not so awful," Gabby said with a smile.

Just then, the alien guinea pig on the screen shot its blaster at a giant evil rat. The rat exploded in three dimensions, splattering virtual furry guts all over Gabby and Satchel. They screamed.

"I take everything back," Gabby gasped. "This movie is awesome!"

"Kind of weird, though, that you picked only alien movies to watch today," Zee said, still bent over her robot bits and clearly unmoved by the giant rat-splosion. "*Outer Space Outrage, Intergalactic Armageddon* . . . It's like you've got aliens on the brain."

"*In* the brain," Satchel clarified. "That's the plot of *Intergalactic Armageddon*. These tiny alien parasites crawl into an astronaut's ear and burrow into his head. Then, when he unwittingly brings them back to Earth—"

Zee wheeled around, her zillion blond braids snapping along with her. "Satch, aren't you the least bit curious about *why* Gabby's so interested in aliens?"

"I *know* why she's so interested in aliens," Satchel scoffed. "It's because alien movies are—" He narrowed his eyes suspiciously as he noticed the knowing smile on Zee's face. "Wait—why are you giving me that look?"

"What look?" Zee asked.

"That you-want-to-tell-me-something-I-don't-want-to-hear look."

"I don't know what you're talking about," Zee said. "I was just going to explain to you that our friend Gabby—"

Satchel clapped his hands over his ears and started singing, loudly and off-key.

"Go easy on him," Gabby said to Zee. "He doesn't want to know."

"Which makes no sense!" Zee blurted. "It's the most incredible news in the universe—literally!"

Zee was right. There was a very good reason Gabby had aliens on the brain, and it had little to do with the truly spectacular splatter-quotient they brought to their movies. Just one week ago, Gabby had learned possibly the world's most enormous secret: aliens were living on Earth, blending in, both unseen and unknown by humanity. The Association Linking Intergalactics and Earthlings as Neighbors, a.k.a. A.L.I.E.N., had shared this secret with Gabby because apparently, if there was one thing aliens on Earth desperately needed, it was great babysitting. And if there was one thing at which Gabby Duran excelled, it was being a great babysitter. Even though she was only twelve, her sitter skills were so spectacular that in addition to sitting locally, she was regularly whisked all over the globe to watch the kids of some of the world's most famous and powerful people.

Gabby's first assignment with A.L.I.E.N. had been only two days ago, and it had gotten so complicated that she'd told her friends the truth so they could help. At least, she'd told *Zee* the truth. Satchel refused to listen. He didn't do secrets because he couldn't trust himself not to let them slip out by accident. He'd still helped, but under the express orders that Gabby and Zee keep him completely in the dark.

This made Zee crazy. It killed her scientifically curious mind that someone could have the chance for mind-blowing information and choose to ignore it, so she kept trying to goad him into asking for more than he really wanted to know.

While Satchel held his ears and sang, Zee turned to face Gabby. "So tell me this," she said, "have you heard anything from Edwina?"

Gabby quickly scanned the room. Edwina was her A.L.I.E.N. connection, and she would *not* be happy if she knew Gabby had let their secret slip. Since Edwina had proven she could pop up almost anywhere, Gabby knew it was best to look before she spoke. When she saw no sign of the older woman, she moved to the floor, crouched down by Zee's side, pushed her 3-D glasses on top of her head, and leaned so close that her dark curls brushed against Zee's blonde braids.

"I've heard nothing," Gabby said. "I thought when the Fremonts canceled for today it meant maybe I'd get an assignment from . . . you know . . . but it's already three o'clock and I haven't heard anything. I don't even know *how* I'd hear anything. Carmen always schedules my jobs, but I don't think Edwina would go through her."

"Um ... Gabby?"

It was Satchel. He sat oddly upright on the couch, the large 3-D glasses bulging off either side of his face. His mouth hung open, and his lips trembled as he tried to form his next words.

"Is there a reason Colonel Jangschmitz is tapping the screen and calling your name?"

Gabby and Zee both spun toward the TV, whipping around so quickly that Gabby's 3-D glasses plunked back down onto her nose.

She wished they hadn't.

What she saw on the screen was *Edwina*. The woman was dressed all in black, but not in her typical suit. Instead she wore the close-fitting uniform of the movie's secret alien task force, her white hair tucked under their signature cap. It was the same uniform worn by the corporal standing just behind her in the shot. He watched Edwina patiently, as if it were perfectly normal for his fellow character to stop the scene and start speaking to a single audience member.

Tap-tap-tap!

Edwina's age-lined finger pounded on the screen again, though in 3-D it felt like she was pounding on Gabby's head.

"Gabby. *Gabby!*"

Gabby broke out of her stunned stupor to blurt, "Yes! Um ... I'm ... um ... how ... ?"

"Eloquent as usual, I see," Edwina said, leaning over Gabby and raising an eyebrow. Edwina always stood tall, but looming out of the Durans' wall-mounted fifty-two-inch high-definition television, the woman was a giant, no-nonsense beast.

"What is happening?" Satchel's voice warbled nervously from the couch.

"The coolest thing ever," Zee marveled.

Gabby scrambled for an excuse. She couldn't let Edwina know her friends had any idea about their secret. "It's a . . . a glitch," she finally said, "in the streaming . . . thing."

"The 'streaming thing'?" Edwina glanced back toward the corporal, who snorted as if he, too, thought this was the most ridiculous explanation attempt in the world. "Honestly, Gabby, you insult me. I'm well aware of what you told Ms. Ziebeck and attempted to tell Mr. Rigoletti, and while I'm not pleased, I recognize the inherent foibles of the prepubescent mind. I also trust you will share our secret with no others, and that Ms. Ziebeck has the sagacity to keep what she knows to herself. As for you, Mr. Rigoletti, should you wish to hold on to your ignorance with impunity, I highly recommend you close your eyes, clap your hands over your ears, and recommence singing."

Gabby didn't turn around, but the off-key warbling be-hind her meant Satchel had clearly taken Edwina's advice.

"So what's up?" Zee asked.

Edwina's ice-blue eyes bored into Zee's. The woman was old, and the high-definition screen brought out every deep crease in her skin, but the glare held such power that Zee shrank into her overalls. The message was clear: Zee was *not* part of this conversation.

"I'll make this brief," Edwina said, focusing back on Gabby, "as this is a terrible movie and I have no desire to spend any more time in it than necessary. I need you to meet me as soon as possible at 3242 Robinson Street. You'll get further instructions there."

"Okay," Gabby said. "Is there anything else I need to know? How long will I be gone? Is there anything I should bring?"

"Colonel?" The corporal behind Edwina looked terribly apologetic for bothering her, but it seemed he had no choice. "Colonel, I'm afraid I need you."

Edwina rolled her eyes and sighed heavily. "One moment," Edwina told Gabby. "I have a line."

She walked several steps back toward the corporal, then spoke in an imperious voice. "I've come to a decision. There's only one way to combat an army of alien guinea pigs: with the world's largest alien hamster ball."

Edwina shook her head, disgusted. "A hamster ball?" she asked the corporal in her regular voice. "That doesn't even make any sense. We were talking about guinea pigs, not hamsters. How does anyone watch this garbage?"

"Beats me," replied the corporal. "Broadway's more my thing. I just do this to pay the rent." Then he straightened and saluted, going back to the script. "Aye, aye, Captain!"

The two grew smaller and smaller as they walked toward the back of their ship. Was Edwina actually leaving?

"Wait, talk to me!" Gabby pleaded, running up to the TV. "I want to know more! I have questions!" She stood on her tiptoes and put both hands on the screen. "Please!"

"Why are you hugging the television?"

The deadpan question came from Carmen, Gabby's sister. She stood at the bottom of the stairs and stared at Gabby. Carmen's alarmingly short, ruler-straight bangs did nothing to temper her look of impassive distaste.

Gabby let out a ridiculously fake laugh. "I know, right? Hugging the television—crazy! Magic of 3-D. I felt like I could touch the uniform."

"You can't," Carmen noted. "It's not real."

Gabby felt her IQ drop several points. This happened a lot around her sister. Carmen was only ten years old, but she was very literal and had little patience for things that made no rational sense. The good thing about Carmen's infallible logic was that she was far more detail-oriented than either Gabby or Alice, their mom, so she excelled at managing the schedules for both Gabby's babysitting and Alice's catering business, plus all their financial records. According to Alice, the girls' dad had been good at those kinds of things, too, and would have been very happy to know Carmen had inherited those skills.

"Why is Satchel holding his ears and singing?" Carmen asked.

"He won't be in a sec," Zee said. She pulled a rag from one of the many pockets of her overalls and hurled it at him. He jumped and his eyes popped open.

"It's over," Zee told him loudly. "You can stop now."

"It's *not* over," Carmen said to Zee. "The movie's still on. You lied to him."

At the sound of Carmen's voice, Satchel broke out in a nervous sweat. He jumped to his feet and wiped his hands on the sides of his jeans. "Oh, hey, Carmen!" he said brightly. "You're here! That's great! Really . . . really great!"

It wasn't unusual for people to get weird around Carmen. She kind of had that effect. She wasn't big on social cues, so she didn't smile or laugh much in conversation, and her natural expression was more of a glare made to shut people down. Satchel, however, had known Carmen her whole life. Gabby knew he wasn't acting weird because of *her*, he was acting weird because he knew he shouldn't talk about what had just happened in the movie, but he also wasn't sure he could keep it in.

"What's up, Car?" Gabby asked.

"Mom wants to know if you need snacks," Carmen answered, but her eyes had locked on to Zee's robot parts, which were still splayed out all over the floor. She raised her gaze to fix on Zee. "Your stuff is touching the Puzzle Place," she said accusingly.

The Puzzle Place was a giant refurbished dining room table. It had a permanent home at the far side of the room, and it was Carmen's official spot for her favorite activity: cobbling together one of her gazillion-piece jigsaw puzzles. To Carmen, the Puzzle Place was sacred. Nothing was allowed to touch it.

"Sorry, Car," Zee said. She stretched out to move the offending bits and pieces from anywhere near the table legs and pack them back into the camouflage duffel bag she reserved for all things Wilbur. As she did, she glanced meaningfully at Gabby. "Actually, I think we're all going to go."

Gabby's skin prickled. She'd gotten so thrown by Edwina's bizarre appearance, she'd almost forgotten the woman's order. Gabby had to go to 3242 Robinson Street. *Immediately*.

"Zee's right," Gabby told Carmen. "Puzzle Place is all yours. We've got to run."

"We do?" Satchel whined. "But what about the movie? They still have to make the giant hamster ball and . . ." He stopped himself as he noticed Zee's meaningful glare. "Oh right. Yeah. We have to go."

"I'm going to grab my stuff," Gabby told Satchel and Zee. "Meet me upstairs, okay?"

Gabby ran up the two flights to her bedroom, leaping the steps in pairs. With every bound, her body tingled with more and more excitement as the new reality of her day sunk in. By the time she got to her room, her heart was thumping, and she was grinning so wide she thought her freckles might pop off.

For the second time ever, she was getting an assignment as A.L.I.E.N. Associate Gabby Duran, official Sitter to the Unsittables.

chapter
TWO

"You gotta let me come along," Zee begged.

Satchel had been so flustered from his encounter with on-screen Edwina that he'd left for home, but Zee and her giant duffel bag were sprawled on Gabby's bed as Gabby scrambled to get her things together. Gabby had already changed out of her movie-day-in-the-house sweats and was now picking through the piles of clean and dirty clothes on the floor to find her babysitting uniform: slightly baggy jeans and a long-sleeved plain-colored T-shirt. It was the perfect outfit—comfortable for running around with kids, but presentable enough for parents.

"I can't let you come!" Gabby insisted. "It's against the rules."

"So was telling me in the first place, but Edwina was cool with that!" Zee countered.

"Did you see the look on her face?" Gabby retorted. "She's not 'cool' with it, she's just not killing me for it. Or firing me. *Yet*. But she could, and then—"

"Then I'd have even less access to the aliens," Zee mused softly, sucking the end of a braid. "I see what you're saying."

Actually, Gabby wasn't saying that at all. She was going to say that without her, alien children would go back to being "Unsittable," a label given to them because alien kids were about as good with secrets as Satchel. Edwina had shown Gabby that if you looked closely enough at the news over the years, it was easy to find bizarre stories that were actually incidents of supposedly human children revealing their true alien identities to wildly freaked-out babysitters. Luckily, the sitters were rarely taken seriously, but A.L.I.E.N. couldn't count on that lasting forever. Sooner or later, the truth would get out, and Gabby had seen enough movies to know what would happen then. Dissection, warfare, world annihilation . . . Nothing good came of humans finding aliens in their midst. That was why alien kids had been declared Unsittable. If they weren't around human sitters, they couldn't blab to human sitters.

Gabby was different. She already knew their secret and had sworn to protect it. Alien parents could count on her to take care of their kids, and the kids left with her could be themselves. Gabby had meant to explain to Zee how wonderful it felt to help these aliens who needed her, but Zee's mind was already whirring down its own path.

"Fine," she conceded, "I won't go with you. Just, like, take pictures of whoever it is. Or better yet, get a blood sample. I have a microscope at home and—"

"No!" Gabby objected.

"I don't mean like at a doctor's office," Zee clarified. "You just maybe take her to a playground or someplace she might slip and scrape her knee. You fix her up, then bring me back the Band-Aid when she's all better."

"Stop," Gabby said.

"I'm just saying, this is a major scientific opportunity!"

Gabby let it go. She had picked her way over the sea of clothing mounds to her all-important purple knapsack and was sifting through it to make sure it held everything she might need. Gabby had found the knapsack in a thrift store when she was only nine, and from that minute she'd always kept it with her. It had just the right combination of large and small outer and inner pockets to perfectly fit everything she needed. In one area she kept basics like ChapStick, snacks, her wallet with her student ID and emergency hundred-dollar bill, and her house keys. Other areas held all her babysitting tricks—the little odds and ends she'd collected over the years to make her knapsack the ultimate playground for any kind of kid. She had the pencil-top erasers she'd decorated as pinkie-puppets, the tiny notebooks filled with codes she'd created for secret spy adventures, the squeeze packets of ketchup she'd use to turn gross vegetables into bloody zombie food kids couldn't wait to wolf down, and the easy-peel cling-on hooks she could stick on walls and ceilings to help with emergency fort building.

The knapsack also held her bag of marbles. Not just any marbles: she'd found these at an amusement park shop where they sat in a giant bin, so Gabby got to pick out each one individually. She'd spent so long marveling over her options that eventually her mom left her in the shop armed with her cell phone while she took a very impatient Carmen around to rides. They'd popped back after each ride only to find Gabby still entranced by the marbles, plucking out one for its beauty, one for its geometric swirls, one for its amazing cat's-eye that seemed to look right at you . . .

In the end, Gabby had gathered thirty completely unique marbles. Since then, whenever she needed something truly mesmerizing for a kid she was sitting, she could always pull out the soft leather pouch and count on the marbles to come through.

"And you tell me *I* carry a lot around with me," Zee remarked. She had crawled to the side of the bed and leaned over it, peering into Gabby's seemingly bottomless knapsack.

"Not done yet," Gabby said. She grabbed the book she was reading for history class and added it to the mix. Always good to have study material for downtime. She'd prefer to bring her French horn to practice, but that was one item that wouldn't fit inside the knapsack.

"Did you finish your report?" Zee asked.

All the sixth graders had been working on a massive history paper since the first day of school, and it was due tomorrow. Gabby pulled out her keys and held up the purple thumb drive she always kept on the ring.

"Completely," she said. "Printing it up tonight."

She tossed the keys back in her knapsack, zipped the bag, and slung it over her shoulder. Zee got up and did the same with her duffel, then the two girls went downstairs.

"Hey, baby!" Gabby's mom, Alice Duran, called when they neared the kitchen. Alice's Einstein-wild hair bounced as she folded the reddish-brown, gooey contents of a giant bowl with a rubber scraper.

"Hi, Mom."

Alice stopped stirring so she could give Gabby a big one-armed hug. The hug pushed Gabby's face into Alice's stain-splotched It's All Relativity apron, but the stain smelled amazing, so Gabby didn't mind.

"Is that graham cracker and . . . pancetta?" Gabby asked. Having a caterer for a mom had trained Gabby's nose to sniff out all sorts of bizarre flavors.

"And kumquat and cayenne," Alice added. "It'll be a cookie, eventually. I saw it on a TV show, but I want to try it out before I use it. There's a batch cooling, or you can grab one of the dark-chocolate bananas from the freezer."

"Thanks, but I actually have to go."

Gabby said it before she realized she couldn't tell Alice *why* she had to go. She couldn't say it was a babysitting job; Alice would wonder why Carmen hadn't scheduled it.

A glance at Zee's backpack inspired her. "I'm going to help Zee with her robotics stuff," she said, then immediately felt the blush crawl up her face. It was a horrible excuse. Gabby didn't know the first thing about robotics. And Zee had been working on her robot downstairs—why would they need to go someplace to do what they were already doing?

"I just need another pair of hands," Zee jumped in, reading Gabby's mind. "Basic stuff. And there's some equipment at the robotics lab that would help a lot."

"She said it might take a while," Gabby added, hoping to give herself as much time as possible for Edwina's job. "Is it okay if I have dinner with Zee?"

"It's okay with my parents," Zee said.

At least that part wasn't *entirely* a lie. Zee's parents would always say yes to Gabby eating with them. They just hadn't said yes specifically for tonight. Luckily, Zee and Gabby both knew Alice was comfortable enough with the girls house-hopping for meals that she wouldn't feel the need to call and double-check.

"Okay by me," Alice said. "Just call and let me know if you need a ride home. And no later than eight—it's a school night."

"I promise," Gabby said, already racking her brain for good excuses she could use if she had to go back on that promise. Edwina hadn't exactly given her an end time for the assignment.

Alice saw Gabby off with another hug, then Gabby and Zee bundled themselves into their jackets and ran outside. A clock ticked loudly in Gabby's head as she grabbed her bike from the garage. Edwina did *not* like to be kept waiting.

Gabby had already slung her leg over the bike and Zee was on her skateboard when the door across the street banged open to reveal the last person in the world Gabby wanted to see.

Madison Murray.

Madison had been Gabby's across-the-street neighbor forever. They were also the two brightest lights in the Brensville Middle School Orchestra. Every solo went to either Madison on flute, or Gabby on French horn. On paper they should have been fast friends, but apparently Madison never read those papers. She had always gone out of her way to rebuff any effort Gabby made to be nice, and her main goal in life seemed to be making Gabby miserable.

"Oh, look!" Madison cried as she stalked across her yard. "It's Gabby Duran, winner of the Screech of Shame Award!"

"Screech of Shame award?" Zee asked.

"Because I missed her big H.O.O.T. decorating session yesterday," Gabby muttered. "The whole thing's owl-themed, so, you know, Screech of Shame."

"But you were working," Zee said. Then she called it out to Madison. "She was working!"

Madison flounced across the street to them, her silken shoulder-length blonde hair glistening in the afternoon sun. She wore black leggings, black boots, and a sleek sweater with a fashion scarf. Gabby couldn't imagine looking that put-together for picture day at school, never mind a Sunday afternoon at home.

"I was working, too, Stephanie Ziebeck," Madison said. She had an unpleasant habit of calling people by their first and last names. "The *entire orchestra* was working on H.O.O.T. Everyone except Gabby."

Despite Gabby's issues with Madison, and despite the fact that she really did need to come through for her babysitting clients, she still felt like Madison was right. Gabby shouldn't have missed yesterday. H.O.O.T. was a huge deal for the Brensville Middle School Orchestra. It stood for Help Our Orchestra Travel, and it was how the group earned the ten thousand dollars they needed to go to MusicFest in Washington, D.C., each December. H.O.O.T. was different every year, with the theme chosen by the H.O.O.T. Honcho. This year the Honcho was Madison, and she'd planned a big auction that would stream live so they could get bids from everywhere.

It was a really good idea, and the list of donated auction items from everyone in town was pretty impressive. In her weekly e-mails and social media blasts, Madison even said there'd be a "Special Can't-Miss Surprise To Be Revealed Soon!" The whole orchestra had buzzed about H.O.O.T. since September, though they stopped a couple weeks ago to get ready for the Fall Concert. That concert had been held the previous Friday, and by the next morning it was again all-H.O.O.T.-all-the-time for the orchestra. The auction was Tuesday after school, and yesterday had been a full-court-press effort to decorate the gym for the big event.

"I'm sorry, Madison," Gabby said. "I really am. I feel awful about missing yesterday. If I could've possibly been there, I would've."

"Prove it," Madison sniffed. "You're not working now. I'll give you an e-mail list. You can send out reminder blasts."

The ticking clock grew louder inside Gabby's head.

"I—I can't," Gabby stammered. "I have to go."

It was as if Madison could smell Gabby's secret. Her eyes narrowed, and she leaned forward suspiciously. "*Where?*"

"Are you kidding me?" Zee exploded. "It's none of your business! Come on, Gabby. Let's go."

Zee pushed off on her skateboard, and Gabby pedaled after her, feeling jumbled inside. Madison was awful, but Gabby didn't like riding off in a huff. She always wanted to try to make things better between them. Still, Zee was right. Madison might not know about A.L.I.E.N., but she *did* know Gabby was hiding something. There was no reason to stick around and give her any clues about what that something might be.

"You know what I'd like to see Madison auction off at H.O.O.T.?" Zee asked as they rode. "Her keeping her mouth shut for an entire week. I'd pay *huge* money for that."

"I would, too," Gabby panted. "At least, as much as Carmen would let me take out of my account."

Unlike Zee, who seemed to have no problems zooming on her board with a giant duffel bag on her back, Gabby sweated and struggled as she furiously pumped her pedals.

"Thanks for riding with me," Gabby huffed, "but once we get close, I need to be by myself, you know?"

"I know," Zee said. But she didn't veer away. Then three

seconds later, she added, "*Or* I could just come with you, then casually skate around in front of the house while you go inside. That way I can get a little peek when they let you in the door."

"No peeks."

"Teeny peek."

"Zee, I can't!"

"Glimpse."

Gabby just looked at her.

"Okay, okay!" Zee relented. "I won't even get close. But call me when you're done. Or before you're done. Or if you get a selfie of you and the kid. Or if the kid licks you and you need help getting the saliva onto a slide."

"I'm hoping to avoid being licked," Gabby said, "but I promise I'll call if I need anything."

"Or come by right after. I have that forensics kit my parents got me. We can lift hair samples or fingerprints with it. Fun, right?"

Gabby rolled her eyes, then pumped her bike pedals even harder. Zee soon veered off to her own neighborhood, while Gabby continued toward her destination. She pedaled so hard her legs burned, and she inwardly hoped whatever child she was sitting didn't scare easily. Her face had to look like a tomato about to explode.

Turning onto Robinson Street, Gabby fully expected to see Edwina's long black limousine sitting in front of 3242.

It wasn't there.

What *was* there was a splintered FOR SALE sign, no cars in the garage, and an overgrown lawn. The lawn seemed to personally insult the gardener next door. Gabby noticed the way he'd pause while pruning bushes along that house's front walk to wipe his hands on his brown coveralls, run them through his salt-and-pepper hair, then send a blue-eyed glare disgustedly in 3242 Robinson's direction.

Gabby worried she'd heard Edwina wrong. Was this really where she was supposed to go?

She pulled her bike to the curb and lowered the kick-stand, then walked up the ragged rock path to the front door. The button for the bell looked rusted, and it crackled as Gabby pushed it in.

No sound.

She peered into the dusty picture windows next to the door, but they revealed only large, vacant rooms devoid of anything but cobwebs and dirt.

Gabby's phone vibrated in her back pocket. She pulled it out and saw "C. Jangschmitz" in the caller ID, which made no sense until she remembered it was Edwina's character in the alien guinea pig movie.

"Hello?"

Edwina's clipped voice chirped into Gabby's ear. "Are you going to stand there, or are you coming to work?"

"I'm here," Gabby said. "But the house is empty."

"Of course it is," Edwina said briskly. "Now get into the limousine so I can give you your assignment."

Confused, Gabby looked up and down the street again. No limousines had magically appeared along the curb or in any of the driveways. "It's not here."

"Not where you can see it," Edwina sighed. "We're a *se-cret* organization. Do you know how much attention a limousine would attract on a suburban street in the middle of a Sunday afternoon?"

Gabby considered mentioning that Edwina had already taken Gabby to a suburban street in the limo, and had twice pulled the giant car up to Brensville Middle School, but she thought better of it.

"Come to the backyard. Through the side gate. It's open. Bring your bicycle."

The phone clicked off. Gabby slipped it back in her pocket and ran to the curb. She peeked around to make sure no one else in any of the neighborhood's cookie-cutter houses was looking her way. She didn't want anyone to think she was breaking in. As far as she could tell, this was the perfect moment. Everyone was either inside or otherwise not around. Even the gardener next door had bent back over his work and wouldn't notice her. She quickly grabbed her bike by the handlebars and bounced it over the weedy lawn until she got to the side gate. The wood was warped, and a padlock sat inside the rusted metal latch that kept it shut.

An *open* padlock, Gabby realized. She slipped it out of the latch, creaked the gate wide, wheeled her bike through, then pushed the gate shut behind her.

From here she could see the side of the house and a small strip of the backyard. Certainly no limo.

"I'm here," Gabby said in case Edwina was within earshot. "Where are you?"

She rested her bike on its kickstand and walked alongside the house. When she reached its rear corner she turned to face the full expanse of backyard . . . and suddenly wondered if she'd ever have an encounter with Edwina that didn't make her feel like she was hallucinating.

The black stretch limo was sitting on the home's raised back deck, nestled comfortably between a barbecue and an outdoor dining room set.

chapter
THREE

For several moments, Gabby just stared at the deck.

Nothing about it made sense. For starters, there was no reason for the deck of an otherwise abandoned and overgrown house to have a shining barbecue and a set of perfectly new-looking outdoor furniture. Given that it *did* have these things, plus a latticed wood overhang and a three-foot-high slatted railing, there was absolutely no conceivable way that Edwina's limousine could have gotten up there, let alone wedged itself snugly between the barbecue, a sofa, and several rattan chairs. But there it was.

Edwina's voice came out of Gabby's rear end. "Please

don't waste time gaping, Gabby. It's terribly poor form. Come into the car."

Gabby jumped, then yanked her phone from her back pocket. It was on speaker, even though she was positive she'd turned it off.

"On my way," she said, but the call had already ended. She returned the phone to her pocket, ran to the deck, trotted up the three stairs, then reached for the limousine's door handle . . . just as it popped open by itself.

Gabby crouched down to peer inside the car. Edwina sat in a far corner.

"Good afternoon, Gabby," she said with a slight nod.

"Good afternoon," Gabby replied. She climbed in and shut the door behind her, then sat across from Edwina, who showed no sign of having just appeared on Gabby's television screen. As usual, she wore a conservatively tailored black suit, with her hair pulled back in a severe bun. She sat stiffly upright, yet managed to look perfectly comfortable at the same time. Her wrinkles were less vivid in real life than they'd been in high-definition 3-D, but her eyes burned with just as much vigor. Looking into them made Gabby feel like Edwina held a secret joke, and somehow Gabby herself was the punch line.

"Edwina—" Gabby began.

"It is my strong feeling," Edwina said, cutting her off,

"that you're about to ask me a series of 'how' questions, including but not limited to, 'How did the limousine get here?' 'How did I get into your poor excuse for a movie?' and 'How did I know you'd be with only Mr. Rigoletti and Ms. Ziebeck when I appeared?' In the interest of time, allow me to assure you simply that the integrity of the dreck you call cinema remains unimpeachable and will be back in its original state should you do something as inexplicable as choosing to watch it again. As for the rest, and to avoid such tedious sidebars in the future, I strongly suggest you accept the following blanket statement: when you need to know something you will, and if such information is not presented in a timely and forthright manner, it's because it's unnecessary for you to have in the first place. Shall we continue?"

Gabby's mouth had stayed open for Edwina's entire speech. Now she snapped it shut.

"Very good, then," Edwina said. She reached up and pressed a button in the ceiling. "Time to go."

There was a loud *WHOOSH*, then Gabby's stomach lodged somewhere in the middle of her throat.

The limo was plummeting. Every organ and all the blood inside Gabby's body lurched upward to prove it, but somehow Gabby herself stayed seated. She shouldn't have. She wasn't wearing a seat belt. By all rights she should have been plastered to the ceiling. Yet still she didn't move. She'd have thought more about how this could be possible, but her brain was squished to the very top of her skull. The few squashed synapses still functioning noticed that Edwina was having no issues with the drop at all. She reached into her bag, fiddled with her tablet, plucked some lint from her sleeve . . . Honestly, she looked a little bored.

Yet just when Gabby had found her larynx in her upper nasal passages and was about to use it to ask what was going on, her insides changed direction and slammed toward the back of her spine. Gabby re-navigated to find her voice.

"Did we just . . . ?" she choked.

"Drop several miles below the surface of the Earth into an underground freeway tube where we can drive at speeds that would make race car drivers' hearts explode?" Edwina asked.

"Um, that wasn't quite what I was going to ask, but . . ."

"Shame," Edwina said. "Because the answer to that would be yes."

Gabby was only mildly satisfied by this response, as it led her to even more questions. She was especially curious about the complete darkness outside the windows. Shouldn't an underground freeway tube involve safety lights of some kind? Gabby almost asked, but she imagined this would fall into the clearly quite large category of Things Gabby Doesn't Need to Know, so she didn't bother.

Suddenly, the limousine shifted direction again and rocketed straight up, hurling every cell in Gabby's body down to the soles of her feet. Her ears filled, popped, then filled and popped again until with a jolt, the car stopped. Filtered light streamed through the tinted rear windows. They were back on land.

Gabby gulped in deep breaths. She felt her heart thrum against her chest as it settled back into place. Her skin grew clammy, and she wondered if she was going into the same kind of shock she had when she met aliens for the very first time.

Across from her, Edwina laced her fingers and extended her arms long, stretching them out. "Wonderful ride, isn't it? Very bracing." She placed her palms on her black wool slacks and leaned forward toward Gabby. "Now get out."

"Okay." Gabby scooted along the leather bench seat and yanked on the door handle. It didn't budge. "It's not opening."

"That's because I don't want you to leave this limousine," Edwina said.

"But you said 'get out.'"

"Not 'get out.' *G.E.T.O.U.T.*"

"Ohhhhh."

G.E.T.O.U.T., Gabby knew, was the Group Eradicating Totally Objectionable Uninvited Trespassers. Their goal was to destroy all aliens, as well as those who helped them. The Brensville Middle School janitor, Mr. Ellerbee, had worked for the group, and two days ago both Gabby and the little girl she was babysitting had nearly become his victims.

"Now tell me," Edwina began, straightening back to her full height, "have you noticed anyone watching you?"

Gabby reached up for one of her dark curls and ran it between her fingers as she thought. "Should I have? I mean, there's Madison Murray, for sure, but she's not . . . She couldn't be . . . *Is* she?"

Hope widened Gabby's blue eyes. It wasn't that she *wanted* A.L.I.E.N. to do something about her worst enemy in the world, but hey, if the girl was part of G.E.T.O.U.T. . . .

"No," Edwina said with a slight smirk that said she knew exactly what Gabby was thinking. "Think harder. Anyone else?"

Gabby kept working her curl as she went back through the last couple days. "I really can't think of anyone. *Is* someone watching me? Like . . . another Ellerbee?"

Edwina snorted. "Were that the case, then Mr. Ellerbee would have been remarkably swift in using his cloning device."

"His *what*?"

"Not your concern. Suffice it to say we changed tactics with Mr. Ellerbee and met some conditions from him in exchange for his help. He will now remain affiliated with G.E.T.O.U.T., but work as a double agent. Already he has given G.E.T.O.U.T. false reports saying their suspicions were unfounded and you've never had anything to do with A.L.I.E.N. As a result, they have officially labeled you 'Alien Unaffiliated.'"

Gabby scrunched her face. "But if I'm Alien Unaffiliated, why would anyone be watching me?"

"Because G.E.T.O.U.T. is highly unprofessional. While it uses bribery to win over helpers like your Mr. Ellerbee, it recruits its most ardent followers through the Internet and during late-night radio shows that cater to lovers of the paranormal, or K.O.O.K.S."

"K.O.O.K.S." Gabby nodded. "Got it. What does that stand for?"

"It's not an acronym," Edwina said. "I'm saying these are ridiculous people. Kooks. Crackpots. Loony birds. Those who are constantly told by society that their conspiracy theories and Armageddon scenarios are balderdash, and are therefore desperate for vindication. Despite your new classification, your name and face are still on G.E.T.O.U.T.'s encrypted Web site, where members can see it, make their own assumptions, and act accordingly."

"They have my picture on their Web site?" Gabby asked.

"Indeed."

Gabby shifted inside her puffy purple jacket. "Do you know *which* picture? Because if it's the one from fifth grade ... I had raspberries at lunch, and one of the seeds caught in my teeth and the guy got me just as I was scooching my tongue around to get it, so I look all mushy and weird. Like when a cow chews cud—have you ever seen that?"

Edwina raised an eyebrow. Gabby felt herself grow smaller.

"But I guess that's not the point," Gabby admitted.

"Indeed not," Edwina agreed. "The point *is*, that while you may not be in any danger, you need to remain vigilant. Should you have reason to feel you're being observed or followed by someone other than your flute-playing nemesis, subtly take their picture with your phone. We can analyze the image and decide if the person is a threat. Furthermore, as part of this added vigilance, you must never contact any of your charges outside of official babysitting duties. Is that clear?"

"Crystal," Gabby said, grabbing her phone and pulling up the Contacts screen. "So what's the best number to text you?"

"Excuse me?" Edwina asked.

"For the pictures," Gabby said. "Of any weird people I see. Shouldn't I text them to you?"

"You don't need a number," Edwina replied. "If you see anyone suspicious, just take the picture. We'll find it."

As Edwina's meaning sunk in, Gabby ran through a mental inventory of all the pictures on her phone. If A.L.I.E.N.

could check them out at will, there were a bunch she needed to delete—starting immediately with the tape-face series she and Zee took at their last sleepover.

"Are you listening, Gabby?"

Gabby shook away images of herself and Zee with tape wrapped around their heads, pulling their noses into ridiculous piggy snouts and their mouths into grotesque frowns.

"Yes!" she said.

"Good," Edwina said. "So G.E.T.O.U.T."

"Right," Gabby said, leaning forward attentively. "G.E.T.O.U.T. What about them?"

"No." Edwina rolled her eyes. "*Get out*. Of the car."

"Oh!"

Gabby blushed, then pulled her knapsack over her shoulder and pushed open the now-unlocked limousine door before climbing out into the glaring sun. After the dark tunnel and shaded car, she had to blink several times before she could focus. Once she did, she gasped with delighted awe.

"Oh, wow! It's like a fairy tale!"

"Fairies tell horrible tales," Edwina clucked as she followed Gabby out of the limousine. "They don't believe in plot on their planet. Chapters and chapters of nothing but flowery description. It's a nightmare."

Alien-fairy storytelling skills aside, the vista before Gabby's eyes was almost impossibly charming. The limo had pulled up next to an arched stone bridge that straddled a gorgeously clear bubbling creek and formed the perfect frame for the lush green hills on either side. A long, cobbled path ran by the creek's bank, then disappeared around one of the hills, as if taunting Gabby with unimaginable delights just beyond her view.

Gabby turned to Edwina for direction. The older woman extended an arm and nodded.

"By all means."

Gabby took her time walking along the path, delighting in the crunch of her purple canvas sneakers against the grass that poked up between cobblestones.

"This is where he lives?" she asked Edwina. "Or . . . *she* lives? I mean, the . . . you know . . ."

"Child from another planet?" Edwina asked. "It's all right, you can say it out loud. It's a secluded area. The aliens are the only ones who live here."

Gabby's eyes widened, and everything around her became instantly twice as magical. She thought about her most recent A.L.I.E.N. clients, Wutt and Philip, and how amazing it would have been if she could have run around and played with them out in the open, without the fear of anyone dangerous recognizing their identity. Her heart pounded again, but this time with excitement. She smiled, seeing so clearly in her head what she'd find when she turned the corner. A fantasy village, dotted with tiny hobbit houses with lush lawns where little aliens of all sorts would race around playing tag, rolling down hills, chasing puppies . . .

Then she made the turn.

Gabby rubbed her eyes, positive they weren't working correctly.

The vista in front of her wasn't what she'd imagined at all. The green hills, bubbling creek, and cobblestone path were all littered with enormous, iceberg-size objects that Gabby recognized, but were so out of place on this field that she felt as if she'd wandered into a postapocalyptic nightmare. She saw large airplanes stuck nose down, or tossed on their sides with their landing gear pointed fruitlessly into the air. She saw an ancient ship the size of her school half-buried in the ground, its tattered sails blowing in the breeze. She saw a bronze statue head tilted on its ear. It was so huge that even from a distance Gabby could tell its eye was larger than her entire body.

And all that was only the beginning. The area was strewn with so many strange and titanic items that Gabby couldn't begin to take them all in. It looked like a giant the size of a mountain had picked up an entire city as if it were a toy box, then turned it upside down and dumped out all the contents.

"What happened here?" Gabby gasped.

"The long answer to that would be slightly different

for each item," Edwina said. "The short version is a single word: Trolls."

"Trolls?" Gabby asked. "Like, the little dolls with the goofy hair and the naked butts?"

"Ideally no," Edwina said. "I generally try to avoid any nude posterior-sharing with those we serve. Real Trolls came here many centuries ago from their home planet. Unlike your previous charges, Trolls can pass for humans without disguise. They go to human schools, work at human jobs, and hold lofty positions in human industries. Yet, like other aliens, Troll children tend to save their most unrestrained and most clearly otherworldly behavior for babysitters. Hence the need for you."

Edwina clopped farther down the cobblestone path, but Gabby barely noticed. She'd spotted something on the closest oversize relic. It was a two-propeller plane, old and rusted, with holes in its side where chunks of metal had been ripped away. The plane lay tilted on the ground, balanced on one wing and one wheel. There was something scrawled on the hull, scratched in shaky block letters as if it were carved with a knife. Gabby moved closer until she could make the letters out.

Earhart.

Gabby's skin tingled.

"Edwina! Edwina!" She ran to catch up with her, then

grabbed her sleeve. "That plane . . ." she panted. "It says . . . It's not . . . I mean, it can't be . . ."

"The plane of aviatrix Amelia Earhart, missing since 1937? Indeed it is. Now please unhand my jacket. Your fingers are sweaty and the fabric requires dry cleaning."

Gabby let go but kept gaping at Edwina. "How is this not shocking to you? Amelia Earhart's disappearance is one of the greatest mysteries, like, ever!"

"It's not a mystery at all. The plane was stolen by a Troll. As for Amelia herself, she was so mortified that she couldn't solve the Troll's riddle, she went back to her home planet without a word to anyone. Except A.L.I.E.N., of course. We had to stamp her intergalactic passport."

"Amelia Earhart was an alien?!" Gabby gaped.

"From the planet Blargh." Edwina sighed. "Lovely place. Hideous name."

Gabby's head swirled. "I'm sorry—is any of this supposed to make sense to me? Because it really doesn't. At all."

"Then allow me to explain. Trolls, as I said, blend in reasonably well with humanity. However, they have some . . . foibles. Chief among these is that they steal."

"They steal *planes*?! And ships?! And big, giant statue heads?!?!"

Edwina looked forward in the direction where Gabby was gaping. "Ah," she said. "That would be the Colossus of

Rhodes. One of the Seven Wonders of the Ancient World. Tallest statue of its day. Toppled in an earthquake in 226 BC. The pieces were deemed 'lost' in 654 AD."

"But they weren't lost?" Gabby asked.

Edwina gestured to the Colossus's grim-set lips. "Does he look lost?"

Gabby didn't quite know how to answer that. After all, the statue was missing the rest of its body. Or maybe the pieces were just strewn elsewhere among the hills.

"Come," Edwina said. "I'll show you the highlights while we walk. We're expected. We don't want to be late."

Gabby trailed Edwina along the cobblestone path. As they passed each gargantuan, hulking item, Edwina explained its history. Gabby almost felt like she was on a school field trip, but one jumbled together with a tumble down the rabbit hole and a fever dream.

"On your left, you'll see the USS *Cyclops*," Edwina said, gesturing to an impossibly huge aircraft carrier sprawled on its side, "a five-hundred-and-twenty-two-foot carrier ship that disappeared in the Bermuda Triangle in 1918. Up here to your right—oh, these are interesting." She gestured to a group of tiny, weatherworn, log-and-shingle houses. "Homes from the Lost Colony of Roanoke, Virginia. Disappeared without a trace around 1587. Historians today expect foul play, of course, but the colonists actually became quite friendly with the Trolls who stole their homes. With their help, the colonists traveled to a far more comfortable place than colonial America, I promise you that."

Gabby's brain was reaching maximum capacity for inconceivable.

"So wait," she blurted. "You're saying every missing thing from every time ever was stolen by Trolls and is right here?!"

"Don't be ridiculous," Edwina clucked. "Only *most* every missing thing from every time ever was stolen by Trolls. And the only ones here are the items stolen by the single family of Trolls who live in this area, and the long line of their direct ancestors. Other Trolls have their own treasure troves. And of course right now you're only seeing the larger items. They keep their smaller treasures closer at hand."

"But I don't understand," Gabby said, shaking her head. "Why is A.L.I.E.N. okay with Trolls taking things?"

"Diplomacy requires compromise, Gabby," Edwina said. "Stealing is the Trolls' greatest pleasure. Plus they always give their victims a fair shot. Trolls can only take something if they ask for it first, and the original owner always has the chance to get their item back by correctly answering a riddle the Troll must provide."

Gabby looked around at the very full field of stolen behemoths. "I'm guessing no one ever answered this family's riddles correctly."

Before Edwina could answer, Gabby realized something. "Google Earth!" she blurted.

Without slowing her gait, Edwina turned and raised an eyebrow. "Is that supposed to mean something to me, or will you be spouting non sequiturs as we walk?"

"It's not a non sequitur!" Gabby insisted. "With Google Earth you can see satellite images of everything on the planet! This is a giant field of massive, enormous things that everyone in the world wants to see. How does nobody know they're here?"

"Honestly, Ms. Duran, if after everything you've seen, you don't think A.L.I.E.N. can handle a little cloaking device, I'm highly disappointed in you." Edwina stopped in her tracks. "Ah. Here we are."

Gabby tore her eyes from the wonders all around and focused on where Edwina was looking. They had neared the end of the cobblestone path and stood in front of a large house with a rounded roof and dappled stone façade. The home seemed to sprout out of the lush, hilly green meadow around it. It was an island of adorable in the middle of a sea of bizarre.

Edwina looked sternly down at Gabby. "Remember," she said, "you now know what Trolls do. If you value your belongings, you will not let the Trolls steal from you. Should you mistakenly do so, A.L.I.E.N. cannot intervene. You'll either have to answer the Troll's riddle, or lose your possession forever. If you don't wish to take that risk, let me know now. I'll cancel the appointment, and, for the time being, the Troll child will return to the ranks of the Unsittables."

The very word made Gabby flinch. Gabby's own sister had been considered "Unsittable," but it was only because Carmen was different. Gabby had been little then, but she still remembered how much it hurt every time another sitter railed to Alice about Carmen's "faults," and why those were the reasons she was never coming back.

Gabby stood taller and adjusted her knapsack on her back. "I'm taking the job," she said. "Let's go in."

chapter
FOUR

As Edwina knocked, Gabby couldn't help but smile. Despite all the weirdness, nothing fired her up like meeting a kid for the first time. It was one of her favorite parts of being a babysitter. To Gabby, every kid was a puzzle-locked box. If you were interested in them enough to figure out the puzzle, you could open that box and completely connect with the person inside. From there, everything else was easy. Gabby couldn't wait to get started with the young Troll. Besides, the house was so cute Gabby could almost smell the gingerbread and apple cider she just knew were waiting inside. Maybe there'd be a pie in the oven, too, and

Gabby could take it out and let it cool on the windowsill when it was done.

Just as Edwina lifted her hand to knock again, the door swung open, and Gabby saw a thick, lumpy pickle of a nose. The nose was attached to a middle-aged woman—a Troll, Gabby assumed—but the appendage was so immense that Gabby couldn't yet take in anything else. Still, she smiled wide and strode to the door with her hand extended, ready to introduce herself like she would to any new client.

"Oh, it's you," the nose—that is, the woman—muttered. "I suppose you should come in."

The Troll woman turned her back, leaving Gabby's introduction to dry up in her throat. Gabby looked up questioningly at Edwina, but she was already walking in. Gabby followed.

The minute she entered, her visions of cider and gingerbread burst. Though the house was a large, charming cottage on the outside, inside it was more like a giant squirrel's den. The main room stretched up through the entire three stories of the home, bending in organic curves like a tree trunk. An *inside out* tree trunk, since the walls were thickly ridged and knotted like bark. Large outcroppings jutted here and there, many tufted in eye-popping shades of fuchsia, lime, or solar flare–orange upholstery. Gabby also saw several large holes in the walls. They looked like mine-shaft openings, and Gabby wondered if the house was really just a main corridor that led to a network of tunnels.

In front of Gabby, the floor was littered with giant haystack-tangles of what looked like junk, but from what Gabby had learned outside, she assumed these were piles of smaller items the Troll family and their ancestors had stolen over the years. The mounds littered almost every space, leaving room only for a few wide walking paths and what had to be a mostly buried kitchen. Gabby half-wanted to sift through the piles and Google the contents against any long-missing treasures, but that wasn't why she was here. Instead she turned to the Troll woman, smiled, and again offered her hand.

"Hi, ma'am," she said. "I'm Gabby Duran. It's wonderful to meet you."

The woman wrinkled her large nose like she smelled something bad. She looked at Gabby's outstretched hand, then at Gabby's face. She leaned so close that her thick mat of frizzy hair tickled Gabby's cheeks, and Gabby could see every double- and triple-humped mole on her face. Then the Troll scrunched her single, protruding eyebrow, locked her black beady eyes on Gabby's, and snorted dismissively.

"This the best you got?" she asked Edwina.

Gabby was surprised by the question, but wouldn't let herself be thrown. She kept her hand out and continued, "I'm really happy you asked me to babysit today, ma'am. I promise your child will be in excellent hands, and he'll have a great time while we're together."

"I didn't *ask* you to babysit," the woman said. "I was forced."

She turned her back on Gabby and shuffled to the wall. Then, to Gabby's amazement, long, thick claws burst out of her fingertips and bare toes. Using these fierce appendages, she scaled the wall, her claws digging into tiny grips in the ridged wood. She pulled herself into one of the tunnel holes and disappeared inside, but she couldn't have gone far. Gabby could hear the woman rummaging around.

"Allynces, it was hardly a matter of force," Edwina called up to the Troll. "You needed a sitter, I have a sitter. That's it."

Items came flying out of the tunnel hole. Gabby dodged to avoid them as they rained down. She saw a rusted 1970s curling iron, an array of plastic brushes decorated with cartoon characters, and an ivory comb covered in ancient Egyptian hieroglyphics.

Allynces emerged from the tunnel holding a large mirror, which she hung on the wall, and a wide-toothed hair pick. Staring at her reflection, she proceeded to give the matted frizz on her head slightly less mat and significantly more frizz.

"We *could* just bring Trymmy with us tonight," Allynces said. "Then we'd avoid this unpleasantness."

Was Gabby "the unpleasantness"?

"You absolutely could," Edwina said.

Allynces sighed. "No. We all agreed no kids tonight." She applied a thick layer of bright purple lipstick and eye shadow as she glared down at Gabby. "I just wish you'd given me a picture first. I mean, look at her. She's not easy on the eyes."

"I'm . . . what?" Gabby stammered.

A loud beeping sound came from Edwina's black bag. "That's me," Edwina said. She unclasped the bag, pressed something inside, then snapped the bag shut again and called up to Allynces, "Have a good night!"

With that, the older woman clopped to the door. Gabby scurried after her.

"Edwina," she said in a low voice, "I know I said I'd take the job, but maybe it's not a good idea. I mean, it doesn't sound like Allynces likes me very much."

"Did I not mention that Trolls can be brusque?" Edwina asked. "That's just their way. They assume they're a million times smarter than any human, and most of the time they're right. You just do your thing, and Allynces and Feltrymm will take you home after dinner. By eight, your mother said?"

"Yes, but . . . Wait. How did you know?"

Edwina raised an eyebrow, and Gabby knew she shouldn't have asked. "Okay, forget that part," she agreed. "But did you say *they're* bringing me home?"

"Indeed," Edwina said. "Have a good night."

She walked out the door, leaving Gabby for the first time ever in a house where she didn't feel wanted. Gabby considered slipping out and running back home, but she had no idea where home was from here. Besides, things would have to be a lot worse than this before she'd run out on a job.

Clanks and jingles drew Gabby's attention back to Allynces. The Troll woman's claws were out again, and she was crawling back down the wall. She had clearly accessorized while Gabby was talking to Edwina; the clangs and clinks were a discordant array of necklaces, bracelets, and earrings. As Allynces got closer, Gabby noticed the earrings looked like ancient gold doubloons. She'd seen similar ones at the mall, but Gabby still kind of wondered if these were the real deal.

"So . . . what can you tell me about Trymmy?" she asked Allynces, trying again for polite conversation. "Does he have any favorite foods, favorite games, fav—"

"Trymmy doesn't need help from a human," the Troll snapped. "You're here only in case of emergency, in which case your sole duty is to stomp three times on that round tile hatch and get him securely into the Holobooth, while you remain here to fight off any danger on your own."

As Allynces retracted her claws and slipped into high heels she pulled from another pile, Gabby replayed her last sentence to see if she could translate it to anything that made sense.

It didn't work.

"Did you say 'hollow booth'?" she asked.

Allynces sighed deeply, then tilted her head and yelled to the upper reaches of the house, "Feltrymm, Edwina sent us one that can't hear!" Then she turned back to Gabby.

Gabby wasn't the tallest girl in her class by any stretch. She only came up to her mom's chest, she was shorter than Satchel, and she was only an inch taller than Zee, all of which meant most adults still towered over her. Allynces, however, even in high heels, had to grab a red upholstered footstool from beneath a hodgepodge of throw pillows, then stand on it to look Gabby in the eye.

"HO-LO-BOOTH," she sounded out.

Gabby winced. She dreaded asking another question, but if this was her main duty, she wanted to be sure she had it right. "And the round tile hatch?" she squeaked.

Allynces rolled her beady eyes, snorted a blast of hot breath into Gabby's face, then strode off the footstool and across the room. She kicked aside a pile of board games, including one chess set that looked like it was carved out of jade, and another covered with figures shaped like U.S. presidents. Once they were out of the way, Allynces pointed to the hatch. It was a single circle of black, made of nothing Gabby could imagine, because it was so incredibly dark that it seemed to suck Gabby in. She had the horrible feeling that if she ever did step on it, the thing would pull her down like a black hole, stretching her deep into an eternity of nothingness.

Gabby felt hypnotized looking at the circle, and realized she was slowly moving closer, which was the last thing she wanted to do. She shook her head to break out of the daze, then stepped away.

"Of course," Gabby told Allynces. "Sorry I missed it."

She told herself that once Allynces and Feltrymm were gone, she'd push the board games back over the hatch.

"So." Allynces crossed her arms. "Trymmy knows where everything is, including his dinner. He can watch one hour of satellite broadcast, but *only* from LR-47, nothing Earthly. If he'd prefer to stay in his room until we return, that's fine with us. We'll be home at seven thirty on the dot, so please be ready. We'll want to get you out of here as quickly as possible."

"Yes, ma'am," Gabby said.

"Here I come, Allynces!"

The deep voice boomed from above. Allynces looked up, and for the first time Gabby saw the woman smile. Gabby followed her gaze to a tall, stocky figure with extra-thick claws scurrying down the wall with acrobatic speed and grace. Ten feet above the ground he hurled himself backward, turned a somersault, and landed directly in front of Allynces. His back was to Gabby, but she could still see the ends of the rose he held in his mouth. He retracted his claws, then with a flourish, he presented the flower to his wife. "For you."

Allynces blushed as she accepted the rose, and Gabby couldn't help but smile. Allynces might not be the nicest being Gabby had ever met, but she and Trymmy's father were clearly in love. It made Gabby feel warm inside, and also a little sad. Her mom always said she and Gabby's dad had been in love like that, but Gabby's father had gone missing in action and was presumed dead when Gabby was only two. She wished she could have seen her own parents act like Trymmy's. Except maybe without the claws.

Allynces pointed over Feltrymm's shoulder. "The sitter."

Feltrymm turned toward Gabby . . . and his wide smile curled into a disgusted sneer.

These Trolls were going to give Gabby a complex.

Like Allynces, Feltrymm had wild dark hair that stood out in every direction. His brow was thick and rippled, and an underbite jutted his bucked-out lower teeth over his fleshy lips. Yet all of that was nearly eclipsed by his thick, pockmarked tuber of a nose. For just a second Gabby imagined he and Allynces kissing, and the careful nasal choreography that would have to happen before such an event could occur.

"Gabby Duran, I believe?" Feltrymm asked. He held out

his hand, which at that moment felt to Gabby like the nicest thing anyone had ever done for her. She shook it and smiled.

"Wonderful to meet you, sir."

"Call me Feltrymm." He remained smiling as he released her hand, but Gabby noticed he held his arm away from his body, like he'd pulled the limb out of a deep vat of sludge. "I'm sorry," he said. "Do you mind if I . . ."

He let the sentence trail as if Gabby would fill in the rest. She had no idea what he was asking, but she nodded to tell him whatever it was, it was fine by her. He smiled gratefully, then rummaged through a tall pile of what looked like hotel toiletries until he pulled out a bottle of hand sanitizer. He poured it liberally over his hands and forearms, then rubbed them together so vigorously Gabby thought he might make fire.

"We should go, Allynces," Feltrymm said, gently taking her elbow. "We're running late."

"Love you, Trymmy!" Allynces called up into the house. "Your sitter's here if you need her, but I'm sure you'll do fine on your own. If you do come down, don't look directly at Gabby after dinner. I don't like when you see scary things too close to bedtime!"

"Really?" Gabby blurted.

She clapped her hands over her disobeying mouth, but Allynces hadn't heard. She and Feltrymm had already slipped down a back tunnel. Since the two were taking Gabby home that night, Gabby sincerely hoped the tunnel led to a garage and not some alien-black-hole-molecule-mixer-upper transporter device.

With the Troll couple gone, Gabby was alone. Well, alone except for Trymmy, who'd been told he could spend the entire night in his room if he wanted. She'd much rather the two of them hang out, but she didn't want to push it in case he felt the same way about humans as his parents did. Instead she made herself comfortable. She slipped off her purple knapsack and jacket, placed them in a clear spot against the wall, then pulled her phone out of her back pocket and texted Alice to say things with Zee were going great and she planned to be home by eight.

"YAAAAAAAA!!!!!!"

The bloodcurdling scream came from high above. Gabby's skin leaped. She looked up, and froze in absolute terror.

A young boy—Trymmy, it could only be Trymmy—hurled himself headfirst out of a tunnel near the ceiling.

"NO!" Gabby screamed. She raced into the middle of the floor and held out her arms, hoping against hope that she could somehow catch him before he smashed into the floor.

Then Trymmy's scream turned to hoots of howling laughter, and Gabby immediately relaxed. She was wrong. Trymmy wasn't falling, he was *descending*. His finger and toe claws were extended, and he hurtled down the wall like a high-speed mountain goat. His mouth spread in a grin, and he looked so happy that Gabby smiled, too. Once he got low enough, he threw himself flat against the wall and rolled down to the bottom. He kept rolling across the floor, barreling right over the strewn toiletry bottles, board games, and throw pillows, then bounced to his feet right in front of Gabby. He spread his arms and leaned his chest forward like an alpha ape.

"That was amazing!" Gabby cheered.

Trymmy scrunched his face. "You're not freaked-out?"

"Should I be?" Gabby asked.

"Most humans are."

Gabby shrugged. "Then I guess I'm not most humans."

Trymmy narrowed his eyes and studied her, which gave Gabby a chance to look at him, too. From a distance, he looked like a totally normal human kid. Gabby pegged him at about ten years old. He was maybe a head shorter than Gabby, though his high corona of curly black hair gave him another six inches. He wore dark blue jeans and a blue-and-red-striped cotton polo top with a white collar.

At closer glance, Trymmy still seemed human. Yet like his parents, he looked like a very *unique* human. His brow was slightly raised and thickened. Gabby could imagine that one day it would stick out as much as his dad's. He had a full caterpillar unibrow, and while at first his face seemed dotted with freckles, Gabby realized it was actually covered in moles. Some of the moles lay flat against Trymmy's skin, while others bloomed out like mini pacifiers. His nose was wide, flat, and so long that the tip of it hung over his top lip. If he really tried, Gabby imagined he could reach the ends of either nostril with his tongue. He wore thick glasses that did him the favor of magnifying his eyes. Without them, his eyes would have been far too tiny for his face. His body was small and wiry, with arms and legs just enough longer than ex-pected that Gabby had to blink hard to make sure she wasn't imagining it.

"You're *sure* you're not like most humans?" Trymmy asked.

"Pretty sure," Gabby said. "I mean, I guess I haven't met most humans. Have you?"

Trymmy didn't answer. Instead he pegged Gabby with a steady gaze as he leaned his head to the left. After a mo-ment, gravity forced one of his larger moles to droop over his mouth. Trymmy caught it between his teeth and worked his jaw gently back and forth, wiggling the trapped mole up and down.

Gabby knew he was trying to disgust her, but it wasn't working. She kept her eyes on Trymmy's as she curled her own tongue in on itself then stuck it out still rolled, so it looked like a tongue taco.

"Ew." Trymmy backed away. "That's disgusting."

"Is it?" Gabby asked. "Or is it just different?"

Trymmy raised his unibrow. "You intrigue me," he said. He nodded to her jacket and knapsack, sitting neatly on the floor. "Can I take your things for you?"

Gabby almost said yes, but then she remembered what Edwina told her about Trolls and their stealing habit. "No thanks."

"Did someone tell you not to let me take stuff?" Trymmy asked. "Or are you smart enough to just know it?"

"Someone told me," Gabby admitted, "but that doesn't mean I'm not smart."

"You're not as smart as a Troll," Trymmy said. "No human is. Did you know I'm five grades ahead of everyone else in my class at math?"

"I did not know that."

"It's true." Trymmy raised his chin triumphantly. "They don't even keep me in class with them for it. I have a special tutor and everything."

"Then maybe you could teach me," Gabby said. "I'm horrible at math."

"I could try, but you probably wouldn't keep up. Truth is, humans can't do half of what Trolls can do."

"You think?" Gabby said. "Try me. Just not at math."

"Okay." Trymmy held his hands in front of his chest.

He'd retracted his claws before, but now he shot them and his toe claws back out again. He grinned. "Follow the leader?"

Trymmy scaled halfway up the wall with gecko-like ease, then circled around so that he was looking right at Gabby. "You coming?"

Gabby pursed her lips and took a deep breath. Just like Trymmy, she held her hands in front of her chest. She squeezed her eyes shut and tensed her muscles so hard she started shaking.

"What are you doing?" Trymmy asked.

With a *whoosh*, Gabby released her breath. She let her shoulders slump and shrugged up to Trymmy. "I tried," she said, "but my claws aren't coming out."

Trymmy laughed.

"I wish they would," Gabby said, "'cause climbing looks like fun. But I guess you're right. Humans can't do half of what Trolls can do."

"Told ya so," Trymmy said.

"But I have some fun stuff we both can do." She walked over to her knapsack. "Now I'm not saying you can *take* any of these things, but we can *play* with anything you want."

Gabby plopped down on the floor, crossed her legs, and started pulling items out of her knapsack and laying them out on her jacket. She did *not* want her treasures to get mixed up with the other piles of random objects in Trymmy's house.

"Let's see, there's pencil pinkie puppets . . . super-secret-code notebooks . . . glow in the dark sticker sheets . . . Oooh, the big bouncy rubber-band ball . . ."

Gabby pretended not to notice as Trymmy slowly climbed back down the wall and edged closer and closer, subtly checking out each treasure over Gabby's shoulder as she laid it out.

"What's that?" Trymmy asked. His voice came from *right* behind Gabby now. She smiled to herself but kept her voice casual. She didn't want to spook him. She wanted *him* to be the one who chose to play. She didn't even look him in the eye when she turned to see where his finger was pointing.

Gabby grinned when she realized. Of course.

"These?" she asked, picking up the very familiar soft leather pouch. "They're the coolest thing I've got."

Gabby spun around on her rear end, held the bag in cupped hands, and raised them to the level of her nose as she looked up at Trymmy. "Want to see?"

Trymmy sucked in his large lower lip, and Gabby saw his magnified eyes dance. She felt his excitement as he reached for the gathered top of the pouch and pulled it open. Gabby's knees bounced up and down with anticipation while she waited to see what he'd say. Gabby never told kids what the marbles were; everyone she showed had their own idea.

The wait was killing her. She almost squealed as he

poked through the marbles, taking some out and swirling them around in his hand.

Finally, he spoke. "These are *so cool*."

His voice was reverent, like he'd just discovered the key to life, the universe, and everything.

"What do you think they are?" Gabby asked.

"You know what they are! They're secret mega orbs! They give you superpowers so you can do battle with each other!" His eyes grew even larger and he smiled wide. "You want to play?"

Gabby was sitting on the ground, but she felt like she was floating on air.

She'd cracked Trymmy's puzzle-lock. She was in.

"I'd *love* to play."

chapter
FIVE

"How does the game work?" Gabby asked, jumping to her feet.

"They're *your* secret mega orbs," Trymmy said. "You should know."

"Right," Gabby agreed, "but, you know, house rules and all, so . . . how do *you* play?"

"Okay," Trymmy began, and his whole body came alive with wild gestures as he described the rules. His larger moles bounced with all the motion. "We each pick three secret mega orbs, but we don't let the other one see. Then we each hide one in our fist and count three . . . two . . . one . . . go!

We show 'em at the same time, and we see who wins!"

"Awesome!" Gabby's curls bounced. She was picking up on Trymmy's energy and moving around as much as him. "But how do we know who wins?"

"Ga-*bby*," he groaned and rolled his eyes. "You *know* what wins. Mostly red orbs are fire, mostly blue ones are water, and the black-and-whites are wind. Water defeats fire, fire defeats wind, wind defeats water. Got it?"

"Got it."

"Okay, now pick your mega orbs."

Trymmy smacked his hands over his glasses so Gabby could choose her marbles. She plucked out three, then held the pouch out to Trymmy. "Your turn."

"Cool," Trymmy said. *"Don't look."*

Gabby tucked her head down and curled her arms over her face so Trymmy would know she wasn't looking, but she was dying to peek. She would have loved to see his focus as he pored over each marble to make sure he chose just the right ones. But that would have broken the rules, and then he wouldn't want to play with her anymore. She had to settle for her imagination.

"Ready," he said. "Let's play."

Gabby snapped open her eyes. Without even looking, she slipped a marble into her right palm, closed her fist over it, and held it out. A second later, Trymmy held out his closed fist, too.

"Three . . . two . . . one . . . go!" Trymmy cried.

They both opened their hands. Trymmy looked down at his red marble with the yellow flare in the middle and shouted, "Fireball power! Fireballs swirl in my hands and shoot across the room to you!"

Looking down at her own white marble with black specks, Gabby cried, "Wind power! I hold my arms up and spin in a circle faster and faster"—which she did—"then *zoom* it right to you!" Gabby lunged toward Trymmy, hurling the "tornado" his way.

"But my fire sucks up the oxygen in your tornado and turns into an inferno! I win!"

Gabby clutched her heart and fell dramatically to the ground. Trymmy laughed. "Okay, get up get up get up," he said. "We're going again."

They played a few rounds, and each time they acted out their power so dramatically that Gabby was out of breath and sweaty. She had just realized she should probably make him take a break for dinner, when he said, "Okay, so are you ready to play?"

"Another round?" Gabby asked. "Sure!"

"No, I mean *play*. For real. Troll-style."

He waggled his unibrow and Gabby laughed. "I thought we *were* playing Troll-style."

"Uh-uh. For that we go into the Holobooth."

He pointed across the floor at the inky circle. Even half hidden by the board games Gabby had pushed back over it, the thing's inky blackness filled her with a dread that was so elemental she couldn't even explain it.

"The . . . Holobooth?" Gabby squeaked.

She'd tried to keep the nerves out of her voice, but Trymmy obviously heard them. His nose seemed to slide even farther over his mouth, and all his moles drooped downward. "You do *want* to keep playing with me, right?"

"Yes!" She said it immediately and forced a smile back onto her face. No matter how much the Holobooth freaked her out, it couldn't really be dangerous, right? After all, it was just some unknown alien technology that made Gabby feel like her soul was being sucked away every time she looked at it.

Gulp.

The happiness on Trymmy's face helped make it better. "Cool! So to open the Holobooth—"

"Stomp on the round tile hatch three times," Gabby finished. "Your parents told me."

Trymmy nodded. Unlike Gabby's curls, his didn't bounce when he moved his head. They remained fanned straight out.

"They kind of also told me it was meant for emergencies,"

Gabby noted. "Are you really allowed to play in there?"

Trymmy rolled his eyes. "It's a safe place to *hide* in emergencies, but that's not what it's *for*. It's for games, I promise. Open it!"

With measured steps, Gabby moved to the hatch. She leaned back and kicked out a sneaker-clad foot to move the board games away from it. Once again she had the stomach-sinking feeling that the blackness was a vacuum, ready to pull her down. She didn't want to step on it. She didn't want to be anywhere near it.

She shut her eyes and stomped. Once . . .

The tile didn't suck in her whole body.

Twice . . .

It felt a little rubbery, and her foot bounced back a little.

Thrice.

"AAAAAH!"

She screamed because this time she *did* think she was getting sucked in, but it was just that the tile slid away so fast she almost fell. She popped open her eyes, quickly adjusted, and pulled herself back to the edge. She peered down to look inside, but all she could see was a simple gray tube. It went down about six feet and looked narrow, like a closed-top waterslide.

Gabby wasn't normally claustrophobic, but the Holobooth seemed like seriously close quarters for one person, never mind two.

"You really think the game will be better in there?" Gabby asked.

"Yes!" Trymmy enthused. Then his eyes and mouth made a sudden O. "One second."

He flashed out his finger and toe claws, then scrambled halfway up the wall until he could duck into one of the tunnels. Gabby heard the sound of rummaging, then a moment later he reappeared brandishing two backpacks. One was large, vinyl, and white with coffee-stained blotches; the other was a soft blue denim about the size of Gabby's own knapsack.

"Jet packs—so we can fly!" Trymmy declared. He slung the white one over his shoulders, draped the blue one around his neck, and scrambled back down the wall. Once he hopped down next to Gabby and retracted his claws, he handed her the blue pack. Though Gabby was dubious about wearing anything that would take up more space in the little tube, she said thanks and shrugged it on.

"You first," Trymmy said.

With trepidation, Gabby took a deep breath and sat at the edge of the round hole. Her feet dangled in. It really did look awfully narrow inside. Still, if this would make Trymmy happy . . .

Gabby squeezed her eyes shut, pushed off from the ledge, and stretched for the floor with her feet. She landed sooner than she'd imagined, and when she opened her eyes, she saw nothing but gray walls, so near they closed her in. Things got even tighter a moment later when Trymmy slid in next to her. Gabby tried to push farther against the wall, but the backpack took up precious inches of space. Trymmy was crushed against her.

Gabby's whole body broke out in sweat. This was *not* a good idea. She thought she'd figured Trymmy out, but this had to be some kind of babysitter practical joke. How could they possibly play a game in here?

Trymmy grinned up at her. "Ready?"

Before Gabby could answer, Trymmy pressed an unseen button, and the tile hatch slid shut.

They were in complete darkness. Gabby couldn't breathe.

"Trymmy . . . ?" Gabby warbled.

"START THE GAME!" Trymmy hollered.

Gabby screamed as a booming sound filled her ears. She felt the sweet relief of space opening up around her, followed by terror as she swung back and up, as if a hook had curled into her spine and yanked her hard. Sparkling lights attacked her eyes, and she closed them, unwilling to see what they might reveal.

"GABBY!" Trymmy's voice somehow sliced through both her fear and the strange booming noise. "Open your eyes! We have to start!"

Gabby obeyed. She screamed again, but this time with

unbelievable delight. Trymmy was *flying*! The white vinyl backpack was a *real* jet pack, just like Trymmy had said! And the booming noise? Gabby realized it was *her own* jet pack! She was flying, too! And the vast world of sparkling lights all around her were stars twinkling through space.

Gabby tilted a little to her right and the jet pack swooshed her gently in that direction. She looked up . . . and *soared*. She tucked her chin to her chest and balled up her knees and squealed as she turned in an accidental somersault that kept the stars spinning even after her body had stopped.

"Trymmy, this is *amazing*!" Gabby cried. "How is this happening?"

"It's a Holobooth," Trymmy said as if it were the most obvious thing in the world. "It knows what I want to do and makes it happen. Now come on, let's play!"

For a second, Gabby had no idea what he meant. They were soaring through space on jet packs—what else could they possibly have to do? Then she noticed Trymmy's clenched fist and remembered the marbles. She plucked one randomly from the front pocket of her jeans where she'd stuffed them and held it out in her fist. She was about to count, but she didn't even open her mouth before a giant 3-D number three appeared in the air between her and Trymmy. The number changed, counting down, as a deeply resonant male voice boomed, "Three . . . two . . . one . . . go!"

Trymmy opened his hand. For the briefest second, Gabby saw a black-and-white marble in his palm, which immediately transformed into a giant blast of whistling wind. At the same time, Gabby opened her own hand. She didn't have the chance to look down and see what it was, but it had to be blue because a massive rush of water exploded out of Gabby's palm and moved in a giant wave toward Trymmy. When the wave collided with the wind, it dispersed into tiny droplets that sprayed over Gabby in a fine mist.

"Trymmy one, Gabby zero," the resonant voice declared. "Prepare for Round Two."

Gabby was breathless. Never in her wildest dreams could she have imagined this. She barely had a chance to take in what had just happened before the voice started counting down numbers and Gabby had to dig into her pocket once again.

"Three . . . two . . . one . . . go!"

Gabby and Trymmy opened their hands. The heat from a massive fireball seared Gabby's face as it flew toward her, but a second later it was doused by another tsunami wave from Gabby. Gabby heard the sizzle and felt the sudden humidity as the water evaporated away.

The game was the greatest experience of Gabby's life. It wasn't just the flying and the powers, either. It was Trymmy. *He* was so into it, whooping and hollering with each win, zooming through space to give Gabby a good-sport high five with each loss. Since the whole game came from his imagination, the powers changed constantly. Water could come in a wave, a geyser, or even a water creature who swallowed its opponent's fire in its gaping maw.

They played until Trymmy was hungry, then went up and grabbed some peanut butter sandwiches. Gabby's heart ached when she noticed Trymmy try to hide his face, as if Gabby might be disgusted watching him eat. She wondered if he had trouble with kids at school. They'd have no idea he was a Troll. They'd just think he was a very different-looking kid. A kid whose nose was so flat, he had to chew with his mouth open if he wanted to breathe. A kid whose nose *tip* hung so low over his lips that it got covered with food, and Trymmy had to lick it clean between bites. A kid whose longer, more dangly moles occasionally slipped between his lips as he chewed and had to be pooked back out again.

"I hope you're not totally grossed out," Gabby said as she leaned toward him conspiratorially.

"What do you mean?" Trymmy muttered, still bent over his elbow as he chewed.

Gabby sighed. "I probably need braces, 'cause I have this space between a couple of my back lower teeth. Every time I eat, something gets stuck there, and I hate feeling it there, so I end up making all these weird, gross faces until I get it out."

Trymmy peeked up from his arm. "Yeah?"

"People don't like to be around it much. You should see my fifth-grade class picture. I look like a cow."

She wasn't lying, and Trymmy seemed to sense it. He smiled, and didn't even lower his head back down when he licked a blob of peanut butter from the tip of his nose.

They went back into the Holobooth after dinner to continue their marble game. Gabby loved it even more now that she knew what to expect. She didn't think once about the time, or when Allynces and Feltrymm might come back, until all of a sudden gravity pulled hard on Gabby's body and she slammed back to her feet. Once again she was squished against Trymmy in a tiny gray tube.

"There you are!" Allynces wailed, and Gabby looked up to see the woman's angry face filling the circle above them. "I told Gabby to hide you down here in case of emergency! I thought something horrible had happened!"

Gabby flushed. "I'm so sorry. It's my fault. I didn't know we couldn't use the Holobooth to play."

"Of course Trymmy can use it to play, that's what it's for," Allynces snapped. "I just don't like that you were *both* down there. I thought the worst."

"I'm so, so sorry." Gabby blushed harder.

Trymmy didn't seem bothered. He climbed out of the Holobooth and hugged his mom hello. They were still embracing when Gabby emerged.

"You're so cuddly this evening, Trymmy," Allynces cooed, hugging him close. "Thank you."

Trymmy turned his head and winked. Warm happiness filled Gabby's chest. He'd given his mom the hug to distract her so she wouldn't stay mad at Gabby.

"Your service is complete, Gabby," Allynces said. "Feltrymm is in the garage. He'll take you home now."

Gabby stuck out her hand. "I just want to thank you so much for entrusting me with Trymmy. He's a great kid, and I hope I get the chance to—"

"Now," Allynces emphasized.

"Right," Gabby said. She started to shrug out of the denim backpack, but Trymmy stopped her.

"Keep it on," he said. "We can play more in the car." Then he turned to Allynces. "I can go with Dad to take her home, right?"

Allynces pursed her lips, but the long hug clearly had her in a good mood.

"Fine," she said, "but you're both in the back."

"Great!" Trymmy chirped. He spun excitedly to Gabby. "Can I grab your stuff?"

Gabby smiled. This happened a lot at the end of a job. The kids felt bad the playdate was ending and they went out of their way to do incredibly nice things for her. She always thought it was really sweet.

"Sure," she said. "That would be great. Thanks."

Gabby watched as Trymmy gathered her things, then ran back to her.

"Let's go!" he cried, and Gabby followed him down a tunnel to a surprisingly ordinary garage and car. They piled into the backseat, and Gabby waited for a ride similar to the one she took in Edwina's limousine. The clock on the dashboard said seven forty-five, and while she had no idea how far from home she was, she assumed it was far enough that only another wild trip would get her back by eight.

She was wrong. As she and Trymmy played the non-Holobooth version of Secret Mega Orbs, Gabby noticed the ride felt completely normal. They might not have even been speeding. It was too dark to see much outside the windows, but then, out of the corner of her eye, Gabby thought she saw the familiar neon window-sign of Bottle Rockets, her favorite candy store. The place was in the Square, a shopping area not too far from home. Was Trymmy's house really that close to hers? Gabby barely trusted her own eyes, until they passed another sign that Gabby would never mistake for anything else, since she saw it every single day.

"That's Brensville Middle School!" she cried. "I go there!"

"Really?" Trymmy said. "I go to Lion's Gate Academy."

This shocked Gabby. "Seriously? I babysit for kids there. I'm there a *lot*. How have I never seen you?"

Trymmy shrugged. He was more interested in the game. "Water beats fire. Your point. Let's play again."

"I can't believe you live close to me," Gabby said as she chose a marble for the next round. "What's your actual address?"

"Don't answer that, Trymmy," Feltrymm's voice sliced from up front. He glared at Gabby through the rearview mirror. "It's information we keep confidential."

Gabby felt hot with shame. No matter how impossibly otherworldly her evening with Trymmy had been, hanging out with him seemed so normal that she forgot this was anything other than a regular ride home. But no. Trymmy and his family were aliens. Aliens with giant stolen artifacts from history all over their property. They would *not* want anyone but the most trusted members of A.L.I.E.N. to know where they lived.

Gabby and Trymmy went back to the game, but all too soon the car pulled up to the curb in front of Gabby's house. "We're here!" Feltrymm said. "Time to get out!"

"I guess you'll need these," Trymmy said, holding out his three marbles.

"Keep them," Gabby said. "That way we can play again next time."

"Didn't you hear me say 'out'?" Feltrymm asked. "Out, out, out!"

"Yes, sir," Gabby said hurriedly, then turned to Trymmy.

"Guess I better take off my jet pack." She shrugged out of the blue denim backpack and reached for her own purple knapsack, but Trymmy stopped her.

"Can I help?" he asked.

His eyes looked wide open and melancholy. She wondered if he was thinking the same thing she was—that there was no way of knowing if she'd ever get the chance to babysit for him again. She smiled. "Of course."

"Turn around, please," Trymmy said.

Gabby did, and Trymmy held out first her jacket and then her knapsack, helping her put them on in true gentlemanly fashion.

"Do I need to explain the definition of the word 'out'?" Feltrymm groused.

"Sorry!"

Gabby quickly slipped from the backseat, but she barely made it out before Feltrymm screeched away, the taillights on his car speeding through her darkened development, then turning out of sight.

Already, Gabby missed Trymmy. If she didn't get to sit for him again, maybe she'd at least run into him the next time she had to meet a kid at Lion's Gate. That would be coincidence, so it wouldn't be the same as breaking Edwina's no-contact-outside-of-official-sitting-jobs rule.

Walking up her lawn, Gabby realized her knapsack felt a

little strange. As a rule, it weighed enough that it sunk down her back a little, but now it sat high on her shoulder blades. Maybe Trymmy had played with the straps. She swung it off to take a look . . .

. . . and realized it wasn't her purple knapsack at all.

It was the denim backpack. Gabby's jet pack. When she'd had it on just a few moments ago, it had been empty. Now there was something inside. Something heavy enough to make the weight feel *similar* to her purple knapsack, but not quite the same.

Gabby unzipped the pack. Inside was a plush Good Luck Troll doll—the kind with the wild hair and naked butt, like she'd mentioned earlier to Edwina. This particular doll was about a foot tall, with bright purple hair, a happy smile, and a butt that wasn't naked. In fact it wore jeans and a white T-shirt, with one word scrawled in marker across the shirt.

"GOTCHA!"

Gabby couldn't believe it. Edwina had warned her, but she'd let it happen anyway. She hadn't blinked an eye when Trymmy had asked "Can I grab your stuff?" She'd thought he was being sweet.

But no. He'd been doing what Trolls always do. He'd been stealing. And now he had Gabby's purple knapsack.

chapter
SIX

This was bad.

Gabby *needed* her knapsack. She couldn't not have it. Her keys, her wallet, her babysitting tricks, her history book . . . they were *all* in the knapsack. Her *thumb drive* was in the knapsack, with the history paper that was due tomorrow!

Gabby raced down the street and screamed at the top of her lungs. "TRYMMY! FELTRYMM!"

But the car was long gone, and so was her backpack. All Gabby saw was a woman with a long gray braid down her back, who was walking her equally gray standard poodle along the sidewalk. The woman wasn't one of Gabby's neighbors, and clearly didn't care for Gabby's outburst. Her green eyes flashed a wicked glare in Gabby's direction, then she led her dog pointedly across the street. Gabby wondered if she should follow them and try to explain, but then she heard a garage door rumble open.

"Gabby?"

It was Alice's voice, and Gabby turned to see her mom pad out their open garage door and down their driveway. As she walked, Alice cinched a red puffy robe more tightly over her pajama bottoms and sweatshirt. "I thought I heard you shouting. Is everything okay?"

"It's fine, Mom!" Gabby called. She quickly trotted back to her house and plucked up the denim backpack she'd dropped on the lawn, then joined Alice next to their car. "I was . . . just yelling good-bye to Zee. Sorry if I was loud."

Alice threw a wiry arm around Gabby's shoulders and pulled her close. "I'm thrilled for the distraction," she admitted. "Let's get you inside."

The garage was packed floor to ceiling with years of memories, regretted purchases, and outgrown clothes and furniture. A single clear path ran from one end to the other, while the rest of the garage could only be accessed through a perilous network of antlike trails that Alice swore let her reach every single item should she be motivated enough to excavate. As the two of them walked toward the inside door, Gabby noticed a large, ragged, and very familiar cardboard box. It was half-full of clothes, stuffed animals, and toys—things Gabby recognized from when she and Carmen were little.

"You're filling the box?" Gabby asked. "I thought you already did this month."

It had been Alice's New Year's resolution to slowly start tackling their garage by filling one large cardboard box a month, then donating the contents to charity. She'd diligently kept to the schedule, even though it hadn't made a dent.

"Getting a jump on next," Alice said, "but I mentioned it to Carmen and she got very worried about Mr. Octopants. I didn't even think she *remembered* Mr. Octopants."

Gabby snorted. Just a little. Alice smiled.

"I know, I know," Alice admitted, "your sister remembers everything. I'm just lucky she brought it up before I finished loading and donated it all." She reached into the cardboard box and pulled out a threadbare stuffed octopus wearing an eight-legged pair of khaki pants. "Packed and ready to go. Can you imagine?"

"Yes," Gabby answered, and both she and Alice shuddered as they pictured Carmen's horror. As they went inside together, Alice held Mr. Octopants at arms' length in front of them, so he could lead the way into the kitchen.

"See? Safe and sound. And look who else I found!" Alice shifted her arms in a flourish to showcase her eldest daughter.

"Gabby was in the giveaway box, too?" Carmen asked. For a girl who was desperately worried about her much-loved stuffie, she barely lifted her head to take in Mr. Octopants and her sister.

"You wish," Gabby shot back.

Carmen was already dressed for bed in a long flannel nightgown and had her favorite dessert arrayed in front of her: parallel rows of blueberries, strawberries, and blackberries, served with a side bowl of whipped cream. The berries were to be eaten one at a time, in the proper order of strawberries, then blueberries, then blackberries, and only after receiving a two-second dip in the whipped cream bowl.

"She wishes no such thing," Alice said as she placed Mr. Octopants on the chair next to Carmen, then breezed over to the refrigerator. "Berries for you, Gabby? I also have chocolate mousse."

"Mousse, please," Gabby said.

Carmen was staring at her.

"What?"

"Where's your knapsack?" Carmen asked. "That one's blue."

Gabby froze. She'd been so involved with Mom and Carmen, she wasn't even thinking about her knapsack.

"She's right," Alice said, frowning. "What happened? You never leave your knapsack anywhere."

"It's...um...it's just with Zee," Gabby stammered. "She spilled robot oil all over it, so she gave me this one to use while she cleans it up."

"Robot oil?" Carmen repeated skeptically.

Gabby was sweating. She pulled off the blue backpack and her jacket. "Something like that. Whatever it was, it spilled."

Peeling off a layer of her clothing did nothing to make Gabby more comfortable. Now her knapsack was back on her mind, and she had no idea if she'd ever see it again.

Then she remembered what Edwina had told her. Trolls had to give riddles to humans from whom they stole. If the human answered the riddle correctly, they'd get their item back.

But how would Trymmy get her a riddle?

Gabby needed to think this out. She was also suddenly desperate to get to her computer. She hoped like crazy she'd saved a copy of her history report onto her hard drive, but she was notoriously bad about that. Still, maybe she'd been more diligent this time....

"Actually, I'm a little tired," she told Alice. "I think I'm going to skip dessert and crawl into bed."

"You should walk," Carmen advised. "Better for your knees."

Gabby scanned her sister's stony face for evidence that

Carmen was joking. There wasn't any, but that didn't mean much.

"I'll do that," Gabby said. "Thanks, Car."

"Mmmm, I don't think so," Alice said. "You won't want to miss this." She placed a bowl in front of Gabby on the table. "I used dark chocolate. I don't want to brag, but the last time I served this, the host gave me a standing ovation. And this will only be here until I take it to tomorrow's luncheon, so believe me, now's the time."

The little glass bowl held a gorgeously swirled mound of rich chocolaty goodness, covered with a perfect dollop of whipped cream and dark chocolate shavings. Gabby may have been worried, but she wasn't nuts. And if she *hadn't* saved a copy of her history report, she was doomed. She'd never be able to re-create the whole thing by tomorrow. Better to enjoy her ignorance while she still could. As for the riddle, Gabby figured Trymmy could only send it to her via Edwina, and the fastest way for Edwina to get it to Gabby was by text. With that in mind, she set her phone screen-up next to her dessert, then sat and scooped a giant spoonful of mousse into her mouth.

She was just digging into her third deliriously thick and gorgeous bite when the doorbell rang.

Gabby froze. Could it be Trymmy with her riddle? She wanted to jump up and see, but Alice was already tightening her robe and striding around the corner to check the peephole.

"Madison Murray?" Alice called a second later.

Gabby choked on her mousse. Then she heard her mother inexplicably opening the door.

"Hi, Mrs. Duran," Madison's voice chirped. "Sorry I'm here so late. Is Gabby available?"

No, Gabby willed her mom to answer. *No, no, no.*

"She's in here eating chocolate mousse!" Carmen called. She smiled impishly for just a second, then turned back to study her berries intently as Madison flounced in.

It was the end of the day, but Madison's tailored blouse and skirt looked perfectly clean and ironed, and her blond hair draped to her shoulders in fresh-blown waves. Even the pink shopping bag she set down next to her looked completely pristine, with crisp folds at every edge.

"Hi, Madison." Gabby forced a smile.

"You have chocolate in your teeth," Madison replied.

Of course she did. Gabby ducked her head and worked her tongue over the entire inside of her mouth.

"Would you like some chocolate mousse, Madison?" Alice asked.

"I can't," Madison said sweetly. "I care about my complexion."

Alice let the insult slide. "And how are things going with H.O.O.T.? It's just two days away, right?"

Madison seemed to glow at the mention of her big event. "Yes! Actually, that's why I'm here. I've decided to honor Gabby with the most important role of the entire auction."

She leaned so close that Gabby could smell whatever lavender lotion or detergent clung to her clothes and skin. "Gabby Duran, you get to be the official H.O.O.T. mascot . . . Hooty the H.O.O.T. Owl!"

With a flourish, Madison reached into the bag and pulled out a giant monstrosity of a brown, fuzzy, person-shaped rug. The arms ended in nappy mittens; the belly had a large circle of what might have been white once, but was now a dingy gray with blotches of uncertain origin; the ankles emptied into extra-large flat plastic flippers.

The chocolate mousse turned to mud in Gabby's stomach.

"I'm supposed to wear that?!" she spluttered. "That's—"

"So precious!" Alice finished.

Gabby wheeled to her mom, positive Alice had to be joking. But no, her mom's face was all round and eager, like she was staring at a litter of kittens instead of a decrepit sheath of matted fur.

"I know, right?" Madison enthused. "And wait until you see the best part!"

Before Gabby could protest, Madison ducked around the back of Gabby's chair and plopped something onto Gabby's head. Gabby was instantly plummeted into a disorienting semidarkness in which she nearly passed out from the mixed scents of mothballs and sweat.

"Wow. You must really hate Gabby." Carmen's muffled voice reached Gabby through the layers of fabric and must.

"Carmen, don't be ridiculous. It's adorable!" Alice crowed.

"I'm wearing an owl head, aren't I," Gabby deadpanned.

"It's so sweet," Alice cooed. "Gabby, you have to see it."

Gabby's mom pulled out her chair, then guided her to the hallway mirror.

"Let me know when you can see," Alice said.

Gabby felt the head tilt and swirl on her shoulders until finally two ovals of mesh netting lined up with her own eyes. Right away, she wished she were back in total blackness. The owl head was the same poofy brown as the body, but with fuzzy white fringes outlining massive goo-goo eyes that must have shifted over the costume's long life because one was cross-eyed and the other stared up and to the left. Add that to the overbite on the bright yellow beak, and the owl looked like it had slammed into one too many trees.

"Don't you love it?" Alice asked. "Now put on the body. I want to see it all together."

"But then you won't be surprised when you see it all Tuesday," Gabby said. "Wouldn't want to ruin that great moment."

Gabby pulled off the head and gulped in fresh air. In the

mirror she saw her face was frighteningly red and sweaty, and her curls stuck out in every direction, as if they were running away to enjoy their newfound freedom.

"Oh good," Madison said. "I'm glad it comes off easily. That way you can unmask when the auction's over so everyone knows how amazing you were running around and dancing and getting the crowd all crazy."

Or more accurately, so everyone could see Gabby look like a giant electrocuted lobster. "Thanks, Madison," Gabby said. "You really thought of everything."

"Speaking of which . . . Mrs. Duran, can I talk to Gabby privately for a second?"

"Of course. Why don't you girls go up to Gabby's room?"

Gabby could think of at least a million reasons why she and Madison shouldn't go up to her room, but she didn't feel like she could say no, so she led her worst enemy upstairs.

"Ew, seriously?" Madison screeched as Gabby opened the door and she saw the wall-to-wall laundry. "How do you live like this?"

Gabby knew she shouldn't care what Madison thought of her mess, but seeing it through Madison's eyes still made her shrink inside. "I was planning to clean it tomorrow," she lied.

"I would hope so." Madison tiptoed along the room's lone strip of visible carpet until she stood in front of Gabby's dresser. Wincing, she ran a finger along its edge, inspected her fingertip for dust, then leaned gingerly against what she clearly saw as an island of cleanliness in a churning ocean of sewage.

Gabby was losing patience. "So, is what you want more or less humiliating than having me run around in a sweaty, disgusting owl suit?"

Madison stood taller against the dresser. "Gabby, I told you—being Hooty is an *honor*. I gave you the part to be nice to you. I want us to be friends."

Gabby searched Madison's eyes for sarcasm and was shocked she couldn't find it. Had Madison actually turned some kind of corner? Was the nasty owl suit her misguided way of holding out an olive branch? Had Gabby's years and years of trying to win her over finally worked?

"Wow, Madison," Gabby said, moved. "That's really great. I always thought we should be—"

"And friends do things for one another, right?" Madison asked.

Inwardly, Gabby slapped herself for falling into Madison's trap. Of course the girl had an ulterior motive.

"What do you want, Madison?"

Madison took a deep breath. Her cheeks grew red, and she looked down at the floor. "I'm in big trouble," she said softly. "I need your help."

Gabby was confused. Once again, Madison looked and

sounded sincere. Was she really turning to Gabby for help?

"What kind of trouble?" she asked.

"It's about H.O.O.T.," Madison admitted. "When I decided to do an auction, Maestro Jenkins didn't think it was a good idea. He said it would be too hard to make the ten thousand dollars we needed. He told me to do something that worked before, like a big carnival, or a bake sale . . ."

"Or the five-K, like last year!" Gabby lit up thinking about it. "That was so fun, remember? Everyone paid to enter, then they bought T-shirts, and we had that raffle at the finish line party, and—"

"Not helping," Madison said.

"Sorry," Gabby said. "But the auction will be great. You've been promoting it like crazy, and you're doing that live streaming thing. Plus, you have that big secret item, right? I mean, that'll be huge."

"It would be," Madison said, "if I had it."

"You don't?"

"I *did*," she clarified, meeting Gabby's eyes for just a second before looking away again. "I mean, I *thought* I did. One of my mom's sorority sisters manages Sukie Elliston. Sukie's on tour, and Mom thought her friend could put together this whole package: concert tickets, backstage pass, hanging out with Sukie. It would have been huge."

"It would have been amazing!" Gabby gushed.

"Sukie Elliston's like the most popular singer *ever*. And did you see that superhero movie she did over the summer? Satchel and I saw it like six times—in the theater!"

Gabby realized Madison's face had paled, and she was staring at Gabby with her lips pursed into a straight, bloodless line. Gabby toned down her enthusiasm and folded her hands together.

"Right," she said. "Not helping again. So what happened to the package?"

"Turns out Mom was wrong. Her friend can't do any of that. Or she *can*, but we found out tonight she *won't*. She's just donating a signed concert poster."

Gabby felt herself deflate at the letdown, but she tried not to let it show. "Okay, but that's something, right?"

"It's not enough," Madison said. "Nothing I have is enough. Not to get to ten thousand dollars. And that means we won't go to MusicFest. Unless some *other* member of the Brensville Middle School Orchestra . . ."

Madison pulled away from her perch and stepped toward Gabby, not even paying attention to the laundry on the floor.

". . . someone who knows *lots* of celebrities . . ."

She moved even closer to where Gabby sat on her bed. Gabby felt like she was being stalked.

". . . and someone who's my very-super-special-good friend . . ."

Madison plopped next to Gabby on the bed and grinned in her face. The grin looked oddly robotic and maniacal. Gabby reared back to get away from it.

". . . unless *that* person calls their celebrity connections right now and gets us a donation as amazing as the Sukie Elliston thing. Then I can announce it just like I'd planned—giving you credit, of course—and we'll go down in history as the team who made the most money for MusicFest ever."

Staring into Madison's eerily intense smile, Gabby considered it. She *did* have celebrities on her babysitting client list. Superstar actors even, like Adam Dent and Sierra Bonita. And she was close enough to them that if she asked, they probably would donate something that fell into the amazing category. Maybe even so amazing that Madison would get huge bids from all over the world with her live streaming auction, and the final price could fund MusicFest not just for this year, but for Gabby's entire middle school career. Gabby could imagine how incredible it would feel, swooping in to save the day. She'd be a hero. The whole orchestra would love her. Maestro Jenkins would love her. Madison would probably want to be her best friend for real.

But Gabby could also imagine how she'd feel *after* the auction, when people she barely knew buffeted her for information about the Bonita-Dents' personal lives. Or asked her to try and get more out of them for other events. Or tried to follow her around so maybe they could meet the actors one day.

There was a reason Gabby kept her client list to herself. She liked the people who hired her for who they were, not their celebrity, and she respected their privacy. Even if it was for a good cause, she didn't want to take advantage.

Gabby reached up and twirled a curl around her finger. "What makes you think I know celebrities?"

"Please, Gabby. We've all seen you get picked up by limousines. And the helicopter on the soccer field?"

Oops, Gabby thought, popping the curl in her mouth. That hadn't exactly been inconspicuous. But when the president of the United States needs a babysitter, sometimes she needs that babysitter *now*.

"Okay, I might know a few celebrities," Gabby admitted. "But I can't ask them for things. I'm sorry. I can help you in other ways though. Like, maybe if we added something to the auction, like a car wash or a face painting booth or—"

"None of that will work, Gabby!" Madison snapped. "Now here's the deal. No one knows I had a celebrity connection, but everyone believes you do. Either you help me, or I'll say *you* were the one who was supposed to deliver the Special Can't-Miss Surprise and you backed out."

"But that's a lie!"

"No one else will know that. And when we don't earn

enough for MusicFest, and we don't get to go for the first time *ever*, everyone will blame *you*. Not me, *you*. And you know what? You'll deserve it, because you're being totally selfish. You're supposed to *care* about orchestra, and you don't. You just care about keeping your special little celebrities to your special little self. So you think about that, Gabby Duran, and if you change your mind, call me. If not . . ."

Madison didn't even bother finishing the threat. She tried to flounce out of the room, but a pair of Gabby's underwear caught on her shoe. She roared in frustration as she kicked it away. "And clean your room!"

This time she made it out. Gabby heard her pound down the steps and out the door.

Gabby flopped back onto her bed. The knapsack, the owl costume, Madison . . . It was too much. And it was all completely unfair! She'd been nice to Trymmy, and she'd always tried to be nice to Madison, but they still went out of their way to wreck her life. What she really wanted to do was dive into a vat of her mom's dark chocolate mousse and forget everything else.

"Hey."

Alice's voice came from the bedroom door. Gabby grunted something that may or may not have sounded like a reply. She felt the pressure of her mom sitting down on the bed.

"I owe you an apology," Alice said.

"For not bringing me more chocolate mousse?" Gabby asked.

"Nope," Alice said, "because *that* I actually did."

Gabby bolted upright. Sure enough, her mom held a bowl of dark chocolate heaven. Gabby grabbed it and took a bite. Already she felt a million times better.

"I owe you an apology for listening in," Alice continued. "I heard what Madison said, and I want to help. I can call her mother and—"

"Don't, please," Gabby muttered between bites. "You know her mom. She'll just stick up for whatever Madison says, even if it's a lie."

Alice opened her mouth to object, but then she closed it again with a sigh. "You're right. Can I have a bite?"

Gabby handed Alice the spoon and her mom skimmed it over the dessert, catching an even ratio of whipped cream and mousse.

"*Am* I being selfish?" Gabby asked. "I mean, I *could* make a call and get something amazing for the auction."

"You could," Alice said. She pointed the spoon at Gabby. "And how would that make you feel?"

"Awful," Gabby said, snatching the spoon so she could grab some more mousse. "Like I was betraying people I care about."

Alice's mouth curled up in a half-smile. "Then . . ."

"But maybe the celebrities wouldn't feel that way!" Gabby interjected. "Maybe Adam and Sierra would *want* to help!"

"I didn't ask how they would feel," Alice said. "I asked how *you* would feel. And if you feel like you'd be breaking a trust, you shouldn't do it. And you certainly shouldn't compromise your beliefs because of some threat by an over-indulged little snoot."

Gabby laughed. "That's the closest I've ever heard you come to saying something mean about anyone."

"Well she deserved it," Alice said. She leaned over and kissed Gabby on top of her head. "You're doing the right thing, baby. And don't worry. I have a feeling it'll all work out."

Gabby couldn't fathom how that could possibly be true, but it sounded good, so for the moment she decided to believe it. After her mom left, Gabby checked her phone, but there was nothing from Edwina, no riddle.

Then she did what she'd dreaded most. She rolled out of bed and moved slowly to her desk. She tapped her computer keyboard to wake up the machine, then murmured out loud, begging the Gabby of the past two months to have been way more responsible and diligent than she remembered her being.

"Please, Gabby," she implored herself as she clicked through files. "Please tell me you saved the history report."

Gabby laughed triumphantly as she saw a copy of the file. She clicked it open . . .

. . . and her whole being sunk as she stared at a bullet-point outline on the screen.

She checked the date on the file and realized it was a month old. Everything she'd done in the past month was *only* on the thumb drive, and the thumb drive was on her keychain, in her knapsack, somewhere with Trymmy.

Gabby buried her head in her hands and gripped her hair. She was in bigger trouble than she'd ever been in her life, and that included being chased by an evil G.E.T.O.U.T. agent who wanted to kill her. The report was due tomorrow, at the beginning of sixth period history class. Ms. McKay had said over and over again that there'd be no extensions. Even if you were home sick, you had to e-mail it in on time. There was no way Gabby could re-create a month's work by then, even if she stayed up all night and skipped every class until history. If she didn't get her thumb drive back, she'd get a zero on a paper that was thirty percent of her grade. She could go from a B to a D. And if her grade fell that low, Alice would pull her out of orchestra. She wouldn't let Gabby babysit. She'd have to give up *everything*.

The room was getting swimmy. Gabby was hyperventilating. She tucked her head between her knees like she'd seen in movies, but it only made her dizzier.

She needed to talk to someone. It was late, but she could call Zee and she would answer. Zee's cousin Kat was in

England for a semester abroad and liked to call Zee at weird times, so Zee always kept her phone on and close by, even at night.

Gabby had already started dialing when she got a better idea. What she *really* needed was Trymmy's riddle. If she had that, she could solve it and get her knapsack back, ideally before sixth period. How could she prod Trymmy to get her the riddle right away?

Edwina.

Edwina had said that if Gabby saw anyone strange following her, she should take a picture and Edwina would somehow see it. Following that logic, Gabby grabbed a piece of notebook paper and scrawled out a message: "TRYMMY TOOK MY KNAPSACK. NEED RIDDLE A.S.A.P. PLEASE!" She snapped a picture, then stared at her phone for ten minutes, willing it to respond. When it didn't, she decided to go to bed but brought her phone with her. If Edwina did reply, Gabby didn't want to miss it. She closed her eyes . . .

. . . and opened them when a duck quacked into her ear.

It wasn't a real duck, it was her e-mail alert.

Gabby grabbed the phone. It said it was five in the morning, and she had one new message.

The message was from TRYMMY01@trollnet.xqz.

The subject line? "YOUR RIDDLE."

chapter
SEVEN

despite Edwina's warning about not having contact with aliens outside babysitting, Gabby didn't hesitate to click the e-mail open. She desperately needed the riddle, and reading an e-mail couldn't possibly put Trymmy in any danger. Besides, how could Trymmy have gotten Gabby's address except from Edwina? That meant Edwina had to approve.

Gabby read the message. It said:

FOR GABBY DURAN
A RIDDLE IN TWO PARTS

I.

You'll find it in a kitchen, any old day.
Take away its blueness, and it'll be okay.
Pull off its tail, and it'll sound like a dove,
When it's good, it makes you things you love.

II.

Life is often a volume of grief,
I need your help to turn a leaf.
My spine is stiff,
And my body is pale,
But I'm always ready,
To tell a tale.

Bring me the object described in these rhymes,
And your knapsack will come back in record time.

She waited for an answer to spring into her head, but when nothing immediately came, she quickly forwarded the e-mail to Zee, then called to wake her up. It was too early for a call, but this was dire. As the phone rang, Gabby moved to her computer and pulled up the riddle there.

"Kat?" Zee mumbled sleepily.

"Sorry, Zee. It's Gabby."

"Gabs!" Instantly, Zee sounded completely awake. "Is

everything okay? Did you get me alien DNA?"

"No, but the alien probably got some of mine. Does DNA stick to knapsacks?"

"Is that a riddle? 'Cause it's way too early for riddles."

"I hope that's not true," Gabby said, then she told Zee everything. Before she had even finished the entire story, she heard Zee tapping on computer keys.

"Okay," Zee said. "I have it on my screen . . . I'm reading . . . I'm thinking . . ."

"Yeah, me too," Gabby said. Then she jumped in her chair and screamed so loud she was afraid she'd wake up her mom and Carmen. "Oh! I think I have it! I think I have the second part!"

"Hit me," Zee said.

"Okay, check it out," Gabby said. "'Life is often a volume of grief, I need your help to turn a leaf. My spine is stiff, and my body is pale, but I'm always ready, to tell a tale.' It's a book, right? It has to be. A *volume*, turning a *leaf*, the *spine*, *telling a tale* . . . and the pale body part is just that the pages are white so you can read the ink!"

"Yes!" Zee crowed. "Now let's look at the first part."

"Okay," Gabby said. "'You'll find it in a kitchen, any old day.' A blowtorch?"

"A *blowtorch*?"

"Yeah. For caramelizing the top of a crème brûlée."

"Okay, Gabs? Think about a *normal* person's kitchen, not a my-mom's-an-awesome-caterer kitchen."

"An anti-griddle?"

"I'm banning you from working on this line of the riddle," Zee said. "Let's look at the rest."

For a moment there was nothing but the sound of the two girls murmuring to themselves as they read the clue out loud.

"Oh! Oh! Yes! I have it!" Zee cried.

"You do?"

"Yeah, yeah! It's all about the third line: 'pull off its tail, and it'll sound like a dove.'"

"What animal sounds like a dove when you pull off its tail?" Gabby asked.

"No animal. The clue is saying you get the sound a dove makes when you pull off the tail of the *answer*—the last letter of the answer. So what sound does a dove make?"

"A dove coos," Gabby said.

"Right! So when you pull off the last letter of the answer, you'll get 'coo'—the sound a dove makes. Pull off its tail and it'll sound like a dove!"

Gabby jounced her knees up and down. They were so close. She could feel it. "Okay, so the answer has to be C-O-O-something." Her whole body electrified as she got it. "COOK! It has to be cook!"

"Totally! And it can go with the other clues. A cook is in

the kitchen, any old day; when a cook is good, it makes you things you love."

"And the blueness?" Gabby asked.

"Just figured that out. It's totally cool, and makes me want to meet your alien even more. Know what cobalt is?"

"It's a paint color, right?"

"A *blue* paint color," Zee affirmed. "But it's also an element on the periodic table, with the atomic symbol . . . wait for it . . . *CO*."

Gabby's eyes grew wide. "So if you take away the *blueness* from 'cook,' you take away the C-O . . ."

". . . and you're left with O-K. 'Take away its blueness, and it'll be okay!' Dude, is it bad that I'm kind of the teeniest bit psyched this kid took your knapsack and gave us this riddle?"

"Yes. Very bad," Gabby replied. "But at least we have the answer. The first part is 'cook,' and the second part is 'book,' so Trymmy needs a cookbook!"

"And whose mom is a caterer with like a zillion cook-books?" Zee asked.

"Mine!" Gabby cheered. "Zee, this is perfect! Now I just have to do the 'bring me the object described in these rhymes' part. That's easy. Trymmy goes to Lion's Gate Academy. I'll grab a cookbook, ride my bike there, and get him before he starts class!"

"Wait," Zee said. "Didn't you say Edwina gave you the

no-go on seeing alien kids when you're not sitting them?"

"Yes, but she also told me I was the one who had to get my stuff back if it was taken," Gabby pointed out. "The riddle says bring him the object—I can't do that if I don't go see him, so that's got to be an exception, right?"

"Totally an exception," Zee agreed. "You're following the riddle instructions. That's what you're supposed to do."

"Exactly," Gabby affirmed. "And if I *don't* get the bag, and I get a zero on my paper, and my grade drops, and I can't babysit anymore, then I can't help A.L.I.E.N. at all."

"You're right," Zee said. "This is the call. We go to Lion's Gate."

"We?" Gabby echoed dubiously.

"We," Zee maintained, "because I can get you there and back fast enough that you won't miss any classes."

"Seriously?" Gabby asked. Lion's Gate Academy wasn't exactly close to Brensville Middle School by bike. Gabby had already resigned herself to skipping her first few classes, but it would be amazing if she didn't have to. "How?"

"Just trust me," Zee said. "Grab a cookbook, ride your bike to our school, then meet me at the robotics shed as soon as humanly possible."

Whatever Zee had in mind, Gabby trusted it would be brilliant.

"Done," she said, then hung up and quickly scrambled

through a shower, getting dressed, and mussing some goo through her curls to tamp down the frizz factor. She tossed everything she'd need for the day into the blue denim bag, all the while rejoicing that she'd be swapping it out for her knapsack in no time at all.

With the house still quiet, she ducked downstairs to pick a cookbook for Trymmy. She figured she'd take whichever one looked the least familiar, since maybe that would be one Alice wouldn't miss. She readied her phone, too, so she could take a picture of whatever book she chose. That way she could order a new copy online and have a replacement before Alice knew it was gone.

Gabby had planned to beeline for the pantry, which doubled as a cookbook library, but then she saw the giant cardboard box on the kitchen table. It was the same one Gabby had seen in the garage last night, only now it was full. Alice must have been motivated to finish loading it after Gabby and Carmen went to bed. Gabby peered into it, just to make sure she didn't see any toys that Carmen might randomly freak out over one day if they were gone.

She didn't, but she did notice something on top of the pile of random odds and ends.

It was a book. The thing was greenish-colored, and very thick and old-looking. Gabby leaned over curiously to look at it more closely. She expected it to be a desperately boring old textbook from her mother's college days, maybe calculus or accounting.

Instead, what she saw on the cover made her almost squeal out loud.

Joy of Cooking.

Gabby's insides danced. It was a cookbook! An old, faded cookbook at the very top of the giveaway pile, which meant Alice didn't want it anymore! Gabby hefted the book and hugged it to her chest—it was perfect!

A little too perfect. Keeping the book close, Gabby wheeled around in both directions. Was Edwina here? Had she put the book on top of the pile? It wasn't impossible. Even though she'd *said* A.L.I.E.N. wouldn't get involved if the Trolls stole anything from Gabby, was it that hard to believe she wanted to help?

It wasn't hard to believe at all, and the small knot of worry inside Gabby finally relaxed. Despite what she'd said to Zee, Gabby had still felt a little uneasy about violating Edwina's no-visits rule, but this was as clear an indication as Gabby could get that the woman approved.

Gabby saw no sign of Edwina, but she knew from experience that meant nothing.

"Thank you," she whispered to anyone who might be listening, then stuffed the cookbook into Trymmy's denim backpack and tiptoed up to her mom's room. Alice was fast asleep, her always-wild hair splayed Medusa-like over her pillow. Gabby knelt down and leaned in close.

"Mom?"

She reached out and shook Alice's arm gently until Alice said something like, "Mmmphmmmblllbrrphlllt."

Gabby took that as a signal to keep going.

"Zee and I have those history papers due today, and we want to go over them together one last time," Gabby lied. She was getting way too good at lying, but she reminded herself that it wasn't a *complete* lie, and in general she only lied when absolutely necessary. "I'm going to ride my bike and meet her at school early. Is that okay?"

"Mbbblllggrrphhmmmbleeee."

"Mom?" Gabby shook Alice's arm again. She couldn't leave unless she was sure Alice understood her, or Alice would panic when she got up and Gabby wasn't there.

Now Alice opened her eyes. "Gabby?" she mumbled sleepily. "Hey, baby. Is everything okay?"

Gabby gave her the story again, and this time Alice nodded. "That's fine. Here, let me get you some breakfast."

She started to roll out of bed, but Gabby stopped her. "It's okay, I'll grab something with Zee. You can rest. The alarm won't go off for another twenty minutes."

Alice smiled. "Thanks, baby," she murmured. "Ride safe. Love you."

She plopped her head back on the pillow and instantly fell back to sleep. Just in case she woke up thinking their conversation was a dream, Gabby scrawled a quick note on the pad of paper on Alice's nightstand—the one where Alice wrote all the wild recipes she came up with as she slept. Then Gabby sidled out of the room, ran downstairs, grabbed her purple jacket, and sprinted to her bike. Luckily, the orchestra members were using all their practice periods to do things for H.O.O.T. There was no way Gabby could carry the backpack *and* her French horn on her bicycle.

Thinking about H.O.O.T. made Gabby a little nauseous, so she pumped her pedals even harder to push it out of her head. The sun was barely up and the frigid morning wind bit into her face, but she was riding so hard that the chill was a relief.

It wasn't long before she pulled her bike up to the robotics shed, which was the least shedlike structure Gabby had ever seen. It was an enormous brick building that, as Gabby understood it, was used generations ago for electives like home ec and shop. For years the school used it only for storage, but when Principal Tate took over the robotics club, he renovated the space and dedicated it to his team.

Was Zee already here? Had Gabby beaten her?

She reached out for the doorknob and nearly fell in as Zee whisked open the door. Her braids clung to her face in sweaty strips, but she was grinning. "Perfect!" she said. "You got the book?"

Gabby shrugged off the blue backpack and tugged out the giant tome. Zee grimaced. "Wow. I'm bored just looking at it."

"I bet that's why my mom had it in the charity pile," Gabby said. "So how are we going to get to Lion's Gate?"

Zee grinned wider, then pushed the robotics shed door all the way open and had Gabby hold it so she could roll something out. The "something" looked like a surfboard, but with four sets of skateboard wheels and some kind of jet booster on the back.

"What *is* that?" Gabby asked.

"It's a surfboard, but with four sets of skateboard wheels and a jet booster on the back," Zee said.

Gabby cringed. "Tell me you don't expect me to ride that thing to Lion's Gate Academy."

"No way! You'd kill yourself!" Zee said.

"Good."

"*I'm* riding it," Zee said, "You're holding on tight." She ducked back inside the robotics shed and came out with her overstuffed camouflage duffel slung over her back and two helmets in her hands. She gave one helmet to Gabby and put the other on herself. When she spoke again, Gabby was only slightly surprised to find she could hear Zee perfectly through a helmet-to-helmet microphone system. It was the kind of detail only Zee would think of.

"Let me get on first," Zee said. "Then step on the back half, hold on to my waist, and bend your knees."

Gabby did as she was told. Zee had tried to teach her to ride a skateboard a thousand times in their years of friendship, but Gabby always toppled over the second both feet were off the ground. This board felt even wobblier than anything Zee had given her before. She tottered precariously, swaying back and forth. She tried to get a good hold on Zee's waist, but it was covered by the camouflage duffel. Gabby's arms could barely stretch around the bag.

"Just promise me you'll warn me before we start," Gabby said nervously. "It'll be worse if I'm sur—AAAAAAA!!!!!"

With no hint at all, Zee stomped her foot on a hidden button, and the engines jumped to life. Somehow Zee had rigged them not to make a sound, but they jolted the surfboard forward at what felt like light speed. Gabby's stomach lagged behind as the rest of her bounced over dirt and grass so quickly her feet flew into thin air. Only a little bit, but to Gabby it may as well have rocketed her into space. She curled her fingers tightly into Zee's duffel bag and tried to will her body to stay upright.

"Get low!" Zee cried through the intercom. "Like me! You'll fall if you stand straight up!"

Zee hunched lower, bending her knees and holding out her arms for balance. Gabby wouldn't hold out her arms for anything, but she forced herself into a knock-kneed squat.

"Are you sure this is a good idea?" Gabby asked through chattering teeth.

"I wasn't a second ago," Zee admitted. "I thought the board might fall apart as soon as it took off. But it's working! Cool, right? I'll get us to Lion's Gate in ten minutes."

Zee was a wheeled-vehicle expert. She knew every skateable back road and path in the entire township. She used them all now, leaning her body to steer through brush, around stumps, and over rutted dirt trails. Gabby tried to close her eyes, but that only made her feel more unbalanced. Instead she focused on a small patch of camouflage like nothing else existed in the world.

Suddenly, a fierce jolt threw Gabby into the dirt in the middle of a thicket of bushes. Zee leaped off the board and crouched next to her.

"You okay, Gabs? I'm so sorry. I should have told you we were stopping."

But Gabby was too transfixed to care. The thicket where Zee had stopped reared up against a beautifully manicured field. Stone steps led from the field down to a lower courtyard, where basketball, handball, and tetherball courts shared open space with a playground, another field, and a sprawl of cabins. The cabins looked rustic from the outside, but Gabby had seen their insides and knew they held the finest in educational technology, plus a kaleidoscope of student art, projects, and writing samples.

Lion's Gate Academy.

Gabby and Zee had made even better time than they'd hoped. It was only seven thirty. The doors to the school didn't officially open until eight, when everyone arrived. Then there was a half hour of before-class playtime, during which Gabby could find Trymmy, hand him the cookbook, get her knapsack, then zoom back to Brensville ideally right on time for her first class of the day.

"Zee, you are a genius," Gabby proclaimed.

"'Very Superior' I'm told is the official classification," Zee said, "but I'll take it."

The two friends settled in the grass and waited. Gabby was too anxious to do anything but watch the field. Zee opened her camouflage duffel bag and spread out her robot parts to work on Wilbur.

Gabby whispered down the last seconds. "Three . . . two . . . one . . ."

At eight o'clock on the dot the fields and playgrounds burst to life with kids wearing the khakis, reds, and blues of the Lion's Gate Academy's uniform. Gabby strained her eyes looking for Trymmy, but from her vantage point every kid looked alike.

"I'm going in," Gabby said. She sprang to her feet, stormed out of the thicket, and ran onto the giant field.

"Hey, Gabby!"

"Gabby Duran!"

"Hi, Gabbeeeee!!!"

Gabby had babysat a bunch of Lion's Gate kids. She returned every wave, smile, and torpedo-slam hug, but all the while her eyes searched wildly for Trymmy.

Then a deep, stern voice boomed, "Gabby? Is that you, soldier?"

It was Gareth, Lion's Gate's head playground monitor. Gabby often ended up chatting with him after class while whatever kid she was sitting hung out on the playground with friends.

"It is," Gabby replied, eyes still darting all around. "Hi, Gareth."

Gareth straightened into a salute. He had been a marine and still looked the part, with bulging muscles and close-cropped hair. He knew Gabby's dad had been in the military and was lost in the line of duty. Out of respect, he always treated Gabby like a fellow soldier, sometimes even an officer.

"At ease," Gabby said, returning his salute. "Hey, do you

know Trymmy? I left something at his place when I was babysitting him yesterday. I'm supposed to meet him and pick it up."

"Trymmy?" Gareth asked, scrunching up his face. "I didn't know he was one of yours. Strange little guy, that one. Don't you think?"

Gabby had always liked Gareth, so she was surprised by his words. Gareth worked with these kids. He was supposed to care about them. How could he call one of them strange? The word was Gabby's least favorite on the planet. It was what people loved to call Carmen when they didn't want to bother to go any deeper. She was "strange" because of her too-short bangs, or the precise way she ate her food, or her lack of comforting smiles in conversation.

"Strange how?" Gabby retorted, and Gareth must have heard the challenge in her voice because he stepped back and blushed.

"'Strange' wasn't really the right word. He's just . . . you know . . . unique."

Gabby raised an eyebrow. "Unique" was the same as "strange," and Gareth knew it.

"Look in the Lost and Found," Gareth finally muttered. "That's where he usually hangs."

"He hangs out in the Lost and Found?" Gabby gawped. "Alone?"

Gareth rubbed the back of his neck uncomfortably. "He seems to like it there."

Gabby shook her head and walked away. At Brensville, the Lost and Found was a smelly Dumpster behind the gym. At Lion's Gate, it had a whole building to itself—a shack that used to house the preschoolers before their new building opened. Inside it looked a lot like a very small department store, with uniform shirts, jackets, and pants—how did kids lose their pants?—dangling off hangers in racks. Shelving units showed off abandoned lunch boxes, notebooks, and even musical instruments, which was a crime against everything Gabby held dear. She looked up and down every aisle and found him in the last one. He was lying on the floor under a rack of blue and red uniform sweaters, reaching up his arms to bat at their hems and make them swing.

"Trymmy?" she asked.

"Gabby!" Trymmy bolted to a seated position, which made the sweater-bottoms hang low on his thick forehead like a hat. "I was hoping you'd come! You got my riddle?"

"Got it and solved it," Gabby said. She shrugged off the denim bag and pulled out the old green-covered volume. "A cookbook. Am I right?"

Trymmy spread his bulbous lips in a smile. "See for yourself." He nodded behind Gabby.

When she turned, her purple knapsack was right there,

sitting on the floor. "How did you . . . ? How did that . . . ? Was that there a second ago?"

"Nope," Trymmy said. "That's just the way it works. The riddle gets answered and the item goes back where it belongs."

Gabby shoved the cookbook into Trymmy's arms, then snatched up her knapsack and hugged it close. "Thank you. I'm still mad at you for taking it, though."

Trymmy got to his feet, unintentionally burying his head in sweaters. "Don't be mad, please? You can't be mad. Stealing is what Trolls do. We can't help it. And you gave me permission. I asked if I could grab your stuff and you said yes."

"Yeah, but I didn't mean—" Gabby stopped herself, because she knew Trymmy was right. She sighed in defeat. "Okay, yeah, I kind of did."

"So you're not mad."

"No." Gabby scooched down on her knees so she could unzip her knapsack and reach inside. Trymmy dropped down next to her.

"Oh come on, you don't think I took anything, do you?" he asked. "I wouldn't do that!"

Gabby pulled out her keys, her purple thumb drive blissfully attached to the ring. She kissed it.

"I didn't think you took anything," she assured Trymmy. "I just had to make sure this was here." She quickly put her keys back, added in the few items she'd had in the blue backpack—his Good Luck Troll included—then shouldered her knapsack and stood.

"Thanks for the riddle, Trymmy. I hope we get to play again sometime."

"Like now!" Trymmy scrambled back to his feet so quickly that all his bigger moles boinged up and down. "Classes don't start for a while. I have my marbles."

He dug into his pocket and pulled out the three marbles Gabby had given him the night before. Gabby's heart melted a little.

"You keep them with you?" she asked.

Gabby thought she could detect the slightest blush behind his sea of moles, but he looked away before she could really tell. "Same pants," he muttered. "That's the only reason."

Gabby smiled. "I'd love to play, but I have to get to school, too." She bent down and wrapped Trymmy in a huge hug. He stayed stiff in her arms, but Gabby wasn't bothered. She was used to that with Carmen. "I hope I get to see you sometime soon."

She released Trymmy and ran, zooming out of the Lost and Found and across the fields. She promised herself that even if she never got to sit for Trymmy again, she'd ask Edwina to arrange a way to see him. It wouldn't be hard. She was at the school often enough. She'd just clear it with Edwina first, then sneak in some extra time at the Lost and Found.

Gabby was panting hard by the time she reached Zee, who must have seen Gabby coming. She was already repacking her duffel bag.

"How'd it go?" Zee asked.

Gabby spun around to show the knapsack on her back.

"You're home!" Zee cheered. She wrapped her arms around the bag in a welcome-back hug.

The two of them were climbing onto the jet-powered surfboard when Gabby's phone rang. Gabby wouldn't have answered, but it was Alice, and Gabby was afraid she was worried. Maybe she'd forgotten about their morning conversation or missed Gabby's note.

"Hi, Mom!"

"Hi, baby. I noticed you took the cookbook."

Gabby felt a quick sting of panic, like she'd done something wrong. "Yeah, I saw it on top of the giveaway pile. Is that okay?"

Alice laughed. "Of course it's okay. How else were you going to get it to Madison? I'm just glad you checked your e-mail this morning. I was so tired when you woke me, I forgot to say anything. I thought I'd have to drive it over to you at school."

It seemed like Alice was speaking English, but the words made no sense. "My e-mail?" Gabby asked.

"Yes, so you saw Madison's. So strange, though—the one I got said she sent it at seven thirty this morning, but that can't be right or you wouldn't have seen it before you left. I'm so glad you did, though, and that you understood and grabbed the book. I do worry she might have hyped it up a little too much, you know? I mean, it *is* a collector's item, but you have to be into that kind of thing. Still, I *have* seen copies go for as much as five thousand dollars."

Nope, still sounded like gibberish.

"Um, Mom?" Gabby tried. "I don't really understand—"

"I know what you're going to say," Alice stopped her, "but I promise I won't miss it. I got it for next to nothing at a yard sale when I first started the business, and I haven't even looked at it in I-don't-know-how-many years. I wasn't even sure I'd find it in the garage. And yes, I know we could sell it ourselves and use the money for other things, but I want this MusicFest trip for you, Gabby. Your orchestra deserves it. You deserve it. For being so strong and brave and principled. It's my pleasure to help."

"Pleasure to help?" Gabby echoed. She was thoroughly confused, but she thought repeating her mom's words might somehow lead to better answers.

"With the book," Alice said. "That's why I dug it up last night, and why I e-mailed Mrs. Murray to tell her all about it and promise you'd give it to Madison at school today."

"At school today," Gabby said. She was still echoing, but clammy fingers of dread had started to crawl up her spine and over her scalp. The pieces were starting to come together, but in a way that made her completely nauseous.

"So have a great day, baby! Bye!"

"Bye," Gabby answered weakly as her mom clicked off. She held the phone away from her ear and just stared at it.

"Gabs?" Zee asked. "Gabs, is everything okay? You look green."

"I have to check my e-mail," Gabby said in a dull monotone.

"Okay," Zee said. "But if you do get sick, make sure to do it *behind* the board. It'll seriously mess up our traction if we have to ride over it."

Gabby nodded, but she wasn't really paying attention. She was reading an e-mail from Madison. It was one of her rah-rah auction blasts sent to her whole list of potential bidders from all over the world, pulled together from both the school's mailing list and from begging everyone for any and all e-mail addresses they could send her way. The subject line read: "THE MOMENT YOU'VE ALL BEEN H.O.O.T.ING FOR IS HERE!" and the body was an extended rave about Madison's long-promised secret surprise auction item—a first edition signed copy of *Joy of Cooking*, a collector's piece that would normally fetch tens of thousands of dollars, but would go for a fraction of that at the Brensville Middle School Orchestra H.O.O.T. Auction.

That was the reason the book was out. It hadn't come from Edwina at all. It had come from Alice, who had promised it to Madison . . . who had just promised it to pretty much the entire globe.

Gabby didn't know when she'd swallowed an elephant, but she suddenly felt one deep in her throat, pressing down on her chest.

"Gabs?" Zee asked. "You okay? Now you look like you're going to pass out."

"I'll be fine," Gabby said dully. "I'll be right back."

Moving like the wind, she raced back down toward the Lost and Found.

She needed to talk to Trymmy. *Immediately.*

chapter
EIGHT

"You came back! You want to play Secret Mega Orbs?"

When Gabby stormed into the Lost and Found, Trymmy had been sitting on the floor, leaning against the wall and distractedly sucking the end of a long mole. Now he was on his feet and smiling wide.

"I can't. . . ." Gabby was breathless from her sprint back to campus, and had to rest her hands on her thighs to gasp in more air. "I just need . . . to talk to you . . . I need the book back."

"What book?"

"The cookbook. I'll replace it with another one. You can

even hold my knapsack until I do." Gabby slipped the knapsack off her shoulders, took a second to dig out and pocket her keys and thumb drive, then held it out to him.

Trymmy shook his head—a move that didn't budge his tall corona of hair in the slightest. "I can't."

"Of course you can!"

"No. I *can't.* I don't even have the cookbook anymore."

"Trymmy, you have it. I just gave it to you!"

"I know," Trymmy said, pushing his glasses back up his wide-potato nose, "but it already went back to my collection."

"What?"

"Remember when your knapsack appeared after you answered the riddle?" Trymmy asked. "It's the same thing, only the opposite. When you gave me the cookbook, it poofed away into my collection."

Gabby shook her head. "That's crazy. I would have seen that. I would have noticed if I handed you a cookbook and it disappeared."

Trymmy shrugged. "Humans see what they want to see. If something doesn't make sense to them, they ignore it or pretend it's something else. How else do you think aliens have been around so long without most of you knowing we're here?"

It was a good point. Gabby couldn't guarantee that the book hadn't poofed away without her registering it. "Okay," she said, smacking her palms down on her jeans, "how do we get it back?"

Trymmy grinned mischievously. "You answer a riddle."

"Trymmy, this is important. No."

"It's not my choice," Trymmy insisted. "It's how it works. I'm a Troll. You *let* me take the book, so if you want it back, you have to answer a riddle."

Gabby scrunched her fingers into her curls with a frustrated groan, then dropped them down again. "Fine. Give me the riddle. I'll solve it right now."

Trymmy widened his magnified eyes and raised his unibrow. "Gabby! That's not how it works. You don't get the riddle right away. I'll e-mail it to you."

"When?!" Gabby wailed.

"It won't be that long," Trymmy said.

They both noticed the sudden increase in noise outside the Lost and Found. It could only mean students were pouring off the fields and filing past them toward the classrooms.

"I gotta go," Trymmy said. "You coming?"

Gabby didn't want to go anywhere without the cookbook, and she certainly didn't want to go to school and face Madison, but she didn't really have a choice. She walked out of the Lost and Found, but the minute they got outside they were met by a sweet-as-honey voice.

"Trymmy! What luck! I was going to wait for you in the classroom, but here you are!"

Gabby and Trymmy both looked up to see a smiling woman, maybe in her late sixties. She wore khaki-colored corduroy pants and a blue button-down shirt, with a long navy-blue Lion's Gate Academy cardigan over the whole ensemble. A matching wool cap was pulled low over her ears and covered all her hair. Her green eyes radiated kindness.

The woman looked oddly familiar to Gabby, but Gabby wasn't sure why.

Trymmy clearly didn't know her either. "Who are you?" he asked.

"I'm Ms. Farrell. I'm substituting for Ms. Roth today. She's ill."

Ah, that explained it. She was a substitute teacher. Subs go to all the area schools. Gabby must have seen her at Brensville.

"I have some fun stuff planned for us today," Ms. Farrell continued. "An off-campus field trip! We're working on algebra, right?"

Trymmy nodded.

"Good. So tell me"—Ms. Farrell leaned in conspiratorially—"why won't Goldilocks drink a glass of water with eight pieces of ice in it?"

Trymmy scrunched his face for a second, then his whole expression spread into a wide smile. "Because it's too cubed!"

Ms. Farrell held up her hand and Trymmy smacked it. They both laughed out loud.

Laughing at math jokes. This was clearly Gabby's cue to go. She peeked at her phone and realized her classes were starting *now*. She'd be late, but if she got back to Zee right away, they'd both still make most of first period. Or better— Gabby could slip into the computer lab and use the end of first period to print out her history paper so she'd have time to go over it before she turned it in.

"Bye, Trymmy," she said. "Talk to you *soon*."

She pointed to him with the last word, stressing its importance, then took off at a run while he walked away in the other direction with Ms. Farrell.

Gabby had almost reached Zee when her chest grew tight. It wasn't from running. She had suddenly realized where she had seen a face like Ms. Farrell's before. The woman Gabby saw last night, the stranger who was walking her dog when Feltrymm dropped Gabby off—*she* had green eyes, too.

But that had to be a coincidence, right? Lots of people had green eyes. What really stood out about the woman with the dog was her long gray braid. Ms. Farrell didn't have a braid. She didn't even have gray hair.

Or did she? All her hair had been covered by the wool cap.

Gabby didn't even realize she had stopped in her tracks until she heard Zee calling from just up ahead.

"Gabs? What's up? Everything okay?"

Gabby didn't answer. She turned and sprinted back onto the Lion's Gate campus. She ran so fast she thought her heart would explode. All the while, she screamed at herself inside her head. Edwina had *warned* her to be vigilant. She'd *told* Gabby that people affiliated with G.E.T.O.U.T. could be watching her. She'd *specifically asked* Gabby to take pictures of anyone strange who showed up around her. But when it actually happened, Gabby didn't even notice.

Gabby tried to breathe. Maybe she was wrong. Maybe Ms. Farrell wasn't the same woman at all. Maybe she was just a fantastic substitute teacher taking a star student off campus for a more interesting tutoring session than he usually got to enjoy.

Then she saw them. Trymmy and Ms. Farrell were all the way at the front entrance of the school, walking toward the visitors' parking lot. Gabby ran even faster, ignoring the searing pain in her legs and her ragged breath. She made it to the parking lot just as Ms. Farrell was climbing into the driver's seat of a light blue compact car. Trymmy was already in the passenger's seat. Though Ms. Farrell was still about fifty yards away, Gabby could make out the back of her head as she bent down to get into her car. The wool cap had slipped upward, revealing the bottom half of a large, twisted bun of gray hair.

Gabby's heart collapsed into her stomach.

"Hey!" she screamed frantically. *"HEY!"*

But she was so breathless she barely made a sound, and so exhausted from the effort she couldn't move. Ms. Farrell's car pulled out of its spot and drove toward the school's exit. She was taking Trymmy away, and there was nothing Gabby could do.

No. There was something. Gabby pulled out her phone and clicked the camera. She zoomed in as close as possible on the car's license plate, then hit the button to take a constant blast of pictures until the car turned the corner and sped away.

Part of Gabby only wanted to collapse in a puddle and cry, but that wouldn't help Trymmy. Instead she plopped cross-legged onto the blacktop, yanked off her knapsack, and pulled out one of the tiny notebooks and pencils she kept for secret spy adventures. Trying hard to control her shaking hands, she scrawled out a message for Edwina:

Trymmy taken, I think by G.E.T.O.U.T. License plate on picture. PLEASE HELP!!!!

She took a picture of the note.

Then she sat.

She had no idea what to do next. She couldn't do anything else to reach Edwina beyond what she'd already done. She couldn't contact Trymmy's parents. She had no numbers for them, and no idea where exactly they lived.

She could only wait. So that's what she did. She sat on the blacktop and let the cold seep through the seat of her jeans and freeze her rear end.

"Gabs?"

It was Zee. Her voice sounded small and worried. It was very un-Zee-like and told Gabby she probably looked as bad as she felt.

"You okay?"

Gabby just shook her head. She kept her eyes on her lap. She didn't want to look at anyone.

"You're sitting in the middle of a parking lot," Zee said. "It's kind of not so safe."

Gabby heard the words, and part of her knew they made sense. She just couldn't fathom doing anything about them.

Zee crouched down next to her. "Want to tell me what happened?"

Gabby couldn't. What she did do was hand Zee her phone. The picture of the note she'd scrawled was still on the screen. Though Gabby didn't look, she knew Zee must have read it because her voice had dropped an octave when she spoke again. "Oh no . . ."

There was silence between them for a moment, then Zee's face loomed right in front of Gabby's. Zee's braids hung like a curtain, blocking Gabby's peripheral vision. All she could see was Zee.

"Here's the deal," Zee said. "This is beyond big-time horrible, but you did everything you could do. And Edwina, she's like Superman, right? I mean, she showed up in your TV. She'll find this car, and she'll find Trymmy. And in the meantime, you can't stay here like this. It's not helping, and sooner or later someone from Lion's Gate is going to start asking questions you're not allowed to answer. Am I right?"

"But it's my fault," Gabby said dully. "The woman who took him, I saw her yesterday. She must have followed us here. I *led* her right to Trymmy. And now . . ."

Gabby couldn't even finish.

Zee looked pained, but rubbed a comforting hand on Gabby's back. "He'll be okay," she said. "I know it. But seriously, we've got to go."

Gabby nodded numbly. She knew Zee was right. It would only make things worse if she had to answer a bunch of questions from Gareth or anyone else at Lion's Gate. She put all her stuff back in her knapsack and hoisted it over her shoulder as she stood up . . . then nearly fell right back down.

Zee grabbed her arm. "You okay?"

Gabby nodded. "My butt fell asleep."

Zee laughed out loud. Gabby mustered up a small smile, but that was the best she could do. As the two walked back across the Lion's Gate campus to the waiting jet-powered surfboard, Gabby said, "I can't go to school. I can't concentrate until I hear. I'll e-mail in the stupid paper."

"No worries," Zee assured her. "I'll drop you at home. Your mom there?"

Gabby shook her head. "She's catering today. But I have my keys. When the school tells her I wasn't there, I'll just say I was sick."

"Cool."

"You don't have to bring me home, though," Gabby said. "You're late enough. I'll take a bus or something."

"Dude, you're so not getting out of a jet-board ride that easily. Come on."

They'd reached the board. Zee shouldered her camouflage duffel, they both put on their helmets, and they were off. When they got to Gabby's place, Zee offered to stay with her, but Gabby said no. Once inside, she trudged up to her room, e-mailed the history paper to her teacher, then slid off her chair and curled into a small ball on the closest pile of laundry.

Never in a million years would Gabby have thought she'd

fall asleep. She was too worried and heartsick and filled with self-loathing. But before she knew it she was lost in a nightmare where she was screaming at the fake Ms. Farrell, who had both Gabby and Trymmy tied to a conveyor belt, their heads moving closer and closer to the world's largest hammer.

BOOM! BOOM! BOOM!

That was the hammer. Gabby could hear it as if it were right there in the room.

BOOM! BOOM! BOOM!

Wait a minute—that wasn't the world's largest hammer at all. It was the door. Gabby's eyes eased open. "Mom?" she moaned groggily.

The door was wide open. No one was pounding on it.

BOOM! BOOM! BOOM!

That same sound again. Was it the *front* door? But it sounded so close.

"Oh for the love of Zinqual, Gabby, look over here!"

No voice could have propelled Gabby out of her laundry nest faster. She leaped to her feet and saw Edwina's angular, lined face filling Gabby's desktop computer screen. Edwina reached up a hand and tapped the screen from inside.

BOOM! BOOM! BOOM!

"Are you quite with me now?" Edwina asked.

"YES!" Gabby lunged for her desk and leaned close to Edwina's face. When Gabby spoke, her words came out in a wild rush. "Do you have Trymmy? Is he okay? Did you get the woman? Was she G.E.T.O.U.T.? Is Trymmy okay????"

Edwina sighed, lowering her eyelids to half-mast. "What have I told you about questions? I will always tell you everything you need to—"

"But, Edwina!" Gabby wailed.

Edwina rolled her eyes. "Yes, yes, I know you're anxious. Fine, then. You'll be happy to know that Trymmy is indeed safe and sound."

Relief poured through Gabby's body and she collapsed into her desk chair. "Thank goodness."

"And thank *you*," Edwina said. "Snapping the picture of the license plate was very quick thinking. We had the woman apprehended before she was two blocks away from Lion's Gate Academy. Without you she likely would have gotten away."

"Thank you," Gabby said, leaning forward onto her desk. "Thank you for telling me and thank you for saving him. I was so scared. . . ."

"Then again, without you she likely would never have gone after Trymmy in the first place."

Gabby took a deep breath. "I know," she said, "and I am so, so, sorry—"

"Sorry isn't enough," Edwina said, her voice edged and her nostrils flaring. "I thought I had impressed upon you the importance of the Unsittables program, and of everything we do here at A.L.I.E.N."

"You did! I—"

"And I believe I expressly forbade you from contacting any of your charges outside of official babysitting jobs."

"I know," Gabby babbled desperately, "but I thought this was different. I thought you knew, and you put the cookbook out for me, and you *wanted* me to solve the riddle on my own—"

"You put a child's life in danger!" Edwina snapped.

"I know," Gabby moaned miserably. "I'm sorry. I—"

"Interesting tidbit," Edwina said, and for the first time ever Gabby noticed stray wisps of hair were flying loose from her normally tight bun. "We questioned 'Ms. Farrell,' who, *exactly* as I'd warned you, is a kook who'd seen your picture on the G.E.T.O.U.T. Web site and decided to investigate on her own. She said she first saw you last night, when you were shouting 'alien-sounding names' in the middle of a residential street."

"I can explain that," Gabby said. "It was my knapsack. My thumb drive with my history report was in it and—"

"No excuses!" Edwina leaned closer, filling the screen with her face from forehead to chin. "I know exactly why you did what you did. I even understand that you missed taking this woman's picture for us, despite the fact that I advised you to be vigilant about strangers. What I can't understand is why you defied my orders and led this woman straight to Lion's Gate Academy, where she saw you talking to a child who is clearly human to most human beings but suspiciously different to a person seeking out aliens. While you were having your terribly important conversation with Trymmy about your precious knapsack, she cleverly asked around and got the information she needed to pass herself off as someone he could trust, and this all happened *right under your nose*."

Every word Edwina said sliced into Gabby's heart. She pulled her feet onto her chair and hugged her legs in tight. She didn't want to cry, but the tears had already built up in her throat and pooled in her eyes. She knew if she opened her mouth they'd spill out, but she couldn't just stay quiet.

"I messed up." Gabby said the words softly, hoping to keep the tears inside, but they tumbled soundlessly down her cheeks anyway. "I was so worried about my paper and the riddle . . . I believed what I wanted to believe. I figured you were the one who gave Trymmy my e-mail address and put out the cookbook, so I thought the rule about visiting didn't count. I shouldn't have done that. You gave me an order. I shouldn't have gone against it without you telling me it was okay."

"That's right," Edwina said.

"I know," Gabby said again, "and I'm so, so sorry. If

anything had happened to Trymmy because of me ..."

She hugged her legs closer as the tears flowed faster.

Edwina sighed, leaning back from the camera. Her eyes looked tired now, and the lines in her face deeper. All of a sudden, Gabby could see every year of Edwina's advanced age.

"I understand why you jumped to the conclusions you did," Edwina admitted. "I did, in fact, give Trymmy your e-mail address, because I saw your note and knew you'd need a riddle. I observed his riddle as well, and even intended to reach out to you this afternoon to see if you'd solved it, and to facilitate you getting a cookbook to Trymmy."

This sounded so kind to Gabby that she almost couldn't bear it. "Really?" she asked.

"Really," Edwina said. Then her face stiffened. "But never did I suspect you would go against a direct command and seek the child out on your own. *Never*."

"It'll never happen again," Gabby promised.

"I know it won't," Edwina said with a finality that made Gabby's heart stop.

"There is a very delicate relationship between A.L.I.E.N. and the Intergalactics we're sworn to protect," Edwina went on. "They need us, but we need them, too, in more ways than you can possibly know. For the balance between humans and aliens to succeed, it is vital that they trust us. They need to know that when a human is affiliated with A.L.I.E.N., that human is someone in whom they can put their complete faith. They must feel utterly confident that human has their best interests first and foremost in his or her mind, to the point where these Intergalactics feel comfortable putting their very lives—their *children's* lives—in that human's hands."

Dread curled inside Gabby's gut. She had a horrible feeling she knew what Edwina was going to say, and she didn't dare breathe for fear it would bring the news faster.

Edwina sighed. A long sigh, with her eyes closed. "I'm afraid, Gabby Duran, that you are no longer Associate 4118-25125A. As of this moment, we must terminate your engagement with A.L.I.E.N."

chapter
NINE

*g*abby felt the air whoosh out of the room.

Three weeks ago she hadn't even known A.L.I.E.N. existed, and now being cut off from the organization felt like being sentenced to a life without breath. She gaped like a fish in a net, her mouth trying to form words that wouldn't come out.

"Edwina," she finally managed, "please. I'll be more careful next time, I swear. Just, please, give me another chance."

A wan smile softened Edwina's face. "If it were up to me, I would, but this goes well over my head. Allynces and Feltrymm were very unhappy when they heard our report.

They demanded a rolling head. If they didn't get their way . . . Believe me when I say there are forces in play here much larger than anything you need to understand."

"So I'm out?" Gabby said, nearly choking on the words.

"We'll be lucky if it's only you," Edwina said. "At the moment, the entire Unsittables program has been suspended."

Gabby's jaw dropped and she gasped. "But all those kids! Like Philip and Wutt and Trymmy—"

"Will currently go back to being officially declared Unsittable, yes," Edwina confirmed. "Which to my thinking will cause even more big-picture problems, but that's a fight I'll be taking up with my superiors. If I succeed, it will be reinstated one day. If not . . ." Edwina's voice trailed off and her eyes looked puffy. Gabby wondered if she was trying not to cry.

It was too much. Gabby sank even lower. Her body felt like it weighed a thousand pounds.

"It's all my fault," she said.

Edwina didn't contradict her. Instead she snapped briskly back to life. "So then," she said in her regular clipped voice, "there are some details to the decommissioning process. First of all, you shall have no further contact *of any kind* with anyone already known to you as an alien, nor shall you attempt to have such contact. Should one of these aliens try to get in touch with you, you are required to terminate this attempt as swiftly as possible. To facilitate this, we have taken the liberty of blocking the e-mails and phone numbers of all your previous clients and anyone affiliated with them from your phone and e-mail accounts."

Gabby nodded numbly. She'd never known how to contact Wutt or Philip, but she'd hoped Trymmy might e-mail her so she could at least say good-bye. Now she wouldn't get the chance.

"Naturally, we also expect you to keep the secrets of A.L.I.E.N. to which you have been privy. Those who have benefitted from the indiscretions you have already made in that arena must also keep their silence."

Gabby nodded again. She knew Edwina meant Zee and Satchel. Zee would never say anything, and Satchel purposely knew so little he couldn't if he tried.

"Maintaining these requirements will stop A.L.I.E.N. from taking more drastic measures, including but not limited to Selective Memory Readjustment."

Gabby leaned forward, her hand nervously reaching up to twirl her hair. "'Selective Memory Readjustment'?" she echoed incredulously. "You mean, you'll erase my brain?"

"*Selectively* erase your brain," Edwina clarified. "Of only those moments that could put our program in jeopardy. And possibly that time in the middle of first grade when you wet your pants during the Pledge of Allegiance—if we're feeling generous."

Gabby's jaw dropped. Even now, the things Edwina said never ceased to amaze her.

Edwina smiled. "However, I have faith it won't come to that. Good-bye, Gabby Duran. It has been a pleasure."

The screen clicked off.

Gabby stared at her own reflection on the monitor . . . until it suddenly flicked back to Edwina's face.

"Oh, I almost forgot," Edwina said. "You need to get to school. You're not an associate now, and I cannot sit by and knowingly let a child cheat herself out of a day's education. Or half a day's education, such as the case may be. Your principal has your excuse for this morning, but should you continue this moping-at-home nonsense, I assure you neither he nor your mother will believe any explanation you devise."

The computer clicked off again before Gabby could respond. This time she leaned close to the screen, staring at her reflection as if it might flick again. She even tapped on the monitor, but the only result was smudgy fingerprints.

Gabby fell back into her chair.

There it was. Her career as an A.L.I.E.N. associate was over. Back to life as Gabby had always known it. She spun around in her chair, staring at her room and thinking about that life. She'd always loved it before. Why did it suddenly seem so small?

Pursing her lips together, Gabby forced herself to her feet. No matter how hollow she felt, she had to listen to Edwina's final order. She had to get to school. She changed into a fresh pair of jeans and a black-and-white flannel shirt that was soft enough to offer some comfort, then grabbed her jacket and knapsack and walked out to the garage. She had only just remembered that her bike wouldn't be there because she'd left it outside the robotics shed this morning, when she saw it sitting in its regular spot. One last helping hand from Edwina.

As she pulled out of the garage, Gabby noticed someone shuffling down the other side of the street. It was a man, maybe ten years older than Gabby's mom, wrapped in ratty wool clothes and a battered jacket. He looked oddly tan and had salt-and-pepper hair that was tamped down on one side like he'd just gotten up. He hunkered over a half-rusted shopping cart filled with recyclable bottles and cans and pushed it slowly down the block.

Something tingled at the back of Gabby's spine. Seeing the man here was odd. Gabby's development was five miles from the nearest store with a shopping cart, and Gabby had never in her life seen someone pushing one down her street. Yet that didn't bother her as much as the distinct feeling that she'd seen this man before. She stared at him until it clicked: he looked remarkably like the gardener she'd seen when she'd met Edwina yesterday—the one pruning bushes next to their meeting place, who'd seemed so disgusted by that house's shoddy landscaping. Despite the cart-pusher's apparently more difficult circumstances, he shared the same hair and build as the gardener. Could he possibly be the same person?

Gabby grabbed her phone and was about to snap a picture when she remembered she didn't have to. She wasn't affiliated with A.L.I.E.N. anymore. Any kook following her now would get nothing out of it but a glimpse into Brensville Middle School life. She pocketed her phone and wheeled away.

When Gabby got to Brensville, she locked her bike in the rack out front, then walked inside. The first person she saw nearly stopped her heart. He was an older man with white hair that grew in a low circle around his mostly bald head, who wore scruffy jeans and a tartan button-down shirt.

Mr. Ellerbee, the school janitor. He was on a ladder fixing a hallway lightbulb, though the last time Gabby had seen him he'd been riding on flying vacuum saucers and trying to destroy her.

Gabby took a deep breath and tried to calm her nerves. She reminded herself that Edwina had told her he was on A.L.I.E.N.'s side now, so she had nothing to fear. Although even if he had still been with G.E.T.O.U.T., it wouldn't impact Gabby. She was no longer A.L.I.E.N.-affiliated. She wondered how long she'd have to keep reminding herself of that.

"Hi, Mr. Ellerbee," she called out with a wave and all the fake confidence she could muster.

Ellerbee looked down but showed no specific recognition of her face. He simply smiled kindly and said, "Oh, hello," in his Scottish lilt. Then he turned back to the job at hand.

Gabby wondered if he'd already messed up with A.L.I.E.N. and had his memory Selectively Readjusted.

As she continued down the hallway, Gabby was thankful she'd arrived during lunchtime. The halls were pretty empty. She didn't feel ready to face a lot of other people. Yet just as she thought this and let herself feel the littlest bit relieved, a new layer of dread settled around her like a lead coat.

She could never have any contact with Trymmy again. That meant she could never get a new riddle, which meant she could never get back the cookbook her mom had promised Madison. It was an infinitesimal thing compared to the fate of the Unsittables program and all the alien kids who needed her, but Gabby knew Madison would make her life miserable for it.

On the plus side, Gabby was pretty sure she had reached maximum capacity for miserable, so maybe she wouldn't even notice.

She got to the cafeteria and peeked inside. Madison and

her group of fashion-doll BFFs were at a table on one side of the room, while Zee and Satchel had their own table all the way on the other side. That meant Gabby had a good shot of getting to Zee and Satch without Madison noticing. Keeping her head down, she started walking toward them.

"Hello," a Scottish accent lilted.

Gabby spun to her left and saw Ellerbee, smiling as he mopped up a spill. He wore the same scruffy jeans and tartan button-down shirt, had the same ring of white hair around his mostly bald head, and even graced her with the same kind expression, but there was no way on Earth he could be the same man she'd just passed in the hallway.

No way on *Earth*.

Hadn't Edwina said something about Ellerbee and a cloning device? If so, it was weird that no one else had noticed there were two of him walking around, but then she remembered what Trymmy had said about humans seeing only what they wanted to see. Maybe it wasn't so weird after all.

"Hi," Gabby said back, then quickly walked the rest of the way and slipped into an empty chair at Zee and Satchel's table. Zee nearly choked on her pork roll when she saw her.

"Gabs! What happened? You hear anything?"

Gabby nodded. "He's fine."

Zee leaned her head back with relief. "Oh good. That's excellent. Totally glad to hear it."

Satchel paused with a forkful of homemade linguini from his aunt Toni's restaurant two inches from his mouth. "Me too. Whatever it was. Which I don't want to know, but I'm glad he's okay." He punctuated the sentiment by shoving the pasta into his mouth and making the loud *mmmm* sounds only merited by Aunt Toni's finest creations.

Gabby's throat turned to sandpaper as she squeezed out her next words.

"But I'm out."

"Out of what?" Satchel asked through a mouthful of noodles. "Oh, out of food! You need lunch!" With his long arms, he pushed a Tupperware container full of pasta across the table to her. "Eat. I've had a ton. It's incredible."

Zee, however, knew exactly what Gabby meant. Her mouth hung open in disbelief. "You're *out*? Like, for-now out?"

"For-good out," Gabby said, then pressed her lips together and blinked quickly to hold back blooming tears.

Satchel didn't need to know exactly what was going on to see that his friend was upset. In a single, gangly motion, he climbed over a chair to sit right next to Gabby. "Are you okay?"

Gabby blinked faster. She sniffled. Satchel was a head taller than her, but he was hunched down enough that she didn't have to look up to meet his eyes. "I will be. It was my own fault. I just . . . wish it was different."

Zee leaned in close on Gabby's other side. "But Trymmy's okay. You said that, right? And that's the most important thing."

Gabby nodded. She blinked down at the pasta Satchel had pushed in front of her. She had no desire to eat, but it was easier to keep hold of herself if she didn't keep looking directly at her friends. Out of her peripheral vision, she saw Satchel and Zee exchange glances. Zee raised her eyebrows in a silent question, and Satchel shrugged uncertainly. Then Zee cringed, as if worried about what she was about to say, but said it anyway.

"Satch and I have been comparing notes," Zee said. "That gnarly old cookbook you delivered to Trymmy . . . does it have anything to do with the signed, first-edition cookbook Madison's telling everyone is going to be the big-ticket item at the H.O.O.T. auction?"

Gabby looked from Zee to Satchel, both of them so earnest and worried for her. She nodded solemnly to answer their question . . .

. . . and then burst out laughing, so hard no sound came out.

It seemed wrong to laugh, really. The H.O.O.T. auction was a huge deal for the Brensville Middle School Orchestra, and it meant a lot to Gabby, too. But it was so much less a deal than risking Trymmy's life, or letting down Edwina, or losing the Unsittables program, that Gabby couldn't help herself. The laughter was contagious, too. After looking at each other with concern for a bit, Zee and Satchel started laughing just as hard.

"So you don't have it?" Satchel snorted as the laugh caught in his nose.

Gabby shook her head, chuckling.

"And you're out," Zee giggled, "so that means you can't get it?"

Gabby chuckled harder as she nodded her head this time.

"Madison's going to kill you," Zee snickered.

"Hard-core kill me," Gabby agreed.

"She'll kill you and *then* she'll kill you even worse!" Satchel burst.

"When are you going to tell her?" Zee asked.

"Eighth period," Satchel answered for her. "That's our next H.O.O.T. meeting."

"Yeah," Gabby said. "I guess then."

Satchel sighed and theatrically pulled out his cell phone. "Better call Aunt Toni and ask her to prep the catering for your funeral," he said. "What do you want, penne or rigatoni?"

That got them all laughing again, and by the time lunch period ended, Gabby actually felt kind of okay about everything, even if she only had two more class periods to live. As it happened, those classes breezed by. Sixth period history was a conversation about their papers, and Gabby was glad she'd had the presence of mind to e-mail hers in. Seventh period French class was spent reading scenes from a Molière play out loud. Gabby probably learned more in those two classes than she had the entire rest of the year. She was so eager to get her mind off things that she hung on the teachers' every word and asked lots of questions.

French class *was* a little tricky, since Madison shared it. She kept trying to catch Gabby's eye, but this was not the place to drop the no-cookbook bomb. Satchel covered Gabby by constantly leaning his long body between Madison and Gabby, no matter how awkward a pretzel he had to make himself to do it. When class ended, Gabby engaged Monsieur Mirabeaux in a very involved conversation about conjugations, so Madison had no choice but to leave before her. After all, Madison couldn't be late to her own H.O.O.T. meeting.

"You missed Saturday," Satchel said as he and Gabby ambled there from the French classroom, "so you haven't seen the gym all done up yet. It's pretty cool, just maybe a little owl oriented."

"Tell me about it," Gabby said. "Last night she brought me a giant owl suit."

"Oh, snap!" Satchel stopped in his tracks. His front shock of hair dropped over one eye. "You get to be Hooty? I totally wanted that job!"

"You can have it!"

"Nah, I couldn't do that to you," Satchel said, walking in his typical slight hunch as they continued toward the gym. "Besides, Madison gave me another job."

"What is it?"

"I'm on recycling," Satchel said. "I run around with a big blue bin and get people to toss their empty bottles at me."

"You mean into the bin."

"Yeah," Satchel said, "I'm sure that's what she meant."

The two of them slipped into the gym, which was abuzz with sound and motion. It looked like the whole Brensville Middle School Orchestra was already there and hard at work. Honestly, Gabby couldn't imagine what else there was to do. The place was amazing. It didn't even look like a gym. It looked like a woodland dream come true. Giant papier-mâché trees filled the corners. At irregular intervals, stuffed owls popped out of knotholes and hooted, then ducked back inside. The noises of birds, a soft breeze, and a brook babbled through the sound system. A raised rock plateau adorned with more trees made up a stage at one end of the room. Even the bleachers and spectator chairs were decorated with leaves, and blue bunting transformed the ceiling into a clear sky painted with white puffy clouds.

"I tried to tell Madison owls were nocturnal," Satchel said. "She didn't listen."

Gabby smiled, but she couldn't laugh. The place was too impressive. It wasn't just the theming either. Madison had the room ready for business. Two of the stage trees held a giant dry-erase board between them. The board was labeled HOOT LOOT! and was clearly where someone would keep a running tally of how much money was raised at the auction. A large screen sat at one side of the stage, and a long table adorned with acorns and vines held a row of computers. And since the whole event would be live streamed, Madison had a camera hooked to a computer on a small raised platform in the middle of the room, ready to record every moment that unfolded onstage.

There was a lot Gabby didn't love about Madison, but she was blown away by all the work Madison had done. Gabby felt ashamed that she'd belittled H.O.O.T.'s magnitude. It might not be life-and-death, and it might not have intergalactic repercussions, but it mattered a lot to everyone here, and that made it important. Gabby hoped like crazy that the other auction items would do better than Madison expected, and H.O.O.T. would be a wild success despite the missing cookbook.

"Okay, everyone!" Madison shouted into the microphone onstage. She held up a bright yellow piece of paper and waved it in the air. "At the end of this period I'm sending you each home with a stack of these flyers for tomorrow's auction! Wherever you go after school, whatever you do, bring the flyers and put them up *everywhere*. We'll have people all over the world participating online, but we want to get the locals, too."

Just then, Madison spotted Gabby and smiled wide. She waved her flyers wildly in the air. "Gabbers! Come on up here!"

Gabby felt sick. She did not want to do this onstage. She shook her head.

"Oh, come on!" Madison chirped. "Everyone, get her up here!"

A chorus of "Come on, Gabby!" and "Go on!" and "Go up, Gabby!" echoed through the room. The orchestra members closest to Gabby—aside from Satchel, of course—surrounded her and gently pushed her forward until she had no choice but to walk, slowly and unwillingly, up to the stage. She climbed the stairs and stood next to Madison, a strained smile on her face.

"I think I've already spilled the beans on this one," Madison began charmingly, "but *Gabby's* the one responsible for our big-ticket item, the first-edition cookbook! Now I know a cookbook doesn't sound like much, but as I said in the e-mail, this one's a major collector's item. Similar copies have sold for thousands of dollars! *Thousands!* So thank you, Gabby Duran!"

Everyone cheered. Gabby even saw Maestro Jenkins, the

orchestra's conductor, cup his hands around his mouth and cry, "Brava! Brava!"

Gabby slipped her own hands into the sleeves of her flannel and rubbed the ends of the cuffs. This wasn't going to be easy.

"So, Gabby," Madison continued, "your mom said you'd give me the book today, so let's have it!" She called to the crowd. "Don't you guys want to see it?"

Of course everyone cheered again. Except Satchel. His face was locked in a wide grimace of impending doom.

Gabby gripped her cuffs tighter, bit her lip, then leaned toward the microphone. Feedback screeched through the sound system and everyone groaned. Once that died down, Gabby tried again.

"I . . . um . . . don't have the cookbook," Gabby said.

"What?!" Madison's hiss echoed through the crowd.

"I'm really sorry," Gabby told Madison. "My mom wasn't lying. She thought we had the book . . . but we don't."

For just a second, Madison's beautiful face contorted into something hideous and zombielike. Then she smoothed herself back to perfection. By the time she spoke, she wore a smile.

"You mean, you don't *now*," Madison clarified, "but you will by tomorrow's auction."

Gabby bit her lip again, but she shook her head. "No,"

she said. "I don't have it at all. I won't. I'm sorry."

The gym rumbled with everyone's groans of disbelief. Gabby tried to slide off the stage, but Madison's shrill, pointed voice pinned her in place.

"But, Gabby, you told me *from the very beginning* that you'd have this book. That's why I stuck with the auction, because *you* told me you had a super-amazing secret item that would earn a lot of money! Without that book, we won't make enough for MusicFest . . . and it'll be *all . . . your . . . fault*!"

Gabby looked out at the crowd. Every single member of the orchestra, except Satchel, stared at her accusingly. Even Maestro Jenkins looked disgusted.

Gabby knew she could take the mic and call Madison out. She could tell everyone that Madison was lying, that Gabby had *never* promised a big secret item, that *Madison* was the one who had promised something she couldn't deliver.

But why? In a sense, Madison was right. This was Gabby's fault. If she had been a worthy A.L.I.E.N. agent and listened to Edwina about not letting Trolls steal her things, none of this would have happened. She'd have held on to her knapsack, wouldn't have needed a cookbook, and when Madison came calling for her big-ticket item, Gabby could easily have given it to her. So no, maybe Gabby wasn't guilty of Madison's *exact* accusation . . . but she was definitely guilty.

"I'm sorry," she said again. She kept her head low as she walked to the back of the gym.

"You just keep walking, Gabby Duran!" Madison barked into the mic. "And don't bother to come back for the auction. That's only for people who care about this orchestra! Satchel, you're Hooty now. You can get the costume from your so-called friend."

Madison said this just as Gabby reached Satchel, and he couldn't help but perk up like a prairie dog.

"Really?" He beamed. "I get to be Hooty?"

Gabby just looked at him.

"Right," he corrected himself. "Friend in need. Way more important."

"It's fine," Gabby said. "I'll bring you the costume in the morning."

She walked out of the gym and straight to the bike rack. This was the last period of the day. Despite Edwina's worries about missing quality education, there was no reason to stick around Brensville Middle School if she wasn't helping with H.O.O.T.

On the way home, she stopped by the playground where she'd taken Wutt, the second alien child she'd ever met. That day had marked Wutt's first time playing with humans her own age, and Gabby would never forget the girl's huge smile or the way her eyes had lit up with glee. Sure, the smile and eyes had been in rag-doll form at the time, but that didn't make their joy any less palpable. Gabby couldn't believe she'd never see Wutt again, or that she'd never be able to bring that kind of happiness to another alien child who so desperately deserved it.

Gabby was about to head home when she noticed someone on one of the playground benches. He was middle-aged, with a natural tan, perfectly groomed salt-and-pepper hair, and an air of sophistication that made it seem like he should be behind a news desk instead of in a park. He wore jeans and a light blue button-down shirt with a blazer. No one else took any notice of him, but in Gabby he triggered a memory. Her nerves prickled when she realized it. He looked like the cleaned-up twin of the man she saw earlier, the one with the shopping cart. Which meant he *also* looked uncannily like the gardener she'd seen at the house next to the one where she'd met Edwina yesterday.

Two of the men could be coincidence. Three could not. Gabby pretended to watch the kids on the seesaw, but she kept the corner of an eye on him. She was close enough to see his piercing blue eyes each time they darted toward her, which they often did. Stranger than that, he kept leaning down to mutter into his chest, like maybe he had a microphone hidden in his shirt pocket.

The Silver Fox, Gabby dubbed him in her mind: a crafty

salt-and-pepper-haired man willing to dress up in different outfits to stalk her all over town. Had she still been with A.L.I.E.N., he'd be a dangerous adversary. She was tempted to tell him he was wasting his time with her, but decided against it. He probably wouldn't believe her. Besides, Gabby thought as she pedaled home, maybe if he concentrated on her, it would keep him away from *real* A.L.I.E.N. agents and associates. So in a way, she was still doing her part to help the team.

It wasn't much, but at the moment it was all she had.

chapter
TEN

When Gabby got home, she went straight to her room, lay down on her bed, and closed her eyes. She felt so drained, she thought she wouldn't wake up until morning, but the smell of incredible food lured her down for dinner, where Alice dished out a savory stew with thick, crusty bread. Carmen of course refused to let the bread touch the stew, even though dipping was half the fun. As they all dug into the meal, Alice regaled the girls with stories of her latest catering assignment: a wedding for two dogs.

"The dogs hired you?" Carmen asked.

"Their owners," Alice clarified.

"They hired you to make dog food?" Gabby asked.

"Yes!" Alice laughed. "But dog food that people can enjoy, too. Like this stew—I'm going to serve it as the main dish!"

Carmen looked at Gabby, who raised an eyebrow. That was all Carmen needed to see. She pushed the stew away.

"I'm not eating dog food," she said.

"Carmen," Alice clucked, "it's not dog food. It's perfectly good people food. I just happen to be serving it to dogs."

"Which makes it dog food," Carmen insisted.

"*Delicious* dog food," Gabby enthused, dipping in her bread for a huge bite.

It really was delicious, but torturing Carmen by savoring each bite made it even better. Gabby polished off two servings while Alice and Carmen debated the definition of dog food. Then Gabby cleared the dishes and poured some animal crackers into a big bowl, which she set in the middle of the table. Gabby and Carmen both immediately grabbed a handful.

"Animal crackers, Gabby?" Alice tsked. "Really? They're so artificial."

"They're not!" Gabby objected. "They're made from real animals!"

Carmen froze, a cracker an inch from her mouth. "That's not true," she said.

"Isn't it?" Gabby's eyes twinkled. Carmen squirmed, and Gabby knew her sister was seconds from jumping up and racing to the animal cracker bag to be sure.

"They're not made from animals," Alice said. "And Gabby, stop teasing your sister. Tell me about the cookbook instead."

Gabby's animal crackers turned into a lump of clay in her mouth. The only good part of that was she couldn't have answered Alice even if she'd tried.

Alice didn't seem bothered. She leaned her elbows on the table and cradled her chin in her hands as she peppered Gabby with eager questions. "What did Madison say when you gave it to her? Is she excited? Is everyone excited? You know, I was thinking, I'm on some Facebook groups for chefs and if I posted something about the auction, I just know that—"

Gabby would have loved to play along and not tell Alice the truth, but it wouldn't help. Even if Alice didn't hear anything before the auction, she'd certainly find out when she showed up for the event. Gabby took a big drink of water, then blurted it out in a single word.

"MomIlostthecookbook."

That said, Gabby snatched several more cookies and shoved them into her mouth to glue it shut again.

Alice shook her head as if clearing it out. "I'm sorry," she began, "did you just say you *lost* a five-thousand-dollar book?"

"We had a five-thousand-dollar book?" Carmen repeated. "Why isn't that in my list of our assets?"

"Because we don't have it anymore, Carmen," Gabby snapped.

"Don't get snippy with your sister," Alice said. "She's not the one who lost a five-thousand-dollar book."

"I know. You're right. I'm sorry." Gabby felt like she was saying "I'm sorry" a lot these days. "I don't know how it happened. I had it in my bag this morning, and then when I looked inside to give it to Madison, it wasn't there."

This was a ridiculously awful story, Gabby knew, but she didn't have the energy to think of anything else. She hoped like crazy her mom would just go with it.

Alice raised her eyebrows. "So the book magically disappeared?"

"Impossible," Carmen said. "There's no such thing as magic."

"I don't know what happened to it," Gabby said, floundering. "Maybe my bag came unzipped. Maybe it fell out on my way to school."

"Maybe?" Alice asked. "Wouldn't you know? Was your bag unzipped when you got to school?"

"Five thousand dollars could buy us a year's worth of groceries," Carmen noted.

Gabby pressed her hands to her forehead. She tried to block out Carmen and answer her mother. "I can't remember. . . . I think so. . . . Yes? Maybe?"

"It would also cover our fall school-shopping budget for ten years," Carmen added.

Gabby leaned heavily on the table and shouted, "Stop with the factoids! We don't care! We know! It's a lot of money and I lost it!"

Some little sisters might have burst into tears if they got yelled at like that. Carmen didn't. She just stared at Gabby impassively and blinked. But that was enough to drown Gabby in guilt. She thumped her head onto the table.

"I'm sorry, Car. It's not your fault."

"I know," Carmen replied matter-of-factly. "I'm not the one who lost two years' worth of gas money."

Gabby felt Alice's hand smoothing her hair. "It's okay, baby," she said soothingly. "It's okay."

"It is?" Gabby's words were muffled by the table.

"It is," Alice assured her. Then, after a long moment she asked, "Gabby, you're not just *saying* you lost the book so we can use the money for ourselves, are—"

Gabby lifted her head before her mom was even finished. "No! It's not that at all! I know you wanted me to use the book for H.O.O.T., but it really is gone!"

Alice moved her chair closer and pulled Gabby in for a hug. "Okay," she said. "I'm sorry. I just had to ask. But you're so responsible. This kind of thing really isn't like you. Is it school? Are you stressed out about work?"

This seemed like Gabby's only reasonable out, so she took it. She made up a story about school getting harder, and midsemester progress reports coming out, and the huge pressure of the just-turned-in history paper. Alice said she understood and promised to help Gabby with whatever she needed so she wouldn't get overwhelmed. As for the book, Alice told Gabby not to worry about it. Accidents happened, and if it *did* fall out of Gabby's bag, there was still a chance someone would find it, know it was the book from Madison's mass e-mail, and get it back to the H.O.O.T. auction.

Gabby, of course, knew this was impossible, but since she couldn't explain why, she simply let it go. She went to bed early that night. The last thing she thought before she fell asleep was that if there was one okay thing to come out of her being decommissioned from A.L.I.E.N., it was that she could stop lying to her mom and Carmen.

The next day was H.O.O.T., and Gabby knew she should tell her mom and Carmen that she wouldn't be the one in the Hooty outfit, but she couldn't do it. She'd had enough scrambling for explanations for a while, and besides, it was impossible to tell *who* was in the Hooty suit once it was on. If they didn't pay close attention to the bird's height, they could totally believe it was Gabby wearing it and not Satchel. She'd just have to ask him to maybe do her a favor and not unmask at the end.

Gabby dreaded seeing Madison on the bus that morning, but it turned out luck was with her. Madison wasn't there. Her mother must have given her a ride for the big day.

Yet once Gabby got to Brensville Middle School, her luck ran out. At least three orchestra members "accidentally" tripped her as she walked down the hall, two attached LOSER signs to her back, and one affixed a note to her locker that said FRENCH HORNS BLOW. Given that that's exactly what French horns do when used properly, Gabby tried to tell herself the note was simply a statement, not an insult.

Once Gabby delivered the Hooty suit to Satchel, she, Satch, and Zee slipped outside. The fall morning was cold enough that most students were staying indoors until class started, so this seemed like a good place for Gabby to avoid further harassment.

"How long do you think they'll hate me?" Gabby asked.

Satchel thought about it. "How many more years until college?"

Just then, something small and round bounced off the top of Satchel's head. He winced and his hand flew to the spot.

"Oh snap!" he complained to Zee. "It was a joke. You didn't have to hit me."

"How could I have hit you?" Zee held up her hands, which were completely occupied with chunks of her robot-in-progress.

"You threw something at me with that remote control thingy," Satchel said.

"It's a vise-clamp hand, not a remote control," Zee shot back. "And even if it was a remote, it wouldn't be a 'thingy.'"

Gabby wasn't listening to either one of them. She'd followed the small, round projectile with her eyes as it bounced off Satchel's head. It had landed among some leaves in front of him. Gabby bent down and gently ran her fingers through the fall foliage until she felt something cold and hard. She picked it up. It was a red marble with a yellow flare in the middle.

Gabby's blood rushed faster. She wasn't sure if she did or did not want to see what would be waiting for her when she looked up.

She tilted her neck back. Clinging to the outside wall of the school, only six feet or so above Satchel's head, was Trymmy, his thick claws sunk deep into the brick. His head was pointed downward, and gravity made his larger moles droop pendulously from his face. When Gabby met his eyes, he grinned and waggled his head back and forth, purposely making the moles shimmy and dance.

Gabby spoke to Zee and Satchel, but she didn't take her eyes off Trymmy. "Satch, unless you want to see something you will never be able to un-see, I suggest you head inside."

This may have been the wrong thing to say. Immediately,

both Zee and Satchel snapped their heads back to follow Gabby's gaze.

"Dude!" Zee enthused. She dropped her work to the ground and whipped out her phone, clicking the camera open. Gabby reached out and grabbed it out of her hands.

"Zee, you can't!"

"But Gabs, *look*!"

Now that he had an audience, Trymmy was showing off. He turned in wild circles along the wall, then released his fingers and let his toe claws hold him as he extended his body out like a flagpole.

"Stop!" Gabby hissed up to him. "Someone could see you!" Then, realizing three people had clearly *already* seen him, she added, "Someone *else*."

"I think my brain just melted."

It was Satchel. He was frozen in place, his neck craned back, his eyes wide. If Gabby looked closely enough, she could see the fibers of his sanity unraveling.

"Zee," Gabby said, "you've got to go. You have to take care of Satchel."

"You can't be serious," Zee said. "Do you not see what's going on up there?"

"I *am* serious!" Gabby insisted. "None of us want our memories erased."

"I do," Satchel said numbly.

Gabby raised her eyebrows at Zee, urging her to leave. Zee rolled her eyes.

"Fine. But you seriously owe me." She moved to Satchel and placed one hand on his back and one on his arm, easing him toward the door. "Come on, Satch. Easy does it. You can fall asleep in class and pretend this was all a dream."

Once they disappeared inside, Trymmy leaped off the building, did a triple somersault in midair, and landed at Gabby's feet. "Ta-da!"

"*SHHHHHH!*" Gabby hissed. She looked around frantically. A.L.I.E.N. and G.E.T.O.U.T. could be anywhere. She leaned close to Trymmy and whispered, "You can't be here. I can't be seen with you."

Behind his glasses, Trymmy's eyes widened with hurt and surprise. Then he just looked defeated.

"Right," he said. "You're a human. Of course you don't want to be seen with me."

"No, that's not what I mean! Not at all! But, Trymmy, people have been watching me. People like Ms. Farrell. And A.L.I.E.N. fired me. If they see me with you, I'll get in huge trouble. You have to go!" Gabby stopped herself, then asked, "Wait . . . how did you even get here?"

"I'm homeschooled now," Trymmy said, "but my new teacher's super-old and fell asleep, so I snuck out and rode my bike."

He grinned, proud of himself, but all Gabby could think was how dangerous it had been for him to be all alone in a world crawling with potential Ms. Farrells. She couldn't send him back on his own, but she couldn't escort him home either, and she *certainly* couldn't let him stay anywhere near her.

She needed to find someplace safe where she could think.

When the idea came to her, she wasn't sure if it was brilliant or completely insane. But there was a man close by who knew all about aliens, and who was working closely enough with A.L.I.E.N. that he wouldn't hurt Trymmy, but ideally not so close that he'd automatically report Gabby and Trymmy for being together.

The fact that this man had tried to kill her the last time they hung out put only a slight damper on Gabby's conviction.

"Come with me," Gabby whispered. "And stay close."

With Trymmy at her side, Gabby opened the door to Brensville Middle School and peered in. The halls were empty. First period had already started. Gabby could only hope things stayed that way as she and Trymmy made the long walk to her destination at the other end of the building.

They made it halfway across. That's where the main entrance of Brensville sat, in the very center of the school's long hall. The large glass wall and doors were on Gabby's left as she walked, so she kept Trymmy on her right. She also peered out toward the doors before she crossed that vast central area, and made sure no cars were pulling up to drop off latecomers. Gabby truly thought she was safe as she hustled Trymmy along to the other side of the main hall, until she heard the worst sound ever.

"Gabby Duran, what are you doing out of class?" Madison Murray squealed.

Gabby made her body as wide as possible as she wheeled toward Madison. She even held out her arms to try to hide every bit of the Troll behind her.

"Madison!" Gabby squeaked. "What are *you* doing out of class?"

"*I* have a late pass," Madison crowed. "I got permission from Maestro Jenkins to put up more flyers for H.O.O.T. around town this morning. When the auction crashes and burns, at least I'll be able to say I did everything I could."

Gabby felt sweat tickle her upper lip. She hoped Madison would think it was her own intimidating presence that made Gabby nervous and wouldn't realize Gabby was keeping something from her.

"Good plan," Gabby said. "Totally. See you this afternoon in French class!"

She gave Madison a huge smile and waited for the girl to leave, but Madison didn't move. Instead she scrunched her perfectly arched eyebrows and clip-clopped her low-heeled shoes closer to Gabby. Gabby leaned back, hoping to keep Trymmy hidden.

"You're acting weird," Madison proclaimed. "Even for you. What are you hiding?" Madison's eyes grew round with realization. "It's the cookbook, isn't it? You have it!"

Madison lunged to the left, but when Gabby lunged that way to block her, Madison made a quick change and ran around Gabby on the right.

On top of everything else, Madison had catlike reflexes. Gabby promised herself she'd remember that in the future.

Gabby wheeled around, already floundering for ways she'd explain Trymmy . . . but Trymmy wasn't there. Aside from Gabby and Madison, the hall was empty.

Where had Trymmy gone? Could someone have snatched him away from right behind her? Gabby wanted to run down the halls screaming his name, but that would only make matters worse.

"See?" Gabby said with forced cheer. "Nothing there."

Madison's face pinched in suspicion. She folded her arms tightly over her ruffled blue blouse.

"You're keeping secrets, Gabby Duran," she said. "I told you before I'd find out what you're up to, and I will."

As her nemesis spoke, Gabby noticed something high up in her peripheral vision: a child-size figure crawling out from behind a trophy case.

So that's where Trymmy went. He must have jumped behind the case when he heard Madison, then crawled up the wall. Now he was scuttling down from ceiling height but stopped just a couple feet above Madison's head.

"Are you even paying attention to me, Gabby Duran?" she demanded.

"Of course! I totally am!" Gabby insisted. But she was really paying attention to Trymmy, who clung to the wall with his toe claws, folded his arms against his chest, and tossed his head in a perfect Madison imitation. Gabby had to bite hard on her cheeks so she wouldn't laugh.

Madison huffed and moved her hands to her hips, with no clue that her every move was being mirrored on the wall behind her.

"You're lucky this isn't my hall monitor period and I have to get to class," she huffed. "Otherwise I'd take you to Principal Tate myself and you could explain to *him* what you're doing."

Above her, Trymmy shook his finger scoldingly and arranged his already unusual features into a mask of cartoonish disapproval as he mouthed Madison's words along with her.

"But you *do* have to get to class, right?" Gabby reminded her. "You said you have a late pass, not a free period pass. Wouldn't want to see you get in trouble."

Madison's pink lips crunched into a puckered line. "No," she agreed. "We wouldn't. I'll leave the getting in trouble to you." She wheeled on a heel and flounced down the hall, turning back to add, "How is the orchestra treating you? Not so great, right? If you ask me, your only smart move is to drop out. That or bring me the cookbook. Toodles."

She waggled her fingers, then strode away.

"Good thing I came to your school," Trymmy said, hitting the floor and wiping wall dust off his khaki pants. "Sounds like you need that cookbook."

What Gabby needed was to get Trymmy someplace less conspicuous before first period ended and the halls filled with people. She grabbed Trymmy's hand.

"Run with me," she whispered. *"Now."*

They sprinted down the hall in the opposite direction of Madison and didn't stop until they were right outside Mr. Ellerbee's janitorial closet. Unfortunately, Ellerbee's space was directly across the hall from Principal Tate's office, and Gabby and Trymmy hadn't exactly been light on their pounding feet.

"Who's running in the halls during class?" Principal Tate's voice wailed from behind his door, and Gabby heard the screech of his chair pushing back from its desk. Frantically, she yanked open Ellerbee's door, shoved Trymmy inside, then followed him. She shut and locked the door just as Principal Tate's door opened behind them.

The closet was tiny, and Trymmy and Gabby found

themselves practically in the lap of a small man with a white fringe of hair around his otherwise bald head. The man sat tilted back in the room's one chair, hands clasped behind his neck. His feet were propped up on the lower shelf of a unit crowded with cleaning supplies and his few personal items. He wore the exact same outfit as yesterday: jeans and a tartan shirt.

"Why hello, wee ones!" he lilted in his Scottish brogue.

"Hi!" Trymmy said.

Someone banged on the door. The knob rattled.

"Ellerbee!" Principal Tate boomed. "I heard a student running down the halls. Is someone in there?"

Gabby spoke quickly to the man who looked like Ellerbee. "You're a clone, aren't you?" Gabby asked him. "I need the real Ellerbee. Is he around?"

"Ellerbee?" the principal's voice called again from outside the door.

"One moment!" Clone-Ellerbee called. Then he winked at Gabby and Trymmy, got up from his chair, and reached for a plastic bucket on a high shelf. When he tipped the bucket forward, a square of linoleum flooring slid open to reveal a carpeted stairway. Clone-Ellerbee smiled and nodded down to it.

Principal Tate banged on the door again.

"Go on with you," Clone-Ellerbee urged quietly. "Right quick now."

Once Gabby and Trymmy had descended several steps,

the panel slammed shut above them. Gabby's ears immediately felt thick and full of cotton.

"Soundproof room," a Scottish brogue called up from below. "Plays with yer ears at first. Yeh'll get used to it. Come on down. I won't hurt you. Not getting paid to these days."

Trymmy looked questioningly at Gabby. She nodded confidently, even though she wasn't at all positive she'd made a good choice. The two of them descended the stairs and saw the exact same nearly bald man they'd seen up above, only this one wore a full kilt and a well-worn black T-shirt with a picture of the Loch Ness Monster and the words I BELIEVE on it. Like the clone above, he leaned back in his chair with his feet up, but the chair down here was thick leather, and his feet weren't on a dinky shelving unit but a massive computer console. The console jutted out below a collection of giant screens flashing so many different programs that Gabby got dizzy trying to make sense of them all. The room's other furnishings included a refrigerator, stove, microwave, hot tub, and several structures that looked like giant black marble works of abstract art, all folds and curls. She wondered if one of them was the cloning machine.

"Welcome to my humble abode," Ellerbee said. "Put it in over the weekend, your people did."

"A.L.I.E.N. did this?" Gabby asked.

"Aye," Ellerbee said. "Carved the whole room out of

nothin'. Little present for me, along with the clones to do my cleanin' work. All I do in return is stick close with those G.E.T.O.U.T. types, poke around their Web site, give your people a heads-up if anything goes awry." He kicked back from the computer console, rolling his leather chair across the room to the fridge. "Want some haggis? I can warm one in the microwave. Nothing like a little sheep entrails in a stomach casing to get the blood flowing, eh? You and yer Troll friend might like a bite."

"How do you know I'm a Troll?" Trymmy asked.

"Yeh're in the database," Ellerbee said, rolling back to the console so he could tap a few computer keys. "Not you specifically, but yer kind."

One of the big screens on the wall flickered to show a drawing of a short, hunched-over humanoid with a thick brow, pickle-shaped nose, and skin mottled with moles so large they looked like small planets. Trymmy stepped closer to the screen to stare at it. Gabby couldn't blame him. It was a pretty insulting representation.

Yet when Trymmy spoke, his voice was full of awe. "Grandma?"

Once again, Gabby reminded herself never to make assumptions about alien life. She turned her attention to more pressing matters.

"Mr. Ellerbee," Gabby said, "can I ask you to please not

say anything to A.L.I.E.N. about the two of us being here?"

"If it's not on the list of things they pay me to do, I don't do it, I can promise you that. All I ever wanted was a life of leisure, and now that's just what I've got. I even have time to take up the bagpipes! Wanna hear?"

Before Gabby could answer, he reached under the desk, pulled out the massive instrument, and began to play, filling the room with off-key bovine wails. The sound was a crime against music, but it would give Gabby and Trymmy some privacy. She leaned down to look him in the eye.

"Okay, we need to get you home like *now*, but I can't be seen with you, and I don't like the idea of you going alone. Do you have your cell phone? Can you call your parents to pick you up? They don't have to know you were with me."

"You're just going to get rid of me?" Trymmy asked. "Aren't you even going to ask why I came and found you?"

Gabby sighed. She didn't mean to be impatient, but she couldn't help thinking that Edwina could show up at any minute, memory eraser in hand. For a moment Gabby wondered if the erasing would hurt, but then she realized even if it did, the pain was probably one of the things she'd forget.

"You're right," she admitted, "I should have asked. Why did you come find me?"

"To give you this."

He pulled a piece of folded paper from his pocket and

gave it to Gabby. She opened it. The words were laid out like a poem, but Gabby knew what it had to be.

"A riddle," she said.

Trymmy nodded. "I tried e-mailing it, but the e-mails bounced back. I tried calling you, too, but you never answered."

"I would have, I promise," Gabby assured him, "but I never got the calls. A.L.I.E.N. must be blocking you. It's my own fault. I messed up. Big-time. You could have gotten really hurt because of me, and now A.L.I.E.N. won't let me see or talk to you ever again."

Gabby winced as she said that last part. It felt like she was smacking Trymmy with her words, and Trymmy reacted like she'd done just that. He recoiled and scrunched up his face in disgust.

"How is that fair?" he asked. "You're not the one who took me away from school. And it's not even like anything bad happened. They got Ms. Farrell right away!"

"But what if they hadn't?"

"But they did!" Trymmy pooked out his lower lip in a pout that covered the tip of his nose. "Do you even know why I took your backpack in the first place?"

"Of course I do," Gabby said. "Trolls steal."

"Yeah, but it's not like we *have* to steal. I took it . . ." He lowered his head and told the last part to the floor. "I took it so I could see you again. I like playing with you. I thought we were friends." A big sigh, then he added more softly, "And I don't have any other friends."

Gabby could actually feel her heart melting down into her body. More than anything, she wanted to hug him. She wanted to tell him he was right, they *were* friends, and she'd come over and play with him whenever he wanted.

But she couldn't.

"I'm sorry," Gabby said. "I wish things were different, but they're not."

Trymmy lit up with an idea. "But we can *make* it different! We can be secret friends and play together anyway! We'll meet right here. I can come over through that Holobooth!"

He pointed to one of the more tubular black marble fixtures in Ellerbee's man cave.

"That's a Holobooth?"

"Ours is underground so you couldn't see its shape, but, yeah, that's what they look like," Trymmy said. "And you can use them to travel. Just step into a Holobooth, think real hard about another Holobooth, and you can go there. So I can come here and meet you whenever we want!"

Trymmy was so excited he bounced up and down, and his grin was infectious. Part of Gabby was dying to say yes and start planning their adventures, but she knew there was no way.

"I can't," she said. "Even if A.L.I.E.N. said it was okay,

which they *won't*, your parents don't want you around me. I can't go behind their backs. It's not right."

Trymmy opened his mouth to object, but no words came out. He just stared up at Gabby, his eyes suddenly so sad and hopeless that Gabby had to look away. She refolded his riddle and handed it to him. "You should probably take this back," she said. "I shouldn't really hold on to anything from you."

Trymmy held the paper a moment, then darted to Ellerbee's console and grabbed a pen. He scrawled something beneath the riddle. "This is my cell," he said, "and it's a number A.L.I.E.N. doesn't have. I know they're here to protect us and all, but my parents still like us to keep some things to ourselves. If you call from a phone that's not yours, A.L.I.E.N. won't know."

He held out the paper, but Gabby shook her head. "Trymmy, I can't."

"Just take it. Maybe you'll change your mind." He shrugged sadly, then added, "And if not, you'll have something to remember me by."

That was too much. Gabby threw her arms around Trymmy and hugged him tight. He stiffened, but Gabby wouldn't have expected anything else. When she pulled back she took the paper from him.

"Only because you really want me to," she explained. "Not because I need it to remember you."

Trymmy nodded. "So now what?"

"You said you can travel through the Holobooth, right?" Gabby asked. "Does that mean you can take it home?"

"Yeah," Trymmy sighed.

With his back slumped, he trudged to the Holobooth. The thing looked completely solid to Gabby, but he pressed some invisible trigger spots until a small portal slid open, then stepped inside. Magnified by his glasses, his eyes were two giant pools of melancholy. They caught Gabby's and wouldn't look away until the Holobooth door slid closed and cut them off.

As the booth hummed to life, Gabby folded Trymmy's riddle and put it in her jeans pocket. She felt something else in there and pulled it out. It was the red marble with the yellow flare, the one Trymmy had thrown down from the school wall to get her attention.

Gabby ran to the Holobooth and banged on it. "Trymmy! Trymmy, wait! You forgot someth—"

The booth stopped humming. Its panel slid open to reveal only emptiness inside.

Trymmy was gone, and Gabby would never see him again.

chapter
ELEVEN

"You were his only friend and now he can't see you anymore?" Zee marveled as she fussed with some wiring on what looked like a tiny military tank. "That's awful."

Gabby had left Ellerbee's den in time for her second period class. Now it was morning break, and she, Zee, and Satchel were spending the twenty minutes hunkered in a corner of the hall. This had two benefits. First, Gabby was tucked away enough that she was less likely to face further retribution from vengeful orchestra members. Second, it kept Satchel away from the outside of the school, which he was afraid was now crawling with thick-clawed spider-children.

"Yeah, that's seriously raw," Satchel agreed.

Gabby had her feet on the floor and her knees hugged tight, but now she peered up at Satchel in amazement. "Satch, are you actually listening to this conversation?"

"Half-listening," Satchel pointed out. "Only to the parts that sound kind of not totally insane."

"Fair enough."

"So what are you going to do?" Zee asked.

"What *can* I do?" Gabby asked back. "I mean, even if he was a regular kid, if his parents don't want me around, I can't be around. And even if they *did* want me around, it's not great for someone's babysitter to be their only friend, right?"

"Probably not ideal," Zee said. She put the tank on the floor, then pulled a remote out of her pocket and made the tank roll toward Gabby. "Unless it was a robot babysitter. Then it'd be pretty cool."

"What would you do about the kid if he weren't, you know…" Satchel spun his entire lanky body in an exaggerated spy-scan of the teeming halls, then leaned in and lowered his voice to just above a whisper. "… *what he is*."

"Good you whispered that," Zee chided him. "Super-incriminating words."

Gabby tilted her head back and considered his question. "If he was just another kid, I'd try to help him meet other friends. I'd take him to the playground, or the park, or we'd just ride bikes around where I knew we'd see other kids. Then I'd introduce him around until he found someone he clicked with. And he *would*—kids always do—I've seen it happen a jillion times. The perfect friend for Trymmy would just have to be really specific. Someone who isn't huggy or hand-holdy, who loves games with a lot of rules, who's hyper-crazy smart and doesn't get their feelings hurt easily, who's so super-logical they can figure out riddles in their sleep . . ."

Gabby suddenly realized both Zee and Satchel were looking at her with wide eyes and dropped jaws.

"Oh snap," Satchel breathed.

"What?" Gabby asked.

"Gabs, listen to yourself," Zee said. "Don't you realize who you're describing?"

Gabby ran over the list in her mind, and soon her own eyes and jaw mirrored her friends'.

"Holy macaroni," she intoned.

She sat up tall on crossed legs and jangled her knees up and down. Now that she'd realized it, she wanted it to happen *now*. It was perfect!

"But how? How do I get them together? Even if I somehow arrange for them to get to the same place at the same time, I know them. They'll never talk to each other on their own. I'd have to be there, and he can't be seen with me."

"I've got it!" Satchel snapped. "An invisibility potion!"

Zee rolled her eyes. "There's no such thing as an invisibility potion."

"Oh yeah?" Satchel countered. "How about kids with claws who climb walls and people who talk to you out of the TV? Is there such a thing as those?"

"That was one you probably should have whispered," Zee pointed out.

Satchel blushed and hunched over, abashed. "Sorry. Just sayin'."

"No, you're right." Gabby's eyes danced as the idea came together in her head. "I need something that'll make me invisible . . . *like the Hooty suit!*"

"That would totally work!" Satchel cried. Then he frowned. "Except I get to be Hooty." Zee elbowed him in the ribs. "I mean, unless you need the suit more," he added. "Then you can totally be Hooty. No problem at all."

He sighed heavily, but Gabby didn't have time to feel bad about dashing his owl dreams. More pieces were clicking together in her head.

"This is good," Zee encouraged her. "Now how will you get Trymmy to H.O.O.T.?"

"He gave me that number," Gabby said. "He wants to see me. I could probably just ask him."

Gabby suddenly reeled back and gasped like she'd been shot.

"Gabs?" Zee worried.

"You okay?" Satchel asked.

"So, so, *so* okay!" Gabby nearly shouted. Then she lowered her voice back to an excited hiss. "You guys, I can tell him to come to H.O.O.T. for the answer to the *riddle*! And if we give him the answer there, he'll give us the cookbook!"

Zee grinned. "Which you can give to Madison during the auction!"

"And save our MusicFest trip!" Satchel finished.

The bell rang for class. They knew they had to get up and leave, but they were too wired to move.

"Let's see the riddle, quick," Zee said.

Gabby pushed her rear off the floor so she could dig into her jeans pocket and pull out the paper. Satchel and Zee huddled on either side of her so they could all read it together.

I never was, am always to be,
No one ever saw me, nor ever will see.
I can't be bought, I can't be sold,
The young have more of me than the old.
And yet I am the hope of all
Who live and breathe on your terrestrial ball.

Bring me this riddle's answer, I pray,
And get what you seek without any delay.

"Anything?" Gabby asked hopefully.

"Not yet," Zee said. "Let's think about it during math."

"I'll think about it, too," Satchel said. "It'll be easy. I have a free period."

"That's great!" Gabby exploded with another idea. "Spend it in the library, and look up anything you can find about Trolls and riddles."

Zee tilted her head dubiously. "You think he'll find the answer there?"

"No, but Edwina told me the stuff we know as folk tales is based on real interactions with aliens," Gabby said. "Maybe Trolls have a pattern, a certain kind of riddle they always like to ask. Or maybe they look for answers that are kind of similar."

"Maybe," Zee agreed. "Worth a try."

By now the halls were empty, and they had to run to class to avoid a late slip. Yet before they did, Gabby borrowed Zee's phone and used it to text a quick note to the number Trymmy wrote on the paper.

I have the answer to your riddle, it said. *Please find a way to come to the H.O.O.T. auction at Brensville Middle School, 4 P.M.–6 P.M. Try not to come alone—I want you to stay safe!*

Knowing Trymmy, Gabby was sure he'd text back before

she could even hand the phone back to Zee . . . but he didn't.

"How do we even know if he saw it?" Zee asked.

"I guess we don't," Gabby said. "We just have to hope."

She also had to hope that if he *did* see it, he'd show up. In the meantime, Gabby needed to crack the riddle. She spent math class sitting in the very back row with Zee, where they tuned out Ms. Emery and worked. For thirty-nine minutes of a forty minute class, they successfully passed notes back and forth, mulling over the possibilities of each riddle line, and their teacher had no idea.

Or so they thought.

"What is the ratio," Ms. Emery said several decibels louder than anything she'd said throughout class, "of time in minutes that Gabby Duran and Stephanie Ziebeck spent chatting with each other today to their time spent participating in class?"

When Ms. Emery finished the question, she was standing right between Gabby's and Zee's desks. Both girls sat up straighter and faced forward like the model students they were *not*, and a hot blush coated their cheeks.

"Yes, Margo?" Ms. Emery called to one of the many students with their hands high in the air.

Margo del Vecchio, one of Madison Murray's little minions, chirped, "The ratio of time in minutes that Gabby Duran and Stephanie Ziebeck spent chatting with each other today to their time spent participating in class is thirty-seven to two."

"Good answer, Margo," Ms. Emery said, "but would you really give them the two? It seemed to me they were paying attention for only point-five minutes. Anyone else have thoughts?"

"I saw Zee stare at the active board for a minute," one girl said, "but I'm not sure if she was paying attention or thinking about something else."

"I could hear them whispering the whole time," added a boy in the front row, "so I'd say they were paying attention for zero minutes."

"I counted twenty notes passed between them," another boy said, "and if each note takes one-point-five minutes to read and respond to, that's thirty minutes."

With each comment, Gabby and Zee sank lower in their seats. When the class bell rang, Ms. Emery put one hand on each of their desks and leaned in close.

"When you waste school time, you don't learn, you don't do well on tests, you don't get good grades, you don't get into college, you don't get a good job, and you don't succeed in life. If you don't mind that, by all means, have more days like today. It's only your future."

Yikes.

Gabby said good-bye to Zee and went to the library for her next period, which she had free. She curled into one of the big reading armchairs, but she had trouble thinking. She was too mortified by Ms. Emery's words, which now echoed in her head.

It's only your future.

It's only your future.

Future.

"Future!"

Gabby shot upright and cried the word out loud, then realized every head in the room had swiveled to face her. She smiled sheepishly.

"Future . . . tense," she explained lamely. "Studying French."

No one seemed to care. They turned away with annoyed clucks and sighs. Once their attention was off her, she yanked Trymmy's riddle out of her pocket and climbed back into the chair, legs tucked under her and feet on the seat like she was preparing to spring off. When the period ended, she couldn't get to the cafeteria fast enough.

"'I never was, am always to be,'" she recited once she, Zee, and Satchel were gathered over trays of tacos so good that Satchel was totally ignoring his home-packed meal. "That's the future. 'No one ever saw me, nor ever will see.' You can't see the future. 'I can't be bought, I can't be sold.' You can't buy or sell the future. 'The young have more of me than the old.' The young have more of a future, because they're younger. 'And yet I am the hope of all who live and breathe on your terrestrial ball.' Everyone hopes for things in the future! That's the answer! The answer is 'the future'!"

"Oh snap!" Satchel said around a mouth full of ground beef. "That totally works!"

Instead of her food, Zee chewed on the end of one of her braids. "It's awesome, Gabs, but isn't there a last part?"

"'Bring me this riddle's answer, I pray, and get what you seek without any delay'?" Gabby asked.

"Yeah, that. How do you bring someone the future?"

Gabby twirled a curl around one of her fingers. "Not sure," she finally admitted. "Satch, did you find anything when you were looking stuff up?"

Satchel snorted. "Only that you should never mess with Trolls. Most of the stories go like this: A Troll offers this crazy amazing prize to a person if the person can answer a riddle. If the person gets it wrong, they have to pay up something huge, like all their money, or their kingdom, or their firstborn kid. But the prize is so super-awesome and the Trolls seem so warty and hunchbacky and un-smart, the person always says, 'Yeah, I'm in, riddle me up.' And every time, the riddle's this mega-impossible harder-than-*Moby-Dick*, no-way-to-get-it tangle that the person gets wrong, and the Troll takes everything."

"Which is kind of what we already knew," Gabby said.

"Yeah," Satchel agreed. "The only chance a person ever has with a Troll is to turn everything around and give *the Troll* a riddle so hard it stumps him. If that happens, then *boom*, the Troll has to give back everything he's ever taken from anyone ever. Pretty cool, right? From the stories I saw, it's happened, like, twice, in forever."

"It's interesting, sure," Zee said, "but it doesn't tell us anything about getting the future so we can give it to Trymmy."

Gabby sighed, knowing Zee was right. "I guess the bright side is that everyone already knows I messed up and the cookbook's gone. It's not like they'll be shocked if we can't figure this out and I don't get it back for the auction."

That's when Satchel started whistling and looking up at the corners of the room. Even if Gabby hadn't known him since birth, she'd have known he was hiding something. *What* he was hiding became evident maybe five minutes later, when two orchestra members, trombonist twins Eddy and Teddy Yadrinsky, stopped by the table on their way to get dessert. They wore huge matching smiles as they leaned in on either side of Gabby.

"I knew all along you were just messing with us, Gabby," Teddy said.

"Yeah," Eddy agreed. "No way would you do anything to screw up MusicFest."

They patted her on the back in unison, then walked away

without waiting for a reply, their smiles even sunnier for having spoken to her.

Satchel had now gone from whistling to *humming* at the corners of the room. With his pointed nose, he looked like a giant, off-key songbird.

"Satch?" Gabby asked.

She was distracted by a pair of arms wrapping around her shoulders, pulling her head into someone's chest.

"Gabb-eeeeeee!"

The someone broke off the hug and knelt down next to Gabby's chair. It was Lilah Hartmann, a clarinet player who had the school's longest hair. She'd never cut it in her life and it hung down her back in a long, dark braid.

"I'm so, so, so, so, so excited you're bringing the cookbook to H.O.O.T.! I already texted my mom, and she's in this online cooking group that's going *crazy* for it! I just know we'll get enough money for MusicFest now!"

She gave Gabby another giant hug, then skipped back down the aisle.

This time when Gabby turned to Satchel, he was staring at something deeply fascinating he'd discovered under one of his fingernails.

"Forgive me, Gabby," a voice rang out, "I never should have doubted you."

That voice Gabby knew well. She winced inside, but

pasted on a huge smile to face Maestro Jenkins, the head of the Brensville Middle School Orchestra.

"Hi, Maestro."

"I was so distraught when I first heard that you'd pulled the book out of the auction. I have to admit, I was starting to wonder about your commitment to our orchestra. That was wrong of me. I look forward to planning our MusicFest trip, and to your considerable part in the concert we play there." Maestro Jenkins took Gabby's hands in his, held them just a moment—were there tears in his eyes?—then strode back to his own table.

Gabby scanned the room to make sure no one else was coming for her. No one was, but way too many orchestra members were looking her way with giddy smiles on their faces.

She slipped out of her seat and under her table before any more of them could approach. The cafeteria floor was grimy with dust and random stickiness, and the underside of her table was blobbed with unnamable ancient dried foodstuffs. Gabby stayed low so her curls wouldn't catch in any of it. She crawled across to Satchel's long, denim-clad legs, and tugged on them until he joined her. Being so much taller, he had to scrunch into a small ball and his top flap of hair totally grazed something that once was a pork roll, but Gabby wasn't concerned.

"What did you do?" she hissed.

"I couldn't help it," he said. "When I was walking to my last class, Andrew Lewis was talking dirt about you to, like, half the brass section, and I got mad. I pulled him aside and told him you *did* have the book, and he should expect it to appear by the end of the auction."

"Why would you say that?"

"I told you! I didn't like the way he was talking about you."

"But now everyone's expecting me to have the book!" Gabby wailed.

"Well, you will. You figured out the riddle."

"Not how to give it to him! And what if I'm wrong? Or what if Trymmy doesn't even show up?"

"Then you're in huge trouble," Zee admitted, slipping under the table to join the conference. "The stuff you dealt with this morning will be nothing. They'll be out for blood. Speaking of which . . ." She looked suspiciously up at a red blotch just over her head on the underside of the table. "We've really got to get out of here."

Sliding under the table was a lot easier than sliding back out. Gabby had to contort her body to get around the chairs and stay low enough that she didn't scrape herself on the table's edge. By the time she slithered back into the open, she could feel her face was red and her hair was a frizzled mess.

Naturally, this was when Madison showed up.

"Looking good, Gabbers!" Madison chirped, a huge smile on her face. "Good news! Everyone's so happy about the cookbook, we're putting you back in the Hooty suit!"

"Wow," Gabby said ruefully, "that *is* good news."

"Isn't it? Now why don't you give me the cookbook so I can lock it up with the rest of the auction items?" Madison's eyes narrowed and though her voice remained peppy, her smile grew cold. "Unless this is all a lie and you don't actually *have* the cookbook to give me."

"Of course she has it," Zee said, stepping between Gabby and Madison, "but she's not going to give it to you *now*. She'll do it at the auction. It's more dramatic that way, in front of your live feed and all. Plus she doesn't trust you to keep it safe."

Madison glared down at Zee, then back at Gabby. "I don't believe you," she said. "I don't think you really have it. But that's okay. If you do, my auction's a success and I win. If you don't, the orchestra hates you more than ever and won't play with you anymore . . . and I win!" She took a deep cleansing breath and pulled herself a little taller. "Thank you, Gabby Duran, for making my day soooo much better."

She turned on her heel and practically floated out of the room.

"You told her I'd give her the book at the auction?" Gabby railed to Zee. "In front of the live feed?"

"I was buying you time!" Zee retorted. "Plus I didn't like the look on her face, all smug and I'm-better-than-Gabby."

Gabby collapsed back into her chair. "I love that you guys stick up for me," she said to Zee and Satchel, "but now I am seriously doomed if I don't get the riddle answer to Trymmy."

"I've got it!" Satchel snapped. "We find a fortune-teller! Then we'll know how this all ends up. If it's bad, we get you on a plane to another country right now."

"This isn't a spy movie," Zee said. "She's not going to another country. Besides, if we had a fortune-teller, the first thing we'd ask is how to give someone 'the future.'"

"A fortune-teller," Gabby mused. "You guys, that's it!"

"It is?" Satchel asked. "'Cause I wasn't actually a hundred percent serious. But if you like the idea . . ."

"I don't like it, I love it!" Gabby smacked her palms on the table and leaned forward, her eyes bright. "I know *exactly* how to give Trymmy the future!"

chapter
TWELVE

*G*abby had been riding Satchel's delivery bike for the better part of forty-five minutes. He had an after-school-and-weekend job delivering pizzas for his aunt Toni's restaurant and always rode the bike to school so he could start work once classes ended. Even days like today, when H.O.O.T. would keep him from any deliveries until much later, he still preferred the bike to the bus or getting crammed into a car with all his cousins. That's why it was available for Gabby. It was an incredibly cumbersome vehicle, with a brutally heavy metal rack on the back, and Gabby weaved back and forth along the shoulder of the road, fighting for balance the whole way.

It was the word "fortune-teller" that had done it. Once Gabby heard that, she knew what she needed for Trymmy, and she knew exactly where to get it. Satchel and Zee had offered to accompany her, but the trip there and back on the bike would take the rest of the school day, and she didn't want them to skip classes and risk getting in trouble. It was the same reason Gabby had said no when Zee offered to take them all on the jet-powered surfboard.

Gabby panted heavily and her heart raced, but it was only partially because of the ride. She'd let so many people down lately—Edwina, Trymmy, the orchestra—and now she had a chance to make at least some of it right. She was so desperate to succeed, it left her gasping for air.

Finally, Gabby weaved Satchel's bike into the Square, a shopping area that straddled Brensville and the next town over. It was a great place for hanging out, filled with unique shops and built around a small park, with lots of wide side-walks. Gabby steered the bike as best she could past coffee shops, yoga studios, and little boutiques, then pulled up to Bottle Rockets, the greatest candy store in the world. Walking in, Gabby faced aisle after aisle of the most unique treats in the universe. Or maybe not in the *whole* universe, but since she was no longer with A.L.I.E.N. Gabby would never really know.

Normally, Gabby would spend hours perusing all the treats. She'd pore over the wall of sodas in bizarre flavors like salty watermelon. She'd stare in awe at the Double Decker bars from England, and the chocobanana, soy sauce, and grilled potato Kit Kats imported from Japan. She'd ponder the merits of an entire aisle of candies made from bacon.

Today, however, she ignored all of that. She wasn't here for candy, she was here for the store's other draw: kitschy toys and memorabilia. These were on round tables scattered between candy stacks. Gabby whizzed past each of them, looking for one specific item amidst the joy buzzers, squeezy stress dolls with bulge-out faces, and Chinese finger traps.

Then she saw it.

A Magic 8 Ball.

She picked it up. The clear fortune-telling window of the ball showed through the square packaging. Gabby looked away and thought hard.

Are you something that represents the future?

She held the package still and waited as an answer floated to the glass surface.

It is decidedly so, it said.

"Yes!" Gabby cried.

She raced to the counter, but when she got there she gasped out loud.

The cashier was a man maybe ten years older than her mom, tall and lean, with a deep tan, crinkles along the sides of his blue eyes, and salt-and-pepper hair. He wore scruffy black jeans and a Bottle Rocket T-shirt. He was good-looking for someone his age, but that wasn't why Gabby gasped. She gasped because she had seen him before. On the playground, dressed in a blazer and watching kids play. On her street, wearing rumpled rags and pushing a shopping cart. In front of a house, pruning bushes.

It was the man she'd dubbed the Silver Fox.

Gabby's brain went a little fuzzy. She hadn't been concerned about the Silver Fox before, but now she was specifically hoping to be around Trymmy. She could *not* have some crazy G.E.T.O.U.T. kook around her when that happened. Gabby had made that mistake once. Never again.

The Silver Fox seemed far more relaxed than Gabby. He smiled. His laugh lines grew deeper.

"Have I seen you before?" he asked.

Gabby didn't like his smile. It looked like the smile of a snake just before it leaped out of its coil and struck. Or like the smile of Madison Murray.

Show no weakness. That, Gabby figured, was the smartest thing to do. If she acted like a totally normal kid who would never even suspect she was being followed, maybe he'd think that's exactly what she was.

"I don't think so," she answered his question. "I'm in a bit of a hurry, though, so if you could just ring me up . . ."

"No problem," he said. As he did, he nodded to a bright yellow piece of paper. Someone from the orchestra had clearly been here with the flyers. "You know anything about this?" he asked. "Brensville Middle School H.O.O.T. Auction?"

Gabby shook her head, staring down at her purchase so she didn't have to look at him as she lied. "Sorry, no. Why?"

The Silver Fox shrugged and handed her a receipt. "You just seem like the right age to know. Word around the store is that the big secret item is a first edition collectible cookbook. Pretty amazing find, right?"

Gabby shrugged. "Not my kind of thing," she said. She stuffed the Magic 8 Ball into her knapsack, ran out the door, hopped clumsily onto Satchel's delivery bike, and pedaled toward school. She looked over her shoulder a few times to see if Silver Fox was following her, but he wasn't. Good.

Between the wobbly bike and her wobbly nerves, Gabby didn't get back until the tail end of eighth period. That meant she missed the bulk of orchestra class time, which everyone was supposed to spend at the gym doing last-minute H.O.O.T. preparations. Gabby got there as fast as she could, and tried to walk in unnoticed. Maybe she could blend in and pretend she'd been there the whole time.

"GABBY!" the whole room chorused.

Gabby waved and returned all their smiles, then sidled next to Satchel.

"They didn't think I was coming, did they?" Gabby asked him under her breath. "They thought I ran off and wouldn't bring the book."

"Every one of them," he agreed under his breath. "They were all cursing your name."

"S'okay," Gabby said with a smile. "I have the future."

"Sweet!" Satchel cried.

"Gabby Duran," Madison called sharply over the on-stage microphone, "I realize time doesn't apply to you, but it's the end of eighth period and we're going to open the doors soon. I suggest you get into your Hooty suit!"

Gabby rolled her eyes. She wanted nothing *less* than to get into the Hooty suit, but it was necessary for her plan to work. Satchel sighed sadly as he handed her the shopping bag containing the giant atrocity, and Gabby lugged it to the girls' locker room. The place smelled about as fresh and clean as the inside of an old sock. The good part about that, Gabby supposed, was that the dank musk inside Hooty's head might feel comparatively refreshing.

Gabby quickly realized she should have brought some-one to help her into the costume. She thought the body would slip on like a pair of footy pajamas, but there was so much extra fabric she practically got lost in it. Once she'd struggled into the limbs and slipped her feet into the un-comfortable plastic flippers, she had to nearly dislocate her arms to fasten the zipper. By the time she put on the head she was already sweaty and exhausted, and she hadn't even started her H.O.O.T. mascot duties.

She peered into a mirror. Hooty's mesh eyeholes gave her a very small field of vision, but her reflection proved what she'd remembered: that there was no way to see it was her inside. If Trymmy *did* show up, he technically wouldn't be seen anywhere near Gabby. That meant A.L.I.E.N. wouldn't know she was breaking their rules, and *that* meant she wouldn't have her memory erased.

Things were coming together. Now she just had to hope that Trymmy actually arrived, that she was able to get him where she needed him to go, and that she'd been correct when she'd figured out the riddle in the first place. Gabby tried to convince herself those were small hurdles to leap.

She strode out into the gym, dangling her knapsack by its straps. Even muffled by the owl head, the roar of the crowd was deafening. Gabby couldn't believe it. In the time she'd been wrestling with her costume, the place had filled. Every chair on the floor was occupied, and plenty of people sat in the bleachers that rose on both sides of the room. Almost everyone held one of the cardboard owl-mask paddles the orchestra had crafted for bidding. Some waved them around, others held them up to their faces, and at any given moment half the audience was hooting.

Gabby smiled inside her giant stuffed head. It was pretty impressive. She hoped things went well.

"Hooty!"

Gabby heard the cry and turned to see her mom, Carmen, and Zee. They sat on the lowest row of bleachers, with Zee and Alice on either side of Carmen. Even though both Alice and Zee were crunched against people on their non-Carmen side, they each sat a good six inches away from Carmen to make sure she had her space. Gabby ran over to them, dragging her knapsack low by her side. It was a dead giveaway to her true identity.

"Gabby, you look so cute!" Alice cried as she fished in her purse. "I need to take your picture."

"Not Gabby," Gabby insisted. "Not here. Just Hooty." She slipped her knapsack to Carmen. "Can you hold this, please?" she asked. "And keep it with you. It's important."

"It's really not," Carmen said. "Not compared to global warming, or unrest in the Middle East, or—"

"It's important to *me*," Gabby clarified. "Please hold on to it." She needed the knapsack to stay safe, since it held the Magic 8 Ball. It also served her to have the bag specifically with Carmen.

Gabby turned her owly face to Zee. "Heard anything?"

Zee shook her head no. No response from Trymmy. Would he even show?

Just then, Madison's voice rang out through the gym. "Good afternoon, everyone, and welcome to our auction! Can I hear a hoot?"

Madison cupped a hand to her ear, and everyone in the gym (except Carmen) responded with a spirited *"HOOT!"*

"Woo-*hoot*!" Madison cheered in return. She was dressed on theme, in a green dress with leaves of silk for the skirt. A crown of red flowers circled her hair, which hung loose except for one Zee-like braid on either side. She looked like a beautiful woodland fairy, minus the wings, and for a second Gabby wondered where in the world she had changed. She certainly hadn't been with Gabby in the sweaty locker room.

"We'll officially start the auction and live stream in a minute," Madison continued. "We just want to give everyone time to get here and settle in. In the meantime, for your entertainment, I present our mascot, Hooty the H.O.O.T. Owl!"

Every eye in the room shifted to Gabby. That's when she realized that in all her frenzy to get ready, she hadn't planned what she'd *do* in the owl suit.

She tried giving her arms a flap.

The room erupted in cheers.

Energized by the crowd's response, she pranced around the room, flapping her wings and leaping as well as she could in the flipper feet. Gabby could hear people roar with laughter, but she *really* knew she was doing a good job when Madison cleared her throat loudly over the microphone.

"Thanks, Hooty! That's all for now. Go sit on your egg."

That got big laughs, too, and Madison kept the crowd's attention by launching into the first item up for bids.

As time passed and Gabby anxiously watched the door for Trymmy, she couldn't help but notice how successfully the auction was going. Bids came in from the crowd in the gym, they came in from online. . . . It seemed like everyone was wrapped up in the energy and wanted a piece of the action. Each item got bids, even the jack-in-the-box, whose pop-up clown didn't have a head. Apparently, an eighth grader named Eric Carlyle thought it would be the perfect instrument for torturing his baby sister.

Still, Gabby understood why Maestro Jenkins had warned Madison against an auction in the first place. Items were selling, but they weren't making a lot of money. Even higher-priced lots like Gabby's night of free babysitting only got two hundred and fifty dollars. Two hundred and fifty dollars was a ridiculously huge amount of money for a night of sitting, but the orchestra needed ten thousand dollars to make it to MusicFest, and the tote board with their running total was nowhere near that number.

Gabby was about to stroll her owly self outside to see if Trymmy was anywhere near the building, when something so terrible caught her eye that if she could have laid an egg, she would have.

Someone new was sitting next to her mother.

Someone Gabby recognized. A very charming-looking middle-aged man with a tan, laugh lines, and salt-and-pepper hair. He wore broken-in jeans and a blue T-shirt that brought out his startlingly blue eyes.

It was the Silver Fox. With a wide smile, he leaned close to Alice Duran and whispered something in her ear. She threw back her head and laughed, then looked around conspiratorially before whispering something back to him that he clearly found terribly amusing.

Holy fricassoli.

Were her mom and the Silver Fox *flirting*???

For a second Gabby stopped breathing. This was a bad choice not only for the obvious reason, but because when she started up again she had to take a very deep breath of noxious owl-head must.

A G.E.T. O.U.T. agent flirting with her mom? Using her mom to get to her? Gabby didn't care who she did or didn't work for anymore, this was unacceptable. She marched as stridently as her flipper-feet would let her and loomed over the Silver Fox, hands on her hips.

"What do you think you're doing?" she snapped.

If the Silver Fox was surprised to find a giant owl yelling at him, he didn't show it.

"Hooty!" Alice cried happily. "I was hoping you'd get a chance to come over. This is Arlington. Arlington, this is Hooty the H.O.O.T. Owl." She dropped her voice to a stage whisper. "Actually it's my other daughter, Gabby." She put her fingers to her lips, warning him to keep silent about it.

He nodded solemnly and his voice was soft. "Gabby Duran . . . I think I've read something about you."

"In the local papers, I'm sure," Alice said. "Gabby had a big solo last week in the orchestra's fall concert."

"That must be it," the Silver Fox said, though Gabby was sure he'd actually read about her on the G.E.T.O.U.T. secured Web site. She glared daggers at him, then realized all he was seeing was the cross-eyed demented smile of Hooty the H.O.O.T. Owl.

"It's so funny Arlington sat here," Alice said. "He used to write for *Fabulous Foods* magazine. I've read his articles! Isn't it amazing that of all the places in the gym he happened to sit down next to me?"

"Amazing," Carmen deadpanned.

Gabby's thought exactly. She had to get this man away from her mom, but how?

"Hooty!" cried Madison from the podium. "Have we lost our mascot?"

The last thing Gabby felt like doing was a Hooty bit right now, but then she got an idea. She grabbed the microphone from Lilah Hartmann, who was taking bids at one of the computers, and called, "I'm right here, Madison, and this time I'm doing a great big Hooty the H.O.O.T. Owl Dance with a lucky member of our audience! Hit it!"

"What?!" Madison spluttered. "Hooty, you're not supposed to speak! And we don't have dance music for—"

But Zee had Gabby's back. She had already hopped up, pulled out her phone, and plugged it into the amp system. Hip-hop music blared, and Gabby started a ridiculous dance, flapping her wings and waggling her tail feathers. The crowd loved it and clapped along. Gabby then pointed a wing at Silver Fox. He shook his head as if embarrassed, but Gabby danced his way, pulled him up by the hand, and spun him onto the floor, *far* away from Alice. He danced gamely along with Hooty, then Gabby pulled in another volunteer: Alana Mulloney, a waitress at Toni's. Alana's ex-husband had just remarried, and she'd been telling everyone in the restaurant that it was her turn to find someone. Gabby knew she would go nuts for a handsome guy like the Silver Fox.

417

Sure enough, Alana threw one arm around Silver Fox's waist, took his hand, and led him across the floor in a wild tango he could only try to follow. Gabby waved her wings in the air to get the crowd cheering. They roared.

"That's enough of that!" Madison cried. "Don't want to keep our online viewers waiting too long between bids. Next up is a three-pack of personalized sessions with nutritionist Sheila Cormsby, redeemable in person or online. Do I hear one hundred and fifty dollars?"

Gabby flapped her way to Zee and told her to cut the music, then said, "You have to keep that guy busy. He's G.E.T.O.U.T. I don't want him near my mom, and if Trymmy and his parents come, I need him far away from them."

"On it," Zee said. "I know exactly what to do, just need a little time."

"No problem," Gabby said. "I'll get Satch."

She raced up the bleachers to Satchel, who was back on his original duty.

"Recycling collection!" he called down rows. "If you've got recycling, I'm collecting it!"

Several cans and bottles flew toward him. Satchel ducked and lunged acrobatically to catch them in his large blue bin.

"I need your help," Gabby told him. "See that guy?" She pointed out Silver Fox, who had already settled back into his seat next to Alice. "I need you to keep him far away from my mom. Can you help me?"

Satchel considered. "Can I tell him I'm with the CDC and we need to quarantine him because we believe he's been exposed to a rare and deadly contagious virus?"

"You can," Gabby said, "but he might not believe you. Maybe something a little more school-centric."

"Got it," Satchel said. He put down his bin, straightened his shirt, and raced excitedly across the gym. "Congratulations!" Satchel cried, pumping the Silver Fox's hand up and down. "You're in seat number four hundred and twenty-eight A! That means you win a special behind-the-scenes tour of the Brensville Middle School gymnasium!"

"No, thank you," Silver Fox demurred. "I'd rather not. I was just up, and—"

"Oh, go on," Alice said, laughing. "It's all part of the fun."

Gabby smiled inside her suit, watching Silver Fox's discomfort. If he wanted to keep up his charade of being an innocent, charming guy, he had no choice but to obey. Gabby relished the way Silver Fox's back hunched in defeat as Satchel led him up the bleachers, prattling brilliantly about nothing.

"So if you count the steps to the top of the bleachers, you'll see they're actually representative of the number of athletes Brensville Middle School has sent to the Olympics over the years. An interesting choice, since if we send any more, we'll have to add more stairs and possibly raise the ceiling...."

Satchel's tour took care of the Silver Fox for quite a while. By the time the so-called Arlington collapsed back in his seat next to Alice, Zee was ready. She had run out of the gym after speaking with Gabby, only to return to her seat next to Carmen, this time carrying her camouflage duffel bag. When no one was looking, Zee took out a small cylindrical robot that moved on tanklike wheeled tracks. Once Zee placed it on the floor, the robot zipped past Carmen, past Alice, and came to a stop under Arlington's chair. Then it reached up one wiry arm and used its gripper fingers to unclasp the Silver Fox's watch. The robot carefully eased the watch off Arlington's wrist, then zoomed at top speed down the floor.

"Wilbur!" Zee shouted loud enough for Arlington to hear. She leaned over Alice and Carmen to tell the Silver Fox, "I'm so sorry. I was testing Wilbur's stealth grip, and I think he took your watch!"

"Who?" Arlington said. "My what?"

"Your *robot* Wilbur?" Alice asked.

Zee nodded. "I'm really sorry."

By then Arlington had looked at his wrist and felt it, as if the watch might be there and he just didn't see it. "I don't ... Where did it ..."

"Over there!" Zee cried, pointing to Wilbur scooting unnoticed under legs and chairs as it zoomed at top speed toward the far end of the gym. Arlington leaped up to give chase, and Zee grinned with satisfaction as he scrambled hopelessly after the speedy robot. Gabby noticed Zee fidgeting with her hands and wondered if Wilbur's remote controls were tucked away in one of her palms.

While Satchel and Zee handled the Silver Fox, Gabby kept busy. She did her Hooty routine whenever Madison asked, but mostly she watched for Trymmy.

There was no sign of him.

Gabby stayed hopeful, but that got harder the more time passed.

All too soon, the list of items up for bids dwindled down to just a few. The auction was hurtling to a close, and Gabby had to face the facts.

Trymmy wasn't coming.

Gabby had failed.

The minute she realized it, all the energy drained out of her. She didn't want to be a happily dancing owl anymore, she just wanted to be alone. She slunk to a far wall near the gymnasium door and slid down it.

All her life, Gabby had cared the most about just a few things: her friends, her family, babysitting, and her music. She put tons of energy into all those things, and they all thrived. She had a great relationship with her mom and Carmen, she and Zee and Satchel were inseparable, she was a terrific babysitter, and she played French horn like no one she had ever met.

Working for A.L.I.E.N. was the first new thing Gabby had cared about in forever. She'd cared about it deeply. She'd only gotten to sit for three alien kids, but each one of them was incredibly special, and they'd trusted her to keep this huge secret that meant everything to their very existence. She'd wanted so badly to be worthy of that trust, and she'd worked really hard to do a great job, but for the first time ever, that wasn't enough. She'd failed. She'd lost the position she loved. Now all she wanted more than anything was to make one little boy's life better—and she knew exactly how to do it!—but she wouldn't get the chance.

She was about to take off her head, slip out the door, and go home, when she heard a voice next to her.

"Why are you hiding back here? Don't you *give a hoot* about the auction?"

Gabby wheeled her stuffed head around.

It was Trymmy. His mouth was curled in a sidelong smile, pleased at his joke. Allynces and Feltrymm stood just behind him. They looked around at the decorations distastefully.

Gabby couldn't believe it. She inwardly thanked herself

for not pulling off the Hooty head. Allynces and Feltrymm never would have let her get away with what she was about to do if she weren't a giant, friendly-looking owl. She grabbed Trymmy's hand with her wing and pulled him down the line of bleachers. He resisted at first.

"Hey! What are you doing? Let go of me."

"It's me," she said through the mouth hole. "Gabby."

"Gabby?"

"Shhh."

She noticed that neither Silver Fox nor Zee was anywhere to be seen, which was good. Zee must still have him on a wild-goose chase to find his watch. Gabby pulled Trymmy all the way to her knapsack, which sat in front of Carmen. Adrenaline and clumsy wings made it almost impossible for her to pry open the zipper, but she finally managed. With a breathless flourish, she pulled out her recent purchase and held it out to Trymmy.

"A Magic 8 Ball," he said. "Cool."

"It's not just 'cool,' it's the answer to your riddle: 'the future'!"

"But 'the future' isn't the answer," Trymmy said.

"Sure it is!" Gabby insisted. "'I never was, am always to be'—the future. 'No one ever saw me, nor ever will see'—the future. 'I can't be bought, I can't be sold'—the future."

"You can sell futures in the stock market," Carmen said. Gabby hadn't realized her sister had been paying attention.

"You can?" Gabby asked.

"You can," Trymmy said.

"And is that the whole riddle?" Carmen asked.

"No," Trymmy replied. "It ends, 'The young have more of me than the old. And yet I am the hope of all, who live and breathe on your terrestrial ball.'"

Carmen shrugged. "The answer's 'tomorrow.'"

Trymmy smiled. "Yeah. It is." He extended a formal hand toward Carmen. "I'm Trymmy."

Carmen didn't take it. "Carmen. Got any more riddles?"

"You have no idea."

"I have *some* idea. There's a limited permutation of words in the English language."

"What if I speak another language?" Trymmy asked.

Carmen thought a minute. "I'd need more data." She gestured to the spot next to her that Zee had vacated. "You can sit if you want. Just not too close."

On Carmen's other side, Alice had been watching this curiously, and now she clapped a hand over her mouth to stop from gasping out loud. Gabby understood why. Carmen didn't invite *anyone* to sit down and talk to her. Social overtures weren't generally her thing.

Allynces and Feltrymm had been running after Trymmy.

They caught up now, just as Trymmy took a seat next to, but several inches away from, Carmen.

"You can't run off like that, Trymmy!" Allynces snapped, but she didn't get anything else out before Alice jumped up to effusively introduce herself.

"Are you Trymmy's parents?" she asked. "I'm Alice Duran. It is *wonderful* to meet you."

Gabby had been so entranced by Trymmy and Carmen hitting it off that she hadn't seen this coming. Fire smoldered in Allynces's eyes as she turned from Alice to Gabby. "Alice . . . *Duran*?" she asked.

"Yes," Alice said, not realizing the sudden temperature drop in the room. "That's my daughter Carmen, and *this*"—she gestured to the owl suit—"is my other daughter, Gabby."

Both Feltrymm and Allynces were fuming now. With her identity blown, and the Silver Fox nowhere in sight, Gabby went ahead and pulled off the owl head. It was a massive relief to gasp fresh air, even though she was sure her face was bright red, her hair was everywhere, and her head smelled like the inside of a sweat sock.

"I can explain," she said.

"*GABBY DURAN!*" Madison squealed from the podium. "I'm so glad you revealed yourself, because we're down to one last item. Please bring us what we've all been waiting for . . . the cookbook!"

"Right, the cookbook!" Gabby called out. Then she turned to Trymmy. "Carmen answered the riddle. You can give me the cookbook now, right?"

"*Carmen* answered the riddle," Trymmy said. "You didn't. The book stays with me. Those are the rules."

"You have to play by the rules, Gabby," Carmen agreed.

Allynces leaned down and took Trymmy's arm. "Trymmy, let's go. We're leaving."

"So soon?" Alice asked.

"Yes," she insisted, then turned to Gabby. "And *you* will be facing the stiffest punishment from our mutual acquaintances, I assure you."

"GABBY!" Madison cried.

Gabby heard the voice, but through a fog.

So that was it. On top of everything else, Gabby was going to lose her memories. She wouldn't remember Wutt, or Philip, or Trymmy.

If A.L.I.E.N. was at all merciful, she wouldn't remember Madison, either.

"GABBY DURAN, YOU LISTEN TO ME RIGHT NOW!" Madison wailed through the microphone, making it screech with feedback.

"I don't have the cookbook, okay?" Gabby shouted loud enough for her to hear. "I don't have it!"

A murmur of disbelief spread through the gym.

"Really, Gabby?" Madison boomed from the stage. "We still need two thousand dollars, which the cookbook could easily get. Are you telling me you're going to fail the orchestra so we can't go to MusicFest?"

"Yes, that's exactly what I'm telling you," she replied. "Auction's over."

Somewhere, dimly, Gabby understood that people were shouting things to and about her, and the crowd was breaking up and getting ready to go. Gabby didn't care about any of it. Only one thing was on her mind. She wanted to come through for Trymmy, even if she was doomed to forget every moment of what she'd done.

Using both owl wings, she pulled Allynces by the arm.

"Get off me!" Allynces cried, batting at Gabby's wings, but Gabby held on so she could say her piece.

"Mrs. Vyllsk . . . Mrs. Villis . . ." Gabby gave up trying to remember her last name and just called her by her first. "Allynces," she began again, keeping her voice low so Trymmy wouldn't hear and be embarrassed, "I know what's going to happen to me, and honestly, I'm fine with it. I deserve it. I messed up, and probably you're all safer if I don't remember anything about any of you. But please. Don't take Trymmy away just yet. Did you know he spent all his free time at Lion's Gate Academy hiding in the Lost and Found?"

"I'm aware," she said coldly. "Humans aren't kind to those who look different."

"*Some* humans aren't kind. But maybe Trymmy only had no friends because he never found the right people. Just look. *Please*."

She pointed toward Carmen and Trymmy, who were speaking in machine-gun blasts back and forth as if there were no one else in the gym. Neither Alice nor Feltrymm could take their eyes off them.

Allynces was looking now, too. Slowly, she moved closer and Gabby followed.

"You shouldn't like riddles so much," Carmen said. "They're easy. Puzzles are hard."

"*Riddles* are hard," Trymmy said. "They take razor-sharp mental acuity."

Carmen shrugged. "They take logic. What's bought by the yard and worn by the foot?"

"A carpet," Trymmy answered. "The man who invented it doesn't want it. The man who bought it doesn't need it. The man who needs it doesn't know it. What is it?"

"A coffin," Carmen said. "A thing there is whose voice is one; whose feet are four and two and three. So mutable a thing is none that moves in earth or sky or sea. When on most feet this thing doth go, its strength is weakest and its pace most slow. What is it?"

"It's a . . ."

Gabby, Alice, Allynces, and Feltrymm had been watching the volley like a tennis match, and they all held their breath as something flickered in Trymmy's eyes. He pulled himself a little taller and arched his unibrow knowingly.

"It's a . . ."

The knowing look faded. He tipped a mole into his mouth and sucked on it as he contemplated. Then he grinned.

"I don't know," he said.

"You don't?" Gabby asked.

"Nope." He turned to Carmen. "What is it?"

"A person," Carmen said. "One voice, but the feet change. Four feet as a crawling baby, two feet when he can walk, three when he's old and needs a cane. The more feet, the slower and weaker he is. Even an old man with a cane can get around faster and lift more than a crawling baby."

Trymmy's grin spread even wider. "Yeah, that's true, but I didn't get it. You stumped me. Hey, want to play Secret Mega Orbs?" He pulled two marbles out of his pocket, then looked at Gabby. "Can I grab more orbs?"

Gabby nodded, and Trymmy dug into her knapsack to pull out the sack of marbles.

Trymmy's mother turned to Alice. "I'm afraid I didn't introduce myself. Allynces Vyllskryn. This is my husband Feltrymm. And our son, Trymmy."

Alice, Allynces, and Feltrymm kept talking, but Gabby didn't hear it because she was distracted by a scream in her ear.

"What is wrong with you, Gabby Duran?!" Madison wailed. Gabby saw she now looked less like a woodland fairy and more like a volcano about to erupt.

"Madison, I'm sorry about the book."

"The one that's sitting at your feet?!" Madison shrieked.

Gabby looked down. Sure enough, a thick greenish-colored tattered volume of *Joy of Cooking* sat on the floor in front of her.

Of course! Carmen had stumped Trymmy with a riddle! Everything he'd ever stolen would be returned to its rightful owners! Gabby's heart leaped as she scooped the book into her hands and presented it to Madison.

"Yes, this one!" she cried. "I have it right here! Let's auction it off and get to MusicFest!"

"Are you insane?!" Madison wailed. "Look around you! Everyone left! You said it was over! The online people logged off! It's *done*!"

Gabby looked around. Madison was right. The gym that had been teeming with people a few minutes ago was now practically empty. No one manned the dark computer tables. No one sat in the chairs on the floor. A small group of Madison's friends huddled by the stage, and only a few stray knots of students and parents dotted the gym floor and bleachers.

"Great work, Gabby," she sniped. "Thanks to you, we missed MusicFest by two thousand dollars. Good luck having anything to do with anyone in orchestra after this."

"Two thousand dollars, you say?" Feltrymm piped up.

Gabby hadn't even realized that he, Allynces, and Alice had stopped talking, but all three of them were now focused on Gabby and Madison. Madison had clearly also not known she was under parental scrutiny. She straightened out her green dress, stood a little taller, and tried to put on a good face for her audience.

"Yes, that's exactly what I'm saying. And it's all Gabby's fault."

"We bid five thousand for the cookbook," Allynces said.

Madison looked like she'd been whomped in the face with the world's largest pillow. "*Five* thousand dollars?"

"Yes," Feltrymm agreed. "That should cover everything with a little extra padding."

Allynces dug into her purse. "To whom should I make out the check?"

"The Help Our Orchestra Travel Fund," Madison said in a daze. When Allynces handed her the check she added, "Thank you. Thank you very much."

Then Madison wheeled away from the group and held the check in the air. "I did it!" she screamed. "I got the money! We're going to MusicFest!"

The small knot of Madison's besties turned and squealed. They raced toward Madison, who met them at the center of the room. "We have to get Maestro and tell him—*I* saved our trip!"

Together, the girls ran out of the gym.

"I don't understand at all," Alice said, her brows knitted. "Gabby, you told me you lost the book."

Thankfully, Gabby didn't have to answer. The sound of pounding feet took her attention, and she wheeled around to see a red-faced and breathless Satchel and Zee burst in across the gym. She excused herself and raced over to them.

"Wilbur was running low on power, so we had to stop Silver Fox another way," Zee said in a fast, panting whisper.

"She had the robot lead him to the laundry room and we locked him in," Satchel added.

"But he's out now and he's coming this way!" Zee finished.

That's when Gabby heard more stomping feet. The Silver Fox had emerged from the bowels of the gymnasium and was storming, head down, toward Allynces, Feltrymm, and Trymmy.

No. Gabby would *not* let this G.E.T.O.U.T. agent any-where near the Trolls. She waddled across the floor as fast as her flippered feet would let her. The Silver Fox noticed her when she was still several feet away. "Oh," he said with a friendly smile. "Hello."

Instead of responding, Gabby threw herself onto her stomach, for the first time grateful that Madison had made her wear a giant carpet. The owl suit skated across the shiny, slick gymnasium floor, and Gabby covered her face with her wings as her body barreled into the Silver Fox's legs and knocked him to the ground. He sprawled forward. When he rolled onto his back to get his bearings, Gabby was right there, leaning over him to stare down into his face.

"There's no way I'm letting you use my mom to get to me," she said menacingly, "and if you think I don't know who you are, you're crazy."

"Who am I?" he asked frantically.

"G.E.T.O.U.T.," Gabby hissed.

"I would love to, but you're on top of me!"

"What is going on?" Alice cried, walking their way. "Gabby, are you okay? Arlington?"

She held out her hand to the Silver Fox and helped him up while Gabby rose to her owl-feet. "You can't trust this man, Mom. He said he writes for a magazine? I saw him selling candy at Bottle Rockets."

Arlington's face brightened as he smiled and nodded. "Yes! You're the girl who came in to buy the Magic 8 Ball. I didn't recognize you with the owl head on. And I said I *did* write for a magazine. Now I'm working on a novel. I'm afraid I have a quirky habit of living like my characters to get inside their heads. I've worked at the candy store, as a gardener, in a law office . . . I even spent a day as a homeless man just to make sure the details I wrote were real."

"That's remarkable," Alice said.

Her eyes shone with admiration, and Arlington looked down at her with equal fondness.

Gabby's stomach rolled over. Was her mom seriously falling for this guy's story? Not that it was an unreasonable story. It kind of made sense. And Gabby certainly didn't have *proof* that Arlington was with G.E.T.O.U.T. It wasn't like he was chasing down the Trolls, who were only sitting half a gym away.

Still, for whatever reason, Gabby felt queasy watching the two of them. That she knew.

"Gabs?" Zee said softly. "You okay? You look a little pale."

Gabby realized Zee and Satchel were both looking at her worriedly. She smiled. "Yeah. I just need a second. I'll be right back."

She flipped her way to the girls' locker room and headed for the stalls. She didn't think she'd actually throw up, but better safe than sorry. She pulled open a stall door, then backed away screaming.

"Hello, Gabby," Edwina said.

The woman was standing stock-still, right there in front of the toilet. As always, she was dressed all in black and wore an expression of pure business. As if lurking in a bathroom stall was a perfectly normal part of her day.

Gabby took a deep breath. Now that the shock had worn off, she knew exactly why Edwina was here, and she supposed she was ready. She stood taller and tried to look dignified in her owl body.

"Just promise me it won't hurt," she said.

"What exactly do you not wish to hurt?" Edwina asked.

"Aren't you going to erase my memory?"

"That was meant to be my assignment, yes," Edwina said. "We've of course been keeping an eye on you and knew you were going to defy direct orders. But then things changed."

"They did?"

"Indeed. My superiors received a very forceful text message from Allynces. She not only insisted that you remain affiliated with A.L.I.E.N., but she has already booked your services for the next three Wednesdays after school."

"Booked me to babysit?" Gabby asked. "But doesn't that mean . . . ?"

A hint of a smile played on Edwina's lips. "The Unsittables program is officially back in business."

"It is?" Gabby was elated, but also confused. "And I'm still in it? Even after I went against your orders, and led G.E.T.O.U.T. to Trymmy, and—"

"You made mistakes," Edwina said, "but you also acted out of great love and respect for another being, even though it meant putting the memories you value at risk. Nothing speaks more to the mission of A.L.I.E.N."

Edwina leaned down a bit to look Gabby in the eye, and Gabby was surprised to see Edwina's own eyes were a little misty. "Allow me to add that I am very proud of you, Gabby, and it is a personal honor to reinstate you as Associate 4118-25125A. Well done."

Gabby flushed with pride. "Thank you."

"By bringing Trymmy to your sister, you also did quite a service to humanity. You'll recall Trymmy's collection encompassed items from his grandfather's thieveries as well as his own. Thanks to Carmen's riddle, they're now all back with their rightful owners. At this very moment, for example, researchers are going quite apoplectic over the sudden discovery of Amelia Earhart's lost plane." Edwina clip-clopped toward a back door that Gabby was quite sure hadn't existed the last time she was in the room.

"There's also an item that you, in particular, might find interesting," Edwina added. "I suggest you check your pockets."

With that, she pushed open the door and left.

Gabby tried to obey, but she couldn't reach her pockets through the owl costume. With her hands still covered by a layer of wing, she fought to unzip the back, then let the costume slip down to the floor. As she stepped out of the flippers, she reached inside the pockets of her jeans.

Her right hand touched something hard and flat.

She pulled it out. It was a silver rectangle with rounded corners, attached to a chain of beaded metal. A second rounded rectangle dangled from the other end of the chain.

Dog tags. Military dog tags. Gabby held them up to look more closely, and the name on them stopped her heart.

Steven Duran.

Gabby's father. He'd gone missing in action when Carmen was a baby. His body was never found.

How had Trymmy's grandfather ended up with his dog tags?

"Edwina! Edwina!" Gabby raced out the door after her. The outdoor chill blasted Gabby's face, but she didn't even notice. She ran over the grass and into the street, calling Edwina's name and looking for the limo, but it wasn't there.

Edwina was gone.

Now Gabby felt the cold. She tried to go back the way she came, but the door was once again gone. Instead she circled around and walked through the gym's main entrance. She could see everyone from here. Carmen and Trymmy hadn't moved; they were still playing with the marbles. Allynces, Feltrymm, Alice, and Arlington had pulled out a circle of folding chairs and now chatted like old friends.

Zee had powered Wilbur back up, and she and Satchel were maneuvering the robot through an obstacle course of woodland decorations.

Gabby had a million questions. About her dad and Trymmy's grandfather, about Arlington, about what came next for her and A.L.I.E.N. Yet as she looked at the group in the gym, she knew she'd have time for all that later. When Edwina came for her again, Gabby would be ready. In the meantime . . .

Gabby looked at her father's name on the dog tags. Smiling, she hugged her hand around them, slipped them into her pocket, and walked out to join the group. She was thrilled she wouldn't lose her old memories, but she was more excited than ever to make some new ones.

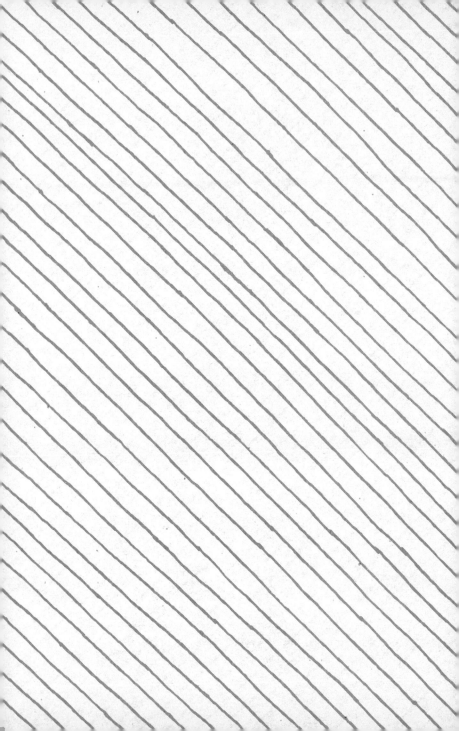

Acknowledgments

We are beyond thrilled to present Gabby Duran to the world, and we know it never could have happened without the amazing efforts of so many people. First and foremost, we'd like to thank the amazing Jane Startz, for being the ultimate matchmaker and bringing the two of us together. Jane's vision is unparalleled, and we're honored to have her in our corner. Equal thanks to Kane Lee, for his always-insightful notes and excellent story sense. Together, Jane and Kane are a formidable team and Gabby's world would never have become what it is without them.

Next, we'd like to thank our incredible team at Hyperion. Our editor Emily Meehan had the vision to see everything Gabby could become, and we're so grateful she brought us under her wing. Together, Emily and Jessica Harriton are an editorial dream team. Their story notes were dead-on, and inspired us to dive eagerly and excitedly into each rewrite.

Thanks also to copyeditor Jody Corbett, who ran through the manuscript with a fine-toothed comb. She made sure we never contradicted ourselves in the details, and called us on all our verbal tics. Thanks to publicist Jamie Baker, for working so hard to tell the world about Gabby, and get her story onto everyone's radar. Finally, thanks to Marci Senders, whose eye-popping cover design made us squeal with glee in dolphin frequencies, then jump up and down and do a giant happy dance.

On a personal note, Elise would like to thank and hug and get all gushy over her husband Randy, daughter Madeline, and dog Jack for their unending love and support. She sends a huge thanks to Annette van Duren, her longtime and wonderful agent. She'd also love to thank all the rest of her friends and family individually . . . but that would take up way too much space. Instead she'll single out one: Sylvia Allen. Mom-Mom Sylvia, you make 98-years-old look GREAT!

Daryle would like to profusely thank Liz Lehmans and Jeannie Hayden for their long-term support of Gabby Duran in all of her many incarnations, and Jack Brummet and Keelin Curran for their help in making the Gabby project happen. She'd also like to thank Dan Elenbaas for the opportunity to create Gabby in the first place, and Farai Chideya for putting Gabby in Jane Startz' able hands. To

Cynthia True, Erik Wiese and Marya Sea Kaminski, thanks for always helping with the tough decisions and giving your advice so generously.

Most of all, we want to thank YOU, our fabulous readers! We do the writing, but Gabby comes to life in your imaginations. Thanks for hanging with her, and we hope you'll join us for Book Two!

Much love,
Elise and Daryle

Acknowledgments

We are extraterrestrially excited to continue Gabby's adventures, but no secret dossier happens without the help of enough people to fill the files of A.L.I.E.N. itself. First and foremost, we owe an enormous THANK-YOU to everyone at Hyperion. We are completely humbled by your dedication to Gabby Duran, and all that you've done and continue to do to get her stories out to the world. We are truly eternally grateful.

More specifically, we want to heap a galactic-sized shower of appreciation onto Kieran Viola! Kieran is the most amazing cheerleader, supporter, champion, and friend to us; plus she's also a staggeringly brilliant editor. She has an eagle eye for story and character, no doubt because she's an author in her own right, and you should all check out her books, which she writes as Kieran Scott and Kate Brian. That's right, she has aliases—of course she's the perfect editor for us.

Huge thanks also to Emily Meehan. Emily, you're the reason we're at Hyperion, and we're so thankful you fell in love with Gabby and believed in her right away.

Julie Moody, thank you for your editorial eye; and thank you, Marci Senders and Sarah Not, for your incredible cover ideas and artwork. To our copy editor Jody Corbett, thanks for saving us from all the mistakes we make that we're too close to see. Jamie Baker, we can't ever rave enough about your publicity genius. The swag you made for book one has us doing giddy dances to this day. We loved meeting you in person at the L.A. kickoff, and can't wait to see you again!

Elke Villa, Holly Nagel, and Molly Kong, thank you for your boundless enthusiasm and passion for Gabby. With the three of you in her corner, she can't help but succeed!

Jane Startz, without you there would be no Gabby, and—even more tragically—the two of us never would have met. Thanks for bringing us together and for all your constant hard work and support. Thanks also to Kane Lee and Jake Holm for all your help along the way.

Annette Van Duren and Matthew Saver, agent and lawyer extraordinaire, thank you for working tirelessly on our behalf. We can never thank you enough.

Finally—and this one's really cool—thanks to everyone at Disney Channel for OPTIONING GABBY FOR TELEVISION!!!!! It's still early, so we can't say much about what the Gabby show will be, but it's in Team Mouse's capable hands, and we can't wait to see what they come up with!!!!

Now the personal stuff. It's not a book until Elise thanks her husband, Randy; daughter, Maddie; and dog, Jack-Jack, for their constant support, love, and treat mongering. Thanks also to all her friends and family, and a special shout-out to early readers Rahm Jethani, Grant Yabuki, and Everett Nellis; to Mrs. Finklestein's 2015–2016 third grade class at Carpenter Community Charter for totally adopting book one; and to the kids at CHIME Charter and their wonderful librarian, Heidi Mark, for their excitement about Gabby and her adventures.

Daryle would like to profusely thank Liz Lehmans, Jeannie Hayden, Suzanne Downs, Karen Miller, Wes Hurley, and Bob and Nancy Young for all of their support and encouragement, and Jack Brummet and Keelin Curran for their help in making the Gabby project happen. She'd also like to thank Dan Elenbaas for the opportunity to create Gabby in the first place, and Farai Chideya for putting Gabby in Jane Startz's able hands. To Cynthia True, Erik Wiese, and Marya Sea Kaminski, thanks for always helping with the tough decisions and giving your advice so generously.

But the biggest thank-you of all goes to YOU—every single person who picks up a Gabby Duran book and dives in. We've been lucky enough to meet a bunch of you, and nothing makes us happier. Thanks for joining us on another Gabby adventure; keep reaching out and saying hi, because we love to hear from you, and we hope you'll join us soon for yet another secret dossier about the adventures of Gabby Duran!

Much love always,
Elise and Daryle

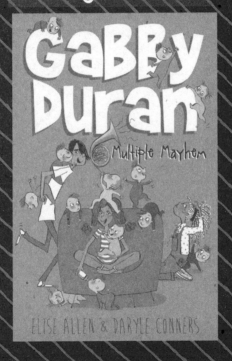

chapter
ONE

*g*abby Duran raced through the woods, her breath scratching her throat. She could barely see. Only tiny slats of the late-afternoon sun squeezed through the thick canopy of leaves. Gabby raised her arms to shield her face from the branches snapping at her with every step, but she didn't dare slow down.

If she did, he'd catch her.

He'd catch her if she kept running, too. He was a born hunter. He'd hear her sneakers pounding on the crinkled dry leaves. He'd hear her gasping for air. It was only a matter of time.

Gabby needed a place to hide. She needed it fast.

Finally, she saw it: a darker spot in the gloom. A cave-like opening at the bottom of a huge tree trunk. She veered toward it and dropped to her knees, then scooted back on the ground until she was curled up inside, her arms hugged around her bent legs.

She felt better, but she didn't feel safe. She was still panting, her breath coming out in white-from-the-cold puffs that would surely give her away. She forced herself to breathe more slowly. In . . . out. In . . . out.

Better.

Gabby grinned. He'd never find her here.

But then she heard the sound. A ceaseless slither, a body sliding over dried leaves, moving closer . . . closer . . .

Gabby's heart pounded. She ducked her head and hid her mop of curls under her arms, making herself as small as possible.

The slithering grew louder. Gabby squeezed her eyes shut. Maybe it wasn't as close as it sounded. Maybe.

Suddenly the slithering stopped. Gabby didn't dare breathe.

Maybe he didn't see her. Maybe he'd move on.

Then a freezing dollop of goo landed on her hand. It chilled her to the bone, but before she could even react, the chill oozed up her arm, slicking between her shirt and the

sleeve of her purple puffy jacket. It emerged as an icy blob against the skin of her neck, and . . .

"Aaaaa!" Gabby squealed out loud. "Okay, you found me!"

Gabby uncurled herself and tried to look at the glob, but it pressed so tightly against her neck it was impossible to see. As if realizing this, the creature extended a bulbous green pod out in front of Gabby's face. The pod was shaped like a head, and it widened in the middle as if it was smiling . . . which it was.

"You're too good at this, Glolc!" Gabby gushed. "No matter where I hide, you always find me."

Glolc's green, quivery head-shape shimmied with laughter. Then he hopped into the air, snapping his elastic-slime body away from Gabby and into a beach ball–sized sphere. Glolc hovered for a second, then Gabby caught him in her arms as he fell.

"What do you want to play now?" Gabby asked. But before Glolc could answer, Gabby's cell phone rang from the back pocket of her jeans. Still sitting inside the tree trunk, Gabby struggled to reach it, rocking to her right and trying to balance Glolc in one arm, but Glolc quickly solved the problem. He extended an amoebalike blob from his body, wrapped it around the phone, then snapped it back into place. Glolc disgorged a smaller tentacle to press TALK, then extended the phone to Gabby's ear.

"Hello?" Gabby said.

"Hi!" chirped an upbeat and very human female voice. "It's Esleil—I'm home!"

"Oh, great!" Gabby replied. "We're playing outside. I'll have Glolc back in no time."

Glolc clicked off Gabby's phone, dropped it, then melted into a giant splotch of green ooze that glopped heavily over Gabby's arms.

"I don't want to go, either!" Gabby laughed. "But it's time. Your mom's back. And I promised *my* mom I'd be home for dinner."

Reluctantly, Glolc congealed his body back into an amorphous mound and rolled out of the tree hole. Gabby scooted out after him, adjusted the ever-present purple knapsack on her back, and moved with him through the woods. Looking down at the little blob, Gabby tried not to giggle. Glolc only came up to Gabby's knees, and he resembled nothing so much as a beanbag made of lime Jell-O, but the way he slumped over as he slithered along on his protruding pseudopods made him look just like a human kid disappointed his playtime was about to end.

Gabby was so entranced by the way Glolc moved that she forgot to look where she was going. Her foot came down on something firm but strangely squishy.

She looked down and saw the lifeless body of a young boy staring up at her. Her foot had landed on his arm.

"Oh my gosh!" she gasped. "I can't believe we almost left this here! You have to get in."

A lump of Glolc's body turned toward Gabby. It looked at her pleadingly.

"I know, but your mom said you could only have it off in the woods." Gabby thought a second, then smiled. "Tell you what—once you're in, I'll break out the string and we can play cat's cradle."

Glolc's gooey form undulated as he thought it over, then he slithered closer to the unmoving body. He extended a sausage-thick section of himself toward the boy's nose, then the nostril flared wide as Glolc's gloopy green mass slid inside, an explosive sneeze in reverse.

A second later, the boy's brown eyes focused. He wrinkled and rubbed his nose while he sat up. "It's so uncomfortable in here," he complained. "Everything pinches. How do you stay cooped up like this all the time?"

"I manage," Gabby said.

She shrugged off her knapsack and rummaged inside until she found her favorite cat's cradle string. Gabby had showed Glolc the game when they first met and he'd loved it right away, but his gloppy pseudopods couldn't handle the

intricate finger motions. He could only play when he was inside his human suit.

As Gabby and Glolc tromped through the woods, trading the string back and forth between them, Gabby marveled over how normal it all was to her. Only two months ago, she nearly went into shock after she saw an eight-year-old boy transform into a gigantic slug-monster. Now she was playing cat's cradle with someone who had just been an oozing sludgeball, and it was as normal as having a stuffed-animal tea party while soaring over the Atlantic Ocean in Air Force One.

Okay, the tea party thing *sounded* unusual, but to Gabby it wasn't. The president of the United States was one of her best babysitting clients, and her other regulars included rock idols, movie stars, sports heroes, and of course all the neighborhood kids she could fit into her schedule. Some people called Gabby a "super-sitter," but Gabby didn't agree. She just loved kids. *All* kids. She didn't buy it when people said some were "difficult" or "impossible." Gabby thought anyone who said that kind of thing hadn't worked hard enough to figure out what the kid was really all about.

That's why Gabby was recruited by A.L.I.E.N., the Association Linking Intergalactics and Earthlings as Neighbors. As Gabby understood it, A.L.I.E.N. was like an embassy for aliens living on Earth. The group knew that

humanity would rise up in a giant panic if they knew about the aliens, so A.L.I.E.N. helped by creating things like Glolc's human suit. They also helped by finding Gabby, a babysitter who would keep their secret and wouldn't panic if a Flarknartian morphed into a piano, or a Pimsplilite burst into flames, or a Yabukerant cast off its human form and became an amoebic beanbag blob.

Gabby and Glolc emerged from the woods into Glolc's grassy backyard, where Esleil waved down to them from the porch. An ancient, pea-green Toyota Corolla with peeling paint spluttered in the driveway next to the house. Its license plate read 4118-251, the first seven numbers of Gabby's official A.L.I.E.N. Associate number. This was Gabby's ride home, and her heart raced a little at the sight. Normally, Gabby hated to leave the kids she babysat, but today she couldn't wait to get home. Her mom had promised she had "something big" to share with Gabby and her little sister, Carmen, at dinner.

True, Gabby's mom, Alice, was a caterer, so at dinnertime "something big" was usually an oddball delicacy like deep-fried onion rings served as a puffy foam, or fish roe consommé. But there was something about the way Alice said it, a gleam in her eye that told the girls this wasn't just about the food. It was something bigger. Something better.

Gabby said quick good-byes to Esleil and Glolc, ran to the Corolla, swung off her knapsack and tossed it inside,

then slid in herself, yanking hard to slam the squeaky door behind her.

"Let's go home!" she cried happily, though of course no one answered. A thick, orange, nubby carpet separated the back of the car from the front.

Gabby sighed. She didn't need the luxury of the limos Edwina, Gabby's main contact at A.L.I.E.N., usually drove, but she did miss the company. Edwina was an older woman who always wore her hair in a severe bun, sat tall and cold, and spoke to Gabby mainly in riddles, clucks, and exasperated exhortations that Gabby stop asking so many questions. Still, Gabby liked talking to her.

Unfortunately, Edwina was "on assignment" somewhere in the outer reaches of the universe. Gabby didn't know much about the larger workings of A.L.I.E.N., but she got the sense that the organization wasn't exactly perfect. Edwina hadn't been happy about leaving for her current mission, and she told Gabby before she left that she *certainly* wasn't going to trust anyone else with the hands-on business of running the Unsittables program in her absence. For the last week, Gabby had received all her A.L.I.E.N. assignments via code. Her rides arrived in random, ramshackle vehicles, always marked with her Associate number, always with the driver walled off so he or she couldn't communicate with Gabby in any way.

Gabby's foot bobbed up and down excitedly as she thought about her mom's big surprise. Gabby and Carmen both started winter vacation in a week, and their mom had been hinting that it would be great to "take a break." Could she be planning a family trip? They hadn't had one in . . . well, ever, really. When Carmen was little it was too hard, and since their mom's catering company took off, Alice always ended up working over school holidays. Sure, Gabby herself went all over the world to babysit—just last week she'd traveled to Washington, DC, to play French horn with the Brensville Middle School Orchestra at MusicFest, but a trip with Alice and Carmen?

It would be unbelievable, no matter where they went. Especially if . . .

Gabby's hand floated toward her chest. She felt her dad's army dog tags hanging under her shirt. The tags had mysteriously appeared in her pocket after one of her babysitting assignments. Gabby still had no idea how it had happened, but that was okay. She was just grateful to have them. She wore them around her neck every day.

Gabby squeezed the dog tags tightly. As the edges dug into her palm, she wondered . . . could her mom's surprise be a trip to Costa Rica to see Dad's family? The aunts and uncles and cousins Gabby and Carmen had never met? Could Mom be planning a reunion with the family Dad

had lost touch with years before he went off to war and disappeared?

Gabby smiled, picturing it: her little family of three swarmed by boisterous relatives telling wild stories about her dad's life. They'd take Gabby to her dad's favorite spots, feed her his favorite foods, pull out old photo albums . . .

"Oof!"

The seat belt dug into Gabby's stomach as the car jolted to a hard stop. But Gabby only smiled. She threw the car door open and raced up her front walk.

One more minute and she'd know her mom's surprise.

She couldn't wait.

chapter
TWO

*g*abby threw open the door, and cried, "I'm—"

Before she could say the word "home," weird sounds from the kitchen stopped her short.

She heard laughter. *Girly* laughter. And male laughter, too. And a rhythmic *thump . . . thump . . . thump* like the slow, heavy footsteps of a movie monster's relentless approach.

What was going on?

Gabby edged out of the foyer and turned the corner into her kitchen.

She immediately wished she hadn't.

Alice Duran stood in front of the stove. Her normally

Einstein-wild brown hair was tamed by a beaded head-band, and instead of her usual stained catering apron, she wore sleek dark-wash jeans, high-heeled boots, and a funky ruched burgundy top. She had makeup on and giggled as she did a juggling act with three or four limes. The number changed because every few tosses she'd fling one of the limes mid-juggle to the man standing just a few feet away from her. Watching her delightedly and laughing with glee, he'd catch the lime, then wait a moment and toss it back to her so she could seamlessly work it back into the juggling.

The man was Arlington Brindlethorp. He was about ten years older than Alice, with dancing blue eyes, a lush head of salt-and-pepper hair, and tan skin that crinkled winningly when he smiled. Most women, including Alice, would look at him and see a very good-looking and charming older man.

Gabby looked at him and saw the enemy.

When Gabby had met Arlington, she'd had every reason to believe he was secretly a member of G.E.T.O.U.T., A.L.I.E.N.'s enemy. G.E.T.O.U.T. wanted to eject all aliens from the planet and destroy all alien-sympathizers. They'd nearly killed Gabby once, and even though she was now on their official Not Affiliated With A.L.I.E.N. list, Edwina had warned her that some members still had their eyes on her.

Arlington, or the Silver Fox, as Gabby and her best friend, Zee, had dubbed him, totally seemed like one of those members. He kept showing up around Gabby in different disguises, as if he were spying on her. He'd even attended the Brensville Middle School Orchestra fund-raising auction where Gabby was supposed to meet one of her alien charges.

That's where he'd met Alice. He had "happened" to sit down right next to her and "coincidentally" had all kinds of things in common with her. He'd even explained all his different costume changes before Gabby could throw them in his face. He was "a writer," he said, working on "his novel," who liked to "live like his characters to get inside their heads."

Yeah right.

Gabby hadn't bought it then, and she hadn't bought it for a second of the past six weeks of Arlington and her mom's flirty phone calls, cutesy coffee dates, and "random" run-ins. He was completely despicable. Gabby had to remember that no matter how happy and girly and glowy Alice got around him, he was only using Alice to get dirt on Gabby.

He was a spy. He *had* to be a spy. Who would actually name a kid Arlington Brindlethorp?

Thump ... thump ... thump.

Gabby ripped her eyes from Arlington and her mom

to the source of the thumping. Carmen sat at the kitchen table, methodically pounding her head on top of one of the giant, leather-covered books she used to keep track of the family's schedules, finances, and businesses. Even though she was only ten, she was by far the most organized and the best one in the family to handle those kinds of things, though you might not guess it from watching her thump her head.

"Oh, come on, Car!" Alice cajoled as she kept juggling limes. "I'm doing well! I haven't dropped one yet!"

Gabby stepped farther into the room. "Mom?" she asked. "What's going on?"

"Gabby!" Alice wheeled to face her, letting all four limes drop to the floor. She winced. "Oh, shoot."

"I've got 'em," Arlington assured her. "Go ahead."

As Arlington knelt down to collect the limes, Alice pulled out Gabby's chair from the table. "Come. Sit. And, Carmen, you can stop thumping. I'm not juggling anymore."

"That wasn't why I was thumping," Carmen said in her straight-faced monotone. She did stop thumping, though, and instead stared across the table at Gabby. Carmen liked to cut her own bangs so they made a razor-sharp line extremely high on her forehead. Right now those bangs and the rest of her straight brown hair curtained a look of barely contained fury.

Gabby knew the glare wasn't directed at her, but at Arlington's presence in their kitchen. Carmen hated Arlington even more than Gabby, and she didn't even know he was a spy. Gabby took it as a sign that her own instincts were dead-on.

Gabby eyed Arlington warily as she spoke to her mom. "So, um . . . you have something to tell us?"

"Something *big*. Yes!" Alice agreed. She nodded to Arlington, then swept Carmen's books off the table and onto a counter. Arlington, meanwhile, opened the oven door. A delicious aroma blasted Gabby's nose, and she realized her mom had been warming the one dish both she and Carmen agreed was their favorite: grilled cheese and bacon sandwiches with a side of thin-cut sweet potato fries.

"Perfect, right?" Alice asked. "But wait—there's more!" She darted to the fridge and pulled out four tall glasses of frothy yellow delights. "Pineapple-coconut smoothies! *With* bendy straws," she added, jointing Carmen's straw so it pointed right at her face, just how she liked it. Carmen remained stone-faced.

"I am *very* impressed with your girls, Alice," Arlington said as Alice laid out the food. "If these are their favorite dishes, they have excellent taste."

"Is he staying for the whole meal?" Carmen asked.

Gabby bit her cheeks to keep from smiling. If she'd

asked that question, she'd have gotten in trouble for being rude. But Carmen said what she thought, no matter what, and Gabby loved her for it.

"Yes, of course he is!" Alice said. "In fact, Arlington is what I want to talk to you about."

Alice pursed her lips and glanced quickly at the Silver Fox. She rubbed her palms on her jeans. She took a deep breath and slowly blew it out.

Was she nervous? She looked nervous. Gabby couldn't think of one good reason why her mom would be nervous about Arlington, but she could think of a million bad ones. One of Gabby's hands crept to the dog tags around her neck, while the other grabbed the smoothie so she could wash down the bile rising in her throat.

"You both know Arlington and I have become very good friends," Alice began. "He's a wonderful man, and if you give him the chance, you girls will think so, too. I hope you will, because Arlington and I—"

Gabby choked. She coughed uncontrollably, gasping for air as spots danced in front of her eyes. She heard the scrape of a chair and felt the Silver Fox reach over to pat her back, but she lurched away and fell onto her knees, her head against Alice's lap.

"It's okay, baby, it's okay," Alice said soothingly. "Just breathe."

When Gabby finally got some air, she looked up, wild-eyed and desperate. "You can't marry him, Mom. You can't! You don't understand—"

Alice's face scrunched. "Marry him? Honey, we've barely known each other two months! I was trying to tell you we're going to start *dating*."

Stunned, Gabby plopped back onto her rear end. "Dating? But . . . haven't you already been dating?"

Alice blushed. She twirled a finger around a stray burst of hair. "Well . . . yes . . . kind of . . . but I didn't think you girls knew. We were trying to keep it from you until we were sure it was something real. . . ."

"You didn't," Carmen said. "We knew. Doesn't make sense, though. You like Dax Rawlins, the guy on *People* magazine's Sexiest Man Alive cover. Arlington doesn't look anything like Dax Rawlins."

"Dax Rawlins, huh?" Arlington asked playfully.

Alice turned red. "I like his movies," she said. "They're very gripping."

Arlington's eyes twinkled until Alice looked away, blushing even harder. The flirting was too much for Gabby to handle. "Is there any more smoothie, Mom?" she asked.

"Of course."

As Alice got up to fetch the drink, Arlington cleared his throat. "Gabby, Carmen, I want you both to know I'd never

rush into anything that made either of you uncomfortable. I care about your mother very much, and that means your opinions matter to me a great deal. I hope we can get to know each other a lot better."

He looked so earnest and hopeful, Gabby wanted to throw her smoothie in his face.

"Sure," she said instead. "I bet we'll find out all kinds of things about you." She raised an eyebrow just to make sure he got the point, then stared until he looked away.

So much for Costa Rica. If this announcement was Mom's "something big," then the trip had been wishful thinking. At least it wasn't marriage. The dating thing was bad, but it wasn't forever. Gabby could stop it once she had solid proof Arlington was up to no good.

"I'm done," Carmen said. She shoved her plate and glass aside, then grabbed her books back from the counter. She flipped open the one containing all their schedules. "Tomorrow. Mom—no appointments. You just have to prep for Saturday's Hanukkah party at Kesher Shalom."

"Latkes with sour cream and homemade applesauce, brisket, and cauliflower-leek kugel. I already made plans to drop you at the Square for a playdate with Trymmy so you won't be bored while I work."

Gabby inwardly giggled as Carmen looked darkly up

at Alice. Carmen hated the term "playdate." Not because it was babyish, which had been Gabby's complaint at that age, but because it was so inaccurate. Carmen wasn't going on a date, and she wasn't doing anything as frivolous as playing. She and Trymmy engaged in deep conversations about life's great matters. And when they whipped out the chessboard it was no mere game, but a serious tournament of wits.

With a sigh, Carmen looked back down at the scheduling book. "Gabby," she began, but Gabby cut her off. She didn't want to discuss her babysitting around the Silver Fox.

"Can you tell me later, Car? These fries are so good I can't even think about anything else."

Now it was Gabby's turn to get a dark look. Carmen always gave out the next day's schedule over dinner. *Always.*

"You're working tomorrow for Claudia R. and James Q. Kincaid," Carmen continued as if Gabby hadn't interrupted her.

Gabby got chills and sat up straighter. She looked furtively at the Silver Fox. "Claudia R. and James Q. Kincaid?" she repeated. "That's how they gave their names?"

Another glare from Carmen. "I wouldn't have said it that way if that wasn't how they gave their names."

"Is something wrong, Gabby?" the Silver Fox asked, and

Gabby tried not to sneer. Of course he'd been watching her body language and saw the way she reacted. Of course he'd love to know why.

"Not at all!" she crowed way too loudly. She leaned back in her seat and draped an arm over the back, super-casual. She even tipped the chair onto its back legs. "Just listening to Carmen. Regular babysitting business. Nothing unusual."

But her heart thudded in her ears, because those names weren't just names, they were *code*. Normally Gabby found out about her A.L.I.E.N. clients through Edwina. With Edwina away, they were coming through Carmen like her human clients did, but with a major clue. They'd book with both parents' names, along with a middle initial for each.

"You'll go see them right after school. They're at—"

"You don't need to tell me the address!" Gabby blurted, sweat pooling now all over her body. No way did she want Arlington to hear where her alien clients lived.

"5429 Lockhaven Square," Carmen continued. "It's close enough that you can walk."

"Or I could give you a ride," the Silver Fox offered. A knowing smile played on his face. Gabby wanted to whack it off with the remnants of her grilled cheese.

"That's so nice of you, Arlington!" Alice gushed. "Gabby, what do you say? Wouldn't that be nice?"

"Very nice," Gabby lied through gritted teeth, "thanks. But I'd rather walk. I like walking after school. It's good. Walking is. Really good."

Gabby thumped her chair back down to all four legs and inwardly smacked herself for acting so blatantly weird. Could she make it any more obvious that these clients were aliens???

"You're watching a real baby this time, so you'll actually be babysitting." It made Carmen crazy when Gabby watched anyone over two years old and still called it *baby*sitting.

"A baby?!" Alice's eyes widened. "Ohhhh, I want to meet the baby! Can I come meet the baby?"

"I'd like to meet the baby, too," Arlington said. "I love babies."

"You do?" Alice gasped.

"Always have. Truth is, the biggest regret of my life is I never had one of my own. A little bundle I could hold and cuddle...."

He mimed rocking a baby in his arms, smiling down at it and cooing. Alice looked transported. Too transported.

"Bummer you're dating Mom, then," Carmen said. "She's too old to have babies."

Both Arlington and Alice looked like they'd been doused with a bucket of freezing cold water. Gabby was pretty sure she had never loved Carmen as much as she did right then.

Arlington was the first to recover. "Age doesn't matter. Your mom's healthy as a horse. Me too! I went for my physical just last week, and the results could be from a man half my age. Virility, thy name is Arlington!"

Ew. Gabby needed to change the subject *immediately*. "I can't let you guys see the baby anyway. I never bring anyone to work with me."

"I know, I know," Alice sighed. "You're very responsible that way and I'm proud of you. Now who wants dessert?"

Gabby somehow survived the rest of the meal without saying much more to the Silver Fox. Afterwards, Alice wanted everyone to go downstairs and watch a movie together. Carmen agreed only because she could work on her latest giant jigsaw puzzle, but Gabby said she had to study and practice her French horn. Which was true, but was really just an excuse to get away from Arlington and think about Claudia R. and James Q. Kincaid. What would they be like? Would they look human, or like nothing Gabby could even imagine? And an alien *baby*—she'd never sat for an alien baby before. Would it be very different from taking care of a human baby?